BY CHRISTOPHER LEHMANN-HAUPT

The Mad Cook of Pymatuning
A Crooked Man
Me and DiMaggio

THE
MAD COOK OF
PYMATUNING

A NOVEL

CHRISTOPHER
LEHMANN-HAUPT

Simon & Schuster

New York   London   Toronto   Sydney

SIMON & SCHUSTER
Rockefeller Center
1230 Avenue of the Americas
New York, NY 10020

SIMON & SCHUSTER and colophon are
registered trademarks of Simon & Schuster, Inc.

For information regarding special discounts for bulk purchases,
please contact Simon & Schuster Special Sales at 1-800-456-6798
or business@simonandschuster.com

Book design by Ellen R. Sasahara

Manufactured in the United States of America

1   3   5   7   9   10   8   6   4   2

Library of Congress Cataloging-in-Publication Data
Lehmann-Haupt, Christopher.
The mad cook of Pymatuning : a novel / Christopher Lehmann-Haupt.
p. cm.
1. Boys—Fiction. 2. Camps—Fiction. 3. Games—Fiction. I. Title.
PS3562.E435M33 2005
813'.54—dc22
2005049907

ISBN-13: 978-0-684-83427-6
ISBN-10: 0-684-83427-8

For Philip M. B., Richard M., and Hugh N.,
who know who they are and helped me to see
what the Mad Cook was

ACKNOWLEDGMENTS

THE EVENTS AND CHARACTERS in this story are entirely fictional, but many people helped me to make the fiction seem plausible, particularly my editors, Chuck Adams and Michael Korda, who patiently guided me back from dozens of dead ends, and my wife, Natalie Robins, who read so many drafts that it's a miracle she could keep the story I was trying to tell straight in her mind. Any missteps that remain are entirely my own doing.

Others helpful too in more ways than I can count were Alan Aronstein, Bennett Ashley, Richard W. Baron, Carol Bowie, Fred and Betsy Bowman, Lisl Cade, Philip Conti, Ernest Frankel, Lana Hartzell, Dalma Heyn, Noah Lehmann-Haupt, Rachel Lehmann-Haupt, Elexis Loubriel, Min Martin, Walt Mason, Victoria Meyer, Noreen Mullen, Lynn Nesbit, Tina Simms, Randy Smith, Norma Starchesky, Harold Trout, Chet Walford, and Leah Wasielewski.

Finally, three books proved invaluable sources for lore on the American Indian: *The Death and Rebirth of the Seneca* by Anthony F. C. Wallace, with the assistance of Sheila C. Steen (Vintage, 1972); *Hamatsa: The Enigma of Cannibalism on the Pacific Northwest Coast* by Jim McDowell (Ronsdale Press, 1997); and *500 Nations: An Illustrated History of North American Indians* by Alvin M. Josephy Jr. (Alfred A. Knopf, 1994).

Pounded him as maize is pounded
Till his skull was crushed to pieces,
Till his skull was crushed and softened
Soft as were the brains within it.

Passage from "The Hunting of Pau-Puk-Keewis" in
The Song of Hiawatha, by Henry Wadsworth Longfellow,
the latter two lines of which were expurgated

THE CAMPFIRE

THE STATION WAGON that had met our train bounced along the dirt road that led to the entrance of Camp Seneca, raising enough dust to make me feel I was riding a stagecoach into some earlier time in history. Adam Lister was driving, despite nearsightedness that required what looked like a pair of thick camera lenses. Because of a remote manner that was partly the result of this handicap, we called him "mister." Mr. Lister.

"Can I go swimming as soon as we get there?" Peter asked, his bright blue eyes sparkling.

"No," I said. "Everything begins with the softball game." I yawned, tired from staying awake most of the night on the train from New York City, a lot of the time answering my little brother's nervous questions.

"Do I have to play?"

"Yes," said Mr. Lister. "Everybody plays."

"You'll have fun," said Buddy Stemmer from the seat behind us. He was a quiet, fourteen-year-old senior camper, so straightforward and reliable that several summers earlier I had coined the nickname Steady Bomber for him. It had stuck. Steady's good looks bordered on prettiness, like what people sometimes said about mine.

"I'm not good at softball," Peter said.

"That doesn't matter," said Bordy Udall from the front passenger seat. He had ridden out with Mr. Lister to meet the train. Bordy was short for Borden, and we sometimes called him Elsie (after the Borden's Dairy cow), but only behind his back. He was the head counselor of the camp and, at six feet six inches and 270 pounds, an offensive lineman for the University of Pittsburgh football team. He had an incongruously high-pitched voice that made Peter smile.

Next to Steady Bomber, Bernie Kaufman—a small, stoop-shouldered fourteen-year-old who didn't look like a senior camper but was—sat practicing his long-necked five-string banjo, just as he had tried to do on the train all the way from New York, until the other passengers made him mute his strings by stuffing tissue between them and the fretboard.

"I didn't know you had a brother, Muller," Mr. Lister said.

"Jerry's actually my half brother," Peter said.

"We have the same father," I said. I lit a cigarette on a new lighter I had been given as a high school graduation gift, and inhaled deeply.

"How old are you, Peter?" Bordy asked. He reached back and tousled Peter's nearly white blond hair.

"I'm nine."

Bordy whistled. "That's old enough to qualify." I think he was covering up his surprise. Peter looked more like seven.

"Qualify for what?" Peter asked with a worried frown.

"For everything," Bordy said.

Peter smiled at Bordy's teasing and looked out the window. The station wagon was passing the old farmhouse that served as a place for the counselors to socialize, and where Woody and Win Wentworth, Camp Seneca's owners, sometimes stayed, especially during the off-season. Gazing at the house, which was built so close to the road that it looked as if it was trying to escape the land it was on, I thought of the sharp taste of the hard cider in the cellar. The Wentworths' old Chrysler Town & Country, with its wood side panels, was parked next to the house.

"This is Peter's first long time away from home," I announced, trying to explain his apparent fearfulness. "Right, buddy?"

"Your brother will take good care of you," Bordy said. "The five weeks will go by like nothing."

"I know," Peter said. "And Woody and Win will be waiting to make me feel right at home."

"Sorry, they won't," Mr. Lister said. "Win's not here yet."

My heart sank. I had sort of a crush on Win, something I probably shared with half the other campers, but which I kept fiercely to myself. "Why isn't she here?" I asked.

Mr. Lister said nothing. He was concentrating nearsightedly on the road in a way that I always found both pitiable and annoying. I was glad Bordy had come along with him to brighten the atmosphere.

"If I like camp, can I stay longer?" Peter asked bravely.

"Not possible," I said. "Ten days after boys' camp ends, girls' camp begins." I felt really bad about Win's not being there. Not only did I have a crush on her, but her calming presence was essential to what I loved about Camp Seneca, and this summer especially I was counting on her influence.

Peter tapped one of the crutches I was holding upright. "How are you going to play softball, Jerry?"

"If I use just one crutch, I can pitch."

"Where did you say you broke it?" Bordy asked.

"Stowe, Vermont," I said. "The snow was wet. I caught an edge."

"No, I meant which bone?"

"Oh. The tibia. The big one below the knee."

"I know where the tibia is," Bordy said lightly. Blue smoke from my cigarette drifted in the air.

"Will the Indians be playing softball too?" Peter asked.

"I told you: there aren't really any Indians," I said. "Only one, Chief Wahoo, and he's just pretend."

"This year we got a real one," Mr. Lister said abstractly, still concentrating on the road.

"What about Chief Wahoo?" I exclaimed.

"Gone," Lister said. Everyone fell silent, apparently waiting for him to explain, but he said nothing more. The only sound for a few seconds was the tinkle of Bernie's banjo.

"If they never had a real Indian before, why is it called Camp Seneca?" Peter finally asked. "Who named it that?"

"The owners," Bordy said. "Indians are a way of learning about our history. And they teach us about nature."

"Oh," Peter said. "That's neat."

LOOKING BACK nearly a lifetime later, I realize now that I had an instant foreboding of how truly horrific that summer of 1952 would be. From the moment we arrived, Camp Seneca just didn't seem the same as it had been in previous summers, partly because of Win's absence, partly because of other disturbing changes.

But I guess I fought not to recognize what I was feeling because I wanted so much for this summer to be successful. What it came down to was that I wanted my brother, Peter, to have the best possible time he could. Partly for his sake, of course, but more because, in truth, I had an ulterior motive: I figured that the better the time Peter had at camp, the more it would impress my father that Peter and I could get along well together, and that I could be a great older brother. Peter had always seemed to like having me around, but I wanted to build on that now. I hoped that Dad would take note, and would ask me to move in with him and his wife, Karla, and, of course, Peter. It was something I really wanted. Even though I was going off to college in the fall, I needed a comfortable place to come home to on vacation, a place where I could have some privacy. And I figured there might be a room for me in the new house in Connecticut Dad had somehow managed to buy despite his always complaining about the meager money he made on his small rare-book business.

More important though, I just had to get away from my mother's small two-room apartment in the Bronx, where things had gotten too depressing.

As we approached the entrance to Seneca, I flashed back to the night before I left for camp, when I had come home and found my mother drunk again. *I don't want that to happen anymore,* I thought. *I don't even want to think about that evening.*

But despite my high hopes for the summer, I guess I sensed trouble the moment the station wagon turned into the camp's main entrance. I looked at the two tall totem poles that framed the gate; their cheerful colors and grotesque carved faces suddenly struck me as being at odds with each other, just like my feelings at that moment. The camp also looked seedier somehow than I remembered it. I noticed right away that a couple of the rails had fallen off the fence that surrounded the riding ring to our right.

Beyond the ring, some kind of slimy-looking green scum floated on the surface of the camp's small lake, though its dock and diving float gleamed with fresh white paint and the two red canoes and assorted water wings on the rack near the narrow dirt beach shone brightly. To the left, where the entrance road curved around to the main grounds, stood two small cabins, one of them used by the Wentworths, the other by whoever was the camp's second in command—Chief Wahoo during previous summers—and beyond them, the mess hall. It struck me now how drab the buildings looked, and how much smaller, even shrunken, the campgrounds seemed.

The wagon lurched to a stop at the outermost of the two cabins. In front of it stood Woody, surrounded by the camp's staff, a few of whom I recognized, and Chunky, the camp's big black mutt, who looked like a cross between a black Lab and something considerably wider. To the right of Woody stood Nora Laird, a pretty redheaded woman who was the camp's nurse. On his other side towered a tall, unusual-looking man with his silver-and-black hair in a ponytail, wearing a fringed buckskin suit decorated with beadwork. I had never seen him before. I guessed he was the real Indian Mr. Lister had referred to, Chief Wahoo's so-called replacement.

After climbing out of the wagon and collecting our trunk and duffel bags from the back, I couldn't help looking around for Win. Maybe she was somewhere greeting the parents and visitors who were still present. But Mr. Lister was right; she was nowhere to be seen. In summers past she would be standing behind a long table on which plastic lanyards braided by campers the previous summer would be neatly laid out, each bearing a tag with a camper's name and cabin assignment printed on it. Win would hand them out, welcome each camper by name, ask him if he was hungry, and see that he got something to eat if he was.

This summer everything seemed to be different. There was a kind of unease about the place.

In Win's absence, Mr. Lister mounted the steps of the mess hall, blew a whistle, and began rapidly calling out names and cabin assignments from a clipboard he was carrying. Finding it hard to hear him clearly, campers and counselors crowded around him on the steps, jostling for a view of his clipboard. Then, in the midst of this turmoil, Early McAdams, a wiry Southerner who, like me, was a junior counselor, came through the door behind Mr. Lister and grabbed his arm, trying to get his own view of the clipboard. Lister, annoyed, tried to elbow him aside. McAdams, who normally kept his hot temper in rein, suddenly whacked Lister's head with his open right hand. Lister's glasses flew off and he began flailing at Mac blindly, as the children around them went flying. Mac stepped back, took aim, and shot a fist at Lister's right eye, catching him squarely. Blood ran down his cheek and he covered it with both hands, dropping the clipboard. Bordy charged up the steps, threw his arms around Mac's shoulders, and pushed him away. Nurse Laird led the bleeding Lister inside the mess hall, to the infirmary. The children who had fallen down were brushed off and comforted, and an uneasy order was restored, with Bordy filling in for Lister, calling out the cabin assignments.

This incident left me breathless and upset. Mac had always struck me as slightly dangerous, but I had never seen him lose it so completely before. But since Peter had stayed out of the fray and didn't seem overly upset by the incident, I tried to calm myself down so I could get us settled into the camp's routine. After waiting our turn, I learned from Bordy that both Peter and I were assigned to cabin one, the first of the nine cabins along Cabin Row, seven of them containing about ten campers each. Our senior counselor was Len Lawrence, a big, warmhearted guy who kept his scalp so closely shaved that it shone. I was the junior counselor in the cabin, and Steady Bomber was the senior camper. The three of us would make a good team. And because Len was also the assistant head counselor and would be given all the responsibilities connected with that position, I would be left more or less in charge of the cabin, a big job for someone just turned seventeen. A sense of excitement began to overwhelm my dismay.

After all, I reminded myself, deep down I loved Seneca and thought that its slightly wacky philosophy of surprising the campers with unexpected challenges made it something special, even unique. I was intrigued with Woody's high sense of drama: his drive to create unusual situations that only he could dream up. He believed that the sometimes scary twists he put on routine camp activities were good for the children; that by either meeting or failing his challenges they got to know themselves better and became more equipped to face real life. I thought this testing would be perfect for Peter, particularly as our dad wanted Camp Seneca to "toughen him up a little," as he liked to put it.

Of course, I also loved the camp for giving me in Win Wentworth and Chief Wahoo an alternative family, something I seemed to want a lot. I knew that this need had come from my parents splitting up six years ago, with my having to go live with my mother, who had remained single and developed her drinking problem, while my father, who had gotten remarried (to the woman he had had Peter with three years earlier), spent most of the rare time I saw him lecturing me about standing up for myself and becoming more independent. But I didn't understand the roots of my feelings, and it would take me a long time to see what was really going on.

Despite his silly name, Chief Wahoo was smart and sensitive, a Jewish guy from Cleveland who was a public school administrator of some kind and knew a lot about literature. Over the summers, he and Win had come to feel a little like parents to me, and they were accepting and even admiring of me. Now I was going to have to get along without him.

But there was one thing to be happy about this summer: I was looking forward to having Tommy Osborne around. He was a classmate at my boarding school I had managed to recruit as another junior counselor. Woody was always urging us to look for good people to bring to Seneca, and I thought that Oz, because of his athletic, musical, and acting abilities, and especially his interest in Indian lore, would be absolutely perfect. I was amazed when he accepted my invitation, as he was out of my social league at school, and Seneca was the very opposite of the kind of elite place I imagined he probably preferred, like one of those fancy camps up in Maine. But then again, he struck me as being very self-assured and politically astute—everything I wasn't—and I guess he wanted to test himself in a different social setting. And Seneca, which drew its seventy-odd eight-to-fourteen-year-old campers from lower-middle- and working-class families in the Pittsburgh area (along with a smattering from Virginia, where Woody and Win had gone to college), would certainly provide Oz with that.

If I had only known how wrong I was.

As Peter and I hauled our luggage down to our cabin, I began to look around for Oz. I was sure he was here already; his family was rich and he had arranged to fly to Pittsburgh and catch a ride up here with the Wentworths or one of the counselors who also lived there. He was probably playing softball already.

LIKE EVERYTHING at Seneca, the opening-day softball game was controlled chaos. It was supposed to throw everybody together after they arrived, including the odd parent and visitor and the few women at the camp, who would also play: Nurse Laird and whoever was her assistant this summer; Eve and Sukie, the kitchen help; and of course Win, so important to life at the camp. Aside from being warm and comforting where Woody was a little remote, Win seemed to restrain him from going too far with his games and not-always-so-funny tricks.

The game was played under the most difficult conditions. The diamond was laid out at the lower end of a downward-sloping, rectangular meadow about the size of a football field, with turf that was so uneven that the ball would rarely bounce predictably. Right field was shortened by the cabins housing the latrine—called the Kybo (for *Keep your bowels open*) and the communal shower, the last of the nine cabins that edged the field. Behind them was a dark and gloomy forest, dense with undergrowth, considered off-limits because the camp property didn't extend that far. Supposedly it belonged to a neighboring farmer who didn't want us trespassing there, not that anyone would want to. We called this the Forbidden Woods.

Batters whose balls hit either the Kybo or the shower house could not advance beyond first base. If you hit the ball over these buildings and into the underbrush, you were automatically out. No one would dream of looking for the ball in that thicket, not even in the brightest daylight. Further complicating the game was a handicap imposed on all the grown-ups—or the men, at least—which required them to bat from the wrong side, so that anyone right-handed had to swing lefty, and the other way around.

Despite all these obstacles, the game was taken very seriously. It might look disorganized, what with players stopping to greet new arrivals, or visitors leaving, or the action slowing at times to let the smaller campers take extra balls and strikes, and no one keeping track of the batting order or even the number of outs. Yet beneath the game's chaotic surface, important individual contests were going on, little games within the game to determine who would be the leaders among the counselors and older campers that summer. The stated point of the game was to mix everyone together smoothly, but what was really at stake was the children's allegiance to the staff.

THE GAME was under way when Peter and I got to the field. Everyone seemed to be participating except Bernie Kaufman, who was leaning against the side of the backstop, practicing his banjo. Since I could do it on one crutch, I offered to take over as pitcher, the position I normally played, and the one thing I could do despite my handicap. Peter joined a group of half a dozen eight- and nine-year-olds who were backing up the catcher.

A couple of the counselors, bald Len Lawrence and big Bordy, football teammates at Pitt, were already in a contest to see who could hit the highest pop fly. In contrast to their fooling around, Jeff Small, the camp's maintenance man, tried hard to get a hit, though as usual he struck out on three awkward swings. As always this surprised me, since Jeff somehow looked like an athlete despite his lanky frame and his salt-and-pepper goatee. In obvious disgust with Jeff's ineptness, Early McAdams—who was easily the camp's best athlete, and very popular among the campers despite his hot temper and the fact that he was only a junior counselor, like me—swung gracefully and hit a soft line drive just over the heads of the infielders. He seemed unperturbed by his earlier fistfight with Lister.

Following Mac, a pretty girl I had never seen before came up to bat. She was tall and long-limbed, with yellow hair that she wore in a ponytail, and she had a sharp-featured face with green eyes that gave her a slightly Asian look. When Mac yelled from first base, "Come on, T.J. Hit one, girl!" I guessed that she was the girlfriend he had always talked about bringing to camp. On my first pitch she poked a blooper that fell just beyond the reach of two converging outfielders. Watching her run gracefully to first base, I couldn't help thinking she was even prettier than Mac had boasted, and that her presence was one of the few positive new things about camp this summer, even if she did belong to him.

"Nice hit," I called to her as she took her lead off first base. In response she gave me a shy smile.

Next up was my schoolmate, Tommy Osborne.

"Hey ho, Jerry Muller!" he cried out to me as he stepped to the left of the plate. He had on cutoff jeans and a bright red T-shirt and a new baseball cap with the words "Camp Seneca" stitched in script above the bill. He looked shiny and expensive, and it worried me a little that his preppyness might not go over so well with the mostly working-class counselors at Seneca. But he was a star at our school and I was eager for the camp to see his talents.

"Great to see ya, Oz," I shouted back. "But you're a rightie, so you gotta bat left-handed. That's the rule."

"If you say so." He moved to the other side of the plate, adjusted his glasses, and hit my second pitch to right field, high over the latrine, and into the Forbidden Woods.

"You're out! You're out!" everybody cried, impressed with the length of the drive yet peeved by his ignorance of the rules. It made no difference, though, since nobody was keeping an exact score. The important thing was that Oz had announced his presence.

As ALWAYS, when the sun got lower and the air began to cool, we broke for supper. Normally this was an Indian-style feast of corn and squash and nuts and berries with baked fish—or even rabbit for those who could stomach it—all cooked over a stone grill deep in the forest below us called the Big Woods, by the campfire site. But with Win and Chief Wahoo missing, Woody switched the feast to one of his movable barbecues, a portable grill that he had designed for just such occasions.

"Are you learning the softball rules now?" I said to Oz as he, Peter, and I got in line for our hot dogs and potato salad.

He lifted his Seneca cap and ran his right hand through his ash blond hair and pursed his lips with a little twitch of amusement. "I don't get it," he said, looking off toward the Forbidden Woods. "Why not at least try to find the balls hit in there?"

"Too much trouble," I said. "Besides, it's off-limits, not part of the camp property."

"Well, okay."

"How was the trip out here?" I asked.

"Smooth."

"You drove up from Pittsburgh with Woody?"

"No. Uh, the bald one."

"Len Lawrence."

"Yeah."

With nothing more to say, I followed Oz's gaze and looked into the darkening woods. A chill came over me. The lowering sun had high-lighted a single large, dead tree deep into the woods that loomed above the newer foliage. Silhouetted against the orange glow of the setting sun, its network of black branches suggested a skeletal hand clutching for the sky. In my three summers at Seneca, I had never noticed it before; maybe it had died since last year. But the sinister sight of it now somehow reflected the changed mood I was sensing about the place.

"Look at that tree," I said to Oz.

He followed my gaze. "What about it?"

"I don't know. I just never noticed it before."

He shrugged.

"I think it's depressing," I said. I took a cigarette from a pack in my shirt pocket and lit it with my lighter. I waited for the pleasant wave of light-headedness to come over me.

"You got one of those for me?" a female voice asked from behind me.

I turned around and found Mac's girlfriend standing behind me in the line. She had an arm around Artie McAdams, a yellow-haired boy of eleven or twelve who was Mac's younger brother. I caught the sweet scent of her hair. "You're T.J.," I said.

"That's right," she said.

"I'm Jerry Muller. This is my brother, Peter. He's new at camp." I gave her a cigarette and offered her a light. "We've heard a lot about you."

"Hi, Peter. Who's 'we'?" she asked me, drawing on the flame.

"I mean the camp."

"I hope good stuff."

"Sure." I looked around for Mac but didn't see him. "What's your job going to be?"

"I'm Nurse Laird's assistant. Speaking of which, why the crutches?"

"I broke my leg. The cast just came off."

"How'd you break it?" Artie asked.

"Skiing."

"Skiing!" Artie exclaimed. "Where do you do that?"

"At the school I go to."

"My, my," T.J. said. "I never went skiing."

"The school's in Vermont."

"Ain't you the lucky one!" She blew out smoke. "So what were you saying is depressing?"

"That tree. It's kind of scary looking."

"I could go and chop it down," Artie volunteered. "I ain't skeered of it."

"I don't think we need to do that," I said.

T.J. put her hands on Artie's shoulders and squeezed them. "Maybe we can go take a look at it one day during free time." She looked up at me and raised her eyebrows, either mocking me or conveying an invitation. I couldn't tell.

Flustered, I turned back to Oz, but found that he was up by the barbecue wagon, being served and talking to Woody. I took Peter's arm and closed the gap.

Woody stopped talking to Oz as I approached. "Hello there, Jerry," he said to me. "This must be Peter. How are you doing, young man?"

"Good," Peter said shyly.

"Where's Win?" I asked.

Woody looked down and busied himself with the hot dogs on the grill. "She'll be here soon enough," he said.

"But not in time to run the campfire, huh?" I said. "Who's gonna summon the spirits?"

Woody gestured at Oz. "I was just telling your schoolmate here: we've made some big changes. We have a new man for the Indian program."

"I think I noticed him when we got here." I took two paper plates and began to load them with food. "What's his name?"

"Buck Silverstone. Going to show us how it's done. Next?"

"Why wasn't he at the softball game?" I handed one of the plates to Peter. "I thought everybody was supposed to play."

"Oh, you'll see. You'll see. Next! There are big surprises in store."

I shredded my cigarette and started to lead Peter after Oz.

"Oh, Osborne," Woody called after us. "Don't forget, I want to talk to you when I get through here."

"What's that about?" I asked Oz when he, Peter, and I had found a place to sit. Other children, including Teddy Wentworth, Woody's seven-year-old son, joined us.

"I'm not sure," he answered. "Something he wants me to do at the campfire."

"Right," I said, trying to hide the mixture of jealousy and pride I felt. I had never been singled out for this kind of attention. Yet it made me feel good to see that Woody was already treating Oz as someone special.

———

WHEN WE WERE finished eating, most of the counselors and campers went off to their cabins to unpack and get ready for the evening's events. All the parents and visitors had left by now. The shadows were getting longer and the air was a lot cooler. But a few of the campers were still hanging around the softball diamond, playing catch. When they saw me and Peter helping to clean up after the barbecue, they called me over to the diamond and asked me to pitch to them, which I was happy to do. Peter tagged along.

I was about to call an end to the playing because it was getting so late when Oz came jogging up to us, apparently done with his meeting with Woody. He was ready for more softball, and insisted that he and I divide up the dozen or so remaining campers and begin a whole new game. I looked around for an older counselor or two to help supervise things, but the only adults in sight were Eve and Sukie, the two kitchen girls, who, along with T.J., were smoking cigarettes and talking.

So we started playing again, with Oz and me pitching for our respective teams, and we went along for a couple of innings without much happening except for a few infield dribblers. The dark was coming on fast now. Oz suggested that to speed things up we start calling balls and strikes, and he called T.J. over and directed her to umpire from behind the backstop. The game intensified when Oz put his smallest player up to bat, who, having virtually no strike zone for me to pitch to, naturally got on base with a walk. Oz then lofted a hit deep beyond the outfielders and circled the bases behind his miniature batsman.

When our turn at bat came, I followed Oz's lead and sent Peter to the plate. After he walked, I got a hit (although someone had to run for me), and then Steady Bomber smacked a home run. The score was 3 to 2 in our favor. Mischievously, I suggested we call it a night.

I was half kidding, although I knew we really should stop. It was getting so dark we could hardly see. Swallows or bats—I couldn't tell which—were swooping in the air above us, and some of the smaller children, still in T-shirts, were shivering from the cool air and starting to complain. In past summers, Win would have come down from her cabin and in her soft but commanding voice suggested that we save the rest of the game for another evening. But Win wasn't around, and Oz wouldn't hear of stopping. We had played only four and a half innings, he said, and the game had to go at least seven to be official. Besides, he had last licks coming. So despite my feeling that the game should end, we went on playing in the deepening darkness.

Pitching harder, I got his side out quickly, and he did the same to ours. It was now too dark to be able to hit the ball solidly, so I placed infielders on either side of me and they were able to run down the few weak grounders Oz's team managed to hit in the next half inning. But we couldn't do any better in our turn up, so it all came down to the bottom of the seventh. This would be it, we all agreed. Even if the score ended up tied.

As Oz's team prepared for its last licks, we could hear people coming out of the cabins and drifting down toward where the campfire would take place. The site was a little ways into the Big Woods, which bordered the lower end of the meadow we were playing on. You entered the Big Woods through a gate made of totem poles that was a smaller version of the camp's main entrance. The softball players were sensing that they might be missing out on something, and little Teddy Wentworth even began to whimper that he didn't want to play anymore. To cheer him up, Oz sent him to bat out of turn, which wasn't such a sacrifice since Teddy was so hard to see in the dark. Just as Oz hoped, I walked him on four pitches.

Now Oz himself came up. I threw the first pitch as hard as I could, but I heard a thunk at home plate and a soft whizzing past my right ear. He was pounding toward first base, chortling and urging little Teddy to run. His team was cheering wildly.

As the runners began to circle the bases, I figured I'd better head in the direction that the ball had been hit and, when the outfielder could get it to me, carry it back to home plate myself without risking a throw to Steady. I switched my crutch from my left arm to my right and started out toward second base. By first planting the rubber tip way out in front of me and then hopping forward on my left leg, I could cover ground at a surprising speed.

I didn't have to travel far. Just past second, Peter came out of the dark and handed me the ball. I switched it to my left hand and took off hopping and swinging, hoping that I could beat Teddy and Oz to home.

I saw that it was going to work. I could hear Oz nearing third base, but I realized he couldn't move any faster than little Teddy in front of him, so I knew I still had plenty of time. I would be waiting at home when Teddy got there. I would tag him out and either force Oz back to third or tag him out too.

But again Oz found a way to one-up me. When the slab of home plate came into view, I saw that I was moving too fast to stop myself in time. That would have been okay if Teddy and Oz had been moving at the speed I'd expected them to. I would have overrun the base path, turned around, and hopped back in time to tag Teddy out. But as I began to brake myself I became aware of a single set of pounding footsteps and low laughter just to my right. Oz had picked Teddy up in his arms and was carrying him along at top speed.

Then, just as I reached the baseline, I got my legs tangled and went flying. An instant later I felt an explosion of pain and heard a loud ringing in my head; suddenly I was lying on my back.

As the ringing faded, I began to hear the sound of crying. I rolled painfully onto my stomach. Peter ran up and knelt beside me. "Are you okay?" he asked.

Except for my aching head and shoulder, nothing seemed to be seriously wrong with me. "I think so." I looked up and even in the dark I could see the outline of Oz crawling on all fours toward the sound of crying. T.J. was moving too, running and then throwing herself onto her knees. I couldn't see little Teddy, but I was sure it was he who was in tears. I lay there for a moment, wondering if I had tripped on something, and considering the very real possibility that Oz and I and Peter would be heading home tomorrow.

I sat up and felt around for my crutch, found it close by, and struggled to my feet. Oz and T.J. were kneeling together in the grass. I was about to join them when Mr. Lister appeared out of the dark. A white gauze patch covered his right eye, and he was clearly annoyed. "It's campfire time now," he said coolly. "Go get your remaining campers from the cabin and take them to the campfire area."

"Sorry, Mr. Lister, but we've had an accident here," I said. "A child is hurt."

He looked in the direction of Oz and T.J. "The nurse's assistant can take care of it. It's not your worry."

"I feel it is," I shot back.

"The director wants us all at the campfire as soon as possible," Mr. Lister barked. "Get moving."

I took a step, but in the direction of Oz and T.J. "It's okay," she said. "Teddy's okay, I think. Just a couple of bruises. You fellas go ahead. I'll get him to the infirmary and we'll look him over. Go on ahead to the campfire."

"You sure?" I asked.

"For certain," T.J. said.

I turned away and Oz fell in step with me and the campers as we headed for Cabin Row. "You win," he said, nudging me.

"What do you mean?" I asked, lighting a cigarette.

"Final score three to two, so you win."

"Oh, right." As if it mattered.

He punched me lightly on the shoulder. "I'll get you next time."

WHEN WE GOT to the campfire site, it was still pitch-dark; the campfire had not yet been lit. *What was Mr. Lister's hurry?* I wondered as we were guided by a flashlight beam to our places. I steered Peter and the three younger campers I had fetched from my cabin to an empty spot at the inner edge of the circle, a space that gave me room to sit with my bad leg stretched out and to lay my crutches beside it.

The flashlight beam bounced around the circle, lighting up one expectant face after another, then went out. No one spoke above a whisper. Peter sat close to me and grasped my right hand with both of his. I could feel the cathedral of tall pines overhead and smell the needles. It was a spot I had always loved, especially at night, when it made me feel as if I were in a vaulted cocoon and the best of the camp's spirits were watching over and protecting us.

A spotlight attached to a tree overhead came on and lit a small area about six feet to our right, where the circle of campers was broken by a passageway. Through this walked the tall man I had seen standing next to Woody when we first arrived, the man he called Buck Silverstone. He was now dressed in leggings, a loincloth, a leather vest, and a feathered headdress. The exposed parts of his lean, muscular body glistened in the spotlight as if oiled. His nose jutted out from a surface of intersecting planes, his eyes were dark shadows. As he lifted a feathered pipe to his mouth, Steady Bomber stepped out of the dark, wearing only a loincloth. He struck a match against a stone in his hand and held it to the bowl of the pipe. Silverstone drew on it, and exhaled a cloud of smoke. He handed the pipe back to Steady and lifted his arms, extending them above his head and spreading his fingers. From the angle I was watching him, he seemed to tower way above us.

"Oh, Great Spirit of Fire, we come in peace." His voice was deep and resonant. "Show us that you hear my words! Grant us now the warmth of your light."

An explosion, loud like a cherry bomb, came from somewhere high off to our left, causing Peter to flinch in my lap and the children all around me to squeal. I looked up and saw a ball of fire begin to blaze like a giant firefly where the explosion had sounded. It burned in place for an instant, then began to hurtle down at us with a loud roar. Voices buzzed as it approached, and from somewhere outside the ring of campers Chunky began to bark. When the ball of fire hit the woodpile, a thunderclap sounded, a wave of heat washed over us, and a wall of flames leaped high in the air. The blaze revealed a circle of astonished faces.

I began to move myself and the children back from the fire, thinking that where we were sitting would be too hot. But the flames died quickly, leaving a smoldering campfire that looked as if it had been burning for hours. You could have roasted marshmallows on it right then. I didn't understand how he made that happen, but it sure was impressive compared to the bonfires of previous summers. Chunky expressed his reaction by continuing to bark hysterically.

The spotlight came on and once more lit up the area where Silverstone was standing, just off to our right. He took the peace pipe again from Steady and raised it with both hands toward the fire. "Great Spirit, Tarachiawagon," he intoned, "Master of Life, Holder of the

Heavens, who decides the fate of battles, the clemency of the seasons, the fruitfulness of the crops, and the success of the chase: we offer you brave young Buddy Stemmer, the first of our young men to sit in vigil the whole night through and greet the dawning. By spending the night alone with only a blanket and false-face mask to cover him, and tending a fire lit without matches, he has come to know his animal helper, the Great Bear. Accept him, O Great Spirit, into the Society of Faces."

Steady stepped into the circle of light. Silverstone turned to him and touched him on his forehead with the pipe. Steady stood still a few moments, and then retreated back into the dark. A breath of cool night air swept over the audience and fanned the flames of the campfire for a moment.

"What's a Society of Faces?" Peter piped up in a frightened voice.

"Silence!" Silverstone roared, and Peter flinched against my side.

"Sorr-eee," I whispered, squeezing Peter's shoulder and wondering when Steady had sat through this so-called all-night vigil by a fire lit without matches. After all, hadn't he been with us coming from the train station this afternoon?

"And silence the dog, please," Silverstone called over to his right. In response, someone got up and led Chunky away.

"Campers," Silverstone chanted, remaining still, as if at attention. "Let me tell you who I am. My white man's name is Buck Silverstone. You will call me Buck. You will know me as the man running Camp Seneca's Indian program. You will think of me as the leader of a game we are playing."

His body relaxed and he began to pace back and forth as if in deep thought. Low whispering came from members of the audience here and there around the fire. "But my name is not really Buck Silverstone and I am not playing a game. I am actually a member of the Seneca tribe, and a descendent of warriors and prophets. My true name is Redclaw. I am of the Wolf clan." He began to pace again, toward us and away from us. "Redclaw, a warrior's name. Although I am working for Mr. Wentworth and helping him to run his camp, my mission is to redeem this land that once belonged to my ancestors, this very land that the camp now occupies."

Is he kidding? I wondered.

He stopped pacing and his head swung back and forth. I could feel his eyes on us. He raised his voice. "For though this place was named Camp Seneca in the spirit of make-believe, the land it is on was, in fact, once part of the Five Nations, the Iroquois." In a lower voice he added, "The white man took it for himself."

Peter leaned his head closer and whispered to me. "Is he right?"

"I don't know," I said. "Listen."

"You campers will help me in this mission. In the next weeks you will learn something of Seneca ways, and the older among you will do as Buddy Stemmer has done. You will be initiated through Seneca ritual."

His body sagged imperceptibly. "That is all I have to say to you now. Let us commune with the spirits as I leave you." He turned to face the fire again, with his right hand removed something from a pocket of his vest, and raised the hand in the air. "Partake of this sacred tobacco, O mighty Shagodyoweh, who live on the rim of the Earth, who stand towering there, who travel everywhere on the Earth caring for the People."

With his raised hand he tossed something into the fire. In response it flared up again in a roar of flames. All of us held our breaths and leaned back from the heat. Then, abruptly, the fire died down again, and we looked back to where Redclaw had been standing. He was gone.

"Wow!" said Peter amid a general chorus of gasps and murmurings. "Are . . . are we really on Indian land?"

"No, Peter, it's just a game, to make what we do here seem more realistic." *I hope.*

"Really?" he asked nervously.

"Guaranteed." I put my hand on his head and turned it so that I could see his face. "How are you doing?"

"I'm fine," he said brightly. "I'm not even homesick."

"That's good. You'll be sure to tell me if you are."

"I promise. When do you think Mom will write?"

"I bet we get a letter tomorrow."

"Really?"

"I happen to know she wrote us even before she and Dad left for Europe."

He smiled, but then his face clouded over. "Boy, that Buck guy is something."

"Don't worry about him," I said with all the assurance I could muster.

But in truth he *was* a little scary; he had put on a very impressive performance, overdone just enough to let us know it was unreal. It was typical of everything Woody did at Seneca, and part of what made the camp so unusual.

In fact, Silverstone's performance made what I knew was coming next seem anticlimactic. It was time for Woody's traditional opening-night campfire story, and I thought he would have to work especially hard if he were to cast his usual spell.

But then something else broke the mood of Buck Silverstone's performance. When the spotlight came back on, Mr. Lister was approaching me. He was carrying a picnic basket.

"Is little Teddy okay?" I asked.

He stooped next to me. "The boy's arm is broken, but he's basically all right. Woody wants to talk to you and Osborne. You're to report to the director's office first thing after breakfast."

"Okay," I said, grasping my crutches and struggling to my feet. "We'll be there." *Oh, my God! Are we in trouble!* I took a cigarette out.

"No smoking here," Mr. Lister said and began to move away.

"What's the picnic basket for?" I asked him.

"It's a morning snack for the campers who are sleeping in the tree house tonight."

"Do you want me to deliver it?" I asked, disliking myself for trying to be ingratiating.

"That's okay. Look after your kids."

I sat down and the spotlight went out again. Five or six more eight- and nine-year-olds, seeing the group around me, came and sat next to us. Shadows moved just beyond the dim firelight. A figure I recognized as Woody stepped out of the dark and seated himself close to the fire, where Silverstone had been. Chunky, apparently calmed, followed and stretched out next to him. The flickering flames reflected in Woody's eyeglasses.

"You campers on the other side of the fire, come closer," Woody said. Shadows moved in the dark beyond the fire, and the group gathered around Woody. I put my arm around Peter, knowing that what was about to happen would be scary. Things were beginning to seem back in control again. I looked around to see if Oz had arrived yet, but in the dim light I couldn't find him.

Woody began to speak in a low voice, and the murmuring around the fire quieted. "Once, not so many years ago, at a famous vacation lodge on an island in Lake Pymatuning—not far from here, as you know—a strange man came to work in the kitchen. No one knew where he was from, or anything else about his background. No one knew if he had a wife or family, or even where he lived. All anyone knew was that he worked very hard and never spoke a word.

"He was an assistant cook whose main job was meat cutting. He worked at a chopping block in a corner behind the kitchen's main stove. He worked all day with his back to the rest of the kitchen help, cutting up meat with a set of sharp knives and a huge meat cleaver. He was a big, powerful man, maybe six-and-a-half feet tall. But he worked with great delicacy, chopping, cutting, carving, fileting, boning."

Woody mimed these gestures with his right arm above his head. The huge shadow of his arm moved against the backdrop of trees behind him.

"Mornings they would bring him a side of beef, or a whole hog, or a crate full of chickens or ducks, and by quitting time there would be a pile of steaks, hams, filets, hamburgers, chicken breasts, drumsticks, or chops. All neatly piled up and ready to cook or freeze. This man was not too pleasant to look at. He had long, greasy black hair, and a scar that ran from the corner of his left eye across one side of his mouth to his chin. It gave him sort of a snarling look. But he minded his own business and worked the days away, chopping and slicing and sharpening his cutlery."

A coal popped in the fire. I still wondered how it had been made to burn so low so quickly. Peter pressed against me and other children moved closer.

Woody went on: "As time passed, this man worked away quietly. He would be the first to arrive in the morning and the last to leave at night."

Woody was quiet for a moment. Peter whispered, "What's going to happen?" I squeezed him tighter.

"But then an odd thing occurred," Woody went on, his voice a few degrees more tense. "One morning the head cook came in and noticed his assistant working away at his chopping block, cutting up meat. The only trouble was he was cutting up something the head cook hadn't given him."

Murmurs sounded among the campers.

"The head cook was a meticulous, orderly man, a small Oriental person, maybe Chinese. He distinctly recalled that he hadn't supplied the butcher with meat the night before. Yet there the man was, chopping and cutting."

"What could it be?" somebody asked.

Woody raised his right hand for quiet. "The head cook didn't know, but he decided to overlook the mystery. Maybe he had forgotten giving him meat. Or maybe the assistant had somehow found the key to the meat locker, and fetched himself something to work on.

"But the next morning the same thing happened. This time the head cook was sure he hadn't given his assistant any meat to cut up. And he'd kept the key to the meat locker with him for the night. And yet the man was cutting up something big, much bigger than a chicken, though a little smaller than a cow. It was something with very long limbs too."

Woody lowered his voice. *"And with hairless skin!"*

"Eeuw!" someone near me groaned.

"What does that mean?" Peter whispered. "What was he cutting up?"

"Remember, it's a story," I said.

"Well," said Woody, "the cook decided that his assistant would have to be confronted. He went and stood behind the big man and tapped him on the shoulder." Woody reached out toward the fire and tapped the air.

"But nothing happened. The assistant cook went on chopping away with his big meat cleaver, hacking at the piece of flesh in front of him. So the head cook tapped him harder. This time the man stopped chopping. But he didn't turn around. He just stood there.

"So the head cook poked him in the back a little harder, and he said, 'Excuse me, mister!'"

Woody paused. Then he shouted, "HAH!"

Peter jumped so hard that his head banged my chin. Other children laughed nervously. Someone on the far side of Woody got up and retreated into the dark.

Woody went on. "The assistant cook said, 'Hah!' And then he yelled, 'Aieeeee!' Then suddenly he spun around, and as he did so he raised his cleaver sideways to the level of the head cook's neck. And with a single stroke, he cut off the man's head. The cook fell dead on the spot, of course, and his head went bouncing along the floor.

"Then the assistant cook let out a scream and ran out of the kitchen, waving his meat cleaver over his head."

Peter twisted and looked up at me with a stricken face. "Will they catch him?"

"Just wait," I said.

The night breeze, as if on cue, began to fan the flames harder. Woody raised both his hands, as if trying to calm the wind. "Well, of course someone called the police right away. And a dozen state troopers showed up with dogs as soon as they could get a boat to the island where the lodge was. But the Mad Cook had disappeared. So the police broke up into three parties, each with a dog, and began to search the island. That wasn't going to be easy, because the island was mostly wooded."

Woody stood up and began to walk in place. "They searched and searched, but they couldn't find the Mad Cook anywhere. They figured he had swum to the mainland. So they headed back to their boat, which was a big, fast police launch.

"But just by chance, one of the younger troopers had strayed away from his group. Without a dog."

"Uh-oh," several children moaned.

"He was right in the middle of the island, deep in the trees, and he was lost. He wandered around for a while, and then he suddenly noticed what looked to him like trampled undergrowth." Woody raised his voice a third of an octave. "The trooper saw freshly broken twigs and ferns with their undersides turned up.

"Then he saw a piece of torn cloth hanging from a broken branch. The branch stuck out between two large tree trunks that formed a sort of archway. The young trooper stopped walking." Woody stopped moving and crouched ever so slightly. "He stood stock-still and listened as intently as he could. But he couldn't hear anything except the usual sounds of a forest—insects chirping, and birds chattering, and wind in the treetops.

"He carefully removed his pistol from its holster and began to walk slowly toward the archway. He couldn't see beyond it, but he kept on walking closer and closer.

"When he got up close, he stopped and listened again. He could hear no unnatural sound.

"He took a step forward. Now he was right next to the trees. He took another step. And another." Woody approached the fire. "He was between the trees and nearly through the arch. He took another step. And then . . ."

Woody looked off into the distance on the far side of the fire.

"Aaaaaaaaiiiiiiiiiii!" a man's voice cried out in the dark somewhere off to the left of us. "Help! Help me! It's the Mad Cook!"

A spotlight came on, more powerful than any that had been lit earlier, and was aimed where the voice was coming from. Bright as day, it revealed Tommy Osborne standing between two big tree trunks that formed an archway just like the one Woody had been describing. Oz was looking back over his shoulder with his mouth wide open in terror. He screamed again, "Aaaaahhhhhh!"

"What's wrong?" yelled Woody in a loud, stagy voice.

Oz turned his face back to us and seemed about to run when a white-sleeved arm reached out from behind one tree trunk and grabbed him. Then a huge figure stepped out. He had long disheveled hair, a greenish yellow face with bulging eyes and a dramatic scar running down one cheek.

The man suddenly raised a meat cleaver over his head and brought it down on Oz's shoulder. A shower of blood sprayed around Oz as he collapsed in a heap at the foot of the tree trunks. The monster roared, "Aaaaarrrrggggggggg!" and raised the meat cleaver again. Children around the campfire stood up and screamed. Peter leaped up and threw himself into my arms.

And then, as he stepped into the full glare of the spotlight, the Mad Cook placed one hand on the top of his head and pulled his hair upward. His features began to stretch out grotesquely. We heard a rubbery popping noise, and suddenly Bordy Udall was standing there with a big grin on his face.

"Joke!" he yelled. "Joke!" He bent down and helped Oz up. Oz smiled and waved and reached under his collar and pulled out what looked like a deflated football bladder that was dripping dark liquid and had soaked his shirt.

The spotlight went out. As my eyes began to adjust again to the dark, I could see the dim outlines of the campers standing still in stunned silence. A few cried out in relief. Those who had started to run away began drifting slowly back.

"Good show," Woody shouted into the dark, clapping his hands. "Great show!"

"So it was all a joke," Peter said, leaning into me with his arms around my neck. He was snuffling back tears.

The night wind was blowing hard now.

"Yes, it was just a trick," I said, hugging him hard, trying both to reassure him and to keep him warm. *But not a very entertaining one,* I thought, suddenly seeing the whole thing through Peter's eyes. *Not a fun story at all for a little kid. More sadistic than funny. Has it always been that way and I never noticed before?* I wondered. *Or is something really different this year?*

MR. GARVEY'S WOODS

O F ALL THE confused images that crowded in on me as I woke up the next morning from a night of bad dreams, the most unsettling was the memory of tripping and falling down as I was running to cut off Teddy and Oz. It wasn't like me to stumble that way, and I wondered if something could have caused it. I guess it was possible that I might have tripped over my own crutch, although that wasn't the way it felt. But what object could possibly have been out there in the middle of the infield? A tree stump? A stake in the ground?

Sunlight was flooding the cabin and a light breeze was blowing through the screening just above my bunk. The air felt cleansed of the threatening elements from last night. The old clock I had placed on the ledge near my head said seven-fifteen, fifteen minutes before reveille. Everyone in the cabin looked to be sound asleep still, among them Steady Bomber. He and I had stayed up late talking about his so-called all-night vigil, which, he admitted to me, he had not yet done, though Buck was planning it for him shortly.

So Buck had a streak of bull in him.

More important, the deep sleepers included Peter, just across the aisle from me. I was relieved that the wild softball game and the scary campfire hadn't kept him awake or given him nightmares. My plan to give him a great summer was still workable, despite the changes in Seneca I sensed.

I had a few minutes before everyone had to be up, so I quickly scribbled a postcard to let Karla and Dad know that Peter and I had arrived safely at camp, and addressed it to my father's secretary, Irma Schrifftgauer, care of his office in New York, so she could forward it to them wherever they were in Germany. When I was finished, I still had enough time to walk down to the softball field and see if I could find something that might have tripped me.

I PUT ON some fresh clothes, pulled my crutches from under the bed, and went out the screen door. The air was cool, the dew glistened on the grass, and the shadows of the trees on the other side of the meadow made their morning stretch toward the cabins. Above, the sky was clear—it had all the markings of a perfect day. But even from a distance I could see nothing anywhere inside the base paths that could possibly have caused me to fall the way I did last night.

I was standing in the infield, puzzling over what could have happened, when Woody's recording of a wake-up bugle call came blaring from the mess hall. Voices began to sound in the cabins. Children's heads appeared in the windows. Chunky came bounding down Cabin Row. I gave up on solving the puzzle of what caused my fall and started back to my cabin. As I paused to greet Chunky with a pat on his neck, I sensed something hovering nearby, something forbidding, as though a shadow had darkened the promising day. I looked around, then glanced up and saw the dead tree, its tangle of bare branches still scoring the sky with skeletal fingers. It felt oddly as though it were staring at me.

AFTER BREAKFAST Oz and I reported to Woody's office, a small room in a corner of the mess hall. Mr. Lister made a big deal out of taking us there, interrupting our after-breakfast coffee and herding us to the office door. I even had to skip my morning cigarette, not allowed in the mess hall, but outside, behind the kitchen. But I was so nervous about the meeting that I didn't protest. Woody hadn't shown up yet, so Oz and I sat down to wait for him, while Mr. Lister stood by the door, his eye patch magnified by the thick lens of his glasses.

Oz and I exchanged guilty glances but said nothing. His Seneca cap rested on his lap. I looked around Woody's crowded office, which, in addition to the usual furnishings, held a number of items peculiar to this camp. On the wall behind a file cabinet were shelves holding a selection of books with titles like *History of the Indian Tribes of the United States, Atlas of the North American Indian,* and one named simply *Indians.* Next to the shelves hung a picture frame containing arrowheads arranged in an arc. On the floor opposite the desk stood a large model fort. Inside were toy soldiers lined up in ranks and files, and surrounding it were Indians getting ready to attack. But what dominated the little room was a huge bearskin draped over a coat tree. The bear's forearms reached out and mauled the air with extended talons. Its large head grinned malevolently with gleaming eyes and gaping jaws. It might have looked alive if it hadn't been wearing Woody's Indian headdress with its trail of multicolored feathers.

On the wall behind the bear's head was mounted a double-barreled shotgun.

WOODY STRODE IN, followed by Chunky. He returned Mr. Lister's salute, then went and stood behind his desk. He looked at Oz and me.

"Men," he finally said, "I naturally wasn't pleased about my little Teddy getting hurt last night."

I tried to speak, but something caught in my throat and all that came out was a squeak.

Woody splayed his fingertips on the desktop and leaned his weight on them. "Not because he's my son; I don't like seeing anyone get hurt. You understand?"

Oz and I both nodded.

Woody leaned back and folded his arms. "But having made that clear, men, I want to say that I also like what happened last night." He looked at Oz, whose mouth had opened a little. So had mine.

"Yes, you heard me right," he continued. "I liked the spirit and intensity of your competition. It was real and it was exciting. Little Teddy will never forget that experience for as long as he lives. And he'll be the better for it." He looked at Mr. Lister, who nodded in response. "That's what the Camp Seneca experience is all about. Right, Adam? Competition. Building character. Sorry about your eye."

"It's okay," Lister said.

"Good," Woody said, turning his attention back to us. "We probe for people's weaknesses, and when they're exposed, we teach them how to overcome them. Everything we do this summer, from the Snipe Hunt to the Sham Battle to the Olympic Games, is designed to be a test of each camper's mettle. The strong ones will grow. The flawed ones will crack. That may sound harsh, but if you're weaklings, life will break you anyway in the long run."

He looked out the screened window behind the bench where we were sitting, and frowned. "And leaders will emerge. Men who can take the initiative, carry the message to Garcia. That's what I want."

He pounded his fist on the desktop. "And that's what my son experienced last night. A test of his mettle. Little Teddy will learn from that. So, good work, men."

Oz and I looked at each other, but neither of us said anything.

Woody nodded again. "Now, let's talk."

He lowered himself into his seat and leaned forward, his hands sliding along the desktop. "Of course," he said in a strained voice, "I'd just as soon you didn't repeat any of what I just said to my wife." He ducked his head as if avoiding a blow. "She would kill me."

"Where *is* Win?" I asked.

Chunky whined at the sound of her name.

Woody sat back. "Well, she'll be along pretty soon, pretty soon."

"When?"

He hesitated. "I don't know exactly. But soon."

Silence hung in the room. Woody reached into his desk drawer and took out a pack of cigarettes and a lighter. "Anyway, men," he began, tapping out a cigarette for himself, "wasn't that something last night? The campfire I mean."

"I didn't know we were on Seneca land," I said.

"Maybe not literally," Woody said, snapping the Zippo open and lighting his cigarette. "Buck Silverstone was just speaking metaphorically. Kind of appropriating these grounds for his Indian program. But all around here, yes; there is Seneca land." He blew out smoke. "Just east of us was the great Allegany Reservation, home of Cornplanter and Handsome Lake, the religious prophet. And of course, north of that were Cattaraugus and Buffalo Creek."

"How did Redclaw do that with the fire?" I asked. "I mean, get embers right away."

"Buck. It's Buck. Redclaw's only his warrior name."

"Buck," I said.

Woody squinted thoughtfully. "I'm guessing the embers were there to begin with and the fireball burned away whatever was covering them. But I don't understand many of his tricks, and believe me, he's got a load of them."

"Pretty neat," Oz said.

I thought about bringing up Steady Bomber's nonvigil, but decided it might seem to be making trouble to do so at this point. "Can we smoke?" I asked instead.

"Go ahead," Woody said.

I lit a cigarette and offered Oz one. He refused.

"Buck's a find, all right," Woody said. "He's going to make Seneca's Indian program richer than it's ever been before."

"I sort of miss Chief Wahoo," I said.

"Yes, of course," Woody said. "But life goes on." He paused, and for a moment it felt as if he had drifted away. Then he focused again and looked at us. "Anyway," he continued, "here's the drill. This evening I want you two to take the junior campers to Garvey's Woods."

In this annual ritual, we took the campers arrowhead hunting. First we would warn them to be very quiet because we were trespassing on property owned by a farmer named Mr. Garvey, who had a terrible temper and didn't want us there. Then someone, usually a local farmer playing the part of Mr. Garvey, would come charging out of the woods, shouting and carrying on and threatening to "pepper" us with his shotgun. We mockingly called it one of Woody's character-building exercises, but I had to admit that surviving a seemingly dangerous experience made the children feel good. It built up morale. Usually, though, we didn't subject the kids to this little game until a week or so into camp, when they'd gotten to know each other better.

"So soon?" I asked.

"Sure."

"Just the youngest campers?"

"The eight- and nine-year-olds. That'll be about a dozen or so kids."

"Just Oz and I?"

"Plus Mac. It works much better with just younger counselors."

"Okay. But should we do every single scary part?"

"No, no, no," Woody answered. "Only a mild version. That's why I want you to go right after supper, while it's still light. Don't build it up too much. Garvey isn't even going to have his shotgun. He'll just shout a little, carry on. The arrowheads are already planted."

Oz looked at me questioningly. "What's this Garvey's Woods?"

"A make-believe place," Woody explained. "That is, the place exists—the woods—but they belong to a local farmer who couldn't care less if we trespass. There is no real Mr. Garvey."

"Sounds like fun," Oz said.

"Who's going to be Garvey?" I asked.

"Buck Silverstone."

"Gee," I said, thinking of the Pa Kettle types we had used in the past, "he doesn't seem quite right for the role."

"You'll be very surprised."

"Where are these woods?" Oz asked.

"A ways from here . . . ," I began.

"No," said Woody. "This year we're going to do it in the woods behind the cabins." He waved his hand over his right shoulder, in the direction of Cabin Row. Chunky lifted his head and yawned.

"The Forbidden Woods? But that's really 'no trespassing,'" I protested. "I don't get it."

"Why?" said Woody, exaggerating his puzzlement, I thought.

"Because . . . because," I sputtered. "For one thing, we tell the children not to go in there." I looked at Oz. "We lose at least three softballs a year in there that we don't even bother to look for."

Oz looked at Woody sheepishly. "I hit one in there last night. I didn't know."

"It's the Forbidden Woods," I repeated.

Woody shook his head. "We've got permission from the farmer who owns that land."

I took a deep breath. I didn't understand why he had to make changes in what had been a comfortable routine, and I really felt that this was not a good one. "Well, for another thing, the arrowhead hunt in Mr. Garvey's Woods has a mystique of danger, of a place you go to at your own risk. Why do this right next to where the children sleep?"

"Not a problem. We're going to do it on the other side of those woods. About half a mile down the road from here. You'll go in from the meadow there. And just a little way in. You can tell the kids that the farmhouse over there is Garvey's."

"But the children will know it's the same woods . . . the Forbidden Woods . . ."

"No, they won't. They'll be confused. We'll load 'em in the truck and Jeff'll drive 'em around first so they don't know where they are."

I shook my head. "But there're so many other woods around here! Why go there at all?"

"Buck wants it that way. So that's it," Woody said, slapping the desk lightly. "You don't realize what a good thing we have in him."

"I guess I don't."

Instead of ignoring me, as he would have previously, he looked at me thoughtfully. "He represents something we haven't had at Seneca in the past, a different culture, a fresh way of seeing things. Best of all, a way of getting closer to nature. If that doesn't fit with what we're used to, it's good. It'll make the campers' experience richer, seeing a clash of ideas."

That actually does make sense, I thought.

Woody liked what he was saying. "We have a little melting pot here. Your friend Osborne here is part of it too. He also comes from a different background. You too."

"What do you mean?"

"Well, you guys aren't blue collar exactly. It's good, it's good. I like the diversity. And I'm especially pleased to have people from the East

Coast. But you're a little different." He stared at us as he said this, his eyes intense.

Oz looked at me. I shrugged.

"But that's neither here nor there, and I didn't mean to get off on that," Woody said, appearing more normal now. He put the cigarettes and lighter back in the drawer, stood up, and addressed Mr. Lister. "Adam, let's get the day going. Call the people for our strategy meeting." He turned back to us. "Go down to your cabins and help your kids get ready for inspection. I'll assign the group for Garvey's Woods at morning assembly. You're dismissed. Good hunting."

We got up and went to the door. Oz put on his cap.

"Oh," I said, turning back to Woody. "Should the group include little Teddy?"

"Of course. Why not?"

"I just thought, with what he's been through . . ."

"Back onto the horse, back into the water."

". . . and anyway, doesn't he know about the trick?"

"I honestly don't know. But what does it matter? Now get to it."

Mr. Lister opened the door and we filed out.

I FELT UNEASY about doing Garvey's Woods so soon, especially for Peter's sake. Now that I was beginning to see the camp through his eyes, I would have liked him to get more used to things before going through another of Woody's make-believe dramas. Woody sounded an awful lot like Dad with all his talk of testing and probing for weakness. The big difference, though, was that Woody at least practiced what he preached. Whereas he was rugged and in good shape, there was nothing tough about my father—he liked eating and drinking too much, plus he pampered himself. Not that he was fat, but he was soft as whipped cream, and he hardly ever exercised, or at least not that I could see. As for physical strength, even with my bad leg I was in better physical shape, unfortunately something I found out shortly after my skiing accident when Dad and I got into an argument and started shoving each other. It wasn't his strength but his terrible temper that I was scared of, which was a holdover from childhood.

That was the problem with my big campaign to move in with him: I had almost as many difficulties with him as I did with my mother. Almost, but not quite. And being with Peter more often would make up for it; and with Karla, who was so much more reasonable than my mother. And just getting away from that apartment and having my own space—that was an important thing too.

AFTER CABIN INSPECTION, when the recording for drill call sounded, the whole camp gathered at the front steps of the mess hall for morning assembly and listened to Mr. Lister bark out the day's activities and the list of who would be doing what.

"The juniors will be going arrowhead hunting after supper." This provoked muttering among the veteran campers, and a mention or two of "Garvey's Woods."

"And the first half of cabin seven will be sleeping in the tree house tonight." Cheers from cabin seven.

Woody stood beside Mr. Lister with his arms crossed and his head tipped back as he scanned the assembly from beneath the long bill of his cap, like a marine general inspecting his troops. Chunky stood beside him. Buck Silverstone was nowhere to be seen.

WHEN ASSEMBLY WAS OVER, I fell into the day's routine as if the previous summer had never ended. One of my duties was to be assistant riflery counselor, under Len Lawrence, so I spent the morning at the rifle range, inspecting targets, calling out scores, and policing up the spent .22 shells. These were somewhat tedious tasks, because I had to change the targets after each round of shooting and be sure all the shells were picked up before we left. Yet I found the repetitiveness reassuring.

The range was in an area that had been cleared in the Big Woods, and the back of the range was up against an old barbed-wire fence that divided the camp's property from that of the farmer who owned the Forbidden Woods. In fact, you could say that the fence divided the Big Woods from the lower part of the Forbidden Woods, except that it was impossible to see any difference in the trees at that point. The firing lanes were laid out so that we shot into a particularly dense part of the Forbidden Woods. Staring into the gloom beyond the fence, I wondered what Buck Silverstone could have in mind by placing Garvey's Woods over there. I was not looking forward to our visit there tonight.

"Jerry, will you help me again?" Peter called out.

"As soon as I get through with the targets."

Peter's arms weren't long enough both to brace the rifle butt against his right shoulder and to hold the barrel steady with his left hand, and without my help he kept firing into the ground. When I held the barrel steady for him, however, he complained, saying that he wasn't doing it himself. He couldn't make up his mind which way he wanted it, and he was growing steadily more frustrated.

When I got back to the shooting gallery I lay down on the mattress next to him to brace his rifle again.

"Why don't you give him a pistol instead?" a voice behind us said.

Both Peter and I looked back. Buck Silverstone was sitting next to Len on the balustrade in back of the mattresses. He was wearing jeans and a blue work shirt. In contrast to Len, whose bald head was wet with sweat, he looked cool and relaxed, and almost genial, certainly a different person from the man at the campfire the night before.

I looked at Len, who shrugged.

"That would be neat," Peter said. "I can hold a pistol."

"We don't have any," I said.

"Then get some," Buck said.

"Could we?" Peter asked.

"We'll have to ask Woody," Len said.

"I doubt if it's in the budget," I added. "Besides, a pistol is awful hard to aim properly."

When the round was over, I went to change the targets again.

"You could make your life a lot easier," Buck said when I got back. He was still sitting on the railing next to Len.

"How?" I asked, as I lay down next to Peter again.

Buck stared in the direction of the targets for a few seconds. "Maybe I'll show you sometime."

I looked at him, trying to divine the intent of what he had said, but he kept staring off in another direction. I wanted to ask him why he had moved Garvey's Woods, why he was changing everything, but with Peter there, it didn't seem the right time.

IN THE AFTERNOON, I took part of cabin one to the crafts room. There, under Bordy's supervision, the children began various projects like making the traditional Indian costumes they would wear during upcoming rituals: loincloths, single-feather headdresses, moccasins, and the like. I wondered if Buck would do something different with these as well. Win still hadn't shown up, and her absence made being in the room, which also served as her office, feel strange. But the time went quickly, and as I watched the kids' growing excitement, I could feel myself continuing to relax.

Halfway through the session, Mr. Lister arrived back from town with the day's mail. As he sorted the pile on Win's desk, I spotted a thickish envelope with Gothic script on it that I instantly recognized as Karla's handwriting. There was also a postcard from my mother, with a photo of the Capitol on one side, and on the other, two lines of wavering script that read, "Having a grand time here in Washington! Hope you're doing well. XXX Mom."

When I got back to the cabin I opened Karla's letter and found a smaller envelope addressed to Peter and a single-page handwritten letter to me:

Jerry my dearest!

I am always so nervous writing to you auf Englisch, but here I go with that. As you know, this is being written before we left for Europe (and you go to camp), so there is not much of news to tell you and Peter about us.

But I do want to say this, Jerry, that I so much hope our plan for the summer will work, that your father will be really impressed with your good care of Peter, and that you will be soon joining our little family once again. My dear Jerry, it is so important thing that you and your father get along better together and that you make this effort to do that. I do not like it when you fight, especially coming to blows. That makes my job so much harder, you know!

Your father is sometimes so very difficult to understand. It is as if he is missing a sense—do you call it the "six sense"—about people, especially the children.

Anyway, Jerry, enough about this. By now you are at the camp and I hope it is as exciting as always! Are there any pretty girls for you? Please don't let them steal your heart away from me!

And please, please take such good care of my Peter. You are so so important to him, Jerry.

Your Karla

When I had finished reading my note, I called Peter over and gave him his letter from her.

"How come there's no stamp?" he asked.

"She sent it in a letter to me . . . to save a stamp, I guess."

He read the letter standing by my bunk. I thought his eyes got a little moist.

"You okay?"

"I'm fine." He looked at the letter again. "Do you think you'll really be coming to live with us?"

"I hope so."

"Me too."

Despite my pleasure at the words in Karla's letter, I soon began feeling listless. Maybe I hadn't gotten enough sleep, or maybe it was the weather. The heat seemed to thicken during the day, and by late afternoon the atmosphere had begun to feel oppressive.

AFTER SUPPER, Oz and I rounded up the fifteen junior campers assigned to go to Garvey's Woods. Chunky joined us on the walk. In the group were both my brother and little Teddy, now wearing a gleaming white cast on his arm. I asked him how he felt. He said he was fine; the break was a hairline fracture, and he could even swing his arm around. He demonstrated by whirling it over his head. I felt a little better about him.

At the farmhouse near the back entrance to the camp, a long green pickup truck was waiting for us, with Jeff, the camp's handyman, at the wheel. It had a tarp mounted above its bed, and when I looked at the sky, I understood why. The air had turned hazy and thunderheads loomed on the horizon.

After counting heads to be sure all the juniors were there, we climbed aboard the truck and squeezed ourselves onto the wooden benches that ran along either side of the truck's bed. When Chunky began barking, Oz lifted him onto the bed, where he immediately lay down. All but one space on the benches were filled when Mac and T.J. showed up to join us. T.J. wasn't assigned to this outing, but I figured she was using the expedition as a chance to spend some time away from camp with Mac.

After Mac pushed T.J. up onto the truck bed, she sat down in the remaining bench space, opposite me, next to Oz. When Mac began to climb up himself, Oz stood up to give him a hand. Mac accepted the lift, and then used its momentum to propel himself into Oz's vacated seat. Oz looked around, then shrugged and lowered himself to the floor with his back against the cab window. I gave Mac a dirty look, but he just stared blankly at me. T.J., however, lowered her eyes and blushed.

The truck took us a few miles over hard-top back roads, past fields of ripening corn. The tarp made it hard to see where we were going, which probably was also part of the plan. After a while, we turned onto a dirt road that I recognized as the one that led to camp, but I don't think any of the children noticed. We rattled along a little way, then came to a stop about a quarter of a mile from the camp entrance. I lowered myself from the truck bed, took my crutches, and began to help the children down. I saw that we were parked by the opening of a stone wall that ran along the road. Beyond the wall lay a broad meadow full of tall grass and wildflowers, backed by tall woods. To the left, in the middle of the meadow, were a farmhouse and a barn with a silo. Off to the right were woods of newer, shorter growth, and above these smaller woods stood the leafless tree I had noticed before, its dead fingers clutching for the sky. I suddenly realized that I was seeing the Forbidden Woods from the other side.

I looked around to see if anyone else had noticed the distinctive tree. T.J. was staring at it, and catching my eye, she gave me a quizzical look. I put my finger to my lips, and she said nothing.

When everyone was off the truck, including Chunky, I told Jeff to come back in an hour or so. We then assembled at the opening of the wall, just beyond which was a path that went off through the tall grass, in the direction of the Forbidden Woods. Since the group would go no faster than I could move on my crutches, it was agreed that I would walk the point, and that Oz would bring up the rear. I hoped that Mac and T.J. would go off on their own, but they stood listening to my instructions to the children and fell into step at the end of the line.

I set out on the path with everyone else behind me, except for Chunky, who decided to trot along beside me—a bit of a surprise, as I wasn't much of a dog person and the feeling was usually mutual. I had decided I wasn't going to tell the children about farmer Garvey. I was counting on Buck simply to show up and warn us off in a friendly way. Judging by his mood at the firing range this morning, he was fully capable of being a genial Garvey.

The ground was firm enough to support the tips of my crutches, so I was able to move along quite briskly. The children were chattering excitedly, including Peter, who seemed to have bonded with Teddy. I liked being in charge. And to my pleasant surprise, when I looked back to check on the kids, I found T.J. walking directly behind me without Mac, who must have been somewhere in back. The sun was lowering behind us, but there was still plenty of light. The thunderheads, however, were moving closer, and a wind was beginning to make the treetops hiss.

"You get along good on those things," T.J. said.

"Lots of practice," I grunted. *I like your company.*

"There's your old tree," she said, pointing up at the treetops.

I stopped to look, and everyone stopped behind me. We were about thirty yards from the edge of the woods, and from the angle at which we were standing you could see only the tree's topmost dead branches, which were swaying slightly in the rising wind. All around us grasshoppers zoomed in the tall grass like tiny whirligigs, as if warning one another of the intruders and, perhaps, the coming storm. The sun was hidden now, and the woods looked so dark that I thought about calling off the expedition, but we had come a good distance already, the children were all excited, and Buck would be ready to perform his act. I figured we might as well go ahead.

"What's going to happen?" T.J. asked softly. "It looks a little gloomy in there."

"It's okay," I said, though in truth I wasn't feeling all that confident. I turned around, leaning on my crutches. The children crowded around me and T.J. Mac circled around the group and moved in next to her. Out of the corner of my eye I saw him take her hand and try to draw her aside, but she pulled her hand away.

Oz came forward and stood beside me and Chunky. "Let me talk to them," he said in a low voice, taking off his cap and brushing back his blond hair.

"Keep it tame," I said.

"Okay, kids," he said softly, as if not wanting to be overheard by anyone who might be nearby. "Listen up a minute. Many years ago— over a century ago—a great battle was fought here . . . on this field and in those woods over there."

"An Indian battle?" Peter asked.

"That's right," he said. "Between the Five Nations of the Iroquois and the Adirondacks."

"Did people die here?" Teddy asked.

"Hardly any—," I began.

"Well, of course they did," Oz cut in. "Many died. It was a bloody battle." He looked around and pointed to a rise in the ground nearby. "That's probably one of their burial mounds right there. There're bound to be others."

The children looked around and murmured.

"Are there ghosts?" Peter asked me.

"No. No ghosts."

The children looked doubtful.

"Sure there are ghosts," Mac drawled.

"Not that you'd see in broad daylight," I said quickly. "Maybe once in a while at night. Indian spirits. But very peaceful."

"I'm not going in those woods," another child said.

"Wait. Look," I said. "There are arrowheads lying around in there, just for the picking."

"Arrowheads? Wow!"

"That's right," I said. "Beautifully shaped stone arrowheads. They've been lying there for years. We're going to see if we can find some."

"In those woods?"

"That's right." I hesitated.

"You better warn 'em," Mac said.

"There's just one thing," I went on. "We have to be very quiet."

"Mr. Garvey?" one of the children said, his tone questioning.

I tried not to react to this. "We'll be trespassing, sort of. The woods belong to the farmer who lives back there in that farmhouse, a man named Ebenezer Garvey. He doesn't really like people walking around on his property."

"If he lives back there, why hasn't he stopped us already?" one of the children asked.

"He spends his time in the woods," Oz said.

"What'll he do if he catches us?" Peter asked.

"Well, he'll just tell us to please leave."

"I'm not so sure. He's mean," Mac said, grinning mischievously.

"He's okay," I said. "But we've got to keep alert." I took a deep breath. "If anyone sees him, just yell, 'Here comes Garvey!' and we'll get out of there. He won't do anything."

"What if he's got a gun?" Teddy asked.

"He won't have a gun," I said firmly. "Anyway, he's pretty lame, and if he gives us any trouble, we'll just outrun him."

"Come on, enough standing around," Mac said. "Let's go yank the old guy's beard." He started off toward the woods. A half dozen of the children ran after him, slapping their mouths with open hands and letting out whooping war cries. The other nine held back.

"Shhh. Quiet," I said. Peter and another boy had taken hold of my right crutch to prevent me from following.

"It's okay," I said, pulling my crutch free. "You'll have fun. Nothing bad'll happen, I promise."

I started moving again, with the two boys next to me and the rest in back, herded along by T.J. and Oz. The woods loomed just ahead of us, but as we approached they seemed less dark inside. I saw that the path we were following led into the trees.

When we reached the edge of the woods, Mac and the six children who had raced ahead with him were waiting for us, as if reluctant to go farther on their own. I went past them, took a few steps into the woods, stopped to call the others to follow me, and continued in.

The woods were not dense, consisting mostly of young birches and alders, with a mixed undergrowth of moss and assorted shrubbery. But the air felt different—mustier—and smelled slightly of mold. The wind was less noticeable, and could be heard mostly in the tops of the trees above us. Invisible strands of a spiderweb tickled my face. The children fell silent as we made our way slowly along. I thought I heard an owl hoot somewhere in the distance.

I followed the path past a thick tree stump about six feet high with a rotten log lying next to it, crawling with insects. Just beyond the log was a large rock covered with lichen. At the edge of it I spotted the first arrowhead that Woody must have planted.

I came to a stop and turned around. The children nervously gathered in front of me. Oz, Mac, T.J., and Chunky stood a few feet in back of them.

"Okay," I said quietly. "Let's start searching."

Oz spoke up. "This is where a big ambush is supposed to have started the battle. There should be lots of arrowheads."

The children looked around tentatively. No one wanted to move away from the group.

"Teddy," I said, pointing up the path. "Why don't you search that rock there."

Teddy took a few hesitant steps past me. An animal suddenly moving in the distant underbrush made him flinch.

Oz walked back along the path to the tree stump and went around it a few feet away from the path. "Over here looks good. Come on, Peter!"

Peter followed him back along the path and stopped to gaze at the undergrowth. Oz gestured, "Come on. Come on. Start searching. There's got to be some around here." Peter moved slowly toward him.

"Hey!" said Teddy, behind me. "I think I found one!" I turned and saw him run to the rock and pick up his prize. "Lookee!" he shouted, holding it up with the hand of his uninjured arm.

His find seemed to embolden the other children. They began to drift away from the path, and Teddy gave me his find for safekeeping, then moved past the rock to look for more. I found myself standing alone with T.J. I looked for Mac and saw him moving with three children into the shrubbery on the opposite side of the path.

I busied myself by scanning the woods for a sign of Garvey. I saw no movement anywhere. I could hear T.J. chewing gum.

"What's gonna happen?" she asked in a low voice. Her green eyes glistened.

"I don't know. I hope nothing."

"It ain't so bad in here."

"I think it's spooky." I looked down at the base of my right crutch and twisted its rubber boot into the dirt of the path. "And it's going to storm."

"Not for a while." She snapped her gum. "We should come in here sometime and look at your tree up close." Strands of her hair had come loose from her ponytail and were hanging down along her cheek. She was sparkling with health.

My face flushed. "I don't know."

A scream, sounding from the path up ahead—a child's cry—made my throat and chest tighten. Chunky's bark came from the same place.

"Teddy found a snake," a child's voice cried. "A big one!"

I swung around, planted my crutches forward, and launched myself along the path past the rock where Teddy had found his arrowhead. I hated snakes—the very idea of a big one made my head swim—but my sense of responsibility for the children had taken over.

About fifteen feet up the path, Teddy came into view. He was standing just off the path, near another fallen tree trunk, paralyzed with fear. Chunky stood beside him, growling and showing his teeth, but keeping a safe distance. Only a couple of feet away from them, half under the trunk, the snake lay coiled. Its triangular head was raised and was drawing slowly backward, forcing its neck into a tight bend. Its tail was lifted and buzzing. Though I had never seen one in the wild before, I knew at once that I was looking at a rattlesnake. I felt both stunned and paralyzed for a moment. I had seen many snakes during the previous summers there, but never a rattler. I had always heard the Eastern ones were found in mountainous areas. There were no mountains near here.

Before I could make a move, Oz came running along the path toward me and lunged for Teddy, snatching him off his feet. Chunky moved away with them. The snake struck empty air and recoiled, still buzzing angrily. A moment later, I felt my left-hand crutch being snatched from under my arm, and there was Mac in front me swinging the crutch through the air and down onto the snake. Children's cries came from every direction. Chunky began to howl.

I saw the snake's lighter underbelly as the armrest of the crutch hit the creature's midsection and rebounded, the two shafts splintering. The snake lashed its tail helplessly, its back broken, as Mac raised the crutch for another blow.

Then a deafening explosion rang out, and I heard a pelting sound, like sudden rain in the treetops, and I saw leaves above us shivering as if a blast of wind had blown through them. Out of the corner of my eye I saw children freeze in their tracks. When I turned to see where the noise had come from, I saw Mr. Garvey standing with a smoking shotgun pointed into the air, and, beside him a black dog the size and shape of a mastiff.

"Leave the snake alone, son," Garvey said.

Where the heck did he come from? I wondered.

Chunky was barking frantically.

If the person dressed as Garvey really was Buck Silverstone, he had shrunk to about three quarters of his size and turned himself into a wiry, angular old man with apple cheeks and a snow white beard.

He had on boots, bib overalls, and an engineer's cap made of ticking. He was missing teeth, and I swear his eyes had turned from black to a piercing light blue. It was an altogether amazing transformation.

"Leave the snake be, son," he repeated in a high, scratchy, old man's voice.

Chunky continued to bark, though keeping his distance.

"Quiet, dog!" Garvey snapped. "See to him, Steel." The bigger dog bounded a few steps forward and barked once. Chunky whimpered and retreated down the path.

As I studied Garvey, I saw that his overalls were baggy enough to allow him to stoop a little without showing it, which was how he had shrunk himself. He swept his glinting eyes back and forth, taking us all in. "You there, boy, come here." He lowered his gun slightly and pointed in Peter's direction. "You."

Peter, on the path, raised his hand to his chest. "Me?"

"Yeah, you. Come here. I won't hurtcha."

Peter looked at me and, when I nodded, took a tentative step toward Garvey.

"Everybody, gather around," Garvey said. He sounded harmless now, even a little friendly. "I want to tell ye all something. Come on. Come on. I won't hurtcha."

I was impressed. If this was Silverstone, he deserved an award for his performance.

Looking at one another, we slowly formed a ragged semicircle next to Peter, about ten feet away from Garvey. I counted heads to make sure no one had strayed. Chunky watched from far down the path. The children were nervous, but seemed to be taking everything in the spirit of fun. Through the foliage above us, I could see dark clouds closing in. The gloom in the woods was thickening.

Garvey took a step toward us and put his foot on a low stump, cradling the shotgun. The big dog sat beside him. Behind them, young white-skinned birches marched up a gradual rise to where low shrubbery formed a barrier. Beyond the shrubbery, the woods turned dense and black, veiling its secrets.

Garvey spoke: "Mind you, it's okay for you to be huntin' arrowheads along the edge of these woods. That's fine."

"You're not gonna shoot us?" one of the children piped up. There was suppressed laughter at the question. I was relieved that they felt they could joke.

"No, I ain't gonna shoot ya." He drew in a sharp breath and scowled. "But I gotta warn ya about somethin' else. As your leaders mighta told you, a great battle was fought here once. That's why there are arrowheads around. Many brave young men died here." His voice dropped to a near whisper. "This ground drank their blood."

"Are they really buried here?" Peter asked.

"They are," Mr. Garvey said. He stood up, limped away from the stump a few steps, and waved his gun at the woods in back of him. "And they are restless, ye hear?" He turned and came toward us, his eyes glittering.

For an instant I detected something of Buck Silverstone in his movements. What was he doing? I wondered. This wasn't part of any script I knew of.

"Listen to me, children, and listen well. I might own those woods, but I can't control what goes on in there. Those are sacred burial grounds, and the spirits that inhabit them don't like what's happening to the land." He looked back at the woods and then back at us. "I seen strange things going on there. So I'm warnin' ya: ya better stay away from here."

"Why would we ever come around here?" Mac asked playfully.

"Don't you know where you are?" Garvey shot back.

My Gosh, he's going to give it away!

"Do you know what these woods are?"

Why is he doing this?

He waved in back of him. "Just yonder are your cabins. Didja realize that?" He raised his voice. "You're practically sleeping in those burial grounds! So beware!"

Damn!

"Don't let him scare you, kids," I said, my voice unsteady. "There's nothing to worry about. There's never been a problem."

"Beware!" Garvey hissed.

"Let's go, children." I started back down the path.

"I see a ghost!" someone screamed.

I stopped and looked back. At the top of the rise behind Garvey, thin wisps of what looked like ectoplasm were rising out of the underbrush. My heart thudded. I was looking at the shape of a small child, its mouth a black circle of woe, its arms reaching out beseechingly.

I blinked and the form dissolved. It was clearly vapor from dry ice or steam from hot liquid, but it was effectively scary nonetheless.

"Let's get out of here!" a child yelled.

Several children were screaming and running away from the path.

"This way, everybody," Oz called out from down the path.

"It's nothing!" I yelled. "It's just smoke." I looked for Peter and saw him running toward Oz.

"It's a ghost. It's a ghost," Mac yelled, cackling with glee.

T.J. began to herd the strays back onto the path. They ran after Oz, who kept shouting, "Follow me to safety." I picked up my broken crutch from the ground and limped along behind on the good one until I got a ways down the path. There I stopped and turned around to take a last look at Garvey.

He was still standing next to a tree, staring at me, his dog beside him. It was the same man, but he was different. He was tall again, younger, more menacing. Now I could see Buck Silverstone.

"What were you trying to pull?" I called out. "You weren't even supposed to bring a gun."

He gave me a look of contempt, raised the gun, and fired it far over my head. Children screamed in the distance. I turned away and moved along the path, feeling as if I might get a load of shot in my back if I lingered. At the edge of the woods, I turned around once more and saw him in the distance. He had picked up the snake by the tail and was carrying it up the rise to where his ghostly vapors were still drifting. His big dog was gone.

When I came out of the woods, the children were scattered over the meadow, some running away and some waiting and watching the woods. The sky had turned a hazy yellow, and the wind was still rising and large drops of rain were beginning to fall. You could feel the tension of a thunderstorm about to break.

I looked for Peter and saw him with Teddy and Chunky, waiting for me on the path. When I caught up with him, he seemed calmer than I expected.

"The kids say the ghosts were fake," he said.

"Of course they were," I told him, putting my hand on his shoulder and squeezing it. "You aren't scared, are you?"

"They sure looked real to me."

"Dry ice or steam, probably."

"Well, I'm never going in those woods again," he said.

"That's probably smart. You'll never have to, anyway, I promise."

THE TRUCK WAS waiting for us at the opening in the stone wall. Instead of Jeff, Bordy stood by the cab. We helped the children and Chunky climb into the back. As I was awkwardly trying to mount the truck bed, Oz told me to ride up front in the cab with T.J. Since I was tired and my bad leg was starting to ache, I didn't argue with him. Peter seemed to be calm, happily absorbed in speculation about how the ghosts had been created. I handed Oz the broken crutch, then with the good one I hopped around to the passenger's side of the cab and climbed in next to T.J.

"How'd it go?" Bordy asked, greeting me.

"What happened to Jeff?"

"He had to fix something in the shower house."

"You can take the short way home," I answered. "The kids know where they were."

"How come?" Bordy asked.

"Silverstone told them."

"How was his Garvey act?"

"He was unbelievably convincing. But then he screwed everything up."

"How so?" Bordy started the motor.

"He tried to scare the kids with ghosts. Did a pretty good job of it too. At least for a while. He even had me going."

"They looked like real hants," T.J. said.

"Well, Woody'll like that."

"I guess. He had a big dog with him, one I've never seen before. He called it Steel."

"Probably borrowed it from someone around here," Bordy said.

"Probably."

From the back of the truck came the sound of children singing. Through the window at the back of the cab I could see that Peter was joining in. "The kids seem fine, but I still don't see why he tried to turn those woods into something frightening."

"Woody'll probably like that too," Bordy said. "Makes everything more exciting."

"I could use a smoke," I said.

"Me too," said T.J.

"Go ahead," Bordy said.

I gave T.J. a cigarette from the pack in my shirt pocket and we both lit up with my lighter. We rode along in silence as we approached the camp and turned into the back entrance, next to the farmhouse. The rain was beginning to fall hard.

"What's the matter, Jerry?" Bordy asked as we pulled to a stop by the mess hall.

"What do you mean?"

"You seem real downcast."

T.J. turned her face to see my response, making me feel self-conscious.

"I'm not down. Things just seem so different this year, and I feel sort of disoriented."

"It's always that way at the start of camp," Bordy said. He tightened the hand brake.

"Where the heck is Win?" I asked. I could see the children climbing out of the truck and dashing with Chunky for the mess hall.

"That's a good question," Bordy said. "Woody says she has business in Pittsburgh."

"What's she do?" T.J. asked.

"She helps Woody in his law office," Bordy said.

"Well, she should be helping him out here," I said.

Mac appeared at the passenger's side window, looking for T.J. He was getting soaked.

"We better get those kids in," Bordy said, opening his door and getting out.

I opened my door and began to climb down.

"Go ahead in, Mac," T.J. said. "I'll be right along."

Mac frowned, but then disappeared from sight.

"Wait," T.J. said, touching my arm.

"What?"

"Get back in a second. We'll finish our smokes."

I slid back onto the edge of the seat and closed the door to a crack.

T.J. blew out smoke. "What was that all about? What went on there in the woods?"

"Why?" I asked.

"You seem so shook up by it."

I looked at her face, wondering if I could trust her. "I'm confused."

"About what?"

"What Silverstone was doing. Some of those kids are going to have nightmares. They're cheering each other up now, but wait'll they get alone in the dark tonight."

"Isn't that what this camp is about?"

"Maybe so. I mean there was always talk about Indian ghosts and so on, but it's going further this summer. Garvey was never so scary before, even with the older kids."

"Really?"

"Yeah. And I'm not sure the burial-ground talk and the ghosts were part of the plan. And why tell them where they really were after we had fooled them by driving there the long way?"

T.J. searched my face with her eyes. "What do you think is going on?" she asked.

Being so close to her made it difficult to concentrate. "I think he wants to keep us out of those woods."

"Or maybe to draw us in."

I thought a moment about that. "You're right. He's certainly building them up."

She stubbed out her cigarette, using the truck's ashtray. "What are you gonna do?"

"Talk to Woody, for one thing."

"What about?"

"About what happened today. About how Silverstone changed things."

"You don't like him, huh?"

"Do you?"

She gazed out the windshield. "He sure is great looking."

"Yeah, he's impressive all right." I pushed the door open and climbed out of the cab. T.J. followed and ran for the mess hall. I went around to the back of the truck and found my broken crutch lying on the floor. I was getting soaked, but I didn't care. It felt good.

As I limped toward the back door of the mess hall, I stopped to look at the Forbidden Woods, a brooding presence no more than thirty yards away at that point, right in back of the staff privy and the flagpole. I felt as if it were watching me, challenging me to enter. I dug Teddy's arrowhead out of my pocket and went to the mess hall door. As I opened it, I expected to find that T.J. had gone to join Mac, but she was standing alone just inside the door, waiting for me.

Something warm flowed in my chest. I was surprised by how good it made me feel.

EVENING ACTIVITIES

INSIDE THE MESS HALL, the tables had been moved to the side and the chairs arranged into rows for watching a movie, a tradition on rainy days. Woody was at the projector, loading whatever film it was we were going to see.

I looked around for Peter and Teddy—I wanted to be sure they had not been too upset by what had happened earlier. When I didn't see them, I decided that someone must have taken the group down to the cabin to change into dry clothes, something I needed to do as well. But some of the things that happened in the woods really bothered me, and I wanted to talk to Woody right away.

"What happened to your other crutch?" Woody asked without looking up from the projector.

"I'll explain if I can talk to you a minute."

"How'd it go?" He was stooping slightly, trying to thread the film.

"Fair. But some bad things happened."

"Everybody all right?" He guided the strip of celluloid onto the receiving spool, humming softly as he worked, basically ignoring me.

"There're things I have to talk to you about."

"Wait'll the movie starts and the kids are settled."

"What are you goin' to show them?"

"The usual."

"The usual" meant a medley of popular song performances by famous musicians like Cab Calloway and the Mills Brothers, something I had seen half a dozen times.

"Meanwhile I'll get dried off," I said.

He didn't acknowledge me as I backed away. I headed down to cabin one.

WHEN I RETURNED with Peter and a couple of my other younger campers, the film was running and Woody was sitting in a chair by the projector. The Sons of the Pioneers were singing "Tumbling Tumbleweeds." Woody was softly singing along. The light of the projector silhouetted the profile of his head, emphasizing its roundness and the way he thrust it forward from his shoulders.

I found a chair and pulled it next to him. "He overdid it," I whispered.

Woody stopped singing. "Who did?"

"Buck Silverstone. He scared us."

"Well, that's the point."

Cab Calloway, wearing a checkered suit, began to sing "Blues in the Night."

"Yeah, but he went too far. He had a shotgun and he fired it."

Woody didn't respond.

"He did other stuff too."

"Was he any good as Mr. Garvey?"

"Yes," I said grudgingly. "I couldn't believe it was him for a while. He even somehow changed size."

"Well, there. That's what I wanted."

"But he didn't follow the script. He really scared the kids. He also told them about the woods. We'd driven the truck around, trying to confuse the kids, but he told them exactly where they were. Now they know they're sleeping right next to the Forbidden Woods. I'm worried they're gonna have bad dreams."

"They'll survive." Woody continued to bob his head to Cab Calloway's beat, as if I wasn't present.

"Oh, yeah," I said urgently. "And I swear he planted a rattlesnake there."

"No kidding?"

"I'm serious. That's how my crutch got smashed. Mac used it to kill the snake. That's what made Garvey fire his gun. I didn't like the whole thing."

"Shhhh. You're talking too loud." Woody looked around to see if anyone was in back of us. "Come see me in my office after taps."

I tried to suppress my irritation. Woody was clearly on board with everything Buck Silverstone did, so he wasn't going to listen to me. And without Win, I had no one to talk to.

As I left the mess hall, the Mills Brothers were singing "Up the Lazy River."

A COUPLE OF hours later, when the children had finally settled down in their bunks and the scratchy recording of taps had sounded, I kissed Peter good night and made my way back up to the mess hall. The rain had stopped and the peeper chorus was loud—friendlier and more inviting than the pale light I could see in Woody's office.

"Take a look at this," he said as I swung my way into his office and took a seat on the bench. I was wondering what it meant that in two previous summers I had never set foot in this room, and now I had been in it twice on the same day.

Another change.

Woody slid a piece of paper toward me and I picked it up. It was a fading black-and-white photograph of a dim interior. It was a picture of a man, viewed from the side. He was addressing an audience seated on tiers of benches. His head was tilted back as if he were shouting or singing, and his hands were thrust forward, holding what looked like a thick rope of beads. He was wearing a black suit and a string tie. His long hair was tied back in a ponytail.

I turned the picture over. In the upper left-hand corner there was writing in ink: "Cold Spring Longhouse, Allegany Reservation, 1947." "What's this supposed to be?"

"It's Buck Silverstone."

"It is? What's he doing?"

"He's preaching. That's sacred wampum in his hands."

"He's a preacher?"

"Correct. In that photo he's in the Cold Spring Longhouse on the Allegany Reservation."

"Yes, I read that."

"That's just east of here. He's the real thing. A descendant of Handsome Lake himself."

"Who's Handsome Lake?"

Woody frowned at my ignorance. "The great nineteenth-century prophet and visionary. A wild man who straightened himself out. Got off the booze and created a religion still practiced by the Iroquois today, a mixture of Indian tradition and Christianity."

I looked at the photo again. "And Buck preaches it?"

"Well, he did at one time." Woody brought the cigarettes and the lighter out of his drawer and lit himself one. "That was taken five years ago."

"Yes."

"He knows the Code of Handsome Lake. Gaiwiio, it's called. The Good Word."

"What's the Society of Faces he talked about?"

"Oh, that's some mumbo-jumbo, I think. But the older kids'll love it. At their age, they love secret societies."

I slid the picture back onto Woody's desk, next to a folded newspaper lying on it. I sat for a moment searching for a polite way to say that I didn't think religion was what Camp Seneca really needed.

Woody offered me a cigarette, and I took one. "But that's not the point," he continued. He picked the photo up and placed it in a file he was holding, on top of another photo. I only got a glimpse of it, but it seemed to show two men in Indian outfits, standing in front of a lodge of some sort.

Buck and Woody? I wondered.

"You've got other photos?" I asked.

He closed the file and put it into the top drawer of the cabinet next to his desk. "Nothing relevant. The point is that Buck is going to teach us about another culture. He's really in a position to know."

I nodded.

"He's going to immerse us in it."

"You told us this morning."

"Well, it bears repeating." He tapped the desktop with his fist and stood up. "Everything we do this summer will be connected to that culture in some way. From the Snipe Hunt to the Olympic Games. Everything!"

I nodded again.

"And it's a culture that in many subtle ways is superior to contemporary civilization," he went on, "not so dependent on industrial capitalism; more in touch with the rhythms of the earth."

"Well, I don't see how what happened out there today is connected." I thought a moment of the snake and the ghosts. "It could have been, I guess, but I don't see quite how."

"What do you mean?"

"Well, the snake, for instance."

"Snakes can be sacred to the red man," Woody said.

"And he tried to use ghosts to scare the kids away from those woods. I mean, he made it look real. He used dry ice or something."

"Couldn't there be an actual sacred burial grounds in there?"

"Is that what he told you?"

"Not really. I'm guessing."

"Well, yes. That's precisely what he said. But why go to the trouble—"

Woody cut me off. "Look, I want you to accept whatever he does. I've asked around and it sounds to me like the juniors had a great experience out there tonight."

"Maybe so . . ."

"Including your brother, let me point out."

"How do you know?"

"Isn't he okay?"

"Yeah, but how do you know?"

"Buck told me."

"Okay." *How did Buck know?* I wondered for a moment. "But what about the shotgun . . .?"

He put his hand up. "Don't ask questions and please don't interfere. It's going to be a new experience for all of us, but I want you to trust it. Buck knows what he's doing. He's been preparing this for a long time. Okay?"

I didn't say anything. I wondered what exactly he meant.

"That's a condition of working here this summer," he said, fixing me with his gaze. "Can you accept it?"

I felt a slight chill in the room. "I'm not sure."

"But you'll try?"

"I'll try."

I stubbed out my cigarette. "Incidentally, does the camp have any pistols?"

"Pistols? Not that I know of. Why?"

"Some of the smaller kids at the rifle range were asking. Peter, actually. They . . . well, he has trouble holding a rifle straight."

"I don't think so."

"Some of the counselors were suggesting . . ."

"It's too dangerous for a kid that small to be shooting pistols. They're hard as hell to aim."

"That's what I told them."

"I don't like it."

"It was Buck's idea, actually."

"Well, it's a good idea. In some ways. But the budget won't allow it."

"I just thought I'd pass it along. In case . . ."

"Well, you did." He stubbed out his cigarette, got up, and opened the door. Our conversation was over. "Okay, then we understand each other. About Buck, I mean."

"I'm not so—"

"That's good."

He isn't going to hear me. I stood up, braced myself with my crutch, and looked around the office. The shotgun was still in its place on the wall.

So Buck used a different one. Does he keep it in his cabin? I wondered.

I turned back to Woody. "May I borrow that newspaper for a couple of minutes?" I hadn't seen one since I got to camp. Win usually made one available with the day's mail.

"Sure." Woody handed it to me. "Leave it on my desk when you're through. The door'll be unlocked."

"Thanks."

"You're walking the bed wetters?" Woody asked as I went through the door.

"Yes. The only one we know about so far is Teddy."

"Well, there'll be more as the summer goes on."

"Yeah, especially if we keep scaring them like we did today," I muttered.

Woody turned off the light and followed me out, leaving the door open. He put his hand on my shoulder. "Things will be okay," he said. "Win's arriving tomorrow."

"That's good," I said, feeling a surge of relief.

Woody nodded at me. I could barely see his face in the dim light coming from the kitchen. "It's going to be a good summer. You'll see."

I hope I do.

As he went out the front door, I turned away and headed for the kitchen. Usually the staff and counselors gathered there for talk and a bedtime snack, and Sukie and Eve served hot cocoa. But tonight it was empty.

There was a saucepan half full of cold cocoa on top of the cooking range. I turned on the burner under it and spread out the newspaper. Twenty minutes later I headed back to Woody's office to return the paper. It was dark inside. I opened the door and stood there, leaning on my crutch and trying to relax by breathing in the cool damp air that was now blowing through the screens. As my eyes got use to the dark, I could make out the file cabinet at the side of the desk. I got a sudden urge to see what else was in Buck Silverstone's file. The back of my neck began to prickle at the thought.

Why not?

I glanced at Woody's cabin. He was still up; through the cabin's single window I could see his shadow moving against the far wall. There was no way to be sure he wouldn't come back to his office.

I better not fool around with the files right now, I decided.

The light went out in Woody's cabin, signaling that he probably had gone to bed. Nonetheless, I felt uneasy about being in his office. I looked out at the camp; there were no lights anywhere. I realized I must be the only person awake.

I turned around slowly, making sure not to knock over anything with my crutch. Then I saw two large eyes glaring down at me. It took me an instant to realize that they were the glass eyes of the bearskin. And far from glaring at me, they were only reflecting a light from outside. But what could the source of that light be? Most likely someone with a flashlight heading for the latrine, or checking up on the cabin seveners in the tree house, I decided. I turned around, glanced through the screened window in back of Woody's desk, and saw nothing but darkness down in the Big Woods.

The light was gone.

Sure enough, when I looked back at the bear's face, its eyes had disappeared into the blackness.

As I moved through the doorway, I heard the sound of a piano being played in Jeff Small's room. I thought briefly about knocking on his door, but then decided against it.

Despite having been around him every summer I'd been to the camp, I realized I didn't know the first thing about him, not even how old he was, or where he was from.

I went down the front steps and headed for cabin one. The air still felt wet and heavy, and my crutch sank into the soft turf. Inside the cabin, the campers were breathing heavily in their sleep. Obviously the experience with Garvey wasn't keeping them awake, but I wondered what they were dreaming, especially Peter. Teddy mumbled something incomprehensible when I gently shook him awake, and he got to his feet as if sleepwalking.

"You got your arrowhead?" I asked him, to see if he had anything to say about the experience.

"Yes. In my trunk." His cast brushed against me.

"How's the arm?" I led him outside.

"Good, but I gotta make number two."

"Aw, Teddy; are you sure?" I dreaded the long walk to the Kybo.

"Yeah," he said in his small scratchy voice.

We set off down Cabin Row. The Big Woods were black.

As I stood inside the latrine waiting for Teddy, I noticed a dim light coming through the small ventilating window high on the far wall.

"I'm going outside for a second," I said.

"Okay," came the sleepy reply.

I hopped out the door. A bright light was shining from the Big Woods, approximately where the rifle range was, and too far from the tree house to have anything to do with the overnighters.

"What's that?" Teddy asked, appearing behind me, still tugging up his pajama bottoms.

"Some sort of flashlight or torch," I guessed.

"Who is it?"

"Maybe someone from the tree house. Or someone working late. Probably getting one of your dad's surprises ready."

"What surprise?"

"Who knows? The Snipe Hunt, maybe. Come on, let's go back to bed." I took his hand and led him up Cabin Row, wondering what surprise indeed was being prepared for us down there in the woods.

THINGS SEEMED BETTER the next day. Peter had slept well. The weather was cool and sunny, without a cloud anywhere. When I had finished breakfast, I told Steady to get the cabin ready for inspection, while I fixed myself a fresh mug of coffee, and went out in back of the kitchen for a cigarette.

After a few minutes, T.J. came over from the women's cabin and joined me. She was wearing jeans and a red flannel shirt.

"Whatcha doin'?" she asked.

"Smoking the evil weed."

"Stunt our growth, huh?" She lit a Lucky Strike with her own small Zippo lighter.

"Oh, you got one too," I said.

"Doesn't everybody?"

"Mine's a Ronson." I dug the lighter out of my shirt pocket and held it for her to see. It was silver and monogrammed with raised letters: "KM to JM—*Ich träum' so viel von dir*—6/13/52."

"Fan-cee! But it's not windproof like mine."

I shrugged.

"Who's KM?" she asked.

"Karla Muller. My stepmother. Peter's mom."

"What's the date?"

I looked at it self-consciously, as if for the first time. "Graduation and also my birthday."

"What's the rest of it? *Itch trowm . . . ?*"

"It's a line from a German song we love. Marlene Dietrich."

"She's German?"

"Marlene Dietrich? Sure."

"No, Jerry," she said impatiently. "Your stepmother."

"Yeah, she's German."

"Does she look like Marlene Dietrich?"

"A little."

"Sexy."

I put the lighter back in my pocket, dragged on my cigarette, and blew out a rolling blue cloud, enjoying the light-headedness that the first smoke of the day always made me feel.

T.J. let smoke drift out of her nostrils. "Tell me about your friend Osborne."

"Well, he's not really a friend. I mean I like him, but we never palled around like."

"Does he have a girlfriend at that fancy school of yours? Are there girls there?"

"Yes, it's coed." I thought a moment. "No, I don't think he has a girlfriend. Not that I know of or can recall." I looked at her. She was waiting for my reaction. "Come on, what do you care? You're spoken for."

"'Spoken for'! My, my."

I blushed. "Seriously . . . What does 'T.J.' stand for, anyway?"

"Thelma John. My daddy, he wanted a boy, I guess."

I looked at her; she was staring at me. I liked the way she cocked her head, as if she were challenging me to find fault. Her high, prominent cheekbones seemed to tilt her almond-shaped green eyes upward. Her skin was pale and delicate, and her lips looked soft and pink, even without lipstick. "Seriously," I repeated, "I thought you and Mac were, you know, practically engaged."

She looked away. "Not really."

"What does that mean, 'Not really'?"

"We're real close . . . good friends. But I haven't even graduated high school yet. I don't think I want to talk about it." She took a quick drag on her cigarette. "Did you all talk to Woody?"

"Woody?" I stalled. "What about?"

"Come on now; don't be going coy on me. I mean about what happened last night with the kids. The ghosts and all."

I dropped the butt of my cigarette and ground it out, then lit a new one. "Yeah, I talked to Woody."

"And?"

"I really didn't get anywhere."

"What do you mean? Did you tell him what happened?"

T.J. was studying my face. Her stare made me feel weak. "I tried to tell him what happened, but he dismissed all of it. He says Buck's an important guy. That we have to trust him."

"Well, do you?"

I thought a moment. "It's Woody's camp. He knows what he's doing, I guess."

T.J. dropped her cigarette and stepped on it. "What about the woods?"

"What about them?"

"What's he doing in there?"

"I don't know that he's doing anything." *What about the light last night!* I thought, suddenly remembering.

"How did he make the ghosts?"

"I don't know."

"Don't you wonder?"

"Yeah, a little. It was probably dry ice." I looked at my watch. Inspection was in ten minutes and I hadn't made up my bunk yet. "I gotta go."

"Me too. What's happening today?"

"Nothing special that I know of. I'll see you around."

She laughed. "Yes, you will."

As she turned away I could make out the shapeliness of her breasts and the narrowness of her waist beneath her loose clothing. *Her figure is like Karla's,* I thought. I felt her almost physical pull, but reminded myself she was off-limits. It was a vaguely familiar feeling that made my stomach tighten.

THE MORNING WENT SMOOTHLY. After inspection, in which Woody gave us eight and a half points out of a possible ten toward the prize of a watermelon for the cabin with the highest weekly total, I got assigned to the rifle range again. When Len and I got there with our campers, we found Buck down by the target stand, hammering away at something.

When I looked closer, I saw that he had built a wooden frame that nearly doubled the height of the stand. The top of the frame held a row of additional targets that were much too high to shoot at. A series of thin wires extended from the new targets to the shooting gallery.

"What the heck . . . !" Len exclaimed. He stood on the gallery, scratching his head.

Buck said nothing, and continued his hammering. He was wearing jeans and a work shirt again.

"What are you doing?" Len called out, walking down to the target stand. Buck stopped his hammering and began to talk to Len, explaining something I couldn't hear. The children milled around, waiting. Finally, the two of them returned to the gallery, Buck leading the way.

"Watch," he said to no one in particular. He stepped between two mattresses and looked to either side of him. "Everyone get back now." From inside his shirt he removed a large pistol, about the size of a .45. He cocked it by grasping the barrel and sliding it back, and slowly leveled his arm, and squeezed off five shots in quick succession. The reports were sharp but not particularly loud. The weapon barely moved in his hand. When I shifted my gaze to the targets after the first few shots, I could see small bits of paper flying from very near the bull's-eye of one.

"Wow!" said Peter, who was standing next to me. "That's neat."

When he was finished shooting, Buck reached above him to the ceiling of the gallery, grasped a small wooden peg that was resting between two nails, and walked it backward with his upraised arm. Through a series of quick maneuvers, the used target was replaced by a new one, all through the use of his wire contraption.

"That's fantastic!" I said, really impressed.

"Save you some trouble," Buck said, without looking at me.

"Woody will really dig it."

"That's something," Len said. "Changes everything."

"How many fresh targets will it lower?" I asked.

"Just two," Buck said. "But that cuts your job way down."

"It sure does," I said. "Now figure out a way to make the empty shells jump into the box without having to be picked up." I walked over to the little bin at the end of the gallery where we stored the policed-up bullet shells. I grabbed a handful and held them up for Buck's inspection.

"That'll be a little harder," Buck said. "But why do you bother to save them?"

"For Indian necklaces and stuff," I said, letting the shells sift back into the bin.

"What kind of gun is that?" Peter asked.

Buck inspected the weapon. "It's a military target pistol. A High Standard Model HD twenty-two."

"Can I shoot it?"

"It's very hard to aim," Buck said. He looked at Len. "Maybe the camp will supply them and include them in the program so the kids can learn."

"I doubt it," I said.

"Awww," groaned Peter.

"The camp can't afford them, and even if it could, they're not weapons for kids. Too big."

While Peter protested, I looked off at the target Buck had shot at. Even from the gallery I could see daylight through the bull's-eye.

"Could I shoot yours?" Peter asked. I noticed that he hadn't addressed Buck by name, and that he wasn't looking at him.

He's afraid of him, I thought.

"I don't want you shooting a pistol," I said.

Buck studied Peter silently. Everyone else was quiet. I could feel tension building. "Maybe sometime," Buck finally said.

"Heck," Peter said.

"Were you doing something down here last night?" I asked Buck.

He shifted his gaze to me. Again the silence built. "No, why?"

"Someone was down here with a light."

Buck said nothing.

I looked beyond the target stand to see if I could see any signs of trampled foliage near the barbed-wire fence. The undergrowth looked normal, and I couldn't go closer to inspect. By building the new target contraption, Buck had removed any excuse for me to take a closer look.

AT LUNCH THINGS got even better. When I arrived with my campers, I could feel a change in the air even before I stepped inside. I pushed open the door and instantly saw Win sitting at the staff table. She looked prettier than ever and she smiled at me warmly when our eyes met. I felt a missing piece fall into place inside me.

As soon as I got my campers seated, I went over to greet her. "I'm glad you're back. We really missed you."

"Hello, Jerry." She smiled without saying anything more. Her attention had shifted to something on my left.

Woody appeared there, slightly out of breath. "Get to your table, Muller," he said. "Let's get things going."

After everyone was seated and he had said grace, Woody clinked his water glass with a knife to signal the beginning of a mealtime variety show, another camp tradition. This would be an opportunity for me to get Oz to play his guitar and sing, something I had been looking forward to.

The campers who had been there before quickly took up the clinking. "We want Woody and Lenny to sing," they chanted. The two men got up from the staff table and went to the open area next to the games corner. Putting their arms on each other's shoulders, they sang "I Only Want a Buddy, Not a Sweetheart" in close harmony, their rich tenor voices soaring sweetly. They were really good, almost professional. Even Jeff Small came out of his room to listen. I couldn't tell what he was thinking of this corny white man's music, but I was glad he had come out because he would hear Oz perform when the time came.

When Woody and Len sat down, the clinking and chanting began again, this time demanding that Bordy do "Herman the Bear," a camp favorite, all about a hungry bear who ate an entire family, then burped them up again. Spoken in a falsetto voice, and with a lisp, it was funny, and Bordy performed it well. The campers applauded uproariously. I noticed that only Buck Silverstone seemed unamused.

When Bordy had sat down, I started to clink my glass and call out, "We want Oz. We want Oz." The children at my table quickly took up my chant. Others did too. Oz, a few tables away, was smiling and hunched over a little, as if he were about to push himself up. Woody was grinning and saying something to Win. I looked at Early McAdams, at the table to our right. His head was tilted at an angle that said, "What is *this?*" and he was looking in the direction of the nurse's office. There I saw T.J. standing in the doorway, watching Oz expectantly. Mac was frowning.

Finally, Oz went to the games corner and took a guitar out of its case and tuned it as he moved to the performing area.

I was suddenly back at school, where Oz's singing was part of almost every gathering, whether formal assembly or spontaneous session in a dormitory room. I took it for granted that his charm would immediately win over everyone at Seneca. I snuck another glance at T.J. and caught her looking at me with amusement.

"What'll it be?" Oz asked. He jerked his head to flip his blond hair back into place, a familiar gesture that suddenly struck me as cocksure.

"'The Princess Poopooly,'" I called out. It was a song I had heard him perform many times.

Oz shrugged and began. As I listened this time, however, I became aware of the lyrics' rather risqué double meaning, something that oddly had escaped me before.

> *Now the Princess Poopooly has plenty papaya,*
> *She likes to give it away.*

I saw that T.J. was now grinning delightedly, and that Mac had noticed. Jeff Small was gone; the door to his room was closed. I began to feel uncomfortable, sorry I had asked for the song.

Oz finished with a few firm strums of his guitar and paused for a reaction. There had been "oohs" and tittering throughout the song. Now some of the campers clapped loudly and hooted, but the pleasure was not general. Win was looking down at her plate. Woody was shaking his head.

"Shoot," I heard to my right from Mac. I saw that his face was flushed and grim. I couldn't tell whether it was the song or something he sensed in T.J.'s reaction that was bothering him. None of his kids applauded.

Artie, Mac's little brother, said loudly, "What kind of shit song is that?"

Mac cuffed him lightly on the side of head. "Hold your dirty tongue!" He looked at me.

"What's the matter?" I asked.

"That ain't a song to be singing to kids."

I looked back at Oz, who was nodding at someone at a table off to our right. Bernie Kaufman, senior camper for Oz's cabin, got up and shuffled to the games corner, where he took out his banjo from its case. As he moved toward Oz, he strapped the instrument over his shoulders, its long neck further dwarfing him as usual. He stood opposite Oz and grinned impishly at him as he tuned up. Together they began to sing:

> *You're so ugly,*
> *Man, you're ugly,*
> *You're some ugly chile.*
> *Now the clothes that you wear are not in style,*
> *You look like an ape every time you smile.*

The children laughed when the song was over. Even Mac was smiling a little.

Oz, looking pleased, began to slap his guitar rhythmically and chanted, "We want Jeff Small to play! We want Jeff Small to play!"

His request was met with silence. Jeff's door was closed.

"Shoot," said Mac, getting up and heading for the kitchen counter. As he passed me he stopped and gave me a hard look.

"What's the matter now?" I said.

"Osborne should leave Jeff Small out of it."

"Why?"

"'Cause he's the help." He moved on.

Buck Silverstone had moved behind Oz and Bernie and was lifting a large guitar out of its case. He ducked his head under its ornate strap and, plucking strings and twisting pegs to tune the instrument, walked over to join Oz and Bernie. He was wearing his leather outfit again and looked like a country-Western musician, even with his black-gray mane, his hawk nose, and his large piercing eyes. Oz mouthed something, tapped his right foot, and began to play. Bernie and Buck joined in after a few notes. The piece was "Wildwood Flower," which soon had the whole camp stomping to its beat. Oz and Buck pounded out the deep lower chords, harmonizing trickily, while Bernie fronted them with a steady flow of higher notes from his banjo.

It was powerful and terrific, and everyone applauded wildly when they finished. I couldn't help but wonder when they had found time to rehearse.

We would have asked for more music, but Woody stood up and began to tap on his glass again. He thanked the musicians for their performances—"We've got real good new talent here this summer!"—and said he had an announcement to make. "Tonight will be the first Fight Night."

There was a mixture of puzzled murmuring and groans.

"For those of you who are new to Seneca, this is the first of our weekly boxing matches," he said. This was a tradition at Seneca, "a character-building experience that'll prepare you youngsters to get along in the real world," as Woody put it. The point of the matches had always been to create sporting rivalry between the cabins, and to give them another opportunity to earn points toward winning the all-around-best-cabin award for the summer. But now, Woody said, with Buck's intensification of the Indian influence on Seneca's program, a new element would be added to Fight Night. "Buck, do you want to say something?"

Buck, free of his guitar now, was leaning against one of the mess hall's supporting posts, a blank expression on his face. *Why hadn't he eaten with us?* I wondered. He pushed himself away from the post with his shoulder and clasped his hands at his chest. He seemed to grow a half a foot in height. "In the great days of my people," he began, his voice a loud monotone, "we formed the Great League of Iroquois nations. One of its purposes was to reduce fighting among the member tribes and to direct all pent-up hostilities and aggressions against foreigners. This was our way of controlling and channeling the traditional blood feud, to direct it outward and to maintain peace within the Great League."

The campers had fallen silent. Puzzled frowns had come over the faces of the younger ones as they strained to understand Buck's words. Jeff had come out of his room again and was listening intently.

Buck paced back and forth a few steps. "Since we have no outside enemies here, we must learn to vent our anger and aggression in another way. We must find a way to settle all blood feuds within the community." He stopped pacing, raising his right hand in a fist. "This will be the purpose of Fight Night! This is how we will maintain the peace!"

There was a moment of heavy silence. Then Woody cleared his throat. "Well, yes, um, blood feuds. So to speak. Uh, by this we mean . . . squabbles, disagreements, and differences of opinion that might develop into feuds. So, as Buck says, we'll be learning the Indian way of keeping the peace."

I could feel the tension ease a little. Forks and knives began to clink as the campers started eating again.

"But of course there hasn't been time for any feuds to develop yet," Woody added. "Except if you count what happened between Mac and Adam Lister on opening day, and Adam's eyes sort of rule him out of fighting. So we'll just have some matches for the fun of it tonight. Right?"

Buck was leaning against the post again. He said nothing.

"Okay then," Woody went on, "here's the format." There would be three classes of boxers: peewee, middleweight, and heavyweight. Each match was to last three rounds. Normally three matches were fought on Fight Night, plus an occasional exhibition by the junior or senior counselors. Tonight was peewee night, Woody said. "There'll be three matches plus an exhibition or two. Mac's agreed to take on whoever wants to challenge him." He looked around for someone to challenge Mac, but nobody spoke up. I was glad that my bad leg gave me an excuse to avoid taking part. I wasn't much of a boxer even when I was healthy.

"Okay, we'll settle that this evening. Meanwhile, finish your meals and proceed to rest time and afternoon activities."

LUNCH OVER, I herded my kids down to the cabin. I felt that the good spirit of the music had been spoiled by both Woody's bringing up Fight Night and Buck's interpretation of it. But I tried to shake off this feeling as I settled the cabin down for rest period. I put Steady in charge and headed back up to the mess hall to get the day's mail. Win was at her familiar post in the crafts room, sorting the mail, standing behind the Dutch door, the upper half of which was open. Chunky lay on the floor beside her.

"We missed you," I said.

She smiled.

"And Chief Wahoo."

She laid a small bundle of mail on the narrow counter that topped the lower half of the door. When she looked at me again, I thought her eyes widened slightly. "You've grown up, haven't you?"

"Yeah, I'm taller."

"How old are you now?"

"Seventeen."

She averted her eyes. "I had some things to clear up in town before I could come up." She was wearing black slacks, a dark red sweater, and, incongruously, bracelets on both her wrists, as if she hadn't quite committed herself yet to the roughness of camp life. "Would you like to see the paper?"

"Please," I said, taking the folded *Erie Times-News* from her while I quickly riffled through the pile of mail. When I saw there was nothing for me or Peter, I glanced at the table behind her. Laid out there were what looked like three papier-mâché masks, waiting to be painted. They had large, staring eyes, long, protuberant noses that were bent at their tips, and mouths that were open and distorted in dramatic expressions: fear, anger, maniacal glee. Each was crowned with what looked like long horsehairs. I hadn't seen them before.

"Is that Buck's project?"

Win shrugged. "I don't know."

"Win, I'm sorry about what happened to Teddy."

Her eyebrows went up slightly.

"I guess we got kinda carried away."

"It's okay. That can happen . . . around here. He's going to be fine."

"That's good."

I took the paper to a table nearby and sat down. After checking the headlines and ball scores, I stood again, folded the paper, and handed it back to her.

"Still rooting for the Yankees?"

"Yup. Always."

I HEADED BACK down to the cabin, feeling uneasy about Win. She seemed different, tentative somehow. She could very well be bothered by some of the same things that were troubling me, yet she also seemed unapproachable. I couldn't think of any obvious way of talking things over with her.

After I handed out the mail, I felt I had to console Peter about the lack of a letter.

"I'm fine."

"You sure?"

"I'm less homesick 'cause you're here."

"Have you written a letter to them yet?

"No, but I will."

Steady excused himself, saying he had something to do with Buck. So I took the cabin group to archery practice, which was held in the meadow below the softball field. Time passed quickly and before I knew it, recall sounded, signaling the late-afternoon swim. By dinnertime my unease had worn off a little and I was back in the camp routine once again.

AN HOUR OR SO after dinner, we gathered at the uphill side of cabin one. A boxing ring had been set up there with gym mats on the ground surrounded by ropes strung to metal poles. Peter was to go first, representing our cabin as a substitute for Teddy Wentworth, who couldn't box because of his arm. I was naturally his manager, so I took my position next to the ring on the opposite side from the Forbidden Woods. Buck Silverstone was standing nearby, providing me my first chance to study him up close. Peter, however, was demanding my attention.

My brother was not an eager contestant, and I had to lift him into the ring and give him a gentle push to get him started. His opponent came out windmilling his arms and caught him on the nose with a wild swing. Though they were wearing sixteen-ounce gloves as big as pillows, Peter retreated to our corner. He was in tears. Woody, who was refereeing the match, called time.

"I don't want do this anymore," Peter told me.

I checked his nose and saw no sign of bleeding. "Okay. Take your gloves off."

Peter looked at me, surprised.

"Come on," I said. "I'll take your place and fight him." Buck was watching us.

Peter stopped sobbing. "That's not fair."

"Why not?"

"You're too big."

I looked at his opponent, who was standing in the middle of the ring banging his gloves together. "Well, he wants to fight. So who's gonna do it?"

"Why does anybody have to?"

"Somebody has to represent the cabin." I reached through the ropes, took him by the shoulders, and held him firmly. "Come on. I don't like it either. But you just gotta go against what you're feeling."

He looked at me doubtfully.

"Okay," I said. "Is it gonna be you, or me?"

He turned back to face the ring. I gave him another little push. When he neared his opponent, he ran into another hard bop on the nose, but this time he got mad and began to swing his arms wildly, landing enough blows to win him the round. As he came back to the corner, I placed a stool in the ring for him to sit on. I massaged his shoulders and neck and murmured words of encouragement as if he were a professional fighter. I even took a sponge and squeezed water over his head to cool him down. My attention seemed to pump him up, and he continued his swinging effectively enough to keep his opponent at bay. By the third round, both his anger and his energy had subsided, but his opponent was tired too. They leaned against each other and threw an occasional weak roundhouse, allowing Peter to coast to a bumpy victory.

I gave him a hug. "That was good. I'm really proud of you for finishing."

He pretended to be indifferent to my praise, but his eyes told me he was happy. Maybe there was a point to these fights after all, I thought. But then he obviously hadn't grown particularly fond of his opponent, so I wondered how exactly this was a way of "making peace," as Buck had put it. When the next bout began, I sat on the ground near our corner of the ring, with the rest of my cabin sprawled on the grass behind me. T.J. had taken a seat next to Teddy, who seemed to have grown attached to her since his accident. Chunky was lying next to them. I caught T.J.'s eye for an instant. She winked at me.

WHEN THE PEEWEE matches were over, Woody once again called for volunteers from among the counselors to face Mac in an exhibition match. "How about it, Osborne?" he said. Oz had been talking with one of his campers and seemed not to understand what Woody was referring to.

Mac was already in the ring, dancing around and looking at the spectators. "Come on, guitar player," he drawled at Oz. "Let's show 'em how it's done."

Artie Mac joined his brother in the far corner of the ring and began to help him put on a pair of eight-ounce gloves, which could do far more damage than the sixteen-ouncers and would require the boxers to wear protective mouthpieces. "Come on, gih-tar player," Artie Mac called.

Various campers called out encouragement.

I snuck another look at T.J. She was looking at Mac with a worried frown.

Finally, Oz stood up, handed his glasses and his cap to Bernie Kaufman, and climbed into the ring next to where I was sitting. He had his lips pursed in a way that he did whenever he was amused by something. He certainly didn't look worried.

Bernie joined him in the corner and helped him with his gloves and mouthpiece. I felt nervous for him because I knew from previous summers how good a boxer Mac was. But then Oz was a good athlete, with fast hands. I glanced at T.J. again. Finally, there was something for me to say to her. "They're probably evenly matched."

Woody, still refereeing, told Mac and Oz to get ready to box. The bell rang, and Oz went to the middle of the ring to touch gloves with Mac. They began by dancing, circling each other, and throwing light jabs, feeling each other out. Mac had a concentrated look on his face, as if he had a hunted animal in his sights. Oz, his glasses off, squinted a little, but he was smiling with his usual confidence. Woody moved around the ring briskly, staying out of the way. I became aware of my heart pounding.

Most of the campers seemed to be cheering for Mac. I kept whispering to myself, "Fast hands, fast hands." But because of T.J., I said nothing out loud. She was following the bout with a slight frown on her face.

Mac and Oz continued to circle and feint. Finally, Mac threw a hard combination, two lefts and an overhand right. All of them missed, though I couldn't tell if this was because of Mac's failure or Oz's elusiveness. Mac faked another hard right and Oz ducked too awkwardly, stumbling and regaining his balance. Some of the campers snickered. Mac grimaced, as if to keep from laughing. I got the feeling that Oz was going to be humiliated. Mr. Lister rang the bell to signal the end of the round.

As Oz came back to his corner, I swung the stool into the ring for him, but he ignored it. He turned around to face the ring, leaned against the corner pole, and waited quietly. Mac, seeing that Oz was standing, bounded up off his stool and pounded his gloves together.

Mr. Lister rang the bell for round two. Mac moved quickly to the middle of the ring, and waited for Oz, who advanced more cautiously. When Oz got within Mac's punching range, Mac began throwing hard roundhouse combinations that backed Oz into a neutral corner. Mac paused a moment, then began to pound Oz's body with looping rights and lefts. He stepped back to gain leverage, and threw an overhand right at Oz's head. Oz raised his gloves to cover his face; Mac dug a left into his stomach. Oz looked helpless, as if he were cowering behind his gloves. Mac began to swing more freely.

But suddenly, it was Mac who seemed to be hurt. I hadn't seen Oz even throw a punch, but Mac was hanging on to him, his legs rubbery. Woody separated them, pushing Mac away toward the middle of the ring. Oz stayed in the corner, waiting for Mac to come back.

From the middle of the ring, Mac began to move toward Oz again, bobbing his head from side to side. Oz caught him with a lightning punch to the chin, one that this time I saw. Mac didn't fall back, but he was struggling to stay standing. Oz threw out a couple of fast jabs. Mac still wouldn't back up, but ducked his upper body to the left and the right as if he thought he could avoid Oz's punches just by bobbing and weaving. Oz settled that by landing a fast, hard right, and Mac went down.

I felt a little thrill of triumph, but the campers were still subdued, not ready to abandon their hero. T.J. didn't meet my eyes, but watched the fighters, nodding thoughtfully, as if what had happened had confirmed something.

Mac got to his feet unsteadily, just as the bell rang. The fighters moved back to their corners. I put the stool out for Oz, but he still wouldn't sit on it. I hoped Woody would stop the fight, but he was watching Mr. Lister, who was timing the break between the rounds. Mac was on his stool, getting sponged off by his brother.

When the bell rang for round three, the boxers moved toward the center of the ring, but Oz held back. Even though the campers were now beginning to urge him on, he only danced from side to side, as if satisfied with having neutralized Mac. Mac gestured with his glove for Oz to move toward him. But Oz kept his distance, still shuffling from side to side. Tired of the inaction, Woody raised his hands before his face and brought them together prayerlike, signaling Oz to engage. At the same moment, Chunky began barking and a deep male voice from in back of me commanded, "Hit him, Osborne! Hit him!" Buck Silverstone had moved away from the corner of the cabin and was standing next to the ring. Chunky kept barking at him, although keeping his distance. Buck's long hair was hanging loose now, flowing back from a face that struck me as softer than I had expected, although I could see the upper parts of his cheeks were pockmarked. He had deep brown, almond-shaped eyes peering out from under the overhang of his brows. His nose was prominent but only slightly hawkish, and the space above his upper lip was long enough to lend him a sullen, slightly hungry look. This was the closest look I had gotten at him so far, and I found him handsome almost to the point of being beautiful. "Hit the bastard!" he said.

Oz stepped forward and threw a right that snaked through Mac's defenses and knocked him across the ring. Mac collapsed on the rope, knocking two of the corner stanchions down. A roar of laughter sounded as he disentangled himself and flopped onto his hands and knees, his face red from anger and the punch it had taken. Woody pushed Oz toward a neutral corner and began to count over Mac. Cries of encouragement went up from the campers.

"Is he hurt?" Peter asked.

"He's stunned. That's what happens if you get hit hard on the chin."

When Woody got to eight, Mac rose unsteadily to his feet. Woody wiped his gloves off against his shirt and signaled the two together to engage again. But Oz refused to press the attack, content to keep Mac at a distance with left jabs. He had clearly decided that the fight was won, and that there was no point in humiliating Mac further.

Mr. Lister banged the bell to end the fight. Oz turned away from Mac to head for his corner, but Mac still stood in the center of the ring, his right glove clamped under the upper part of his left arm. Yanking his right hand out of the glove, he clenched it into a naked fist and came charging toward Oz. Reacting too quickly, I made the mistake of yelling, "Look out, Oz!" Oz responded by turning his head to the right just as Mac's fist arrived. If he hadn't turned, it would have glanced off the side of his head or cheekbone, but instead it caught him squarely on his nose and mouth. Oz's mouthpiece went flying. Woody grabbed Mac by the other arm and pulled him away, but the damage was done. Blood began gushing from Oz's nostrils and mouth and onto his chest.

"Was that fair?" Peter asked in a high voice, huddling against me.

"No, not at all." I placed the stool so that Oz could sit on it.

"There's blood!" Peter shrieked. "I don't like this!"

I tried to reassure him. "It looks much worse than it is."

Buck leaned over the ropes and cupped his right hand against Oz's mouth while with his other hand he dug in his pocket for a handkerchief.

"You're a jerk, Mac!" T.J. yelled, charging past us and climbing through the ropes. She kneeled in front of Oz, gently moving Buck's hand aside and studying Oz's mouth. "Somebody give me a towel or something," she said. "Don't we have a first-aid kit down here?"

"No. It's up at the infirmary," Woody said.

"I better get him up there."

Buck handed her his handkerchief. She shook it out, balled it up, and pressed it against Oz's mouth. Together they helped Oz stand up and climb out of the ring. The spectators were quiet, except for a couple of children who were chattering nervously. T.J. and Oz began moving toward the mess hall.

"You want help?" I called out to T.J.

"That's okay," she said. "You stay with your kids."

As they moved toward the mess hall, I turned back to the ring.

Everyone was silently looking at Mac. He was sitting on his stool just outside the ring, his head down. His brother and another boy were kneeling beside him, checking his face. Woody was still inside the ring, leaning with his hands on one of the stanchions.

"That was unfortunate," he said softly to no one in particular.

"But it happens," Buck said firmly. He had left the ring and gone back to his stand at the corner of the cabin. "It was a good fierce fight."

Yeah, it was fierce, I thought. *But what was it supposed to teach us? I* wondered.

Woody took a deep breath. "Right! Let's get on with it." He glanced at his watch. "There's time for one more match." He looked around, his sense of command returning. "Anyone interested in another exhibition?"

"Sure," said Buck. He moved to the corner of the ring, stripped off his fringed shirt, handed it to a camper, and stepped over the ropes. His stomach was ridged with muscles.

"Goooood," said Woody, in a slightly hollow voice. "Anyone want to box Buck Silverstone?"

"What about you?" I heard myself say.

Woody shook his head quickly. "No, no. Too old. Too old."

"What about you?" Buck said, leveling his dark eyes at me.

"Yeah, yeah," several of the children said.

I felt my face flush. "I, I ... . can't," I said, slapping my crutch a couple of times. My words felt lame. *The doctor who had removed my cast had told me to get rid of the crutches as soon as I could. Was I pushing myself as hard as my father had urged me to?* Buck wasn't really that much bigger than I was, although he had a couple of inches on me and a lot of muscle.

Big Bordy rose up from beyond the other side of the ring. "I'll box him."

A loud cheer went up from the campers.

"Good," said Buck, backing into our corner and resting his arms on the ropes.

Bordy stripped off his T-shirt, climbed into the ring, and went to the far corner. Artie Mac helped him put on gloves. Despite the fat at his waist, Bordy looked huge and powerful. The campers were quiet. Woody went over to confer with Mr. Lister, then moved to the middle of the ring.

"Okay, campers, the final match of the evening, one that promises to show the true spirit of Fight Night. An exhibition in fisticuffs pitting Buck Silverstone at, uh"—he looked at Buck appraisingly—"six feet four inches and two hundred . . . ?"

"One ninety," Buck said in a low voice.

"One hundred and ninety pounds, versus Bordy Udall, at six six and . . . what are you admitting to these days?"

"One ninety-five," Bordy said in his chirping voice.

Everybody laughed at this obvious misrepresentation.

"Three hundred," Woody said to more laughter. "All right, three rounds unless there's a knockout. Let the fighters come to the center of the ring."

Buck and Bordy joined him. Bordy towered over Buck, who chewed on his mouthpiece and stared expressionlessly at his opponent's chest.

"Look how big Bordy is," Peter said. "Is it fair?"

"Bordy'll be fair."

"All right, men, you know the rules," Woody said. "Neutral corner on a knockdown; mandatory eight-count; no counting after the bell. Keep it clean and do your best. Go to your corners now, and come out fighting."

"I tell you what," Buck said, backing away a step and looking around at the audience outside the ring. "Instead of fighting another exhibition, let's show the campers what Osborne did wrong." He looked at Woody. "Teach them how to defend yourself from a sneak attack."

"Good idea," Woody said. "Fair enough."

Bordy shrugged.

Is Buck scared of him? I wondered.

"Good." Buck moved to the edge of the ring where Oz had been standing when Mac had hit him. He looked back at Bordy. "Take your gloves off like the Southern boy did."

Bordy pulled his hands free of the gloves and handed both of them to Woody.

The campers began to murmur.

Buck averted his eyes from Bordy. "This you must always remember," he announced. "As long as you remain in the ring with your opponent, keep your eyes on him." He looked back at Bordy. "Go ahead and attack me." He appeared to look away again, but from the angle of his head I could tell he was still watching him.

Bordy came slowly across the ring with his bare right fist raised. He began to pantomime hitting Buck's face from behind with a lazy, looping, roundhouse punch. It had traveled about halfway when Buck said loudly without seeming to look at Bordy, "No, no. Don't pretend. Make it real."

Bordy threw a quicker punch. Before it had arrived, Buck had spun around and blocked it with his wrist like a fencer warding off an opponent's foil.

"Can't you throw a real punch?" Buck asked coldly.

Bordy set himself again. He did a quick bob of his head and shoulders and lashed his right fist out. The punch seemed about to land when Bordy was suddenly staggering backward, struggling to keep his balance.

Again I hadn't seen whatever had done the damage, but Bordy had his guard down and Buck was stalking him, measuring him. The camp was holding its collective breath. Woody moved closer to Bordy, I guess to be ready to stop the fight if necessary. Bordy looked drunk, but Buck kept stalking him like a cat after a bird with a broken leg. He hit him a tremendous left hook and then a right and then a combination of lefts and rights so fast that I couldn't keep count.

"Stop it!" I yelled.

Woody tried to get between them, but Buck pushed him aside and hit Bordy once more, a solid blow to the upper lip and nose. Bordy went down on his back, blood gushing from his mouth and splattering Woody's face and T-shirt.

"That was horrible," Peter said, starting to cry.

I pulled him onto my lap and hugged him. His whole body was quivering. *Was he shaking like this in Karla's arms that time I knocked Dad down and she had to beat me off him with her shoe? If Peter complains about this evening to them, how am I going to explain it?*

Buck stood over Bordy for a moment, breathing heavily. When he saw that Bordy wouldn't get up, he walked back to his corner, holding out his gloves for Steady to remove. "That's how it's done," he said. He climbed out of the ring and slipped on his shirt. Chunky had returned. Buck feinted throwing his right fist at him, which backed him away yipping in fear, then disappeared around the corner of cabin one.

Bordy was still down, but moving his arms and legs, struggling to sit up.

"Towel here," Woody said. He was kneeling next to Bordy, trying to help him. He looked around. "Children, things are going to be okay."

"Get a towel," I told Peter. "There's one at the foot of my bed."

Peter dashed off. It was almost dark now. I heard the cabin door slam and Peter was back, carrying a white towel. I helped him through the ropes and he carried it to Woody, who took it and pressed it to Bordy's face. I was relieved to see Bordy sitting up. He took the towel from Woody.

"Are there going to be any more exhibitions?" I asked, an edge of anger in my voice.

Woody shook his head as if coming to his senses. "No, no. We're done for the night." He seemed to pull himself together. "All right," he said, looking at his watch. "It's free time now. Forty-five minutes till taps. That's it for Fight Night."

I rounded up my kids and herded them into the cabin. The fights had left a bad taste in my mouth. As soon as Peter was settled down, I wanted to withdraw and be alone.

I felt disgusted with Camp Seneca.

AFTER TAPS, I lay on my bunk in the dark, waiting for the children to fall asleep. The violence of Fight Night had brought my earlier doubts about the summer to a boil. I felt particularly upset because I had collaborated in the nastiness by making Peter join in. The damn place had infected me. Fight Night was supposed to "keep the peace," Buck and Woody had said. Like hell! When the evening was over you could have cut the tension with a cleaver.

Looking back, I can see now that I was both overreacting and underreacting to things as they were developing. Knowing now what was going to happen, I should have taken Peter and gotten the hell out of camp immediately, no matter what the consequences. In this sense I was underreacting.

But at the same time, I had no hard evidence to go on, only my somewhat overwrought feelings. In this sense I was overreacting, as I guess any teenager would do.

In any case, as I lay in the dark I began to consider seriously if my summer campaign to rejoin my father's family wasn't in trouble. I didn't know what Peter's state of mind was—once again, he had gone to bed without a fuss, and seemed to be sleeping soundly now—but he couldn't have loved the evening. Sure, his own boxing match was a triumph, but the two other bouts had obviously upset him.

Of course, those fights had upset me as well. If things went on this way, the friendship that already existed between me and Peter would be damaged, and he and Karla and Dad might end up blaming me for the whole thing. So much for proving to them that Peter needed me! Maybe it was time to start thinking about getting both of us out of this place.

Could we just pack up and leave? I wondered.

The trouble was, Dad and Karla were counting on their time together in Europe to be relaxing, and if we cut out now, they might feel as if they would have to come home early. Besides, there really wasn't anyplace for us to go: the house in Connecticut wasn't ready, the apartment in the city had been loaned to someone, and my mother had sublet her place for the summer and gone to stay with friends in Washington, D.C., where she was helping to gather signatures for a petition to denounce Senator Joe McCarthy.

Even if I could, I certainly didn't want to go back to my mother's tiny apartment in the Bronx. If I could help it, I never wanted to set foot there again.

I balled my hands into fists and pressed them against my eyes, remembering what life with my mom was like. *I recalled coming in that night and finding her asleep on the couch, the bedclothes fallen to the floor, her nightdress up around her waist. I tried to awaken her, but she was drunk again. She simpered flirtatiously, as if she didn't know who I was; she talked of being on a late date with a handsome young visitor. I told her to go to bed, but she insisted that she would get up and fix me dinner. Then, carrying the tray, she staggered, lost her balance, and let the dishes crash to the floor.*

It was just too painful. I never wanted to live there again.

I just had to move back into my father's house, and if achieving that meant getting Peter away from camp early, then the idea was worth exploring. Maybe I could write to Karla and get her ideas about a possible place to go to. I could explain that camp had changed for the worse and that Peter would be better off somewhere else. This would at least raise the possibility of leaving. And it would show that I was looking out for him.

Of course, rationally I knew that by the time my letter reached Karla—forwarded from my father's office to wherever in Germany they were—and she responded, many days would have passed. Still, it might be worth trying.

Despite all the turmoil of Fight Night, the cabin dropped off to sleep quickly, even Steady. It was my night for both pee patrol and delivering the breakfast snacks to the tree house, so I couldn't go to bed yet myself. I figured I had about an hour until I had to wake Teddy and the other bed wetters, so I dug out some stationery from my trunk and headed up to the kitchen to have a cup of hot chocolate and begin working on a letter to Karla.

A few people, including Mac and the kitchen girls, Eve and Sukie, were in the kitchen, seated at the long table. But Woody wasn't there, nor were Win and T.J. And not Oz or Bordy. Eve pointed out the basket of snacks sitting on a table by the back door.

Sukie, a red-faced, chubby girl, brought me my cocoa. I lit up a cigarette and took a deep drag; the first wave of dizziness was a powerful one. When my head cleared I began to work on my letter.

Dear Karla,

I got your first letter yesterday (and Peter got his and will be answering soon). Thank you so much for writing. Your Englisch, as you called it, is really good. You shouldn't be self-conscious at all.

Our trip on the train went fine. We arrived safely, obviously, and Camp is now in full swing. We are both very well, especially Peter, who is having a fine time. He has adjusted to camp life very quickly, does not seem to be at all homesick, and is sleeping well.

Still, I'm having a bit of a problem, and I want to confide in you about . . .

"What're you writing?" Mac asked.

He had sat down on the bench next to me. "A letter. What else would I be writing?"

"I don't know. A dirty song?"

"Very funny."

"Or a song about freeing the slaves?"

"You're a wit." I shielded the piece of paper with my arm and tried to continue writing.

"Who're you writing to?" Mac asked.

"My family." I looked at him. He seemed genuinely curious.

"What about?"

"I don't know; how the summer's going."

"How is it going?"

"How's it going?" I took a deep breath. "I guess I'm still trying to get used to the changes. Now, if you don't mind."

"You mean changes like this guy Buck?"

"Yes. Things like that. I'd really like to get this done."

"And I'd like to talk. This is s'posed to be a time for visiting. You can finish your letter on your own time."

"Why do you want to talk?"

"I feel there's bad stuff between us."

"You're right about that." I began to fold the letter, figuring that Mac was right about "visiting" too.

"He's different, isn't he?"

"Who?"

"Buck."

"Yeah." I found it difficult to meet his gaze. I was still ticked off at him for throwing his sneak punch, but I didn't see much point in bringing it up.

"What other changes?" Mac asked.

"New people."

"You mean like T.J.?"

"T.J. and others."

"You like that change?"

"Sure. T.J. seems nice."

"You better believe she is." He tapped the tabletop with his fingers. "You all finished with school?"

"Yes. With high school." I felt relieved at the change of subject. "I just graduated. But I'm starting college in September."

Mac smiled. His face was chiseled and handsome. "What college?"

"Swarthmore. Near Philadelphia."

"Swarthmore," he said, as if trying out the word. "What kind of school is that?"

"It's a small, private college, founded by the Quakers."

"You Quaker?"

"No. You don't have to be."

"Private. You pay for that?"

"Yes. But I got a scholarship."

His eyes narrowed slightly. "How do you get that?"

I took a pull on the cigarette. "I dunno. Grades, test scores, recommendations from teachers. And need."

"Need?"

"Like if you don't have enough money."

He began to say something, then seemed to think better of it.

"What about you?" I asked.

"I'm a year outta high school. Gonna join the navy in the fall."

"How long?"

"Three-year hitch. See the world."

"See the sea."

"That's what they say."

Somewhere, a screen door slammed. The sound seemed to come from the direction of Woody's cabin.

"Three years," I repeated.

"Won't be bad. I'll be married."

"To T.J."

"That's right."

To my surprise, I felt a sting of disappointment.

"Married, and I'm gonna get trained. Electronics."

I felt glad that I hadn't responded to her flirting. "Does that . . . ? After you get out, can you . . . ?"

"Sure. I'll know about circuits. Radio, television, whatever. Lots of applications."

I stubbed out the cigarette. The screen door slammed again.

"What about you?" he said. "What'll you do?"

I let my breath out. "You mean as a profession?"

"Yeah."

"I have no idea."

"What'll you specialize in? At Swa'thmore."

"English? History? I don't know yet."

"You going to be a teacher?"

"I guess. Maybe. I don't know. Luckily, I don't have to decide for a while."

From the direction of the slamming door, a man's voice said, "Come on." A woman's voice laughed or sobbed. I couldn't tell which.

Mac's mouth was a straight line. "Your friend, Osborne. He went to school with you, right?"

I stiffened involuntarily. "Yes."

"He going to college too?"

"I think so. Yes."

"Same one as you? Swarthmore?"

"No. Somewhere else, out west. Pomona College, I think. In California."

He lifted his chin. "You by any chance know where he was this evening?"

"No, I don't. The last I saw, he was headed for the infirmary with T.J." I braced myself. "Thanks to you."

"You got a problem with that?" he drawled.

"It was a dirty punch."

His green eyes flashed, then looked away. "I didn't hear the bell."

"Bullshit. You took your glove off and hit him when his back was turned."

The man's voice in the distance said what sounded like "Bitch!" I couldn't be sure. A prickling feeling passed over my scalp.

Mac's eyes dropped. "I guess I don't like Osborne."

"You don't even know him."

"I don't like his songs."

"That's a reason to sucker punch him?"

"He's a nigger lover."

"That's your problem."

"He might be messing with my girl."

I suddenly wasn't afraid of him. "If anyone's messing, it's your girl that's doing it."

He flinched. "Where are they now?" he asked.

"I have no idea. I've been down in my cabin. But I would imagine that after he got his mouth fixed up he would want to lie down and rest."

"Yeah, you're right." He twitched a smile. "I guess something got into me. I got me a temper."

I was still wondering whose voices those were outside. "At least it wasn't as bad as Buck with Bordy."

"Tell him I'm sorry," Mac said.

"Tell him yourself."

"I think I will." He stood up. "And I'll tell him to stay away from my girl."

I took a sip of cocoa and unfolded my letter, rereading what I had written. I searched for the words I wanted to put down, while at the same time keeping my nerves alert to any possible sounds outside. Finally, too distracted, I gave up. I pocketed the paper and said good night, then took the picnic hamper from its place on the table and went out through the back door, past the corner where Chunky was sleeping.

I didn't usually leave the kitchen through that door—except for my after-breakfast smoke—but I was trying to stay as far away from the Wentworths' cabin as possible. I wasn't sure that the raised voices were theirs, but the possibility was disturbing. I had never heard them say a cross word to each other, unless I counted Win's gentle reproving of Woody for what she described as his "occasionally getting carried away." I certainly never heard him use the word "bitch."

The night was clear and cool, the moon hanging high overhead. A slight breeze was up, hissing through the trees. As I passed the corner of the mess hall where Jeff Small's room was, I could hear the faint tinkling of the piano. Again I found myself wondering fleetingly why Jeff had seemed to be disdainful of Oz's music.

What dominated my thoughts, though, was the raised voices I had heard. I dug my crutch in to propel myself faster, swung myself forward, and collided with something hard coming at me from my left. It hit me just above my left elbow, and it knocked me down. Luckily, the cover on the hamper prevented its contents from falling out.

"Whoa!" a deep voice said. "Look where you're going."

Against the night sky I could see a figure towering above me, holding what looked like some tool with a long handle.

A shovel?

I braced myself on my crutch and pulled myself up. "Sorr-ee!" I said unnecessarily, picking up the hamper.

"What's wrong with you?" It was Buck Silverstone. He smelled of damp soil.

"Nothing. I'm okay." *Why would he have a shovel?*

"Then why do you need that crutch?"

"Oh. I broke my leg. Skiing."

"When?" He was standing stock-still. I couldn't see his face.

"Uh, January. January sixteenth."

"They put a cast on it?"

"Yes. It just came off two weeks ago."

"It should be fine then."

"The muscles are still weak. I have to build them up. And I can't flex my knee."

He said nothing for a moment, standing there like a pillar in the dark. Then, "You're giving in to it," he said. "It should be fine by now." He strode off.

I said a silent "Fuck you" as I watched him cross the open area. He was coming from the Forbidden Woods when I collided with him. *What in hell had he been doing in there?* I wondered.

I turned and headed for my cabin. I tried putting more weight on my bad leg, but I was tired and it hurt more than the effort was worth. "Fuck you, Redclaw!" I said, out loud this time. I was still angry about what he'd done to Bordy. From now on I would try to think of him as Redclaw. He was not somebody I felt I could warm up to.

I set the picnic hamper on my trunk and took Teddy and two other kids out to pee. I noticed Len's bunk was empty, and wondered where he was. When the kids were back in bed, I got some liniment for my knee, to ease its aching. Sitting on my bunk, I glanced over at Steady's bed; the figure lying there was too large to be him, I realized with a start. I leaned closer. It was Oz. He had his cap on.

"Hey!" I said, a little too loud.

"Shhhhh!"

"Where's Steady?"

"He went off on his vigil." Oz was having trouble getting his words out.

"Are you okay?"

"Keep your voice down," he said. (It sounded like "'eep 'our 'oice 'own.") "Yeah, I'm fine. I took a couple of stitches in the lip."

"That's too bad."

"Not so bad. They took good care of me." He tapped my arm. "We better go outside to talk."

I took my flashlight and the hamper and followed him through the screen door. "Keep me company while I deliver the tree house snacks," I said when we got outside. "Are you up to it?"

"Sure."

We set off down Cabin Row.

He took a deep breath. "It really cools off here at night."

"Yeah, it does. You fell asleep?" I didn't know how to ask him what he was doing on Steady's bunk.

"I guess. I helped Steady get packed."

"Who's looking after your cabin?"

"Bernie Kaufman."

"He sure can pick that banjo. Who's with Steady on his vigil?"

"The bald guy. Len Lawrence."

"'Cause I just saw Buck."

"Yeah. Woody and Len are taking Steady out to an island on Lake Pymatuning. Len's gonna watch him."

"I wonder why Len didn't tell me."

"They were being pretty secretive about it."

"I guess because Buck said at the campfire that Steady had already completed his vigil."

"Yeah, maybe."

"Who told you?"

"Steady did."

"He's a good man, isn't he?"

Oz didn't say anything.

"Why did Len go with him? What is it that Buck's doing?" *What story did he tell them?*

"I don't know."

I didn't think you did.

WHEN WE GOT DOWN to the totem pole gate and entered the Big Woods, we both fell silent. Oz led the way since I didn't have a hand free to carry the flashlight.

The tree holding the tree house stood at the edge of a small clearing. Oz's light beam picked up the rungs of the wooden ladder that led up the trunk to a hatch in the floor of the house. Just off to the right, a small wooden crib attached to a rope served as a dumbwaiter, another of Woody's gadgets. Moving quietly, I placed the picnic hamper in the crib. Its cover would protect its contents from animals for the remainder of the night. The counselor in charge, whoever he might be, would pull it up first thing in the morning.

As we turned to leave, Oz was about to go off in the direction we had come in from, but I pointed him in the opposite direction, toward a tangle of thick undergrowth that divided the woods from the meadow below the softball diamond. By cutting through the undergrowth, we could walk directly to the cabins and save ourselves the trouble of going back to the gate.

"Watch out for branches hitting your face," I whispered to him, using my crutch to clear the way.

"Don't worry."

When we reached the meadow we fell into step beside each other. The moonlight was bright enough to light our way without the flash.

"Who put the stitches in your lip?" I asked him when we were halfway from Cabin Row.

"Nursey. With T.J.'s help. They were great. Almost worth getting hurt."

"Did you, um, spend time with her after?"

"Who? T.J.?" He laughed. "No. Why?"

"Mac was wondering. I saw him in the kitchen a little while ago, and he seemed suspicious."

"Really!" He walked along in silence for a few steps. "How serious are Mac and T.J.?"

"Mac says they're engaged. But she says not really. He's been talking about her for years. This is her first summer at Seneca."

"Well, she wanted to go for a walk with me. She seemed hot to trot."

"No kidding?"

"But she doesn't interest me."

"Why not? She's great looking."

"I don't know. Not my type, I guess."

"I don't understand why she would be disloyal to Mac."

"She probably knows a good thing when she sees it."

"Meaning?"

"Come on, don't be naive. Mac's not going anywhere in life. What would she have to look forward to with him?"

"Well, I'll give him this: he feels bad about hitting you."

"How do you know that?"

"He told me. He may apologize."

"He got carried away. I can see where we would piss him off."

"We?"

"Fancy prep school boys. You know what Woody said about us being different."

"Yeah, I guess."

"T.J.'s not stupid."

"I sort of like her."

"Why not? She's beautiful. A sexy tomboy. Just not my type."

"Still, you better watch it. Mac thinks you're messing with her."

"Don't sweat it." He stopped about thirty feet from cabin three. "Let's not go closer if we're going to talk. Were there any more fights after ours?"

"Sort of." I leaned on my crutch. "Bordy against . . . Redclaw."

"Redclaw?"

"Buck Silverstone. I'm calling him by his warrior name now. In private at least. After what he did to Bordy."

"Big Bordy?"

"It was unbelievable. Bordy was just going easy and Redclaw started beating him up. Wouldn't quit."

"He beat Big Bordy? But he's twice Buck's size."

"Beat the hell out of him."

"Buck's an angry man. I guess he's got a lot to be angry about."

"Maybe so."

"What's the matter?"

I didn't know how much to air my feelings. "I can't figure him out. He makes me nervous."

"Really? I like him."

"Why did he tell us at the campfire that Steady had already done his vigil?"

"A white lie. He was just getting the ball rolling. Introducing his program."

"He's changed the camp."

"I find him impressive. Good at everything he does."

"What's he doing in those woods?"

"What do you mean?"

"First he makes us aware of the woods, by staging the arrowhead hunt in them. Then he tries to scare us away from them. I ran into him before, when I was on my way down to the cabins, and I think he was coming from the woods. With a shovel. What's he doing there?"

Oz took a few steps farther from the cabins and turned around to face me. "I think it's just part of his program. He and Woody have something planned. He's setting something up. Maybe he's eventually going to hold the vigils in those woods instead of on the island."

"Then why try to make the place scary to the kids?"

"Make the ground seem special, sort of sacred. Build up the mystique of it. Teach us about it."

"Yeah. Maybe."

"It's all part of some strange ritual," Oz said. "Like the masks in the crafts room."

"Weird. We never did that before."

"Those are for the vigils."

"Really? Steady took a mask with him?"

"I think so."

"What for? I don't get it. Why are their noses bent?"

"Buck's in touch with something we don't understand. His people all are."

"Who's 'we'?"

"White people. Europeans."

"How the heck do you know all this, Oz?"

"It's obvious, if you know anything about Seneca lore. They have a lot to teach us. Indians have a special relationship with the earth, with all of nature."

"You think?"

"I know. Do you realize that the Iroquois influenced the American Constitution?"

"No."

"They did. Ben Franklin, who was a colonial Indian commissioner, admired the Iroquois League. The Senecas were part of the Iroquois League, y'know."

There was an awkward silence between us. I felt dumb and uninformed. *Maybe I'm not thinking things through.*

"Anyway," he went on, "I talked to Buck after lunch, after the music."

"Okay, maybe I'm wrong about him. What time is it?"

He looked at his watch. "Ten-thirty. Time to hit the hay."

We started back toward cabin three.

"I like this place," Oz said. "I'm glad you recruited me."

"It's amazing you feel that way, after what happened with Mac."

"He just got carried away." Oz opened his cabin door. "Hang in there," he said softly. "This month is going to be terrific."

"I'm glad you think so." *But terrifying might be more like it,* I said to myself.

I made my way back to cabin one, my anger coming back to me. I didn't understand why Oz had been helping Steady pack, or why Buck wasn't supervising the first vigil. No matter how Oz felt, I remained troubled. Camp was too different this summer, and I wasn't at all sure I could adjust to the change.

4

THE SNIPE HUNT

DESPITE MY INITIAL MISGIVINGS, not everything at camp turned out to be going wrong, as I had to concede in the following few days. For one thing, Peter seemed really to be enjoying himself. He apparently suffered no ill effects from Fight Night; the one thing he took away from it was his own victory in his match. In the meantime, he had gotten more and more involved with the kids his own age, and he had become happily obsessed with making a toy pistol. So for the time being at least, with regard to him I had little to worry about.

As for me: looking back, I understand now that I desperately needed to see things as being all for the best that summer. There was in me then an overwhelming urge to deny the presence of any evil in the people around me—the very idea that someone would take satisfaction in harming me—because, I guess, for a child to recognize malevolence in those he counts on to love and protect him would mean having to face that there's really no one but yourself out there to look after you. An almost impossible thing for any child to do, hence his attribution of evil to monsters, hobgoblins, or bogeymen. That summer, even at seventeen, I remained that child. And for a while, that child was content.

But then, on the Fourth of July, a couple of things happened to confuse my feelings again.

AT REST TIME that day, I put Steady in charge of the cabin and headed out to the pond for a swim, taking along the letter to Karla I had begun. Because I spent the morning at the rifle range, I had missed the general swim before lunch, which would have provided a chance to exercise my leg. When I got to the pond—which had been skimmed clean of the algae I had noticed on opening day—I went to the end nearest the camp, by the dam, where the water was deep enough for a diving board to be mounted. I took off my sneakers and shirt and lay them with my towel and crutch on the dam, making certain that my cigarettes and lighter were secure in my shirt pocket. The day was hot and the water looked inviting, but I wanted to work on the letter first. I moved to the end of the diving board and sat down, almost immediately falling into a pleasant semitrance watching the water striders skittering below over the reflection of the clouds billowing above. I thought some more about how the summer was going.

IN THE TWO DAYS since Fight Night, the camp had settled back into its routine. Each morning would begin with Woody playing the scratchy recording of reveille. After breakfast, we would shape up our bunks for inspection. During the day, we did familiar, commonplace things like hiking, swimming, archery, volleyball, and crafts. Each evening ended with lights-out at ten, after the daily contingent of younger campers had been packed off to spend the night in the tree house. Two of the junior counselors would be assigned to cabin watch and pee patrol. The rest of us were free to visit a nearby amusement park or—those of us old enough or willing to lie about our ages—to go drink beer at the tavern on the causeway over Pymatuning Reservoir, named, fittingly enough, the Causeway Tavern. The only condition was that we had to be back in our cabins in time for a decent night's sleep.

Yet despite the familiarity of the routine, the summer was not improving, not for me anyway. Part of the problem was the little changes that were added to the big ones. To my disappointment, there wasn't going to be any Treasure Hunt, a cabin competition that I had always liked, and thought Peter would enjoy. The reasoning was, apparently, that it didn't fit into Buck's Indian program. Then, the Best Camper and Favorite Counselor Awards were eliminated; that meant the usual fierce contest among the counselors for the kids' allegiance would be missing. Buck had decreed that all campers should be judged as equals and that good leaders ought to be determined by skill, not popularity.

I felt more alone than I ever had before, and I also felt oddly homesick, although for what home I didn't know. Even though Win was back, she wasn't around as much as usual. And when she was, she somehow didn't seem present. It was as if she were detached from everything, and I couldn't figure out why.

Oz had got into the swing of camp life, which, of course, was to the good, but his lack of reliance on me was a little disappointing. And for some reason, Steady was not his old self. He had survived his vigil on the island successfully, which made him a hero among the campers. I had wanted to ask him about his experience, but he didn't want to talk about it, and he seemed distracted—not at all the old reliable Steady Bomber.

As JUNE turned into July, the heat became oppressive. Luckily, it still cooled off after sunset, so the camp's Fourth of July ritual wouldn't be spoiled by the weather. This consisted of a bonfire and fireworks preceded by a Snipe Hunt. It was not your ordinary Snipe Hunt, however, the kind in which new campers were sent out into the woods with bags and flashlights to catch nonexistent little birds that were supposed to be driven toward them by others who were in on the joke. No, in Camp Seneca's version, the Snipe Hunt was another of Woody's character-building experiences, to which he was always trying to add new wrinkles, and was reined in only by Win's common sense. As always, I was apprehensive about what tricks he might be adding this year, but I was even more curious to see how Redclaw would adapt the hunt to his Indian program.

———

THE PLOP of a frog into the pond brought me back to the present. I returned my attention to the letter I was writing to Karla, read what I had said so far, and began to write some more:

Still, I'm having a bit of a problem, and I want to confide in you about it. The truth is that camp is kind of different this summer. It's hard to put my finger on any single thing. If I had to, it would be this strange new guy who runs the Indian program. His name's Buck Silverstone and he seems to have cast a spell over everything.

But it isn't just him, it's a lot of other things too. Whatever the cause, Woody Wentworth is different this year, and the way he runs the camp shows it. It's wilder, scarier, and nastier, as if some evil spirit had been let loose on the place. We had something called Fight Night a few evenings ago. Peter participated and did well (he won his bout and was really proud), but there were some really ugly fights, with people actually getting hurt. It wasn't at all like the camp that used to be. And there are a lot of indications that things could get worse.

What I'm really afraid of is that our plan could easily fail or even backfire. Peter could end up having an awful time here and wanting to go home. Dad would blame this on me (since it was my idea that Peter come to the camp) and say he saw no reason for Peter's needing me around in the future. And that would take away my argument for moving in with you and him.

There are really some very threatening signs, and I want to be prepared. So I'm asking you to think about the possibility of our leaving camp early. It could happen very suddenly. I would need some money to travel and live on (since I don't get my $100 salary until camp ends) and we would need a place to go to and stay till you and Dad get home. I can't just walk out of here and hitchhike, at least not with Peter in tow.

I realize this possible change isn't going to make Dad happy, and I realize that you and he were counting on a restful summer. But I have a very bad feeling about things here, so I'm pleading with you for help, just in case.

I miss you a lot and wish that Peter and I were with you.

With much love, Jerry

I folded the letter, slipped it into an unaddressed envelope, and took it back to where my things were lying, putting it into my shirt pocket. I would hide it at the bottom of my trunk and mail it only if necessary. But I felt more at ease, as if I had armed myself.

THAT DONE, I limped back out to the end of the board, bounced a couple of times, took a deep breath, and dove, hitting the water at an angle that allowed me to go deep. The temperature was just right, cold but not numbingly so. When I got short of breath, I kicked my way toward the surface, purposely flexing my right knee harder than my left. As I rose through the murky greenness, I felt something hit the water nearby. No one had been there when I dove in, so when I broke the surface, gulping air, I looked around. Suddenly the water exploded a few feet in front of me and a head emerged, streamlined by a green bathing cap. It took me a moment to recognize T.J., laughing at my startled expression. With a few powerful thrusts of her arms she closed the distance between us.

"Heya," she said. She was chewing gum.

"Jesus! Where did you come from?"

"I followed you here."

"I didn't see you."

"That was the idea. Whatcha doin'?"

"Exercising my leg." I swallowed a little water and began to cough.

"Ain't you the good boy!" She treaded water.

"Actually, I haven't been doing it as much as I ought to."

She tilted her head sideways and moved away a few feet. "You always a good boy?"

I opened my mouth, but said nothing.

She swam closer again, until our faces were almost touching. Then she tipped her head back in the water, as if she were about to backstroke away. But instead I felt her feet touching my knees, then her legs snaking around my thighs. Her arms came out of the water and went around my neck. She pulled me close to her. I took a deep breath and we sank. She grasped me tighter with her legs, pressing her face to mine. Her heels were firmly hooked against the back of my knees, her crotch was pressed against my stomach. I slipped my arms around her and held on. Her mouth engulfed mine. I felt dizzy with desire. Nothing like this had ever happened to me before.

Just as I began to feel short of breath, she let go and dropped away from me. I struggled back to the surface, gasping. I looked around but didn't see her.

A splash exploded behind me and I heard laughter. I spun around and saw her grinning face again, about a foot away from me.

"What's this?" I asked.

"What's it feel like?"

"Good." I coughed, spitting out water. "But . . ."

"It's supposed to feel good." She began to backstroke away. "You goin' into town tonight?" She didn't seem to be the least bit winded.

"No. Tonight is the Snipe Hunt and the bonfire and the fireworks!"

"I meant later. After lights-out."

"Oh. I think I have cabin duty."

"Okay. Some other time."

"Sure." I began to swim after her.

She stopped and waited for me to catch up. "Do you ever get time off during the day?"

"Sometimes, during rest period."

"I thought we could go into those woods sometime, check out your tree."

"I don't know."

"What's the matter? You scared?"

"It's just . . . I don't get it."

She gave me a look of mock concern. "You don't get what?"

"What about Oz?"

"What about him?"

"You seemed, y'know, interested . . ."

She tossed her head. "Oh, he doesn't like me."

"I'm sure he does."

"Well, you're wrong."

"What about Mac, then?"

She leaned her head back and began to swim away again.

I looked at my fingers. They were beginning to wrinkle. I felt disoriented and out of my element. "I don't think Buck Silverstone wants us in those woods," I said, instantly aware of how weak I sounded.

When she reached the ladder and grasped it to climb out, she turned back to me. "Is that enough to keep you away?"

I swam after her and waited for her to climb the ladder. Her thighs were smooth right up to the edge of her bathing suit. When she had cleared the ladder, I began to climb. She was on the diving board when I reached the top. She bounced a couple of times and jack-knifed gracefully, barely making a splash. I waited for her to break the surface. When she didn't, I picked up my crutch and towel and began to dry myself off.

Finally her head appeared some thirty feet away from the board. She was too far away to talk to. I watched her as she swam farther away. I felt deeply frustrated—excited by what had just happened, yet unsure as to what I should do or say next. I checked to see that my letter to Karla was still in my shirt pocket, then put on my shirt, draped my towel around my neck, and headed off.

"Chicken!" she called out.

Exactly, I thought. *But why? Is it Mac? I don't think so. There's something else, some deeper instinct, keeping me away.*

I gave her a half wave and limped off along the path, hoping the shrubbery next to it had hidden what had happened between us from the camp's view.

As I passed Buck's little cabin—Redclaw's cabin—I saw him standing inside the doorway, watching me, his arms folded. He was wearing shorts and a black shirt. "Hey, you!" he said.

With his arms still folded, he was beckoning me with his hand.

I stopped.

"Come here a minute."

When I reached the door, he was still standing in the same position. Since the floor of his cabin was elevated some eight inches off the ground, he towered over me. "What were you doing?" he asked.

Not much, I thought. "At the pond?" I said, stalling.

His dark eyes drilled into mine. "Yes, at the pond."

"I was exercising my leg."

"Let me look at it. Come on inside."

I hesitated.

"Come on. I won't hurt you."

I pushed myself up the front step into the doorway.

"Put your crutch there and lie on the bunk." He pointed at the wall next to the door.

"I was going to get the mail." It was dark inside, but smelled clean. His guitar hung on the wall. There was no sign of either a shotgun or a dog.

He leaned my crutch against the door frame, grasped my right upper arm with his big hand, guided me gently but firmly to the double-decker bunk on the left side of his cabin, and pushed me into a sitting position on the lower bunk.

"My suit is still wet."

He ignored me. With his other hand he forced me to lie down by pushing against my chest. He ducked his head and sat on the edge of the bed and moved his right hand to my leg.

I breathed in sharply.

"What's the matter?" he asked, staring down at my face. "Does that hurt?"

"No, it's just . . ."

His fingers massaged the muscles above my knee. "How long did you say your leg was in a cast?"

"I didn't say. About six months."

"Too long. There's atrophy. You should exercise it."

"That's what I was doing."

"You were fooling with the girl."

My face flushed. *If only.*

"You should throw away your crutch." He massaged the muscles above my knee skillfully. It felt good and I relaxed a little. His hand slid down to my ankle and grasped it. He lifted it and began to bend my leg.

"My knee is bad from a childhood sledding accident," I said quickly. "I can't bend my leg all the way."

He continued to force my ankle toward my haunch. My knee began to hurt.

"That's as far as it'll go," I blurted out. "That's why I need the crutch."

He continued to bend it. The pain grew sharper.

"Stop! That really hurts."

He placed his other hand on my knee and eased up on the pressure. "It's in your mind," he said. "You're fighting me. That's what's causing the pain."

"You're damn right I'm fighting you."

"Look at me!"

I shifted my focus from my knee to his eyes, which were staring down at me out of his swarthy, pockmarked face.

"Relax everything," he said soothingly. He squeezed my knee with his large left hand, and with his right hand began to apply pressure on my ankle again. The pain sharpened and I began to feel panic. My leg was more sharply bent than it had been in years. I held my breath and arched my back as he jackknifed my leg shut.

The pain was gone.

My body relaxed and I could feel cold sweat on my face. When I opened my eyes, Buck was smiling at me. "You did it," he said. "Is there pain now?"

I took a deep breath and let it out. "No."

"You see?"

"But it'll hit when I walk on it."

"You have to fight through it." He turned to a shelf in back of him and poured some water from a canteen into a glass. "Take this."

"No, thanks."

"Open your mouth," he said in a commanding voice.

I sipped from the glass and tasted something bittersweet.

"What is it?" I asked after swallowing.

"An herb."

"What kind?"

"If you work your knee hard, you'll be able to bend it without pain."

"We'll see."

"You could have bent your leg yourself if your mind was right."

I said nothing. I was waiting to feel some effect from the herb.

"What holds you back?"

"What do you mean?" I made a move to sit up, but he put his right hand on my chest and gently pushed me back down.

"Your brother," he said. "Peter is his name?"

"What's he got to do with it?"

"He's a beautiful child. Fair skinned."

"Yeah? So?"

"You try to protect him."

"He's a little kid."

"And yet you don't protect. You made him fight when he didn't want to. How old is he?"

"Nine."

"So there's—what?—a nine-year difference in your ages?"

"Eight. But he's my half brother."

"Ah. How is that?"

"He's the child of my father's second wife."

"And you're by the first?"

"Right."

"So."

"So what?"

He let me up.

"You don't like him," he said. "You protect him from yourself."

"That's not true." I stood and took a step toward the door, but he was blocking my way. "I like him fine."

"You'd understand more if you'd search within yourself."

I averted my eyes. *Of course I like him! I even love him!*

"You should sit on a vigil. Join the Society of Faces."

"What exactly is that?"

"You'll learn when you meet your spirits."

I wanted to say that I didn't have any spirits.

"I'll arrange it for you. I have a place."

"In those woods of yours?"

Something stirred in his eyes. "Perhaps. Not necessarily."

"I think I'll pass. I really should go now."

"You'll go on a vigil."

"No. As a counselor I don't have to."

He handed me my crutch. "I'll arrange it. Before the end of camp. Go now. And get rid of your crutch."

As I WENT to the mess hall, I tried to walk normally, but my knee was beginning to hurt again, and I didn't feel like fighting it. I couldn't feel any effect of the herb Redclaw said he had given me. I was, however, still dazed by what he had said about me and Peter.

It wasn't true, was it? I loved Peter. I had forced him to box that night only because I thought it would be good for him, right? And he was so proud when he won, wasn't he?

I tried to dig deeper into my feeling of uneasiness, wondering if Redclaw could possibly have a point. I had enjoyed Peter from almost the time he was little: he was fun to have as a younger brother, and he looked up to me. We were just like full brothers.

No, not entirely. If I looked at things from a slightly different angle, I had to admit that his arrival had displaced me, both in my father's family and in his affection. And it was because he needed his own room that I had to move in with my mother, and eventually had to go away to school when I couldn't get along with her. Karla was always assuring me that my displacement wasn't because of Peter. But you could definitely look at it that way. Maybe Redclaw was onto something.

But wasn't it precisely to mend this problem that Peter was with me at Seneca this summer? Wasn't it my aim to be a full brother to him again and, I hoped, to move back in with him and make the family whole again? The unpleasant thought suddenly struck me that Peter was just a tool in this project I had undertaken, a means to an end. Maybe I was just using him to get back into the family.

To get away from my mother.

Maybe I was kidding myself—perhaps even deluding myself—and that's what Redclaw had spotted.

Like him or not, he had a knack for getting at the essence of a situation. Maybe I was being too harsh in judging him. *Still, there was something about him that just wasn't right. There were things I wanted to ask him about, but couldn't—like the ghosts or the dog or the snakes.*

INSIDE THE MESS HALL, Mr. Lister was working at a table, laying out burlap bags and flashlights for tonight's Snipe Hunt. He gave me a funny look when he saw me in my bathing suit, but since I had my shirt on he couldn't really say anything.

The upper door of the crafts room was open. Inside, Win was sorting the mail; she had a cigarette in her mouth. When I asked her for the newspaper, she gave me her absentminded smile and handed it to me. I spread it out on a table nearby, sat down, and began to read. Every so often I would look at the infirmary door to see if T.J. had gone back there while I was in Redclaw's cabin, but though the door was half open, I couldn't see her.

I read the newspaper. Taft and Ike were still at it; Senator Joe McCarthy, from Wisconsin, had called one of his colleagues in the Senate a propagandist for the communists. The Yanks and the Washington Senators had split a doubleheader. The Yanks' lead over the White Sox was down to two and a half games. I looked around: there was still no sign of T.J. On page two of the second section, under "Crawford County News," I saw a small headline that read, "Linesville Boy Missing." Linesville was the post office address for Camp Seneca. I felt a shock go through me as I read the article.

> LINESVILLE, July 3 — A 12-year-old boy, Sam Holden, was reported missing this morning after he failed to return home by dark Wednesday evening. According to Police Chief Walter Izenaur, the boy's disappearance was reported by his parents, John and Ann Holden, of West Erie Road, at 10 a.m. Thursday morning. Young Holden had left home early Wednesday morning to trap beaver on Lake Pymatuning. His mother believes he planned to go out on the water in a skiff he kept at the lake. The skiff is also missing. Police planned to begin searching the area shortly after noon today.
>
> When last seen, the boy was wearing a black T-shirt, a denim jacket, blue jeans, and gray sneakers. His parents describe him as five feet tall, with

brown hair, blue eyes, and a mole on his upper lip. Any information concerning his whereabouts should be reported to the police immediately. Chief Izenaur has set up a special phone line, 2167.

When I had finished reading, I looked around the dining room again. Mr. Lister was gone. There was still no sign of T.J. The boy in the article, Sam Holden, was probably just off on some adventure on one of the many deserted islands on Lake Pymatuning. Maybe camping out. The islands there were great for that.

But what if . . . ?

Jesus! I thought back to Redclaw, and to the woods. *No, that couldn't be. Come on! Let's not get carried away!*

I closed the paper and took it back to the crafts room. "I'm done," I said to Win, leaning on the counter to stop myself from shaking. My knee still ached, but the pain was beginning to feel detached and remote.

Win was standing by the window facing the pond, looking out and smoking a cigarette. "Just leave it there on the counter," she said without turning around.

"What about our mail?" I looked at the crafts table, where the masks were lying. There were only two of them now; the third had obviously been taken by Steady. The two remaining had been painted garish colors since I had last seen them. Next to the masks lay several other projects, among them the pieces of what was obviously going to be Peter's wooden pistol.

"Oh, the mail. Of course." Win turned around and stubbed out her cigarette. She handed me a small packet of letters. I hesitated for a moment, trying to think of something else to say.

"Shouldn't you be with your campers, Jerry?"

"I left someone in charge. Buddy Stemmer. I was exercising my leg at the pond."

"How's it coming?"

"Okay." My eyes drifted back to the masks. "One of the masks is gone, I see. Do you know what they're for?"

"You asked me about them before. I really have no idea."

"Sorry." I started to leaf through the packet of mail. There was a postcard from my mother with another meaningless, nearly indecipherable message on it, and a thick letter addressed to me in Karla's hand.

I felt a rush of exhilaration. *Is it the letters, or the herb?* I wondered.

"Jerry," Win said in a resigned voice.

"Yes?"

She shook her head. "It's I who should be sorry." She picked up her pack of cigarettes. "I didn't mean to snap at you."

"It's okay."

She lit another cigarette and offered me the pack. I took one.

"Look," she said. "I've been under a strain, and that man . . ." She stopped herself.

"What man?"

"Never mind." She gave me her cigarette to light mine from.

"Is it okay for me to smoke here?"

"It's against the rules, but we'll make an exception."

"Thanks. Did you mean Red—Buck?"

She looked at me sadly.

I decided to gamble. "It's none of my business, I know, but didn't you help hire him?" My head was throbbing pleasantly. I felt invincible.

Win drew her head back almost imperceptibly. "No. It was entirely my husband's decision."

"But didn't you help interview him?"

"Just once. I don't like it up here in the winter."

"Up here?"

"Yes. Buck doesn't go into the city. Woody would meet him up here."

"And Buck would come from . . . ? I think Woody told me where he lived, but I forget now."

"I don't know. But as soon as Woody hired him, he started living here."

"You mean before camp began?"

"Oh, yes. Ever since last fall."

"All alone?"

"He seems to like it. Of course, on a number of weekends he had Woody for company. The boys would play," she added, speaking almost under her breath.

"Fixing up the camp?"

"Whatever."

"What about Chief Wahoo?"

"Yes. What about him?"

"I miss him."

"So do I."

I felt bursting with energy but couldn't think of anything more to say. Win gave me an expressionless look. "I guess I better get going," I said.

"Give me your cigarette. I'll put it out."

"Thanks." I handed it to her and turned to go.

"And, Jerry, let's keep this conversation between us, okay?"

"Sure. Of course. I don't really like him either."

"Why not?"

"I don't know. He's trying to tell me there's nothing wrong with the leg I broke." I took the packet of mail and headed for the door. Halfway across the room, I gave the infirmary another look, but it was still empty.

I GOT BACK TO cabin one while rest period was still going on, so I lay down on my bunk to read Karla's letter. It had been sent by airmail and was dated June 30, the day after we arrived at camp.

Jerry dearest!

We arrive in Hamburg last evening after a long travel from Frankfurt, where our airplane landed yesterday morning. We are so so tired, but now we get a much-needed rest. The hotel we are staying is quite perfect, cheap enough for your father but still comfortable. He will be able to do his business and we can have some fun. We need this very much, Jerry, this being alone together. It helps this marriage, I am sure.

How are you and my darling little Peter? I miss you very

much. I enclosed a little letter for him. I understand that letters you may write has not reached me yet, because we are traveling, but I hope you and Peter write me soon. Remember to address all letters to your father's office in New York. Irma Schrifftgauer will forward them. I want to know how things go for you. Is Peter happy? This will be good. If you need to call me you can always learn how to reach us by calling Irma. You have those numbers. She attends your father's office at regular hours. She is always home in the evenings. You know you must not do this unless absolutely necessary, because your father doesn't wish his vacation disturbed. But you should know that you can.

I miss playing cards with you and your father and having fun teasing him. He is very serious and busy now, hoping to "drum up" business. Don't forget to write to your mother.

With much love, your Karla

I called Peter over from his bunk and gave him his letter. With a roll of his eyes to let me know he would rather it had come separately, he began to read. I stared at the top of his blond head, thinking, *I can protect you from anything.* When he was finished he looked at me expressionlessly.

"You miss her?" I asked.

"A little."

"The time will go quickly."

"Actually, I'm having fun here."

"That's good."

He shifted his weight from one foot to the other. "Will you be coming home with me when camp ends?"

"I hope so. Sure." I thought a moment and decided not to say anything more. "It's time for you to write home."

He grimaced. "Soon."

"Now, Peter. Right now." I handed him a pen from my shelf. "Take one of the writing boards. When you're done, I'll address an envelope."

"I can do that."

When he had gone back to his bunk, Steady Bomber, who had been lying on his bunk reading, sat up and looked at me glumly.

"What's the matter?"

"About tonight, the Snipe Hunt?"

"Right. We should talk about that. Who's going to be watching which kids."

"I won't be helping you."

I felt a stab of disappointment, but I also felt oddly disoriented, as if it had happened to someone else. "Hey, I'm counting on you."

"I can't. I'm gonna go with Oz and his kids."

I couldn't believe it. "You can't do that!"

He looked at me pleadingly. "Bernie Kaufman, Oz's C.I.T., will take my place. We're switching."

"Oz asked you to do this? Why?"

He shrugged.

"I don't get it." I felt a flash of anger. "Well, it's up to you. Just remember we're a good team for this cabin."

"I know."

I lay back, trying to think in the fog of exhilaration. The battle for camper allegiance might have died down this summer, but it was still affecting me and I sure wasn't doing well if I couldn't hold Steady's loyalty. I could go to Woody about it, but that would be admitting weakness. *Why in the world would Oz do this to me?* I wondered. I had to talk to him about it.

By DINNERTIME, whatever herb Redclaw had given me had worn off, leaving me with an unfamiliar edge of anxiety. At the mess hall I could feel the excitement building among the younger campers over the Snipe Hunt. Woody and Len Lawrence tried to calm things down by singing, and Bordy told "Herman the Bear" for about the half-dozenth time so far this summer. But with the veteran campers bursting with their secret knowledge of what was to come, the buzz of expectancy didn't stop.

Oz was missing from his table. "Do you know where Oz is?" I asked Steady, who at least hadn't left our table.

He shrugged.

Redclaw was seated at the staff table, which was unusual; frequently he would be missing at mealtime. But T.J. wasn't there tonight, and the infirmary door was closed. Mac was watching me, his eyes glaring. He seemed to know exactly what I was thinking.

"What?" I mouthed at him.

He said nothing.

About five minutes later, the infirmary door opened and out came Oz and T.J., looking pleased with themselves. Mac was staring grimly at his brother, Artie, who was staring back with his eyebrows lifted, as if to acknowledge some unspoken message. When Oz and T.J. had made their way to their respective seats, the campers struck up a call for Oz to sing, which he had been refusing to do since Fight Night because of his injured lip. This time he got up, went to fetch his guitar from its case, and announced that now that Nursey and T.J. had trimmed his stitches and the swelling had gone down, he could sing again. He began to strum slowly, singing a melodic, plaintive blues song.

The campers listened with hushed respect and when he finished, applauded. I felt a small surge of elation. Mac continued to look grim.

Over dessert, Woody gave us instructions for the Snipe Hunt. A couple of hours from now, at dusk, we would all gather at the mess hall steps. The new campers would be "separated out" from the group, and they would be the "catchers," since to catch the snipe was the real point of the hunt. Returning campers had done it before, so they would just be helping out this time.

Woody explained that each new camper would be given a burlap bag and a flashlight and then taken out in the woods and placed in an isolated spot. It was important to be alone and far apart from any other hunters so as not to scare or confuse the snipe, which was a very skittish creature.

"What *is* a snipe?" Peter asked.

Woody answered: "It's a smallish bird, very fast on its feet, with absolutely delicious, tender, sweet meat." He resumed pacing, as if addressing his troops. "The veteran campers will serve as bush beaters to rouse the snipe and direct them toward the sack holders. As I said, they've drawn this assignment because they've caught their share of snipe in previous summers.

"Now," he went on, "to catch a snipe you have to squat down like this." He hunkered down with his haunches on his heels. "You lay your bag on the ground and lift up one side of the opening with your left hand and then hold your flashlight well inside the bag with your right hand. Like this." He demonstrated the position. "Then you want to make a clucking sound: cluck, cluck, cluck, cluck. Snipe are very curious and they can't resist light. So the soft light and the sound will attract them. When one of the birds begins to enter your bag, you quickly pull your hand with the light out of the way and slam the bag shut with the other hand. Simple."

Several hands went up. "What if lots of them come?" somebody asked. "What if I want to catch more than one?"

Woody stood again, holding up his right hand for quiet. "That is a problem. If two come in at once, fine. But if you catch one, you won't want to open up your bag to catch more, 'cause the one you've caught will get away. So once you've bagged your first snipe, you better head back to the mess hall. We'll be meeting here when the hunt is over. Maybe cook up a few of the birds for a bedtime snack."

Woody stopped pacing. "Everything clear?"

Hands were still waving, but he ignored them. "Now, let me focus on one detail."

Here it comes, I thought: Woody's special twist for this summer.

"It's extremely important that you get your hand out of the way when the snipe comes into the bag, because there's one thing to know about the snipe around this part of the country. I don't want to scare you, but they can bite. And though they're not fatally poisonous, if their saliva gets into your—uh—bloodstream, you can go a little crazy for a while."

A lot of talking greeted this warning, but Woody held his hand up to silence everyone. "It's not a bad problem. They're small birds and their beaks are dull. A bite won't kill you or do any permanent damage. Still, get that hand out of the way and don't get bitten. Understand?"

"Can't they bite through the sack?" Peter asked me, sounding nervous.

Here we go! "Absolutely not," I said. "Their beaks aren't strong enough."

"I don't think I want to do this."

"You'll be okay, don't worry. I'll stay close by to be sure nothing bad happens, okay?"

"All right," said Woody. "Any more questions?"

"Yes," I said, mischievously waving my hand. "Did Indians hunt snipe? Did the Seneca—"

"Well . . ." Woody cut me off. "I'm not sure about that." He glanced at Redclaw, who was staring off into space. "Of course, we know how important the hunt was to the Indian and how he depended for survival on what he could kill. But, um, this evening doesn't really have much to do with our Indian program. In fact, Buck here is not participating."

I wondered if we were witnessing the evidence of an ever-so-tiny rift between him and Redclaw. After all, Woody had told me that even the Snipe Hunt would be part of the Indian program.

"It's just a tradition," Woody concluded. "Soooo . . ." He looked at his watch. "Let's gather at the steps of the mess hall in about an hour and a half." He looked up. "And after the Snipe Hunt, of course, we'll have our annual fireworks display in the Far Meadow."

The news of the fireworks was greeted with cheers.

I PASSED THE next hour playing shuffleboard with Peter, Teddy, and a couple of my other younger campers. T.J. watched us, fussing over the children. I wanted to find Oz and ask him what was going on with Steady Bomber, but my kids were anxious about what was coming that evening, and it seemed important to stay with them.

When it began to get dark, I took my group down to the cabin to change into long pants, so their legs wouldn't get scratched during the hunt. Then we headed up to the mess hall. Peter continued to stay close to me. Next to the steps, Woody and Bordy were handing out the burlap bags and flashlights. While we waited in line for our turn, Bernie Kaufman told me he would be serving as my C.I.T. for the evening in place of Steady Bomber, if that was okay with me. I told him it was fine, and walked off with him to give him instructions. Peter watched apprehensively.

I told Bernie he would be taking charge of the three older new campers in my group. "We'll place everyone in the area near the rifle range. Not too far apart, so we can keep an eye on them. They're nervous, so I want to keep reassuring them. This should be exciting, not frightening, okay?"

He said nothing.

"You got that, Bernie?"

"Yeah."

Somehow I wasn't convinced.

WE HELPED OUR five campers draw bags and flashlights. On the hill beyond the pond—in the area known as the Far Meadow—the bonfire had already been started. By the light of the fire I could make out the stand that Woody always used as a base for the fireworks, as well as the keg of hard cider he always broke out for the staff and older counselors. I could see the silhouettes of several people working around the fire, but I couldn't tell who they were.

"Why is there a fire burning?" Peter asked.

"That's for the fireworks."

"Can we toast marshmallows?"

"Not tonight. You'll watch from in front of the cabins. The fire is only for the grown-ups and older campers."

"Nuts!"

"Don't worry. There'll be plenty of other times to toast marshmallows."

Peter fell into step with Teddy. My bad leg ached, so I kept it off the ground and hopped along on my crutch. *Screw Redclaw!* When we reached the lower end of Cabin Row the children began to dawdle, hesitant to plunge into the woods.

"Come on," I said, trying to quicken the pace. "Follow me."

The five campers and Bernie fell in behind me. Using my flashlight to show the way, I led the line down the path to the gateway into the Big Woods. Illuminated by my flashlight beam, the faces on the totem poles looked eerie and menacing, but the flashlights of other groups moving in the black distance beyond made the woods seem less forbidding. Bernie and the five children gathered around me.

"I don't think I want to do this," Teddy said.

"Come on," Peter said. "It's gonna be fun." I was surprised by his change of attitude.

"I don't know," Teddy answered. "I feel as if we're surrounded by things that want to bite us."

"Well, we're not," I said. "Believe me, Teddy—all of you—nothing is going to bite you. Nothing."

"What about the snipes?" Teddy asked. "What about going crazy?"

"It's not going to happen. Woody's just teasing us to make it all more exciting."

"I don't know," Teddy said.

"Let's get going," I said. "Bernie, you bring up the rear, okay?"

"Right."

"Keep your flashlights off for now. We don't want to stir up the snipe yet." I turned and went through the entrance, shading my flashlight so that the beam illuminated only the path. As we walked, I thought back to what Redclaw said about my not protecting Peter, and my not really liking him. He was simply wrong. Maybe I shouldn't have encouraged him to fight, but tonight I would be here for him. Tonight I would protect him for sure.

Ten feet beyond, where the path divided, I took the left fork across the bridge to the rifle range, moving slowly in the dark. No flashlights flickered where we were headed; the other groups were all off to our right.

When I got over the bridge, I stopped to let the kids catch up with me. They were moving very slowly.

"Come on, Teddy," Peter said.

"Hurry up," I said, trying to keep my voice low. It was comforting to see the lights of the mess hall in the distance. When the group had caught up, I turned and hobbled on. A dozen steps farther along I could make out the roof of the rifle range gallery, reflected in the moonlight that shone between the trees. I planned to use it as a home base so that the children would have a place to run to if they were truly frightened by anything that happened.

When we reached the gallery, I stopped to count heads. Peter went over to the bin of spent shells and grabbed a handful.

"What are you doing, Peter?" I asked, playing part of the flashlight beam on him.

"For my pistol," he said, stuffing his fist in his pocket.

Several of the shells fell on the ground. I felt a flash of irritation. "One will be enough," I said. *Maybe Redclaw's right,* I thought.

Peter put one shell in his pocket and threw those left in his hand back in the bin. I divided the children between Bernie and me and led my three, including Peter and Teddy, in the direction of the target stand. I positioned each boy among the trees that lined the right side of the range. That way they would be completely in the dark, yet they could see the lights of the mess hall from where they were kneeling. I put Teddy in the middle and Peter at the far end, near the targets but not too close to the Forbidden Woods.

"Can't Teddy be closer?" Peter said, his voice shaky. "He's scared."

"That would spoil his fun."

"I think he's had enough fun."

"I'll keep an eye on him." I directed him into position. "Are you okay with this?"

"I want to catch a snipe."

I went back to where Teddy was positioned. "You okay?"

"I can't see you," he said. "Can't you leave your flashlight on?"

"No. That might distract the snipe."

"Are they coming?"

"Soon. When the beaters start working. Don't forget to make a clucking noise."

I reached behind me with my crutch and began to back away from him.

"I'm right here, Teddy," Peter called out.

I MOVED AWAY from the boys, past the target stand, and stopped. Putting my hand over the face of the flashlight, I turned it on, allowing just enough light to leak out to see the surrounding underbrush. There was no sign of anyone having trampled it, although in the dark it was hard to judge. When I took a few steps farther and allowed a little more light to escape my hand, I saw the strands of the barbed-wire fence that divided the two woods.

"Are you okay, Teddy?" Peter called.

"I think so," came the answer.

"I don't hear you guys clucking," I called out.

"Cluck, cluck, cluck, cluck," they began, very tentatively.

I turned off the flashlight and worked my way quietly back past the targets to the far side of the range from Peter. I could see the glow of Peter's flashlight inside the bag, and off to the right, Teddy's too. The point of a Snipe Hunt was to leave the hunter alone with his bag until he realized the whole thing was a joke, but I wasn't about to do that tonight, especially because I was sure Woody had some kind of twist in store for everyone.

I could hear the soft sounds of clucking from off to my right. Everybody seemed to be okay.

Suddenly an arm went around my neck and gripped me tightly by the throat. I let my crutch fall away, reached up, and tried to loosen the grip with both hands. I was having trouble breathing.

"Are you there?" Peter called out.

A voice whispered in my ear, "Never leave your rear unguarded." The arm loosened and I staggered, caught my balance, and turned around, switching on my flashlight. Woody was standing there, dressed in olive-drab army fatigues and his long-billed cap. He had blacking rubbed under his eyes. Next to him stood Chunky.

I was shaking with anger. "Jesus, Woody! You scared me!"

"What's the matter?" Peter called. "Why is your flashlight on?"

"It's okay," I called back, trying to keep the rage from my voice.

"You'll scare the snipe," Peter added.

"You know by now, Jerry, that in the woods you should be alert for anything." Woody was still standing uncomfortably close.

"I thought the woods were a place of peace. Why do you have that stuff on your face?"

"So flashlights won't blind me. Are your campers all in position?"

"Of course they are."

"I don't hear much clucking."

"Cluck, guys!" I called out.

They responded.

I turned off my flashlight and immediately became aware of a bright light off in the distance. It was flanked by what looked like car headlights and seemed to be moving slowly along the main entrance road in the direction of the mess hall. "What's that?"

Woody looked over his shoulder. The lights had stopped in the vicinity of Woody's and Win's cabin. "Looks like the spotlight on Chief Izenaur's cruiser," Woody said.

I recognized that name from the news story about the missing boy. "Why would he be here?"

"He drops by now and then," Woody said after a moment.

"I've never seen him."

"Well, maybe in the off-season. He's a friend. Win'll look after him. I'm not hearing enough sounds from your campers. Only your brother."

"I'll see to them. I don't think they're having a thrilling time."

Then Woody was gone again, as silently as he had appeared. I retrieved my crutch and moved back to Peter. "You okay?" Chunky had followed me.

"I'm not catching any snipes," he said.

"I think the hunt is almost over." I looked back to see if I could make out Woody moving up Cabin Row. There was no sign of him. The spotlight on the police car, if that's what it was, continued to shine.

"Peter?"

"What."

"How would you like to get out of this place?"

"The woods?"

"No. I mean this camp?"

"Really?" He sounded dubious.

"Would you like to?"

"I don't know. There's a lot that's fun here."

"You think so?" I felt slightly disappointed at his response.

"Well, I'd like to catch a snipe."

I sighed, debating whether to let him in on the joke. Instead I stood for a moment, listening. Off in the distance voices called back and forth, but the children in the bushes nearby had fallen silent. Suddenly I heard what sounded like the flutter of a large bird's wings beating near the target stand. Chunky growled.

"There's a snipe, Teddy," Peter called out.

"Where?" Teddy called back.

I turned to look and felt the presence of someone coming toward me out of the dark.

My body lurched with surprise. Chunky snarled.

"Why are you using your crutch?" I recognized Redclaw's voice. *He had appeared from the direction of the Forbidden Woods!*

I turned on my flashlight. "It's you," I said pointlessly. He was carrying what looked like a burlap sack. Chunky continued to growl.

"Is it a snipe?" Peter called.

"I don't think so," I said.

"Why are you still using your crutch?" Redclaw repeated.

"Because my leg still hurts. Worse than earlier, in fact. Where did you come from? You scared me."

"Didn't that stuff help?"

"For a while. What the heck was it?"

"Never mind. Didn't it help?"

"Sort of."

"You want more?"

"No, thank you."

"You should not be nervous in the dark," Redclaw said. He had moved very close to me.

"Well, I am. Were you with Woody?"

"No. Where is he?"

"He went to see the chief. The police chief. What are you doing with that bag?" I shone my light on it. It looked bigger than the ones being used by the children. I felt reckless from my nervousness and anger at Woody. "I thought you were against the Snipe Hunt."

"What police chief?"

"That bright spotlight." I waved at it with my flash. "It's apparently on top of one of the police chief's cruisers."

He grunted.

A further wave of daring hit me. "Do you think he's here about that missing kid?"

"No, I don't think so."

"Then you know about him, Sam Holden?"

"Of course."

"How?"

"The same way you do. From the newspaper."

In the very faint light, it appeared that he was smiling.

Suddenly a cry for help sounded somewhere in the woods behind us, in the direction of the council fire.

Then came a high-pitched howl: "Awooooooooooooo-eeeeeee-iiiiiii iiiiiiii." It went higher and higher until the flesh on my arms and shoulders began to tingle. Chunky barked and ran off into the dark.

"What's that?" Peter called out.

"I don't know, but don't worry, I'm right here."

"You'd better gather up your kids and get 'em to the mess hall," Redclaw said.

"Why? What's going on?"

"I don't know." Then he disappeared back into the darkness.

I waited, listening to the shouts and cries.

"Mac's bit," a child cried out in the distance. "He's gone crazy!" someone else yelled.

So this is Woody's game. Another character-building trauma! I thought.

"Everybody to the mess hall," called a grown-up voice that was probably Len.

"Come on, Peter, Teddy, everyone," I called out. "Gather round me. Bernie?"

"I'm here." His voice came from the direction of the gallery.

"Round up your campers. Let's get 'em to the mess hall. Make sure everyone's accounted for."

Peter and Teddy were beside me, tugging at my T-shirt. "What's happening?"

"Awoooooooo-eeeeeee-iiiiiiiii," came the bloodcurdling howl again.

"Mac's pretending that a snipe bit him. It's all make-believe."

"It sounds pretty real to me," Teddy said.

"We'll stay with you," Peter said.

I counted my campers and led them across the bridge toward camp. When we got to the totem pole gate, I could hear cabin doors slamming. People were streaming toward the mess hall.

"Oooowwww-ooowww-ooww-ow-ow." The sound came from off to the left, somewhere in the vicinity of the Far Meadow, where the bonfire was. It seemed to be moving closer to us.

The sound of Chunky barking came from the same area.

"Help! Help! Help!" children cried.

"Come on, kids. Let's hurry up." I swung myself on my one crutch as fast as I could. The children trotted along beside me.

"If it isn't real, why are we running?" Teddy asked breathlessly.

"It's part of the game," Peter said.

I reached out to pat his head, but he and Teddy had already run ahead.

We joined the stream of campers and counselors moving up Cabin Row. Flashlight beams flickered like fireflies in the meadow off to our left. I guessed that Mac would keep his distance until everyone was safely in the mess hall. The police car was still parked in front of the Wentworths' cabin, and the spotlight was still on. The Chrysler Town & Country was parked beside the cabin too. Laughter came from inside the dining room.

Sounds continued to come from behind us, down near the Big Woods: "Ooooo-wooooo-woooooo-eeeeeeeeeeee-iiiiiiiiiiiiii" and shouts of "There he is! Look out! Run!"

I pushed my way through the mess hall door. Bernie had herded his campers to the corner of the dining room. Other campers were playing shuffleboard, or clinging to their counselors, depending on their age. In the same corner as Bernie, Oz was sitting with Steady and several of his campers.

A bare-headed gray-haired man in a uniform was standing by the door to Woody's office, which stood open. Next to him was a younger uniformed man. Win was with them, standing in the office doorway; she appeared nervous and distracted. A little apart from them, alone in the corner, stood Redclaw, once again stone-faced and unreadable.

I looked about for T.J. but didn't see her. The door to the nurse's office was closed.

Peter was pulling on my arm so hard I found it difficult to stand. "I want to watch from a safer place," he pleaded.

I squatted awkwardly and put my hands on his shoulders. "Mac'll be fine and so will you." I drew him close to me. "It's all pretend. Remember that. Everything that's going to happen now is pretend too."

"I know. And the policemen too. Right?"

"They're just friends of Woody's, paying a visit." I pushed myself up again. "Let's go over and watch."

I led him over to where Bernie and the other campers from our cabin were now sitting. Most of the camp was crowded into the mess hall. Outside, the shouting moved closer.

Suddenly a sound of stomping came from the front stairs and the front door flew open. Woody stepped inside. He was still wearing army fatigues, but the blacking was gone from under his eyes. "We got him!" he shouted dramatically. "Mac's definitely been bit. He's gone crazy, but we got him! Clear the way, we're bringing him in." He stuck his head outside the door and called, "Bring him in, boys!"

Peter pushed himself closer to me. I looked over to see how Win was reacting, but she was gone and the office door was closed.

Woody strode toward the performance area. "Clear the way here." He pointed to one of the hall's supporting posts. "We'll secure him right here. Can we open the infirmary, please? Just in case we need medicine or bandages?"

Peter's eyes were blazing with excitement.

The door to the office was opened by someone not visible from the outside.

Woody strode back to the front door and looked out. "Here they come now!"

We could hear Mac's howling getting closer. It was accompanied by the jangling of chains. Cries of excitement and panic rose in the mess hall. Peter was bouncing up and down now.

Mac, manhandled by Len and Bordy and followed by Chunky, came through the doorway. His shirt was loose and hanging in shreds. His wrists and ankles were shackled to a chain, and his face was lathered with thick white froth that was surely shaving cream. As soon he entered the hall, he stopped in his tracks, threw back his head and shoulders, and let out a sound that began as a howl and rose to a high-pitched scream, piercing enough to make the inside of my ears itch. Chunky, standing by the entrance, began to howl in unison. Mac appeared to be drunk or was working himself up to do something crazy. It occurred to me that the victim of whatever he was planning to do might be Oz.

Or even me?

Bordy and Len jerked Mac upright and frog-marched him over to the wooden post that Woody had designated. They wrapped the chains around the post and Woody made an elaborate show of securing them with a large padlock.

"There!" Woody shouted. "That should hold him."

Mac howled dramatically and struggled to get loose, snapping the chains against the post and striking out at Bordy, Len, and Woody, but the chains seemed to be holding. When some of the more adventuresome campers approached to get a closer look, Mac drove them back by lunging and snarling at them.

"They better not bother him," Peter shrieked. "They're making him madder." He sounded more thrilled than afraid.

"I'm going to call for help," Woody yelled at no one in particular. He strode toward our end of the hall. "Can you help us with this, Chief Izenaur?" he called out. "Maybe get him to a hospital?"

"Wal, I dunno," the policeman answered, scratching his head, half embarrassed and half pleased to be included in the game. "Maybe you oughta call an ambulance."

I snuck a glance at Redclaw. He was looking on impassively.

"Good idea!" Woody shouted. "I'm gonna do that. Keep a close eye on him, boys!" He hurried past us into his office, followed by Chunky, and closed the door.

Mac began to struggle harder, shaking his chains, throwing his head back, and howling. The foam from his face flew in droplets around him.

"He looks like he's trying to escape," Peter said, sounding almost pleased.

Woody stuck his head out. "Everything okay? Help is on the way."
Mac stopped struggling for a moment.

"Easy now, Mac," Bordy said, standing among the ring of people watching the prisoner from about ten feet away. "Just relax."

Mac let out an enormous roar and gave a mighty jerk of his chains. With suspicious ease, his shackles suddenly came loose and his chains fell in a heap at his feet. He stood for a moment, a dazed look on his face.

"Oh my gosh, he's loose," Woody shouted from his office door.

"It's okay! I got him!" Big Bordy called back, stepping forward and grabbing Mac. Mac immediately threw him to the floor and with another loud roar went charging into the crowd of campers off to his right.

"My God," Bordy cried out. "He's got the strength of ten men. That snipe juice really got to him."

Campers screamed and fell away as Mac, still impeded by one leg iron and a long length of chain, lunged here and there, howling. Most of the campers sensed it was all playacting, so there was as much glee as fear in their cries. The braver ones even baited Mac by dashing almost within his reach. The more timid ones were cringing at our end of the hall.

"Stay away from him, everybody!" Woody shouted. "He's very dangerous."

I had thought from the outset that Mac was building toward something, and I was right. After lunging at a few more campers, he lurched toward the kitchen and went through the door. Through the opening above the counter I could see him moving toward the work table by the stove. A noise like the clattering of cutlery on a countertop followed, and a moment later Mac reappeared in the doorway, brandishing the large meat cleaver.

"Jeeesus!" muttered Woody, still standing at the entrance to his office. "It's the Mad Cook of Pymatuning!"

"What's he going to do now?" Peter yelled. "Oh, oh!"

"Stay close to me," I said.

"I'm fine," he answered, a little irritably. "Here he comes!"

Mac was limping toward our end of the hall and was swinging the cleaver round and round above his head, howling the entire time.

"What's going on?" I said to Woody. "Isn't he overdoing it a little?"

"I think he might be a little high," he answered out of the side of his mouth. "Got into the cider early."

Mac had stopped at our end of the hall. He was grunting unintelligibly, and had the cleaver cocked at his shoulder. Suddenly his focus came to rest on something to the left of us, and his face twisted in what appeared to be real rage. He let out a sudden howl of anger and jerked the cleaver back. I followed his gaze and saw that it had fixed on Oz, who was surrounded by Steady and their campers.

From the far side of the hall, Artie Mac came running. "Don't do it, Early!" he shouted. "Leave him be!"

Mac grunted, swayed, caught his balance, and raised the cleaver higher.

"He isn't worth it! I tole you, even if he *is* messin' with her!"

Mac seemed to come out of a trance. He gave his brother a sharp look, swung his gaze back to Oz again, and lowered the cleaver to his shoulder. Suddenly he stepped forward, snapping his arm down like a pitcher and releasing the cleaver. A collective gasp sounded as it spun through the air in Oz's direction. Peter shrieked. Woody said, "Jesus!" Oz ducked. The cleaver thunked against the door frame against which Oz had just been leaning, and buried itself deep in the wood.

Christ! This is out of control! I thought.

Everyone froze, except Oz. He slowly turned to the door and worked the cleaver loose from the wood. Then he turned back to face Mac, hefting the cleaver a couple of times as if making up his mind about something, his expression a mixture of bitterness and anger. He held the entire crowd transfixed, even Mac, who stood frozen in position, his arm hanging in front of him, as if he'd just thrown a pitch.

After what seemed an interminable time, Oz took a step forward and began to walk slowly away from the canteen door. Every eye in the room followed him. At first he seemed to be moving toward Mac, but then he veered away in the direction of the kitchen. When he reached the counter, he turned slowly to face the room. He stood there for another interval with the cleaver raised in the air. Finally, he lowered it and placed it carefully on the kitchen counter.

"You missed," he said.

Mac let out another exuberant howl and went charging to the front of the hall and out the main door. Some of the campers ran after him, but stopped at the door, waiting to see what he would do next. Others drifted to the windows.

"That was great!" Peter said, more to himself than to me.

"Was that part of the act?" I asked, turning to Woody.

"Christ, no," Woody said. "But he missed on purpose."

"I don't know. I think he's over the edge." I felt sick to my stomach.

Woody hunched his shoulders. "Maybe not." He turned away from me and disappeared back into his office. Mac's roaring began to recede. None of the campers followed him outside.

Woody reemerged from his office, cradling the shotgun I had seen on the wall. Chunky was beside him. "Everyone stay here," he yelled theatrically. "I'm going to have to shoot him."

"He's pretending, right?" Peter yelped.

"Of course," I said, though at this point I wasn't sure of anything.

Woody strode to the front door and went out and down the steps. Bordy, Len, and Chunky followed him. Everyone in the mess hall strained to listen.

The chief and his assistant went over to the screened window and looked out. Together, they moved toward the door.

Mac's howling continued to sound in the distance.

A loud shotgun report boomed out. The howling stopped abruptly.

"Did I get him," Woody yelled.

"Yep, he's down," someone answered.

A hush fell over the mess hall. The police chief and his man stopped and began to talk together quietly.

Suddenly the kids by the door began to laugh and cheer and back up. Then an instant later Bordy and Len pushed their way through the door and held it open for a smiling Woody, who entered dragging Mac, who had his arms raised triumphantly in the air.

The whole mess hall broke into loud applause. Mac was mobbed by the campers near the door.

"Yaaaaaaaaaaaaaaaaaaaaaaaayyyyy," Peter cheered.

I knelt down beside him and put my arms around him. "Remember what I said about getting out of here?" I said in a low voice. "How do you feel about it now?"

"That was pretty scary." He seemed out of breath.

"I'm working on something. Don't tell anybody, but remember that."

"I don't know. Let's see what happens next." He pulled himself away and went running off.

Was I making a mistake? I wondered. *Should I just grab Peter and run? Things were definitely getting out of control, and I didn't know whom I could rely on any more.*

I looked around for Oz but I couldn't find him in the excited crowd. T.J. was standing in the doorway of the nurse's office. She was staring at Mac and the crowd swarming around him. The expression on her face was grim.

As we herded the campers out of the mess hall, I could hear the concussive booms of the first fireworks going off. By the time we were down the stairs, the sky above the Far Meadow was alight with a fiery weeping willow trailing long tresses of red, gold, and bronze, which ended in soft puffs of green and silver. I led my children slowly down to the front of cabin one, where we sat on the ground to watch. Teddy huddled close to me with his hands over his ears. Peter stood on the steps.

Another rocket exploded above us and sent an arching shower of white-and-red sparks. Peter leaped in the air joyfully. Others around us sighed.

"Try to relax and concentrate on what you're seeing instead of what you're hearing."

"Wow, neat!" Teddy said.

The light of sparklers near the bonfire revealed the silhouettes of the half dozen older boys who were helping Bordy and Woody with the display. Several more rockets went up and exploded gaudily. I tried to make out who else was up there, but I couldn't recognize anyone. I wanted to talk to Win and get her take on why the police had come by.

A car motor started up near the mess hall. The police chief's cruiser, with its spotlight still shining, moved slowly up the driveway toward the main entrance. Another car trailed behind it, the Chrysler Town & Country, I was sure. Woody was still at the fireworks stand, so I figured Win was probably driving the Chrysler. Strange for her to go off on her own.

The fireworks display distracted me from my uneasiness, however, and for a couple of minutes more I relaxed. After it ended, I looked for Peter and saw him running in the distance with other kids his age.

He looks happier than I feel, I thought.

I put Bernie in charge of getting our kids to bed, then I headed out to the bonfire. There, I found a kind of bedlam, with people running about while Woody sang barbershop with Bordy, Len, and the kitchen girls, Eve and Sukie, all of whom seemed to be feeling the cider. Win was nowhere around. Neither were Mac, T.J., Oz, or Redclaw. I drew myself a glass of cider from the keg, but since there was no one to talk to, I gulped it down and decided to go looking for Oz. We had bed wetter duty together that night, and though I could handle it without him, I wanted the company. Besides, I was wondering how he was doing after Mac's attack.

I went to his cabin first. Oz's bunk was empty. Steady Bomber was lying awake on the adjoining bed, dressed in just his underpants. His duffel bag sat open on the floor beside the head of his bunk.

"What gives, Steady?" I asked in a low voice. "Are you coming back to us?"

He looked at me sadly. "I'm staying here. I made a deal with Bernie Kaufman."

"You can't just do that on your own."

"You won't let us?"

"Is it what you want?"

"Yes."

"Well, I guess I can't stop you if you feel strongly."

"Bernie's good."

"Not as good as you."

"I'd like to try this."

He said nothing more. I figured I could push him, but why risk hurting our relationship? "Where's Oz?"

"I don't know."

"Did he go to town? We've got bed wetter duty."

"I don't think so."

"Help me look for him?"

He sat up slowly, reached into his duffel for a pair of jeans, and began to pull them on. I took my crutch and went outside to wait. When he joined me we went down to the end of Cabin Row and looked in the Kybo and the shower house. Oz wasn't in either building.

"He's gotta be around here somewhere," I said. "It would save time if we split up. Why don't you take the Big Woods—the rifle range, the council fire, and the tree house. I'll search the other end of camp— the mess hall, the barn, and the farmhouse. Okay?"

"Sure."

"Take my light. When you're finished, come back to the cabins, whether you find him or not. If I'm not there, start waking up the bed wetters. Do you know who they are?"

"Yes."

"We shouldn't let them go too much longer."

He started down the path to the Big Woods, walking quickly. I felt the assignment was a little unfair, sending him off into the woods, but there were grown-up places in the part I was going to search that might make Steady uncomfortable, like Woody's cabin, Jeff's room, and the farmhouse.

I passed the cabins and went across the meadow toward the pond. The air was getting cooler, and the frogs were making a racket. I could barely hear the voices from the bonfire.

What had changed Peter in the middle of the Snipe Hunt? I wondered. Why had he suddenly stopped being so afraid?

As I reconstructed the evening in my memory, I realized the change must have come about while he was looking after Teddy. Seeing Teddy's fear had made Peter feel more brave.

Would looking after Peter work changes in me? I wondered.

No one was at the pond. I wanted a cigarette, but I hadn't been able to find my lighter when I looked for it in my cabin. I made my way back and checked Redclaw's cabin. Empty. I figured Redclaw had gone to town.

Maybe with Win? I thought, then decided that was unlikely.

I looked in Woody's cabin, the mess hall, and the various staff cabins behind the mess hall. Every place was deserted, even Jeff's room. On the way to the kitchen exit I grabbed a wooden match and lit a cigarette, then I headed up the road toward the farmhouse.

Where did I leave my lighter? I wondered.

I remembered smoking a cigarette in the afternoon when I was talking to Win but I lit it off the one she was smoking.

The barn loomed on my left. It was a building Woody had talked about tearing down someday.

The farmhouse was completely dark, but I could hear a sound coming from inside. When I mounted the back steps I recognized the soft plinking of a ukulele, accompanied by a low voice singing.

I ground my cigarette out on the stone step and pulled the flimsy screen door open. The dark parlor smelled of apple cider and mold. I could see the form of someone sitting on the old couch in the corner off to my right.

"Oz?"

He went on singing, playing awkward little riffs on the uke. The smell and the way he was slurring his words told me he'd raided the cider barrel in the cellar. I was surprised he knew about it.

I leaned my crutch against the wall and sat down on the other end of the couch. Oz stopped singing, reached for a milk bottle I could now dimly see sitting on the low table in front of the couch, and drank from it. He still wore his cap. He extended the bottle in my direction and I accepted. The cider was sharp, heavily fermented.

"It's been a wild night," I said.

Oz continued to sing.

"Were you in the woods during the Snipe Hunt?" I asked. "Mac was drunk, y'know."

"So'm I."

"Yeah, but you're not throwing cleavers around."

The air seemed to thicken. "He resents us."

"Why does that allow him to act like that?"

"Drunk, crazy. Thinks we're privileged."

That was true, I thought. "And he's mad at you about T.J."

"Don't care about T.J."

You don't care about me either, do you? I thought. "What's going on with Steady? He told me he's moving to your cabin for good."

"Switching with Bernie."

"Steady's always been with me," I said, feeling a rising resentment.

"Bernie's good man too."

I took another sip of the cider. It made my lips tingle. "We should go walk the bed wetters."

"They can wait."

"Do you really like it here?"

"Here, the farmhouse?"

"No, the camp. Seneca."

"Sure. Why? You?"

"The summer's not working out the way I thought it would."

"Wh'ya mean?"

"I told you . . . something's wrong this year."

He began to strum again. "I got nothing to compare things with."

I felt as if I were aiming an arrow at a moving target. "What does Redclaw do in those woods, I wonder."

"Don't know."

"He was there again this evening."

"Can't help you."

"Don't you talk to him?"

"Sure, but not about the woods."

"Do you know why the police chief was here?"

"Friend of Woody's."

I give up, I thought. He was in no shape to talk. "Let's get the bed wetters."

"Let 'em be like Indians," Oz said. He reached for the cider jar again and took a long drink from it. His hand softly touched my knee. "Do you know what Indians do?"

"What?"

"If they wanna wake up early in the morning they drink a lot of liquid and go to sleep without peeing. Need to pee wakes them up. Like an alarm clock."

"Yeah, I've heard that."

"When you wake up needing to pee, you get a hard-on."

"I know. Sometimes."

"It's time to get up," he said.

"What?"

"I gotta pee."

"Oh."

"Feel," he said.

"We ought to head down to the cabins," I said. "Steady's waiting for us." I reached out in the dark to nudge him. In the air between us, his hand closed around my wrist.

"Steady's a good man," he said. "Feel."

"Come on, Oz." My voice came out as a whine that I didn't like. I tried to pull my hand away, but he was too strong. He pulled my hand to his crotch. Through his pants I could feel his erection.

Oh, shit! I thought, trying to pull my hand back. *I should punch him.*

Then his other arm went around my neck and pulled my head down roughly to his face. His wet lips found mine. The sweet, rancid smell of the cider on his breath made me gag.

I tried to jerk myself free, but his hold around my neck was too strong. He released my hand from his crotch and began to unzip the fly of his jeans.

I succeeded in pushing him away. "Please, Oz, please don't," I whimpered, ashamed at how helpless I sounded. At the same time I felt a bubble of rage start to blow up in my chest.

A low laugh came out of him. He pushed me aside and sat up, his head thrown back, a hiccuping of staccato breaths hissing out of him.

He stood. His hand went to my head, grabbed my hair, and pulled it roughly enough to hurt. "It's okay. Forget it," he said. "Let's go get the pissers."

I found my crutch and followed Oz outside. My neck and shoulders ached, and I could feel the cider burning in my throat. My leg hurt too. I didn't care what Oz was doing now—and I was too numb to know what I was feeling—but I could still hear his erratic footsteps behind me as we approached the mess hall. When I got beyond the corner where Jeff's room was I heard Oz veer off toward the flagpole and begin to retch. I went back to him. He was down on all fours, and heaving violently. I leaned down and cupped my left hand at the base of his neck. His cap was gone.

Finally he stopped and let out a groan. I massaged his neck and left shoulder. I thought he was beginning to heave again, but after a few moments I realized he was sobbing.

"Take it easy, Oz."

His shoulders stopped shaking, but he didn't say anything.

Frogs sounded from the direction of the pond. I could smell the faintest odor of smoke, left over from the fireworks, I guessed.

Oz pushed himself up and stood beside me. He smelled of vomit. "Bed," he said. He took a few steps and tumbled to the ground. "Sleep."

"Come on," I said, taking his arm and trying to pull him up.

"Lemme sleep."

I heard footsteps approaching from the direction of the cabins. "Steady?"

"Yes."

"Help me."

We pulled Oz up and began to walk him clumsily toward the cabins. Oz cooperated for a while, then jerked his right arm away from me, stopped walking, and embraced Steady, who stood there patiently.

"Buddy," Oz said. "My Buddy."

"It's okay," Steady said.

I looked up at the sky. The moon was out now, a half disk hanging above the cabins. A cloud of smoke drifted across its face. My first thought was that it came from the fireworks or the bonfire, but the display had ended long ago and when I looked at the Far Meadow I saw that the bonfire was out. The smoke was coming from another source.

"Let's get him to bed," I said.

We got Oz into cabin three and onto his bunk. He murmured and seemed to drift off to sleep.

"I got the bed wetters," Steady whispered in the dark.

"Good," I answered. "Thanks. You can go hit the sack now. I'm going to stay up for a while." I felt stupid to my bones, and needed some time to think. Oz had certainly surprised me. *No wonder he didn't care about T.J.!*

I moved away from Cabin Row. The smoke was rising in a plume near the dead tree—that much I could see. As it got above the tree-line the night breeze tore it into ragged clouds, which were wafting in my direction.

What could be burning? I wondered.

Could the woods themselves be on fire? The smoke seemed far too concentrated for that, but whatever it was could be dangerous if the fire spread.

Should I go in the woods and see what's burning? I wondered.

The thought made my whole body twitch. I wanted to catch Redclaw at whatever he was doing in there. *Catch him red-handed!* But then I remembered our encounter this afternoon—his liquid black eyes and pockmarked skin—and I suddenly felt drained of curiosity.

I'm not about to go in those woods alone—not tonight, anyway. Things are too weird!

There was something else I could do, and with so many people away in town, now might be the perfect time for it. I thrust my crutch forward and headed for my cabin, feeling determined again. Everything about the camp had turned sour. Something evil seemed to have taken hold. Even Peter seemed to have fallen under its influence. I knew what I had to do. I had to mail the letter to Karla immediately. It was no longer an exaggeration of how bad things were.

And there was something else that I could do. It might not be fair to blame Redclaw for what had gone wrong here, but it felt to me as if he were at the heart of the problem. His presence was the thing that was different this summer, that had changed Woody and Win, and Mac, and Steady, and even Oz. It was as if Redclaw had infected them all and made them reveal their uglier, secret selves. He had made the whole point of Camp Seneca seem negative, if only by announcing at the campfire that we had wrongfully seized his people's land. And he was up to something in those woods. I was sure of that.

I was determined to get to know more about him.

AFTER FETCHING the letter to Karla from my trunk and sliding it into the slot in the crafts room door, I moved to the door of Woody's office, took a deep breath, and gently twisted the knob. It turned easily and the latch clicked open. Win had probably left the office in anger over the Snipe Hunt, and Woody had either gone to town or was sleeping off the cider.

I stepped inside and closed the door. Moonlight bathed the office. I stood there for a minute, waiting for my eyes to get used to the dim light. When I could see the outlines of the furniture, I worked my way behind Woody's desk and awkwardly sat down in the chair, keeping my bad leg extended.

I could see the bearskin's silhouette.

I reached for the handle of the file cabinet's top drawer, gave it a yank, and was relieved to find that it slid open without protest. It dawned on me then that I had left my flashlight with Steady.

I groped in the drawer and, to my relief, found Woody's Zippo lighter there. Using the flame's dim light, I found a file marked "Silverstone." The lighter was burning down, so I snapped it shut to conserve its fuel. I opened the file and counted the number of papers inside. I could feel the glossy photograph Woody had shown me earlier. There were two others beneath it, and three sheets of paper.

Paranoid now, and afraid that if I relit the Zippo above the level of the desktop it would be seen from outside, I got off the chair and lowered myself to the floor. I snapped the lighter on again and saw the photo of Redclaw preaching. I slid it aside, revealing a second photo, this one of Woody and Redclaw stripped down to just loincloths and standing in front of a structure covered with what looked like animal skins. They were smiling and holding up glasses of liquid. This was a side of Woody I never imagined.

The third photograph showed Redclaw standing alone. His arms were flexed in a bodybuilder's pose. He was naked.

I gaped at the picture, dumbstruck. A photo of Redclaw standing naked? Woody had to have taken it. *What in hell did that mean? Was this the real reason behind why Chief Wahoo was gone? Could this be why Win didn't like Redclaw?* A thousand thoughts filled my mind.

Underneath the photographs was a brief letter accepting the job of chief Indian counselor, dated last year, September 21, 1951, and signed "Buck Silverstone." The flame had flickered so low that I could barely see the next two pages in the file. I could tell they contained a long résumé. I had time only to skim them before the last bit of yellow flame flickered out: there were listings of several schools that Redclaw had attended and taught at, including Penn State; several hotels that he had worked for; and years spent in the United States Marine Corps.

A couple of things caught my eye before the light was gone. One was that there was a gap in the résumé from 1947 to 1949, the years after he had preached at that reservation longhouse, as I knew from the date on the photograph Woody had shown me. The other was that he had gone from teaching American studies at Allegheny College in Meadville, Pennsylvania, in 1945, to working at a hotel in Niagara Falls the same year. That seemed an odd leap.

Suddenly the desk was flooded with light, and I stared into the glare of a bright flashlight.

"I'm looking for the newspaper!" I heard myself say, gambling that whoever was holding the light couldn't see what I was doing behind the desk.

"Funny time to be doing that," a familiar voice said. The light beam moved around the room. "Funny place to be doin' it."

"Jeff?" I said, my voice coming out half an octave too high.

"Thass right. Watcha doin' back there?"

Relieved, I put the file away, snapped the lighter shut, put it back in the drawer, and stood.

THE VIGIL

YOU BEST COME WITH ME," Jeff said.

I took my crutch and followed him. He headed in the direction of his own room.

"What was that you were playing the other night?" I asked him. "I mean the simple-sounding piece."

"Never mind that. What were you doin' in the boss's office?"

"I told you. I was looking for the newspaper."

"Come on in. Close the door behind you." He picked up a chair next to the piano, turned it around, and straddled it backward.

I stood with my back to the closed door. "Woody said I could borrow the paper."

"Down on the floor you was lookin' for it? Take a seat." He waved his hand at a wooden chair.

I sat on the chair's edge. "I thought it might have fallen off the desk."

"Into the file cabinet?"

I didn't know what to say to that. To the left of me stood his bunk, with an old guitar lying on it. "You play guitar too?"

"Some."

I began to relax a little. "So Oz was right when he called on you to play."

Jeff scratched his goatee. "Me and him don' belong on the same stage." His tone was disparaging.

"You don't like his music?"

"Don't mean a thing if it ain't got that swing." He smiled brightly. "But let's get back to the subject. Which is, what you were doin' in those files?"

I raised my hands in defeat.

"What you find out about him?" he asked before I could speak.

"Who?"

His eyes got exaggeratedly big. *"Who!* The chief! Mr. *Buck.* You think I don't see things?"

I let out my breath. "What do you think of him?"

"What did you find out, man?"

"Not much," I stammered. "Gaps in the record. Funny jumps from one type of job to another."

Strange photographs.

"What do you mean, funny jumps?"

"One month he's a professor, next he's working in a hotel."

Jeff fixed his eyes somewhere to the left of me. "Man, he's a strange one."

"Why do you say that? What do you think?"

"I think he might be bad news."

I felt a rush of relief at learning he shared my fears. "Why do you say that?"

"I know what I know."

"I thought I was the only one who was worried."

"They playing with fire."

"What do you mean?"

"This Indian stuff."

"What about it?"

He waved in the general direction of the Big Woods. "They makin' like it's all jes' fun and games."

"But that's exactly what it's supposed to be."

"Well, it ain't."

He moved in his chair to face me. "They actin' like his Indians was all jes' good folks, Woody and them."

"Well, weren't they? I mean, y'know . . . close to nature and . . . ?"

"You know who this Tarachiawagon is? Was?"

"Who?"

"Ta-rach-i-a-wag-on. 'Great Spirit, Master of Life, Holder of the Heavens . . .'"

"I never heard of him."

"Sure you did. At the campfire the first night. The man prayed to Tarachiawagon."

"Oh, well. That's what he does. He's like a priest or minister in some new Indian religion. Woody showed me a photo of him preaching."

"Yeah, but that new Indian religion supposed to be influenced by Christianity, and ole Buck, he don't seem very Christlike to me."

"Then who's this guy Tarachy-uh . . . ?"

"See, that's the thing. He's part of the new religion, but he's also part of the old. And the old—"

"Who is he?"

"He's an old god, the Good Twin of the Seneca creation myth. Breathed life into dust to make the first man and woman and like that."

"A creation myth."

"And Shagodyoweh: y'know who that is?"

"Who?"

"Shagodyoweh. The man said his name when he threw tobacco in the fire."

"He did?"

"Yeah. He was Tarachiawagon's Evil Twin, turned into a powerful giant responsible for all the evil in the world."

"Come on . . ."

"You offer him tobacco, he give you great power through the masks, the faces."

"But he was just doing mumbo-jumbo for the kids. He also said we're on Seneca ground. That was just make-believe too."

Jeff let his shoulders slump. "I don't know. I just don't know." He lifted his chin so that his goatee pointed at me. "Why you lookin' in his file, then? Why you bothered by this Buck?"

"I call him Redclaw."

"Why?"

"It's his warrior name, remember?"

"Yeah. So?"

"Well, he seems as if he's looking for a fight."

"That why you messin' in his file?"

"I guess so. It bothered me the way he beat up Bordy boxing. The way he tries to be so scary. He seems so angry."

"Well, there you go! The new religion, the Way of Handsome Lake, is s'posed to be a forgiving one. Buck don't seem so forgiving. He more like the old way, which was based on revenge, the blood feud. Revenge is s'posed to be gone from the New Way. And the masks, they're s'posed to be gone too."

"What about the masks?"

"In the old Seneca way, they were made in the image of the Evil Twin, the Punisher, Shagodyoweh, the giant. Handsome Lake wanted them out of his religion. Buck, he seems to like the masks."

"What were they for?"

"In the Old Way, you put on a mask to express things inside yourself you might not like. The masks let you express those feelings. Join the Society of Faces."

"What the heck is that, anyway?"

"Part of the Old Way too. Not just mumbo-jumbo."

"How do you know all this stuff?"

His eyes narrowed. "I got a life beside this one."

"You went to school, didn't you? You're educated. But you try to hide it."

"I reads." He grinned, mocking me.

I scanned some of the titles of the books on a shelf by the head of his bed. *Patterns of Culture, The Golden Bough, Midwinter Rites of the Cayuga Long House,* by Frank G. Speck.

"You know *The Song of Hiawatha*?" Jeff asked.

"Yeah, a little. Longfellow. 'On the shores of Gitche Gumee, of the shining Big-Sea-Water . . .'"

"Right. The real Hiawatha was founder of the Iroquois League. You know that? Ended the warfare among the Five Nations."

"Right."

"What Longfellow doesn't tell you is how Hiawatha lived before his conversion to being the peacemaker."

"How?"

"He was a cannibal. Ate folks."

"You serious?"

"Yeah, but Longfellow makes it all pretty, sentimental. He even cut the ugly stuff out of his own poem. This here Buck reminds me of that stuff." He stood up. "Here," he said, removing a volume and handing it to me: *The Indians of North America,* volume one, edited by Edna Kenton. "Read that."

"Thanks," I said. It was heavy. "It's so long. I don't know if—"

"You don't gotta read the whole thing. Just, uh . . ." He took the book back from me and riffled through its pages. "Just pages three thirty-six to three forty-eight. The story about Joseph. That'll tell you what I'm talking about." He handed the book back to me.

"I will." We looked at each other. "It's funny that you and I have never talked like this before, isn't it?"

He raised his eyebrows. "I been right here."

"I know. I know." Embarrassed, I looked at the piano keyboard. "So what was that piece you were playing the other night?"

"Don't know. What did it sound like?"

"Very simple, but formal." I tried to hum it.

"Oh." He began the simple eight-note sequence.

"That's it."

"That be the man," he said without looking at me. "Bach. *Well-Tempered Clavier.* First prelude in C major." He stopped playing. "Good stuff."

"It's beautiful." I slapped the book against my thigh. "Look, I'm worried. Will you help me?"

"How'm I s'posed to do that?"

"Isn't there someone you could call?"

"Call about what?"

"You know, about Redclaw . . . Buck."

"What about him?"

I thought for a moment. "Do you know anyone at, uh, Penn State? Or Allegheny College? Those are places he taught."

"Why would I?"

"Well, I mean, you seem to know about his field. Buck taught American civilization, I think. Couldn't you find out about him?"

"That be a white man's world."

"Redclaw's not a white man." I wondered for an instant what exactly I meant by that, but let it go.

"He could pass for one."

"We gotta find out about him."

"Shouldn't you be gettin' back to your cabin?"

I stood. "You're not going to say anything about me being in Woody's office?"

"No."

"Thanks." I opened the door. "Think about someone you could call to find out about Redclaw." *Do I dare risk it?*

He turned back to the piano. "Get along now."

What have I got to lose? I closed the door again. "I'm trying to get out of here."

Jeff's hands hung above the keys. "No kidding?"

"I've written my parents."

He turned his head to look at me. "Why not just go?"

"I can't do that."

"Why not, you wanna go?"

"I'd have to take my brother. I don't have any money."

"He don't pay you, Woody?"

"Yeah, but not until the end of camp."

"So ask for it now."

"I couldn't do that. He wouldn't give it to me early."

"Tell him you need it. Man's gotta give you what he owes you."

"You mean tell him I got a bill?"

"Sure. Folks do get bills."

"Like something for college."

He played a single note softly. "What I'd do."

I opened the door. "Maybe so." I hesitated a moment. "Meantime, you'll think about someone to ask about Redclaw?"

"Don't know about that."

"Well, think about it."

AFTER THE SNIPE HUNT, things got worse at the camp. There was a nasty feeling that affected almost everyone. Squabbling broke out among the campers, leading to several fights. Woody had to put on an extra Fight Night one Tuesday to allow certain campers to have it out with each other and relieve the growing tension. Mac and Oz didn't take part; they apparently had declared some sort of chilly truce. Redclaw showed up but kept his distance, and no one suggested he take part in any more exhibitions.

A sudden plague of accidents hit the camp. Sukie, the kitchen girl, dropped a pot of boiling water at her feet. A camper who had snuck into the barn stepped on a rusty nail and had to be given a tetanus shot. T.J. and Nurse Laird were kept busy tending to cuts, scrapes, splinters, and insect bites.

The weather turned steadily hotter during the daytime. But even during the cool evenings the atmosphere remained tense. It was as if an evil spirit had been unleashed by the Snipe Hunt.

The encounter with Oz at the farmhouse left me angry and confused and questioning everything about my judgment of people. I thought about what he had done and wondered why I hadn't had the guts to punch him. We hadn't seen much of each other since, and the few times I did catch sight of him he was usually with Steady Bomber, who had completed his switch to Oz's cabin. This bothered me particularly, because aside from missing Steady's resourceful company, I learned that as a result of the switch it was now up to me to supervise a vigil to be kept by Bernie Kaufman. Redclaw had decreed that for each senior camper or C.I.T. to be chosen for his ritual, it fell to the junior counselor of the cabin he occupied to watch over him. Bernie, with his lack of interest in anything beside his banjo, impressed me as the least likely candidate for the ritual. I couldn't picture him being able to start a fire without a match, and sitting awake all night beside it with a mask on, trying to get in touch with his inner animal helper. I didn't know when this event would be coming, but I dreaded it.

On top of everything else, I had seen almost nothing of T.J. I would swim as often as I could, but she never showed up to join me again. After, I would drop by the mess hall to pick up the mail and read the paper, always hoping she would come out of the infirmary.

I would skim the news: the Yanks were still in first place; the Republicans nominated Eisenhower and Nixon as their ticket; the search went on for the missing boy from Linesville (his empty boat had been found pulled up on a remote shore of Lake Pymatuning, which made it seem less likely that he had drowned); there was no mention of Senator Joe McCarthy (I wondered how my mother was doing). But none of it seemed real; the only thing etched on my mind was T.J.

Once or twice she came out of the nurse's office to visit me. Each time she teased me about going with me into the Forbidden Woods to check out the "death tree," but then she would dance away without allowing me to talk with her, leaving me to wonder why I couldn't seem to make a move on her.

And one tiny but irritating detail still bothered me: my lighter continued to be missing.

I STILL WANTED like hell to get out of camp. The problem was, Peter was one of the few campers who hadn't been spooked by the Snipe Hunt. In fact, he was happily obsessed with working on his wooden pistol, enjoying a widening circle of friendships among kids his own age, and generally getting into what Woody liked to call "the spirit of Camp Seneca."

And then I hadn't had any response to my letter to Karla. Dead silence! But I was feeling increasingly threatened by the atmosphere of camp and I was convinced that Peter was just being seduced by things he didn't understand. So I was beginning to think about other ways of escape. For instance, maybe I could go somewhere away from camp and try telephoning my dad's secretary to get a number I could call in Europe. Or maybe I could act on Jeff's idea of asking Woody for some of my salary. He wouldn't know if I'd gotten a bill from Swarthmore, for books or something.

Even if I didn't take any of these steps, thinking about them made me feel a little less desperate.

The weirdness I felt was heightened by a fight between Chunky and a large snake that crawled out from under the kitchen help's shack after dinner one evening. The snake struck repeatedly, but Chunky kept darting out of the way and finally grabbed it in his teeth, violently whipping it back and forth to break its spine. It was a rattler.

"What's going on here?" I asked Woody, who had come out of his office.

"Don't worry about it."

"That's the second one this summer," I said. "There aren't supposed to be rattlers around here."

"They sometimes show up."

Jeff, who was standing nearby, muttered something I couldn't make out.

"What do you think?" I asked, stepping closer to him. "We saw a rattler when we did Garvey's Woods a couple of weeks ago."

"Something's not right."

"What do you mean?"

He opened his mouth but said nothing.

"Have you thought about what I asked you?"

He didn't acknowledge my question. "You talk to Woody yet about gettin' paid?"

"No, but I'm working on it."

"Then don't be pushin' me."

Chunky nuzzled the dead rattler. Woody pushed the dog away. He picked up the snake by the tail. "Jeff," he called. "Can you skin it? It'll make a good wall trophy."

"Yes, boss," Jeff said.

THE NEXT EVENING, while we were still eating our strawberry Jell-O and deciding whom to call on next to entertain us, Woody came out of his office. Another day had passed without my hearing from Karla, and Woody's ridiculous appearance that evening didn't improve my mood. He was wearing camouflage army fatigues, a soft-billed cap, black combat boots, and a colonel's insignia. He carried a wooden baton in his right hand, and as he strode to the entertainment area, he slapped the outside of his thigh with the stick.

I glanced at Win, who was still sitting at the head table, but I couldn't read her expression.

"Listen up, men," Woody barked. "Tomorrow, Friday, July eighteenth, the Sham Battle begins!"

Cheers filled the hall. I didn't join in.

"What's a cham battle?" Peter asked above the din.

"'Sham'—it's not 'cham'—means 'fake, pretend.' So, it's a fake battle."

"Can I shoot my fake gun in it?" he asked, aiming his wooden pistol at something across the room.

"Just listen."

"For those who are new here," Woody went on, "here's how it works. We'll divide the camp into two groups roughly equal in ages and sizes. One side will be called the Injuns. They'll be led by Buck Silverstone."

Redclaw was standing next to the main entrance with his arms crossed, wearing his beaded leather outfit.

"The other side'll be the Settlers. Their commander will be me. It'll be the Injuns against the Settlers."

Redclaw pounded one of his fists on top of the other, in a gesture I didn't quite understand.

"What will I be?" Peter piped up. He had tucked his pistol into his belt.

"I don't know," I said. "Maybe you can be my aide-de-camp."

"What does that mean?"

"It would mean you could stay with me and do nothing at all."

"No, I want to be in the battle, on one of the teams."

Woody explained that the Settlers would occupy the cabins and defend the campgrounds, while the Injuns would bivouac in the Big Woods, which would be their territory to defend. "The mess hall, the Kybo, and the shower house will be demilitarized zones," Woody added, "so both sides can use them when necessary without worrying about being attacked. Also, each side's command headquarters will be off-limits to attacks. In my case that'll be my cabin. In Buck's case that'll be wherever he decides. I would guess the tree house. Right, Buck?"

"Most likely," Buck said.

"And as usual," Woody added, "the Forbidden Woods will be strictly off-limits."

Off-limits. Did Redclaw get him to say that?

"I hope I'm a Settler," Peter said. "I'd rather sleep in my bed."

"I'll try to make it so you can."

The battle would last two days and three nights, beginning Friday after supper and ending Monday at noon. The objective would be to "kill" your enemy. The way you did that was to remove the armband he would be wearing. Whichever team had the most armbands come Monday noon would win. The grand prize would be a sit-down banquet Monday evening, with the losing team waiting on the winning one.

"That's about it," Woody said. "Everybody will participate, except the nurses and kitchen staff"—he looked around as if to make sure he hadn't forgotten anyone—"and Jeff Small, of course"—his eyes fell on me—"and Jerry Muller, who's sidelined."

Maybe I'll be more than that, I thought hopefully.

"The Injun side will wear red armbands," Woody added. "Settlers will have white ones. The way to kill your opponent is either to slide his band off his arm"—he mimed the gesture on himself—"or tear it away." He gave an imaginary yank. "Don't worry. It'll be held together with adhesive tape, so it'll come off easily when it's pulled." He looked around. "Each team's captured armbands will be kept under guard at its commander's headquarters, or a place of the commander's choice. Now, are there any questions?"

"How can a little person defend himself?" Peter asked.

Woody put up his hand for quiet. "That's a good question. You'll all have a lot of questions that your counselors will answer over the next couple of days. But one thing I want to make clear right now. We're gonna divide up each side into different classes of fighters so that nobody can be attacked by anyone bigger than he is. Understand that, Peter?"

"No."

"Okay, think of it this way: you and your buddies will able to gang up on bigger kids. But bigger kids won't be able to attack or gang up on little kids like you. Just trust me. Okay?"

"I guess."

"Very good, then," Woody said, laughing. "Any other questions?"

"I got one," Mac said in a stagy voice from his seat at the table next to ours.

"What's that?"

"If I'm dead, is there any way I can come back to life?"

"A very good question. The answer is yes. You can come to life if you get an armband back. And the way to do that is, of course, for one team to steal the other's supply of captured ones, wherever they're kept. That might not be so easy because each team's gonna guard its supply with its best men. But it's an option. Got it, Mac?"

"Got it, chief."

"Good. That'll be it for now. Let's get on with the evening's program."

I snuck a last look toward Win. She was no longer there.

Dinner broke up amid a buzz of speculation over who would be on which team. Arguments began about whether the woods or the camp would be better to defend.

I set off for cabin one, thinking about getting to a phone away from camp. Redclaw stepped into my path. He put a large hand on my right shoulder and fixed me with his black eyes. "Tomorrow night," he said.

"What?" *He can't know about my looking at his file.*

"Tomorrow night is Kaufman's vigil. You'll be his escort."

"But it's the start of the Sham Battle."

He flicked the armrest of my crutch with his fingers. "You're still using this. You're not part of the battle."

"But what about Bernie? He'll be out of action a whole day. Can't we do it after the Sham Battle?"

A spark of irritation flickered in Redclaw's eyes. "His vigil means more."

"What about Peter?"

"What about him?"

"I'd like to be here for him."

"Don't worry. Peter's just fine."

Redclaw touched my arm. "Let's talk for a minute. Come with me." Campers were running everywhere, and their shouts echoed over the meadow. Redclaw quickly walked to the flagpole and turned around, waiting for me to come to him. It made me feel like a supplicant. I was shaking with nervousness. Chunky stood at the side of mess hall, barking at Redclaw but keeping his distance.

Does he smell the other dog on him? I wondered.

I approached Redclaw. "The dog doesn't seem to like you."

"You have to take this seriously, Muller," he said.

"I find that hard to do."

"Let me tell you: in the old days the adolescent braves went out into the woods for days under the supervision of an experienced warrior. They fasted, went without sex, covered themselves with dirt, and even punished themselves by bathing in ice water and gashing their shins with rocks. They had dreams that revealed things." He paused, waiting for me to react.

I worked to keep my expression neutral.

"What I'm asking is a small thing by comparison. But the ritual must be followed strictly, especially the mask and tobacco."

"Tobacco? What for?"

"To sprinkle on his fire, as I did at the campfire. It will help his visions."

"How?"

"He will see things in the smoke."

"Okay."

"He must follow Stemmer's example."

I held his gaze. *Even if you lied to us about when he did it,* I thought.

"Your turn is coming too, you know."

"No. No, thanks."

"Oh yes. You'll see. Your going with Kaufman is a preparation."

"I'm sure the vigil is not compulsory for counselors."

"No. But you'll do it anyway."

"Why?"

"Because you need to. Because you have bad dreams."

"Bad dreams? But I don't."

"You will."

I closed my eyes, trying to break the mood he was creating. "I thought these vigils weren't, y'know, part of the new religion."

He opened his mouth slightly in what looked like surprise. "What new religion?"

"You know, what you're part of."

His eyes narrowed. "Who told you that?"

"Woody did. He said you follow the Way of Handsome Lake. I forget the Indian word."

"What do you know about it?"

"Nothing. But I've heard somewhere that the masks and stuff aren't supposed to be part of it anymore."

He appraised me. "What you say isn't true. In the New Way we partake of the flesh and blood of Christ."

"Really?"

"Sure. Many of my people attend mass. They partake of innocence."

"What's that got to do with vigils and masks?"

"In the Old Way we devoured the flesh and blood of our enemies. We partook of courage and strength. Of youth, eternal youth. The difference is not so great."

"But . . . but I thought Handsome Lake . . . and Christ . . . taught, y'know, forgiveness."

"Perhaps. Tell me something. At home: you live with Peter and his parents?

"No. Why?"

"Ah. Why is that?"

"I'm away at boarding school. In Vermont."

"Yes. But when you're home for vacation?"

"I stay with my mother."

"You were never with your father?"

"I was. For a while."

"I thought so. And you had to move out."

"Yeah."

"Because of Peter."

"Well, sort of. He needed his own room."

"So you moved in with your mother."

"Yes."

"And you didn't like that, did you?"

"No, actually I didn't."

"You don't get along with her."

My face began to burn. "Not really."

"Why did your father support the move?"

"It was his decision."

"Really! Why was that?"

"I don't know." I felt a flash of irritation. "Why does it matter?"

His hand was on my shoulder and his head was cocked to one side. "You speak of the Indian ways as if you know something. Well, maybe soon you will. Together, you and I will explore what's in your heart. We'll see if it's forgiveness. This is something you don't yet know. But I promise you before it's done, you will."

"Forgiveness! For what?" I thought of the time in his cabin when he exercised my knee. *Could that have been when I lost my lighter?* I wondered.

"We'll see what you have to forgive. Meanwhile, take your mission with Kaufman very seriously."

I let out my breath. "Well, I'll try."

"You know where it will be?"

"In Lake Pymatuning? On the island?"

"You know the place?"

"Sure. Not from any vigil, but we've had campfires there."

"It's a good place. I've scouted it."

"Can I ask you something?"

"Of course."

"That time I was in your cabin . . . did I leave my cigarette lighter there?"

"Maybe you left it. I'll look."

"It would have been on your bunk, I think. It's a Ronson. It's got an inscription on it."

"I'll look."

I started toward my cabin, feeling drained. Children rushed by me, still caught up in the excitement of the evening, but my face felt numb and I had trouble hearing them. I went into my cabin, overcome with an urge to lie down. I stretched out on my bunk and tried to fall asleep.

Why do I feel so lousy? I wondered.

It wasn't really so bad to be going on Bernie's vigil. It meant camping out in a beautiful, wild place. It meant sleeping alone under the stars, or at least sleeping alone between periodic checkups on how Bernie was doing.

The only thing I regretted was leaving Peter, but that might not be so bad considering how excited he seemed about the Sham Battle. But Redclaw had upset me, and it went beyond the menace he conveyed. *Why was he reminding me that it was my father who decided I had to move out? How did he know?*

When Peter ran into the cabin with his friends, I called him over. "How're you doing?"

"Teddy says we're gonna be Settlers."

"How's he know that?"

"His dad told him."

"That's what you wanted, right?"

"I love the Cham Battle."

"Sham. Look, I'll be away tomorrow night."

His gaze shifted from mine. "How come?"

"I have to supervise Bernie's vigil at Lake Pymatuning."

"Neat. Will I do that?"

"No. Is it okay with you?"

"You being away? I'm going on a raid."

"That's great." *But is it?* I wondered.

"I'm gonna go play now," Peter said.

"Okay."

I drifted off to sleep. When I awoke it was dark. The overhead light was on in the cabin, and campers were coming and going. Bernie was sitting on the bunk next to me, practicing his banjo. I got up, called everyone inside, and got them to settle down.

"Isn't it our turn to sleep in the tree house tonight?" little Teddy asked from his bed, after I turned out the light.

"Teddy's right," I announced. "But the tree house will be Injun territory in the Sham Battle, so nobody sleeps there tonight. Buck is probably preparing it either to be his headquarters or a place to keep prisoners."

"I ain't going to be no prisoner," somebody said.

"Me neither."

"Tell us a story," another camper asked.

"It's late," I said. I didn't feel up to telling stories.

"Sing us a song!"

"Bernie?" I asked.

"What'll it be?"

"How about 'The Fox Went Out'?" I said.

He started singing, his voice husky and nasal, yet somehow pleasing. The children quieted down. When he stopped after half a dozen verses, the cabin was quiet. Our campers were asleep.

I felt wide awake, though, and decided to go up to the mess hall.

I WAS SITTING in the kitchen, flipping through the book that Jeff had lent me when Woody came out of his office. "As officers in the forthcoming battle, you owe yourselves an evening of R and R," he said to Mac and Bordy. "All of you," he added, waving at the rest of us sitting around: the two dishwashers, Chris and Wimpy; and the women, T.J., Eve, and Sukie. "I've gotta go into town on some business, but I'm officially declaring the mess hall a nightclub for the evening. There're several six-packs of beer in the ice chest, and a record player and some records in my office for anyone who wants to dance. Relax, have fun. Closing time is midnight." He strode away. A minute later we heard a car start up and drive off.

For a moment we just stared at each other. This was definitely unusual behavior for Woody. But sure enough, we found three six-packs of Iron City beer in the ice chest, and there was a record player in his office, along with a stack of records.

Mac took the record player to the dining room and plugged it in. Walking without my crutch—Redclaw had gotten to me—I followed him out with a bunch of records. While he and T.J. pushed some tables aside to make a small dancing area, I went back into the kitchen and found some candles. I lit four of them and placed them on tables around the edge of the dancing area. When we turned off the overhead lights, we had a softly lit dance floor.

I put on "Mona Lisa" and Mac danced with T.J., wrapping both his arms around her. She didn't look at me. Nurse Laird came out of her office and Bordy asked her to dance. Chris and Wimpy danced with Eve and Sukie. When "Mona Lisa" ended, everyone said to play it again, so I did.

Win appeared from the canteen, wearing jodhpurs, a white blouse, and a black blazer. She took a seat at the edge of the dance floor and lit a cigarette. When her eye caught mine, she smiled. I wondered why she hadn't gone into town with Woody.

I played "Mona Lisa" a third time. The couples were dancing closer and slower, even Bordy and Nurse Laird. I stood and limped over to where Win was sitting.

"Would you like to dance?"

"Why, sure," she said. She stubbed out her cigarette and moved into my arms. "Is it all right, with your leg?"

"I think so."

She smelled of perfume and whiskey.

I kept her at a distance. My leg felt fine, but she was moving unsteadily, and holding my hand too tightly.

"Is everything okay?"

Her eyes were black. She had on dark lipstick. "What do you mean?"

"I mean, you look as if you were ready to go out for the evening."

"As if, as if." She took her hand away from mine and pressed it against her mouth for a moment. "You speak so correctly, Jerry. Why do you speak so correctly?"

"I don't know. I . . ."

"Never mind. I mustn't make you self-conscious." She moved ever so slightly closer to me. I stooped a little, to keep the lower part of my body at a distance.

"Mona Lisa" ended. Wimpy, the dishwasher, started it over again.

"What are you planning to do with your life?" she asked.

It took me a moment to realize she was addressing me instead of singing. I replayed what she had said. "I don't know. The next step is college."

"What are you going to major in?"

"English, I guess."

"Of course. And then you'll become a writer."

"I suppose. It's not so easy."

"No, it isn't," she said. "You suppose. But you'll try."

"I will."

"Mmmmhh." She pressed her hand against my back so that it was awkward to pull away. The scent of her hair was sweet, but the strongest smell was still the liquor.

"Where did Woody go?" I asked.

She didn't respond. Her stomach was moving against my groin. When I tried to pull back she moved closer.

"Win?"

"I heard you."

"Where, then?"

"Let's go to the Causeway for a drink."

It took me a few seconds to understand what she had said. My face felt hot. The Causeway was a couple of miles away. It was a dive. "I . . . No, we better not."

"Why not?"

"I have to check the bed wetters."

"Are you afraid of Woody?"

"Well, yes. I mean . . . Where is he?"

"S'okay. I do what I like." She put her head against my shoulder. I could feel her breasts against my chest, her stomach harder against my groin. I lowered my face into her hair. My cock stirred. Everything felt unreal.

What the hell, I figured. "I went into the files last night," I said.

Her hand tightened in mine. "Bad boy."

"I looked at Redclaw's file. Buck's."

She stopped moving. "Let's go outside." She walked unsteadily toward the back entrance, pushed open the screen door, held it for me, then went down the steps and sat on the lowest one.

I lowered myself next to her.

She lit a cigarette and offered me one. As I took it and lit it off hers she pulled the collar of her jacket up and shivered slightly in the cool night air.

The sky was dark. I couldn't think of anything to say.

She said, "I was an English major, you know."

"No, I didn't."

"You can see what I did with it." She reached into the pocket of her jacket, removed a small silver flask, took a long pull on it, and offered it to me.

I shook my head. "No, thanks." I looked in the distance to see if Woody's car was coming back.

"Go 'head. It's cool out here."

I took the flask from her and sipped. My throat blossomed with fire.

"This summer is a little different," she said.

"I'll say." I let my breath out.

Inside, the music finally switched to another song.

"What's Woody trying to do?"

"You have to understand, he lives in his . . . He's a dreamer. This camp is a little world he can make perfect."

"Seems to me he's trying to make trouble."

"He's, y'know . . . utopian."

"Utopian? Then why does he like uniforms? Why does he act as if he were a general?"

She sighed. "Utopians do that."

"Really?"

"Sure. They get carried away. Look at . . . Lenin . . . Stalin. It's what—what's his name?—Senator . . . Joe McCarthy is trying to fight."

I thought about my mother in Washington, gathering her signatures.

"You're comparing Woody to Stalin?"

"No. No," she said with a sigh. "I'm talking about something that's in all of us. Telling other people what's good for them. Bullying weaker people. Threatening them."

"I should go. The bed wetters."

She put her hand on my knee. "What did you find out about him?"

"Who?"

"In the files. About Buck."

"Oh. I looked at his résumé. Jeff caught me."

"Did he tell Woody?"

"No."

"Good." She kept her hand on my knee. "So?"

"Did you ever read his résumé?"

"I didn't."

"Could you?"

"Sure, I could have."

"I mean, could you now?"

"Yes. Of course."

"Would you?"

"Why?"

"There're things in it that don't make sense."

"What?"

"Gaps. Funny changes in jobs. Other things. You'll see when you read it."

"*If* I do."

"Win, you've got to."

"Why?"

"Everything's . . ." I took a breath. "Everything's wrong this summer. Even you."

"What do you mean, even me?"

"You seem troubled."

"Yes."

"I didn't have a chance to see if Buck put down any references . . . someone we could call about him. I can't go back in there."

"So you want me to look."

"Yes, to see if there's someone we can call. Find out more about him. There are photos."

"Photographs? Of what?"

"You'll see."

"Maybe."

"Why did the police chief come that time?"

"When?"

"July Fourth. During the Snipe Hunt."

"I don't know. He's a friend."

I heard footsteps in back of me. A voice said, "There you are!"

I looked back and saw Len. I stood up. Win stayed seated.

"It's time for the bed wetters," Len said.

"I was just going."

Win stayed seated. I wondered what Len was thinking.

I went inside to get my crutch.

THAT NIGHT I had a terrible dream. It was about Peter, only it wasn't exactly Peter I saw in the dream. It was a mechanical monster with staring, empty eyes that looked like Peter and kept coming at me with an axe. And I couldn't stop him. The axe kept going through me. I looked for blood but couldn't find any.

The dream seemed so real that when I woke up I looked at Peter to be sure he wasn't the monster. Climbing out of bed, he waved to me sleepily and began to dress. He was the same person, but I couldn't shake the awful feeling that he had tried to kill me. I wondered how Redclaw had known it would happen.

THAT EVENING, I went to the cabin to get Bernie Kaufman ready for his vigil. I felt resigned to not hearing from Karla and had decided to make the most of the night away from camp. I was even beginning to look forward to it. Being out on the lake alone would be both challenging and fun. I packed a small duffel bag and supervised Bernie as he gathered the few items he would need: a blanket, a change of underwear, his toothbrush. He insisted on bringing along his banjo. When I asked whether it fit with the spirit of the vigil, he said, "Indians dug music." We headed up to the mess hall to draw camping equipment and supplies for breakfast and load them on the pickup truck. Bernie kept muttering: "Why am I doing this? Do I really need to get in touch with my animal helper? If Stemmer's was a bear, mine's probably a gerbil."

"Come on; this is an adventure," I said. "Let's try to get whatever we can out of it."

Instead of the pickup I found the Wentworths' Chrysler Town & Country waiting for us in back of the kitchen. Win was seated at the wheel. This was not unheard of, Win driving people on a camping trip, but it was unusual.

"Woody wanted me to drive you," she explained when I greeted her through the open passenger window. She was freshly made up, as if she had plans for the evening.

"Great," I said, feeling a little uneasy.

Bernie and I loaded everything in the trunk and got in. I sat in front, Bernie in back.

"You got your mask?"

"In my duffel."

"Tobacco?"

"Yup."

"What about starting your fire?"

"No sweat."

"How you gonna do it?"

"Flint and tinder, of course."

"Of course."

When I got into the car Win handed me a letter from Karla. Excitedly, I tore it open, removed an envelope addressed to Peter, and read the opening of the letter to me.

Lieber Jerry,

How does it go with you and Peter? We are now by Frankfurt-am-Main. I am so longing to hear from you. Why are you not writing?

I checked the postmark on the envelope—Frankfurt, July 11—and saw that it had been sent by airmail. It was now—what, July 18?—which meant she should have had my letter mailed July 5, unless

Irma what's-her-name hadn't forwarded it by airmail or it just hadn't caught up with them on their travels.

Damn!

I stuck Peter's letter in the little compartment next to the car radio and asked Win to give it to him as soon as she got a chance.

Damn! Damn! Damn!

We drove in silence, except for Bernie softly picking his banjo, singing the phrase "She gets lonesome too," and trying to smooth out a complex series of notes that harmonized with his voice.

He seemed oblivious to Win's presence.

We turned off the hard-top and drove along a narrow dirt road through dense woods until we came to the edge of Lake Pymatuning, where the camp had an old wooden wharf. Three canoes lay on it, linked by a padlocked chain. I got out, found the key hidden in one of the canoes, and unlocked them. The sun, just above the horizon, was making dark shadows of the lake's many islands. Although the air was still warm, I shivered.

Bernie was standing by the car with his banjo.

"It's up to you to get the canoe in the water and load the gear into it," I told him. "That's part of the deal."

"Oy." He laid his banjo on the ground and went down to the canoes.

I leaned on my crutch and looked at Win. "Thanks for the lift."

She gestured with her head. "Get back in for a second."

I climbed back into the front seat, leaving the door open.

Win kept her hands on the steering wheel and looked straight ahead. "Would you like to go to the Causeway for a beer tonight?"

I knew that the counselors camping out overnight on Pymatuning sometimes paddled back to the dock and got picked up. I thought about leaving Bernie alone. "I don't think so. But thanks."

"Why not?"

Bernie was carrying gear down to the wharf. "I think Bernie's a little nervous."

"Isn't part of the challenge that he thinks he's alone?"

"Still." I touched my leg. "And I don't want to risk straining my leg in the dark."

"I have to talk to you."

Bernie had one of the canoes half in the water and was loading gear into it. "What about?"

"What you mentioned last night?"

"Yes?"

"I took a look at that file today."

"Really? What do you think?"

"That's what I wanted to talk about tonight."

I thought about making the trip back from the island alone in the dark. Redclaw would really love that. "I don't think I can."

"You wouldn't have to walk at all. I could meet you right here."

"I know. But Buck would kill me if he found out. And he easily could." *Woody too.* "I'm sure he'll be checking up somehow."

"Suit yourself."

"Were there any references?"

"No."

"You're kidding! Isn't that unusual?"

"Not really. That's one of the things we have to talk about."

"All set," Bernie called out. He was squatting on the dock, holding the loaded canoe by its painter.

"Be right there." I climbed out of the car and looked at Win through the open window. "Did you read over his job history?"

"Yes. And I see what you mean."

"And the photos?"

"I'll tell you about them too. That's what I wanted to talk about tonight."

"How about tomorrow night?"

"Maybe," she said. "We'll see."

Bernie was waiting on the dock.

"With Woody I never know when I can get away. But there's no real urgency."

"Are you sure of that?"

"We'll get another chance. There was something you missed."

"What was that?" I could hear Bernie moving behind me, coming back to the car.

"I'll tell you when we talk."

I swallowed. "Okay. Tomorrow night."

"Maybe. Take care tonight." She drove away.

I went down to the wharf with Bernie. We got in the loaded canoe and shoved off. Paddling stern I pointed the canoe toward the nearest of several islands.

What did I miss in Redclaw's résumé? I wondered.

I looked back. The car was gone, of course.

"I need this like a *Loch in Kopf,*" he said, digging his paddle into the water.

"What?"

"Like a hole in the head. It's Yiddish."

We glided toward the setting sun, barely able to see our destination in the glare. Bernie's paddling was choppy and he kept trying to adjust our direction, not understanding that only the stern paddler has the leverage to steer the canoe. Nonetheless, we made good time. The air was still, the horizon a splash of orange, the water a sheet of gold foil charred at the edges by the shadows of the shore.

"Stop a second," I said.

I let us coast, hearing the water against the canoe's hull, the slap of a beaver's tail somewhere ahead, the grunt of frogs. Suddenly, I felt free and on my own. Then I saw the darkness of the island ahead of us and felt a sliver of fear.

It's going to get dark fast and I'll be alone.

We dug our paddles in again and surged through the water, passing the first of the islands. I caught myself wondering what might be hiding in its undergrowth.

My nervousness mounted. I wanted to get my campsite set up.

When we came abreast of the island I would be camping on, the light was beginning to fade. I aimed the canoe at a tiny cove. Ten feet from the shore I told Bernie to jump out and beach us. He nearly tipped us over, but he managed to right the canoe and to drag the bow up onto a narrow dirt beach. I got out stiffly with my crutch, and unloaded the gear.

Because I had camped here in previous summers, I knew the general drill. I had never done it alone before, though, so while I was proud to be trusted on my own, I was nervous about messing up. A little way in from the beach I found the campsite in a small clearing and laid out the gear next to the ashes of a long-dead fire. I told Bernie to gather up some kindling and driftwood. While he stomped around in the island's shrubbery, I put up a one-man pup tent and unrolled a sleeping bag inside. Next to the mouth of the tent I arranged a Coleman lamp, the books I had brought along, and my toilet gear. With my gimpy leg it was hard work, but I enjoyed setting up this little home.

When Bernie had gathered enough wood, I piled up a small amount of it to light in the morning, put the carton of breakfast fixings next to it, and covered it with a poncho pinned down by stones to protect it from small animals. Bernie was sitting on a stump tuning his banjo. Dusk was closing in.

"We better get you set up. There's not much light left."

"I don't know about doing this," he muttered. He began to play little riffs.

"Come on," I said.

He stopped playing. "Why can't we just fake it?"

"Because I'm sure they'll be checking up on us."

"I got enough character without sitting under a blanket all night."

I headed for the canoe.

We shoved off. Bernie still had his banjo. I decided to let him keep it even though Redclaw would probably disapprove.

In the gathering darkness, I paddled us away from the cove. Just to the southeast was a smaller island. The fading light silhouetted it against the horizon. The water next to it was deep enough to let me paddle right to the shore. With a thrust on the port side I was able to pin the canoe against the shore while Bernie climbed out. He removed his banjo and blanket.

"You gotta strip."

"Come on!"

"That's the rule."

"You can bend it."

"No, Bernie. I'm absolutely sure someone will be checking on us."

He sighed, and began to peel off his clothes.

"Throw your stuff in the canoe," I said. "I'll bring it when I pick you up in the morning."

"Or later tonight if I can't make it."

"The vigil site is up on that rise," I told him, pointing ahead with my paddle.

"I know."

"You got your flint and tinder? And tobacco?"

He lifted a small pouch and his mask, and held them up.

"Right. Good." The mask had an expression of exaggerated sorrow. "You understand why you've got a mask?"

"I guess."

"Tell me why," I said, trying to sound casual.

"I can't. We're not supposed to talk about it."

"Okay."

His pale body disappeared into his blanket. He turned and moved along the shore to a small promontory twenty feet away from the canoe. With his fire lit, he would be visible from a hundred yards away, which meant I could check on him easily.

I back-paddled away from the shore until I could get a clear view of the little headland. The air remained still, and the water was so calm I could hear the plops of feeding fish.

I let the canoe drift and stared into the shadows of the island. I could just make out Bernie moving around, gathering fuel for his fire, I assumed. When he seemed to have settled down, I waited for the sound of stone banging flint and possibly even the sight of a few sparks. But I saw and heard nothing.

I waited a little longer, letting the canoe drift as the darkness deepened.

After another minute or two, I heard Bernie say, "Shit!"

I started back toward his island, listening for a call for help. Instead I heard a faint metallic click and saw a flame flare up larger than a match would make. The flame held steady until other flames began to lick around it. Bernie had his fire going. The small flame came away again and with another metallic click it disappeared.

I didn't have to think long to identify the sounds: a cigarette lighter. Probably he had hidden it in the pouch with his flint and tinder.

My lighter? I wondered. *Probably not.*

I watched Bernie in the firelight as he wrapped himself in his blanket. He picked up his banjo and unloosed a cascade of notes with that unusual picking style of his. The rhythm was so catchy that I found myself tapping the canoe's gunwale with my hand, as I drifted. Then, realizing I had to catch some sleep so that checking on Bernie during the night wouldn't leave me tired tomorrow, I swung the canoe around and headed back to my camp. As I moved away, the slapping of water against the hull made the banjo sound fade quickly. I suddenly felt alone in the dark.

I didn't feel tired at all, but as soon as I'd secured the canoe I stripped down to my undershorts and T-shirt, unzipped the sleeping bag, and stretched out on top of it. My knee ached from all the walking and bending I had done, so I rolled over on my back, groped for the liniment in my toilet kit, and gave my leg a rubdown. When the heat began to penetrate, I lit a cigarette with one of the few wooden matches in my jeans pocket. By the light of the Coleman lantern I read the rest of Karla's letter.

Why are you not writing? Can it possibly be that you are angry at me?

There is something I have to talk with you, concerning that fight you had with your father. Now that we have had some peace and quiet together and talked things over, I know that he still thinks about it, even if it happened more than two years ago. And it still works its influence on him and the question of your coming back to live with us.

Jerry, I know that he should not have attacked you when we were just "fooling around" (is that how the expression goes?) on the couch that time. He saw it as something different than what it was—innocent "horse's play." You must understand that your father is very very jealous. He was even so angry at me afterwords that he had to fight himself to keep from striking me. He completely misunderstood.

Still, you should not have knocked him down like that when he tried to pull you away. It was completely humiliating for him, and I don't think so good for you too.

So you have to think a lot about your feelings for him and

make them better before you come back to us. You must see that our "plan" depends on more than you and Peter. I cannot have you fighting with your father like this.

There I have said it, and now we never have to discuss it some more. I hope so much that letters are on their way to me from you and Peter, telling me what a good time you are having.

We also are doing very well. Give my letter to little Peter with my kisses and hugs. And for you too. I have such strong memories of you. When you came to take Peter to the camp you looked so delicious I could have eaten you.

Your Karla

I put the letter back in my duffel. What exactly was it that had happened on the couch that time? We had been playing gin rummy and I had picked up a jack she had discarded. She had tried to grab my hand to see my cards and suddenly we were wrestling, with her on top of me. And then my father had rushed at us and begun hitting me, as if I had started it. *What was I supposed to do? I lost my temper completely. I didn't really mean to knock him down. But he tried to beat me up for playing cards with Karla. How am I supposed to react?* Trembling with anger at the memory, I lit another cigarette and decided to try to distract myself by browsing through Jeff's book.

It was a collection of the letters and journals—or "relations," as they were called—of a bunch of French Jesuits who landed in Canada in 1611 and formed a "forest-roaming church" with the aim of knowing the Indian and converting him to their faith. The relation to which Jeff had directed me was written in 1637 by a priest named Le Mercier, and it concerned one Joseph, an Iroquois prisoner of war. Joseph had been given to a Huron chief at the village of Onnentisati, in a district on the high ground near Georgian Bay, in Lake Huron, to compensate him for one of his nephews, who had been captured by the Iroquois, "for it is customary, when some notable personage has lost one of his relatives in war, to give him a present of some captain taken from the enemy, to dry his tears and partly assuage his grief."

Le Mercier's letter described the horrible tortures inflicted on Joseph, during which he had to keep singing and dancing while his torturers enjoyed a feast. They kept complimenting him on how well he was taking it all. Meanwhile Le Mercier and his fellow priests kept telling the poor man about Christ, and promising him a better world when he died. This ordeal went on all night.

I skimmed much of the account, until I got to the end section. Though disturbing, the story was fascinating:

As soon as day began to dawn, they lighted fires outside the village, to display there the excess of their cruelty to the sight of the Sun. The victim was led thither. The Father Superior went to his side, to console him, and to confirm him in the willingness he had all the time shown to die a Christian. He recalled to his mind a shameful act he had been made to commit during his tortures,—in which, all things rightly considered, there was but little probability of sin, at least not a grave sin,—nevertheless, he had him ask God's pardon for it; and . . . left him with hope of soon going to Heaven. Meanwhile, two of them took hold of him and made him mount a scaffold 6 or 7 feet high; 3 or 4 of these barbarians followed him. They tied him to a tree which passed across it, but in such a way that he was free to turn around. There they began to burn him more cruelly than ever, leaving no part of his body to which the fire was not applied at intervals. When one of these butchers began to burn him and to crowd him closely, in trying to escape him, he fell into the hands of another who gave him no better a reception. From time to time they were supplied with new brands, which they thrust, all aflame, down his throat, even forcing them into his fundament. They burned his eyes; they applied red-hot hatchets to his shoulders; they hung some around his neck, which they turned now upon his back, now upon his breast, according to the position he took in order to avoid the weight of this burden. If he attempted to sit or crouch down, someone thrust a brand from under the scaffolding which soon caused him to arise. Meanwhile, we were there, praying God with all our hearts that He would please to deliver him as soon as possible from this life. . . .

. . . fearing that he would die otherwise than by the knife, one cut off a foot, another a hand, and almost at the same time a third severed the head from the shoulders, throwing it into the crowd, where someone caught it to carry it to Captain Ondessone, for whom it had been reserved, in order to make a feast therewith. As for the trunk, it remained at Arontaen, where a feast was made of it the same day. . . . We would, indeed, have desired to prevent this act of lawlessness; but it is not yet in our power, we are not yet masters here. . . . Superstitions and customs grown old, and authorized by the lapse of so many centuries, are not so easy to abolish.

I closed the book. The account was so sickening that it seemed almost unreal. It was sort of funny too, in a very perverse way, the idea of the missionaries trying to sell the idea of a better world to a poor guy for whom any world other than the one he was in would sound better.

I found it hard to imagine anyone alive today behaving this way. It was my inability to imagine evil, again. Anyway, a Huron, not a Seneca or even an Iroquois, had done this torturing. What did Jeff have in mind by lending me this book?

My eyes were heavy. The air felt gently warm on my skin, and the ground under the sleeping bag was not too hard to keep me from relaxing. Beyond the glow of the lantern, the night was a shroud. I closed the book and turned the lantern down until the flame went out. In the dark the air felt cooler. I opened the flap of the sleeping bag and crawled in.

But now I felt wide awake. My skin itched.

I tried to relax each part of my body, beginning with the tips of my toes. When I got to my ankles I thought I heard a noise. The sound of a twig snapping. *Was something out there?* I wondered.

Not wanting to lie in the tent and wait for whatever it was, I slipped out of the sleeping bag, groped for my sneakers, got a small flashlight out of my kit, and snapped it on. I slid out of the tent and stood up. I thought of putting on more clothes, but the effort didn't seem worth it.

I picked up my crutch and made my way through the bushes to

where the canoe was beached. It was still in place, groaning slightly as it was rocked by the water. I stood and listened and stared at the sky. I could no longer see the moon. A cloud cover had definitely moved in.

I heard a scraping sound coming from back at the campsite, as if an animal were dragging the container of breakfast fixings.

I turned off the flashlight and, wielding my crutch as a potential weapon, worked my way back to the tent, feeling suddenly vulnerable dressed only in my undershorts. I turned the flash back on. The tent and food box appeared to be undisturbed.

I limped to the opposite side of the campsite clearing and played the flashlight against the low shrubbery. I still saw nothing. I suddenly imagined a rattlesnake slithering along the ground toward my feet, but quickly realized that made no sense at all.

I could feel my heart beating. I listened closely, but heard no sound. I took a deep breath and let it out slowly, trying to calm myself, then went back to the tent and turned off the flashlight. I sat down in front of the tent, felt with my feet for the opening of the sleeping bag, and began to work my way in.

"Hi!" The voice came from inside the tent.

I exploded backward in shock, knocking over the front tent pole with my left knee and banging the back of my head against a root in the ground.

"Sorry," the voice said. "I didn't mean to scare you."

I groped for the flashlight and turned it on. T.J. was sitting with her legs folded beneath her, dressed in jeans and a gray sweatshirt. Her hair was gathered in a ponytail and she was smiling impishly.

"It's you!" I said dumbly. A dizzying wave of sexual desire swept over me.

"Yeah, it is."

Keeping the light on her, I slid the tent pole back into place. To cover my near nakedness and my sudden erection, I scrambled farther into the sleeping bag. This left me sitting just inside the mouth of the tent.

"You okay?" She breathed deeply so that her breasts lifted. I felt both incredibly excited and incredibly anxious.

"How the hell did you get out here?" I asked.

"I canoed."

"Alone?"

"Of course."

"How did you get to the lake?"

"Hitched."

"How did you get away from camp?"

"Everybody's doing the Sham Battle."

"What about Mac?"

"He wasn't around."

"Did you see Oz?"

"No. I think he's on the woods team." She unfolded her legs and stretched out. Her sweatshirt slid up and I glimpsed the waistband of her pink panties. "Turn that flash off," she said. "You're blinding me."

"I'm sorry." I clicked it off and put it aside. We sat in the dark, about two feet apart. I could feel the warmth coming from her body.

Why can't I just reach out for her? I thought, my emotions in a jumble.

"I don't get it," I said. "How'd you find this island? You've never been out here before."

"Ain't you glad I'm here?"

"Oh my God, T.J.! But how . . . ?"

"Win told me the general direction. Then I saw lights."

"What kind of lights?"

"Fire. On another island. And I guess your flashlight."

"I didn't know you could canoe."

"I'm a country girl."

"How'd you get them unlocked?"

"Them?"

"The canoes."

"There was only one. I found the key under a stone on the floor."

"Only one canoe? You sure?"

"Course. Why?"

"I thought there were two, not counting the one I took."

Who had taken the other canoe? I wondered.

"You're sure suspicious."

"Well, you scared me." *And your boyfriend scares me,* I wanted to say. "Where did you beach your canoe?"

"Next to yours."

"How come I didn't see it just now?"

She laughed. "I hadn't landed yet, stupid."

I felt confused. T.J.'s closeness didn't help. "What'd Win say when you asked her how to find me?"

"You think I'm dumb? She doesn't know why I was asking."

"You sure?"

"Anyway, why would she care?"

"Well, it's sort of against the rules."

"I'm sure she didn't get it."

"You're pretty sharp."

"Tell Woody that. Put in a word for me to be a counselor at girls' camp."

"I will." I reached out and grasped her forearm. "What's happening at camp?"

She moved closer to me. "I told you, nothing."

"I mean, what happened this evening? After we left?"

"Nothin' much. Kids hacking around. They're all fired up 'bout the Sham Battle. Hey, is there room for two in that bag?"

My heart felt as if it were working its way out of my chest. "It'll be a squeeze. But sure, come on."

"Good." I heard the sound of cloth brushing against skin, as she slipped out of her clothes. I saw her pale figure move next to me. I felt her cold feet sliding along my right hip.

"Come on, slide down," she said. Her breath warmed my ear.

I lay back, turned onto my stomach, and worked my way into the bag. She slid in beside me. Her skin was hot against mine. I could smell the sweetness of her hair. She lay on her stomach next to me. I held my left arm stiffly against my side, not knowing where to put it.

We lay in the dark, silent for a full minute, the only sound our deep breathing. I was trying to remain calm, but it was a struggle. My cock was throbbing.

"You ever had a girlfriend?" she asked.

"Sure."

"You ever get laid?"

I paused before answering. "No."

"Almost?"

I said nothing.

"You know why I like you?"

"Do you?"

"Yeah. You want to know why?" She began to massage my neck.

"Why?" I lifted my left arm. I felt the soft material of her panties, the cool flesh of her hip, the ripple of her rib cage. I shifted onto my side and let my left hand come to rest on her right shoulder blade. I felt the strap of her bra against my wrist. She moved an inch or two closer to me. I could feel her breath on my face.

"'Cause you don't come on to me," she said. Her bent right leg slid up along my thigh. I felt as if I were falling in the darkness.

"What do you mean?" I had to catch my breath to speak.

"You don't chase me and flirt 'n' stuff. You act like yourself." She was whispering now, purposely expelling hot little breaths into my ear. I quivered and clasped the back of her neck with my hand.

My voice gulped. "I thought girls liked to be chased."

Her breast pressed against my chest. "Sometimes they like to do the chasing themselves. 'Specially when the guy is so good looking." Her mouth enveloped my ear, and she plunged her tongue inside. It was soft and liquid. Involuntarily I pressed my cock against her.

Her tongue went away. "Oh, good," she said. "I want that." She moved away from me and tried to work her way deeper into the sleeping bag. "Not enough room," she whispered. "Unzip us."

I opened the bag a foot or so. T.J. scrambled out of it and moved around beside me. She put her hand on my left shoulder and pushed me onto my back. I felt her knee against my head and felt her fingers lift the waistband of my undershorts. She was trying to pull them down.

"Come on," she said. "Help me."

"Ruuuuuuaaaaarrrrrrrrrrhhhhhhggg," came an enormous roar from outside the tent, just behind my head. "Rrrrrrrrrrrrrrrrrrrrrrrrrrrrrrrrrrrr rooooooaaaaaaaaaaaaaaaaauuuuuuuuugggggh!"

Something hard hit the side of my head—T.J.'s knee, I realized amid a chaos of sounds and scufflings. When I regained a sense of where I was, I found myself still on my back with the canvas of the tent dragging across my face. T.J. was somewhere near my feet, wrestling frantically with what I slowly realized was the other end of the collapsed tent. She was yelling, "Help, help, help! Get me outta here!"

"Rooooooaaaaaaaaaaaaaaarrrrrrrrrrrgggghhhhhhh," came the sound again. Whatever was making the noise was coming from the other side of the clearing in front of the tent. I scrabbled for the flashlight, and found it under the tangled canvas.

T.J. was still yelling, "Get me out of here!"

"Roooaaaaaarrrrrrrgggghhh," came the sound again, but this time it ended with a series of panted barks: "Rhgh! Rhgh! Rhgh!"

I stood up, snapped on the light, and played the beam across the clearing.

A huge shadow loomed up from behind the clump of bushes. The light reflected a glinting pair of eyes above a row of white teeth. Just below them, shiny black talons waved back and forth.

I was looking at the upper part of a bear.

"Oh my God!" T.J. shouted.

I swung the flash around to where her voice came from. She was standing in her bra and panties, trying to cover herself with the end of the collapsed tent.

"Rooooaaaaarrrr," went the bear, but this time I began to detect something human in the sound. This realization came together with my slowly dawning memory that no wild bears existed in this part of Pennsylvania, and most especially not on a tiny island in the middle of a lake.

"Be quiet," I said in as controlled a voice as I could manage. "It's not a real bear." I played the flashlight beam on the ground until I found my crutch. I picked it up, and with a mounting feeling of outrage yelled, "Okay, you son of a bitch." I raised the crutch above my head and began to limp across the clearing. But when I raised the light beam again, all I could see was a commotion in the shrubbery. I could also hear the sound of low laughter.

Who in God's name is it? I wondered.

I decided to go after whoever it was, even though I couldn't move too quickly through the bushes. I skirted the place where I had seen him, and played the light on the shrubbery beyond, looking for a way to get through without scratching myself.

Finding an opening, I headed in the direction the laughter had come from. Just a little way up ahead, I could hear what sounded like the scrape of boat being skidded into the water. I tried to move faster, but the branches and the uneven footing made it impossible. By the time I stepped clear of the foliage and found myself at the water's edge, I could see no sign of anyone. All I could hear was the wind and the lapping of water at my feet. I aimed the flashlight out over the water, but the beam was too weak, and I could see nothing.

I stood there for a moment trying to figure out what had happened. Suddenly even the foliage around me and the breeze on my face felt threatening.

Was this all a joke? I wondered. *And was T.J. in on it?*

I turned around and found her standing behind me. She was dressed again.

"Did you see anything?" I asked her.

"Yeah. A bear."

"It was a fake. A joke."

"Some joke."

"It was the bearskin from Woody's office. With somebody inside." I studied her face. "Did you know this was going to happen?"

She looked truly stricken. "How can you say that?"

I moved past her into the bushes. "We better get back to the campsite."

"Who the heck did it?" she asked from behind me.

"I don't know. Must have been somebody who followed you." The campsite was orderly, except for the collapsed tent. I set about to put it up again.

T.J. stood over me. "You okay?"

"Sort of."

"They ruined a good moment, didn't they?"

She seemed to have her sassiness back. "They sure as hell did," I said.

"We'll try it again sometime. Maybe in those off-limits woods."

I felt a rush of pleasure. "Let's."

"But looky here. I told you; I took the only canoe that was there."

I put the front tent pole in place and lashed it down. It took me a moment to grasp that she was talking about the canoes at the dock. "So what?"

"So how could anyone have followed me?"

I suddenly felt a chill. "That's true. But they could have known where you were going and got there ahead of you."

"Who?"

"I don't know. Mac, if I had to guess." I put on my pants and shirt.

"Hah! He might could've, but if it was him and he saw us, he woulda done more than stand there and growl."

I put on my sneakers. "Maybe he didn't see us. It was dark. Maybe he just knew you were around somewhere."

"I think it was someone else. It was a joke on you. I think it was a coincidence I was here."

I found my crutch and stood up. "Who then?"

"I don't know. Anybody."

"Well, I'll worry about it later. Right now, I gotta go check on how Bernie's doing. Come on."

"He'll see me. I don't think that's such a hot idea."

"Yeah, you're right. Will you wait for me here?"

"I have to go back. I can't stay out all night. Nursey will have my ass."

I thought a moment. "Why don't you take off while I'm checking Bernie? That way my canoe will cover the sound of yours."

"Don't worry. I can be very quiet."

"Good." I started off toward my canoe.

"Hey, Jerry. Kiss me."

I went back to her. My mouth melted into hers until she pulled away. "I really like . . . ," I began.

"We'll do it again. Better. I promise."

"If Mac doesn't kill me first."

At the water's edge two canoes lay side by side. I slid mine into the water and began to paddle as quietly as I could. The night was completely dark. When I rounded the point of the island, the southeasterly breeze swung me toward Bernie and I found the paddling easy.

I could see no sign of his fire. The rising wind might be giving him trouble, I thought. I beached the canoe in the little cove, climbed out awkwardly, and set off for the vigil rise, using my crutch. All I could hear was the wind, and all I could see were dim shadows.

When I got to the top of the rise, I saw the scattered coals of Bernie's dying fire. By their dim light I could see the dark silhouette of his form stretched out on the ground. I stood still, leaning on my crutch, straining to hear some sound from him above the beating of the pulse in my ears.

His banjo was lying on the ground a few feet away from him. Next to it lay a cigarette lighter. His mask lay facedown in the ashes at the edge of his campfire.

He looked dead.

I stopped again, a few feet away from him. A wave of panic swept over me.

I should never have been fooling around with T.J.! I thought.

I should have been watching Bernie from the canoe.

Then Bernie let out a deep sigh, turned over, and pulled the blanket tighter around his shoulders.

Thank God! I breathed a deep sigh of relief.

I knew I should wake him—after all, this was supposed to be a vigil—but decided to let him sleep. I would come for him in the morning and let him pretend that he had successfully completed the night's assignment.

What the hell! I decided. *Who really cares?*

Not me.

6

THE SHAM BATTLE

THE SUN SHINING THROUGH the open end of the tent woke me early the next morning. I was instantly filled with rage at whoever had played the bear trick on me. But I knew I had to think before I acted.

All the while trying to figure out who had been wearing that bearskin, I got dressed, folded my tent, and paddled over to fetch Bernie, who was waiting by the inlet, yawning incessantly and rubbing his eyes. We cooked and ate breakfast without saying much, cleaned up the camp, and canoed back to the mainland. I guess we both had a lot on our minds.

I was surprised to find Mr. Lister, rather than Win, waiting for us with the pickup. I wondered if she was annoyed at me for not going to the Causeway with her last night, and if maybe she would turn against me now.

Mr. Lister leaned against the passenger door and watched as we unloaded the canoe and put the gear on the back of the truck. He was wearing a white armband, which meant he was a Settler. The patch was gone from his eye, though it still look a little bruised. "I understand you had some trouble," he said when we had all climbed into the cab and were heading for home.

"Where did you hear that?" I shot back.

"I don't know. Around." He seemed surprised that I was challenging him.

"You must have heard something from someone," I said hotly. "Just
what sort of trouble are you talking about?"

"I don't know," he muttered. "Maybe I'm wrong."

I had never seen him back down before. "There was no trouble.
Right, Bernie?"

Bernie's eyes got slightly larger. "Right."

THE TRUCK TURNED into the road leading to the camp entrance.

"Did you happen to pick up the mail on the way?" I asked Lister.

"Win's getting it later. I've been too busy with the Sham Battle."

"How's it going?"

He kept his eyes on the road. "Everything's going according to
plan. The Injuns are ahead by about five armbands."

"Really?"

"As of last night's count. Course there was a big raid during the
night. Mac led it."

"What time was that?"

"Very late. Small hours of the morning."

I did some quick calculations: *that meant Mac could have been on
the island and easily got back in time for the raid.*

"Your brother was on it too."

"No kidding?"

"He even helped make a capture, I think. He's getting to be a
tough little guy."

"I'm glad he's on the Settler team. I don't think he likes roughing it
in the woods."

"Maybe so." Mr. Lister turned the truck into the camp entrance.
"But he was out in the woods all evening."

"He was? Really?"

"Yes, I'm pretty sure." He pointed at the top of the dashboard,
where a white armband was lying. "You're a Settler, Kaufman. Better
put it on. You're neutral, Muller."

"I know."

I kept thinking how pleased my father would be about Peter, but I worried as well that now I might not be able to get him to leave.

When the truck pulled up behind the mess hall, Bernie and I got out and began to unload. The camp felt empty. In the dining room, the members of the Settlers team—all wearing white armbands—were still eating breakfast. They were unusually quiet. Through the opening at the counter, I spotted Peter eating next to Teddy. He looked tanned and rugged, not at all the pale little thing he was when he first arrived at Seneca three weeks ago.

Mac and his brother were at another table, sitting with a group of older campers. Mac was dressed like a frontiersman, with boots and a broad belt across his chest that looked like a bandolier. His presence probably meant that Oz and Steady were Indians.

I was glad not to be part of any of it.

Bernie and I went back out to the truck, got our belongings, and headed down to the cabins. Bernie was walking even slower than I was with my crutch.

"You okay?"

"I'm tired. What the heck was Mr. Lister talking about?"

"I guess you didn't hear much of what went on last night, did you?"

"Are you going to tell?"

"About what?" I knew what he meant, but I wanted him to say it.

"Everything. Me sleeping on my vigil."

I thought about facing Woody and Redclaw. It was one thing to talk back to Mr. Lister. Lying to the people I worked for could lead to trouble I didn't need now.

"I won't say anything about your using the lighter. But I might have to tell them you dozed off."

"Aw, come on!"

"They might give you a break."

He shook his head despairingly. "Tell 'em everything. I really don't give a shit."

I threw my stuff on my bunk and headed back up to the mess hall, determined to talk to Woody about what had happened last night.

As I approached the front steps, Peter came running out, wearing his toy pistol in a shoulder holster sewed crudely out of cloth. He had on a red baseball cap.

"Hey there, mighty warrior," I said, reaching out with my left arm to catch him.

"I'm a mighty warrior, Jerry," he said, hugging me.

"So I hear. You went on a raid."

He broke free and unholstered his wooden pistol. "And Buck Silverstone let me shoot his gun." Grasping the toy in both hands, he stooped and aimed at an imaginary target in the distance. "It was neat! Pow! Pow!"

"You're kidding, Peter! You shot on the raid?"

"No, before. At the rifle range." He was quivering with excitement. "I even hit a target!"

"Hold on—he took a bunch of you?"

"No. Pow! Just me. And he told me about the Windigo. Pow!"

I kneeled and grasped his shoulders. "Slow down, Peter." I pulled the pistol from his hand and stuck it back in his holster. "When did this happen?"

"Right after supper. When it was still light . . . just me and Buck. He told me about the Windigo."

"The Windigo?" I said. "You mean the Winnebagos? The tribe?"

"No. The Windigo. It's a horrible giant that gets into you when you're starving to death. It makes you crazy and awful, and you see things . . . like heads rolling on the ground and animals without any skin, and it makes you eat up anything, even people."

"Hold it . . ."

"Buck said I should learn to shoot it."

Mr. Lister came out the front door of the mess hall. I figured he had been in Woody's office, so maybe now would be a good time to get in to see him.

"I want to hear more about all this. But I have to go see Woody now."

"Buck's gonna let me shoot his gun again."

Again? "Look. It's great that you're having such an exciting time. But I don't want you to go shooting with Buck again."

"Awwww! Come on!"

I held him so I could look him in the face. "You hear me?"

He refused to meet my gaze.

"Have you given any more thought to my idea of leaving camp early? Just you and me?"

"Leave camp?" He frowned. "No."

"We could go to Connecticut. The new house. Have fun."

"I love it here!"

Damn! They got him! I stood up stiffly. "We'll talk about it later."

"I ain't leaving."

"Don't say 'ain't,' Peter."

"Buck's neat."

I went to Woody's office door and knocked.

"Enter," Woody called out.

To my surprise, the room was crowded. Blue cigarette smoke drifted in the air. No one was speaking. I wondered if they had been talking about me.

Don't be paranoid! I quickly told myself.

Woody was sitting behind his desk, wearing a black T-shirt and sunglasses. His white armband was twice as wide as the others I had seen, and made of some lighter, shinier material, possibly silk or rayon. Win, also in a black T-shirt but wearing no armband, was sitting in a chair to his left, studying an open file folder. Bordy and Len were also there, Bordy with a white armband, Len with a red one. Redclaw was there too, wearing long pants and a tunic made out of some kind of soft animal skin. His hair was pulled back in a ponytail and he had delicate paint markings on his face. His wider red armband was a match of Woody's. He looked too big for the room. Chunky was lying on the floor on the near side of Woody's desk.

"What's up?" Woody asked.

"I came to report on Bernie Kaufman's vigil."

"That's between you and Buck," Woody said. "Sit down." He indicated the empty chair next to Chunky.

"I'll stand. There's other stuff to talk about."

"What's that?" He slid an open pack of Pall Malls toward me. "Light up, if you like."

I took one from the pack and accepted the flame from his lighter.

"We were just planning battle strategy here," he said, snapping the lighter shut. "How's the knee?"

"It's fine. A little sore. But that's not—"

"Not much sleep, huh?"

"Enough," I answered quickly. Redclaw was looking out the window. In the dim light of Woody's office, his face seemed more pockmarked than usual. I wondered who was running things in the woods while he was up here.

"You okay, Jerry?" Woody asked.

"I'm fine. I wondered if I could talk to you alone."

"Sure. But we're all family here. Something particular on your mind?"

Why not speak up now? "Yes. I want to lodge a complaint."

"Really? A complaint?" Woody looked at Bordy, who was resting his head on his hand so that his eyes were shielded. "What's the problem?"

I couldn't read his expression because of the sunglasses. "The problem is that somebody played a joke last night."

"A joke? God forbid!" Woody said.

Win continued to scan the file she had open.

"Yes, a joke. And I want you to do something about it."

"What sort of joke?"

"A joke with the bearskin." My voice sounded shaky.

"What about the bearskin?" Bordy and Len had looks of mock surprise on their faces. Redclaw watched Woody expressionlessly.

"Come on! And I know who did it."

"Really? Tell me."

"Mac. I'm sure of it, and if you don't do something about it, I'm going to do it myself. I don't care what it means for the camp." I looked at Redclaw for support, but he was still looking out the window. My head was throbbing and I was edging toward tears.

"Well, I tell you what," Woody said. "I'm not going to do anything about it, at least not to Mac."

"What?"

"I said we're not going after Mac."

"Why?"

"Because Mac didn't do anything to you."

"How do you know that?"

He paused for a few long seconds. "I know that because I was the one who did it."

I found myself short of breath. "Why?"

Woody leaned back in his chair. "No particular reason."

"It scared the hell out of me," I said, sounding whiny. *Did he know T.J. was there?* I wondered.

"Maybe if you'd been on the lookout instead of . . ."

So he did know. "The campsite was all set up," I said. "Bernie was in place. I could have been asleep."

"Look, Jerry. We play jokes on everybody. You know that."

"I thought only on people you want to punish for something."

Len spoke up. "They did it to me on Steady's vigil."

"They did?"

"We do it to everyone," Len added.

"Sure," Woody said. "You're taking yourself far too seriously this summer."

"But I thought the vigils were supposed to be taken seriously." Redclaw was looking at me now, but he still said nothing in my defense.

"Nobody here is exempt from jokes," Woody said. "You know that. It's nothing personal."

Win was staying out of it. "You scared the heck out of us."

"Us?" Woody asked.

I wished I could see his eyes behind the sunglasses. "Bernie and me."

"Oh, yes. Well, is that it?"

"I guess so." I thought I saw a flash of warmth in Redclaw's eyes.

"Anything else?" Woody asked the room.

No one said anything.

He squared a pile of papers on his desk. "Okay, let's wind this up. Buck, you and Len better get back out to your men. And Jerry, you're dismissed now. You've got bunk time coming." He spoke in a softer voice. "The boiler's fired up. Maybe you want a hot shower."

Everyone seemed to be waiting for me to leave.

"Or maybe you should make it a cold shower," Woody added.

Bordy snorted.

I closed the door behind me.

Enraged, I didn't know where I was until I got halfway down to the cabins. I was brought back to my senses by the sound of hammering coming from the direction of the Big Woods.

Cabin one was empty. I sat on my bunk and tried to think. It was too hot to sleep. My clock read nine-forty. I decided to take Woody up on his suggestion, so I got my things and headed down to the shower house.

Near the foot of Cabin Row I saw where the hammering was coming from. One of the teams, probably the Indians, was building something at the bottom of the meadow. The structure was made out of long poles and planking and looked like the scaffolding you'd put up next to a building you were going to work on. Only it was next to the wall formed by the edge of the forest. A narrow platform about seven feet in the air, with poles rising up above it.

What can it possibly be? I wondered.

It was stifling inside the shower house. No one had been tending the boiler, and it was ticking angrily. The needle on the temperature gauge was near the danger point and the pressure bubble was high. In a panic, I got down on all fours to see if the burners were going. Through the little opening at the bottom I saw with relief that only the pilot light was on. The safety gauge had worked and cut off the gas.

When the temperature was right, I stepped under the shower spray.

I loved the feeling of this outdoor shower, the combination of fresh air and hot water on my skin, the feeling of being naked under open sky. I could feel cool air coming from the Forbidden Woods, only a few feet away from me. I began to feel calmer.

How quiet the woods seemed! I was standing wet and naked, and even if dozens of people were hiding in there watching me, I would never know it.

Suddenly it dawned on me that the thing they were building at the bottom of the meadow was a lot like the scaffolding for torture in the Indian book Jeff had loaned me.

I shuddered at the thought and turned to rinse the soap from my body. I didn't like the feeling of having my back to the woods.

I thought about last night. Why would Woody play that kind of trick on me, especially in the middle of an important Indian ritual? *Was something going on between him and Redclaw?* I wondered.

I've definitely got to find some way of getting out of here! I decided. *Maybe a letter from my father will come today.*

I turned off the faucets, took my crutch, and turned to where my towel and clothes were lying.

They were gone.

My first reaction was to cover my groin with my left hand. Then I hopped to where my clothes had been and looked around the corner of the shower house. No one was there. When I turned back to face the showers again, T.J. was standing there. "Oh my God!"

She was wearing tan shorts over her yellow one-piece bathing suit. She had no armband on. She was holding my clothes and towel.

"Hi." She laughed.

"Shit! You scared me. Again."

"You look cute. What are you doing?" she said.

"What does it look like? May I have my towel?"

"'*May I have my towel?*' Oh, yes, you *may.*" She handed it to me.

I began to dry my hair.

"You have free time now?"

I dried off my legs.

"Hey, you're mad at me!"

"I'm embarrassed."

"Come on. I've seen naked guys before."

"You snuck up and scared me. I'm getting tired of that trick."

She hung her head sheepishly. "I didn't mean to. Nursey gave me a couple hours off." She flipped me my underpants and jeans. "We could do something."

"Like what?"

"I don't know. Anything." When I had my pants on she stepped closer. "You accept my 'sorry'?"

I studied her face. "Can you believe it was Woody who played the joke on us last night?"

"Was it? The son of a gun."

"Didn't you run into him on the way back?"

"No. There was a canoe there when I got back to the wharf." She handed me my sneakers.

The canoe meant that Woody had beaten her back to shore.

I leaned against the shower house wall to put the sneakers on. "How'd you get back to camp?"

"Walked and hitched. No big deal."

"Didn't Mac wonder where you were?"

"He was out on a raid."

"That's right."

"Does Woody know I was there last night?"

"I think so."

"Darn. Oh, well."

"What if Mac finds out?"

"Don't worry about it." She looked toward the woods. "Hey, I know what!"

I followed her gaze and saw nothing but the darkness. "What?"

"Let's go look for your tree."

A chill went through me.

"Don't clutch, it'll be a kick." She gave my cheek a wet lick. My head swam. I craned to kiss her mouth, but she moved away.

"What about Mac?"

She tossed her head impatiently. "Forget Mac. Mac's busy. Let me worry about Mac. Ain'tcha curious about what's in there?"

I thought of Redclaw in Woody's office.

"Come on," T.J. urged. "I'll show you something."

"What?"

"You'll see."

"You better put on long pants."

"You're right. I'll meet you by the flagpole in five minutes."

"No. They might see us go in." I thought a moment. "Come back here. I'll wait for you."

"I'll be back faster than a sexy thought hits you."

"You better go like lightning, then."

I moved back into the boiler room and stood beside the front wall to make sure no one heading to the Big Woods would see me. I lit a cigarette and thought about what T.J. and I might find in the woods. Besides the dead tree and maybe the secret of why it was still standing, there might be the source of Redclaw's fire the night of the Snipe Hunt. And maybe we'd see the so-called Indian burial grounds, or whatever he was trying to keep us away from.

Or is he trying to attract us to it? I wondered suddenly. *Maybe it's some kind of trap.*

T.J. returned, Chunky by her side, and we quickly crossed to the edge of the woods. I felt as if we were about to leave one world and enter another, someplace entirely alien.

We stepped over a low barbed-wire fence and forded the little stream that ran along the woods' edge. Chunky followed us hesitantly. The feeling was different here from the far side where we had hunted for arrowheads in "Garvey's Woods." At first we had to fight off brambles and thorned branches. Then the woods turned darker, denser, damper. There was no path to follow, and I found it hard going. The wet ground was covered with small mushrooms. Funguses ringed the many dead tree stumps. The air was thick with rot, and it felt unnaturally quiet. The sounds of the camp had faded.

The coolness that I had felt coming out of the woods was replaced by a humid, stifling heat. Between our sweat and the dampness of the foliage, T.J. and I were soon wringing wet. She led the way, moving as though she knew where she was going, with me hobbling along on my crutch and Chunky panting behind us. Tiny insects added to our misery, swarming around our eyes and biting our necks.

"Shoot, no-see-ums," T.J. muttered.

"No wonder the place is called Forbidden."

"Come on, it's an adventure."

"We should be marking our trail," I muttered.

"How?" T.J. asked.

"I don't know; by slashing the trees with a knife or something."

"We couldn't see the marks in the dark, and that's the only time we would really need them."

"We could leave something shiny," I said.

"What would that be, diamonds?"

We continued to work our way along. I kept as close to T.J. as possible, and I could smell her salty sweat. It aroused me.

"Why is it so dark?" I muttered.

T.J. paused. "What'd you say?"

"It seems too dark for the time of day."

She looked up at the canopy of leaves overhead. "No. It's just all the trees, crowded together. Come on. It has to be only another hundred yards or so to your tree."

I could feel the heat of her body next to me. I could hear the snap of her chewing gum.

She pointed ahead and off at an angle to the left. "It's gotta be somewhere up there."

We started moving again, more slowly, as if something was holding us back. After a few minutes, T.J. stopped. "What's that?" She was pointing at something dark and solid.

"I don't know. Some sort of building, maybe."

"Let's see."

Chunky let out a whine, followed by a low growl.

"Come on, boy," T.J. said.

Instead he backed away and trotted off in the direction we had come from. In a moment he was gone.

"Maybe he knows something."

She shrugged. "Too far from home, I guess. Let's go."

About twenty yards farther we found ourselves facing a barrier made of draped material, green and tan and brown, either canvas or animal skins on a frame. It was hard to judge the size of it in the thick foliage, but we had to look up to see its top.

T.J. stepped through the remaining trees that separated us from whatever it was and disappeared around its right corner. I followed slowly. Up close I could see that the wall was definitely made of animal hides. I stepped around the corner and found myself facing what seemed to be another wall of the structure, about fifteen feet wide and ten feet high, with a gently arched roof. T.J. had disappeared.

One of the hides that formed the wall in front of me was swaying perceptibly. When I jabbed it with the tip of my crutch I discovered that it formed an entranceway. As I slipped through, I could hear T.J. saying, "Holy smokes!" I found myself standing beside her.

A low growling sound came from somewhere in the dark space ahead of us, which was now illuminated only by a single shaft of pale sunlight that glimmered faintly through what looked like a smoke hole in the ceiling. Directly below the opening there were smoldering ashes of a dying fire, contained by a ring of cemented stonework topped by a grill. Although only faint wisps of smoke rose from the ashes, the place smelled acrid. Above the fireplace a large cauldron hung from a chain attached to a rusty tripod. Beyond the kettle yellow eyes gleamed in the darkness.

After a moment of trying to decide whether to run or to stay, I realized that the eyes weren't coming closer. Whatever they belonged to seemed to be secured.

"It's okay," I said.

"Hey there, dog," T.J. said.

A low growl came in response.

I looked around. The space we were in was about ten feet high, fifteen feet wide, and thirty feet deep. The structure was made of unhewed wooden beams running vertically and horizontally and covered with animal hides. The floor was hard-packed dirt, with more animal skins scattered around. On the left side of the space three poles rose from the floor to the roof and supported a tier of platforms that held large baskets, bowls, and what looked like urns. Two shelves near ground level supported mattresses, blankets, and pillows.

Strangely, despite the lack of ventilation, it felt cooler inside the space.

"Geez!" whispered T.J. "What the heck is this?"

"It looks like some kind of Indian hut. It's a . . . whatta you call it? A . . ."

"Whose is it?"

"It has to be Redclaw's."

"Wow!"

I moved farther inside, hoping to inspect the right side of the room. The growling intensified. From this new vantage point I could see that the yellow eyes and growling belonged to a large black dog lying just beyond the fireplace. A chain fixed to its collar suggested that it knew better than to try to charge us.

"It's the dog that was with Farmer Garvey," I said. "I think he called it Steel. Hey, Steel!"

The dog flattened its ears.

"Easy there, Steel," T.J. said.

Steel barked. The sound was unexpectedly high-pitched for such a big animal.

On a shelf in back of the fireplace there was a large glass box that looked like an aquarium, and inside there appeared to be lengths of coiled ropes. With a start I realized that the box held no water, and that a couple of the ropes were moving. Snakes!

I took a step back.

"What is it?" T.J. asked.

"Snakes."

She quickly went to the container. "Rattlers!" she said. "Six of 'em!" The dog's eyes followed her, but he didn't move.

"Christ!" A row of wooden masks hung to the right of the glass container. They were brightly colored and primitive—representing raw expressions of joy and sorrow and rage—and had bent noses like the masks I saw in the crafts room. At the end were a few rubber masks, among them a Mad Cook mask like the one worn by Bordy at the opening-night campfire.

Below the masks a shotgun hung from two wires attached to the cabin's frame. I was sure it was the one that Farmer Garvey had carried.

"Look at this," T.J. said. She had opened a large drawer to the right of the snakes and was staring in.

"We should get out of here."

"Come here and look at this!"

I approached her cautiously and looked in the drawer. Inside it were half a dozen small bones.

"What're these?" T.J. asked.

"From an animal. They look new."

She slid open another drawer, revealing six or seven knives of different lengths and shapes, a cook's repository. One of them was the largest cleaver I had ever seen. *A mad cook's arsenal,* I thought. To their right, in an open felt-lined case, lay a target pistol with the words "Model HD Military—US Property" stamped on its barrel. It looked like the one that Redclaw had fired at the rifle range. Beside the case lay several cartons of .22 caliber bullets.

T.J. reached into the drawer and pulled out a bunch of keys. She jingled them in the air. "I wonder what these are for," she said. She put the keys back, took my right hand, and squeezed it. "This is exciting!"

"Yeah, but what does he do here?"

She opened the drawer below the one with the weapons in it. Liquor bottles—scotch, gin, and rum—and a variety of spices and condiments: salt, cinnamon, mustard, relish, and a large bottle of ketchup.

"He eats here," T.J. said matter-of-factly. She moved toward the far end of the hut. The dog's growls grew louder and he began to strain at his chain. T.J. put her hand to her mouth and let out a piercing whistle. The dog froze, and then lay down.

"What did you do?" I asked.

"Some pups'll respond that way." T.J. approached the dog and knelt. With his head between his paws, Steel looked up at her imploringly. "Good boy." She rubbed his head and massaged his ears.

"Jesus, T.J.," I said.

"It's just a good old dog." She lifted his chain. "He's padlocked. I bet one of those keys would unlock him."

"Let's not," I said.

She rose and moved to the corner. "Look at this!" She was staring at something I couldn't see.

I circled the dog. The walls at the far corner joined a huge tree trunk with its bark stripped away and its wood bleached nearly white. An opening, big enough for a large man, had been cut into it, and the inside looked hollow. The rest of its surface was covered with elaborate carvings, but in the dim light I couldn't make out their details. The tree rose beyond the height of the ceiling.

"Is that the tree?" T.J. asked.

"Maybe. Let's look outside."

She patted the wall and found an opening similar to the one we had entered through at the other end of the structure. I followed her out. She was gazing upward, her body slowly turning. Above us was an intricate dark fretwork, as if the strings of some gigantic black harp had snapped and sprung, scoring the sky with filigree.

"It's just a darned tree," T.J. said.

"Yeah, but it's dead, completely dead." And now, up close, I could see the source of its eeriness: every one of its limbs and branches and twigs was not only bare of bud or leaf, but also weirdly luminous, as if it had been dipped in some immense can of varnish.

"It's your tree, for sure. It looks like somebody painted it," T.J. said.

"Impossible." Just behind her was a small clearing in the woods, bordered by a semicircle of hemlocks. The ground was dotted with rectangular mounds crowned with grass. Two openings near us had piles of fresh dirt lying beside them. "I think we've found those burial grounds," I said.

"Brrrrrr," T.J. said. "I'm gettin' the willies."

"What makes the grass on them so green?"

"It could be where an outhouse stood. That'd do it for sure. Or garbage."

"Let's hope."

"I'm going back inside."

As she moved past me, I went over to the nearest pit and looked in. It was about five feet long, with its corners cut neatly square and its bottom flat. I looked around for a shovel. There was none.

"Jerry." T.J.'s muffled voice from inside the hut. "Come on."

Nothing was in the pit, thank God. *What's it for?* I wondered.

I turned away. The graveyard, if that's what it was, had an eerie peacefulness, with its bright green grass crosshatched by the black shadows of the death tree. But its overall effect was purely frightening. I pushed through the hut's entrance. The longhouse was empty except for the dog. I decided T.J. had rushed to leave, so I started moving toward the opening at the other end.

"Jerry?"

T.J. was lying stretched out on her side near the back of the lower platform, her head resting on her left arm. She had taken her hair out of its ponytail and let it fall across her shoulders. As I drew closer I saw that she had taken off her shirt, removed the straps of her bathing suit, and slid the top down to her waist. Her breasts were fuller than I had imagined, with large pinkish brown nipples. I felt as if a curtain had been lifted.

"Come here."

I advanced to the edge of the platform, laid my crutch on the ground, and sat down.

"Touch me. This place is doing something to me."

I placed my left hand softly on her bare shoulder.

"This is what I said I would show you," she whispered. "Kiss me." She turned her face toward mine.

I put my lips on hers. Her mouth opened wetly and I found her soft, warm tongue. She twisted her chest so that my hand covered her right breast. I felt her nipple hardening. Still kissing me, she lifted her hips and began to slide her jeans and bathing suit down over her hips. I saw the beginning shadow of her pubic hair.

Suddenly she froze, quivering. Her eyes were fixed on something in back of me. I turned to look over my shoulder.

Redclaw was gazing down at us, smiling.

"Jesus!" I sat up, my heart pounding. T.J. scrambled beside me, quickly covering herself.

"Hello, you two," Redclaw said. The big dog was standing beside him, still chained and quiet. Redclaw was patting his head.

"I'm sorry," I said.

"You've been nice to my dog. I can tell."

I could barely catch my breath to get the words out. "There's no excuse."

"For what?" Redclaw asked. "He's a good dog."

"For us being here . . . on . . . on your sacred ground."

"How polite you are."

"We were just curious . . ."

"About?"

"About—I don't know—the tree, about the smoke I saw one night, about . . . about what you're doing in here."

"Well then, let me explain."

"What about your troops? Woody said you were supposed to be with them."

Redclaw smiled. "Don't worry. My troops are fine."

"I gotta go," T.J. said. "I got someplace to be."

Redclaw flicked his right hand. "Run along then."

T.J. started toward the far end of the hut.

I reached for my crutch and stood up. "I'll go with her."

"No. You stay."

T.J. disappeared through the flap. I wanted to tell her to wait for me, but she was gone.

"Sit down."

I put my crutch down and sat again on the edge of the platform.

"Relax." He sat at the head of the platform, folding his legs and leaning his elbows on his knees.

"Can I smoke a cigarette?" I asked.

"You shouldn't," he said, smiling primly.

"It's hard to relax."

"You can do it without smoking."

"I thought tobacco was sacred to Indians. You put some in the council fire. You make the vigil boys use it."

"Not cigarettes. The white man invented cigarettes. That's why I'm reluctant to return your lighter."

"*You* have it?"

"Yes. You left it in my cabin that day."

"It's important to me. It was a gift."

"I know." He pointed a finger. "How's your leg?"

"Okay."

"You're still not pushing yourself."

"I am."

"You still have your crutch."

"I know."

"So. What do you think?" he asked, after a pause.

"About what?"

He waved his hand. "About this. Aren't you impressed?"

I still couldn't relax. Redclaw's polite, deferential manner was almost more unnerving than the cold, unemotional stance he'd previously assumed. "Very. Why isn't it hot in here?"

"The roof is covered with straw to keep the sun off."

"When did you build it?"

"I've been working on it for nearly a year."

"Does Woody know?"

"Of course. He helped on weekends all winter. It's part of the Indian program. It'll be shown to the children in due course."

So this is where those photos were taken! I realized. "Then why all the mystery?"

"What mystery?"

"I don't know. The sacred ground stuff. At the campfire and when you were playing Garvey. You were trying to scare us away."

"No. Just trying to command respect. It *is* sacred ground."

"You mean as a burial ground?"

"Yes. Once, perhaps. But my people died on this land, spilled their blood. Their blood makes the land sacred for us. The children will learn the importance of that."

"Those graves outside—they're real?"

"It doesn't matter. They could have been. The land is haunted, as you say. Do you remember when I was Garvey?"

"How could I forget!"

"Do you remember the ghosts?"

"The smoke you made? How did you do that?"

"What did you see?"

"I saw a crying child."

"Of course you did."

"What was I supposed to see?"

He didn't answer, only smiled slightly.

"What about this tree? How does it stay standing? Why is it shiny?"

"It's petrified. I varnished it to preserve it. With many hands, it didn't take long."

"Many hands?"

"People from the North. From my nation."

"Why?"

"Why paint it? Because the tree is central to the Seneca view of how the world was created."

"I call it the death tree."

"You're wrong. It's our tree of life. Do you see the carvings on the trunk?"

"I can't see the details."

"They tell our story of the creation. I'll show you sometime. Do you see what the opening is?"

"It looks like a mouth," I said.

"It is a mouth. If you looked closer you would see lips and teeth."

"Why?"

"I can sleep in there when it's cold. The tree devours to protect. 'The-Tree-That-Is-Called-Tooth.'"

"I don't get it."

"Never mind. Just understand that to preserve this tree is to preserve my people."

"What about the snakes?"

"Snakes are sacred too."

"Rattlers?"

"Especially."

"Did the one Mac killed with my crutch come from here?"

He considered this question for a moment. "No."

"Then where . . . ?"

"There are rattlesnakes in these parts. I would know that."

"We've never seen them before this summer."

"You have a lot of questions, don't you?"

"You asked what I thought."

"I did. But enough. Let *me* ask *you* some questions now."

"Wait. There's something else."

"What?"

"Back there in Woody's office. What was going on?"

"What do you mean?"

"When I took the vigil too seriously, why didn't you stick up for me?"

"That's between you and me. And it was none of their business."

"You let me hang there."

"You'll see why. You want to stretch out?"

"No, thanks. I want to know why you didn't defend me."

"The mattress is comfortable."

"I'll sit. Aren't you supposed to be leading your troops?"

"Nothing's happening now."

I lifted my legs onto the pallet and crossed them, mirroring his position. "Peter tells me you took him shooting."

"Yes. I like Peter. He did very well with the weapon. You think that's wrong?"

"You told him some wild stories."

"Not so wild. Why is he so much fairer than you? His mother is lighter than yours?"

"Yes."

"K.M."

"That's right. She gave me the lighter. That's why I'd like it back."

"Why did your father make you move out of their house?"

"Apartment. I told you. They needed my room for Peter."

"But you could have shared, couldn't you?"

"It didn't work out that way."

"Why don't you get along with your real mother?"

"We get along all right."

"Why did you say before that you didn't?"

"I don't know."

"She looks after you?"

"Sure. What the heck are you driving at?"

He seemed to be waiting for me to say something more. I fought an urge to fill the silence with talk. *My mother was never there to take care of me. And she drinks. And worse . . .* I thought all these things, but said nothing.

"After your father remarried, how long did you live with him?"

"I don't know."

"You don't?"

"It's complicated. About a year."

"You liked living with them?"

"I guess I did."

"Why?"

"We had fun?"

"Then Peter spoiled something good for you."

I tried to hold his stare, but it was too intense. I felt my face getting warm.

"That's true, isn't it?"

"If it were, what would it prove?" I asked, hoping to challenge him. He smiled as if he'd won something.

"What are you saying?" I sounded as if I were pleading. I still felt uncomfortable, but at the same time I could feel a rising sense of pleasure, perhaps at being the focus of such concentrated attention.

"Tell me about K.M."

"Karla Muller. What about her?"

"Is Karla beautiful?"

"She's pretty enough. German. My father met her during the war."

"He was a soldier?"

"No, they met in London. He was with the O.W.I., the Office of War—"

"I know. What was she doing in London?"

"She hated Hitler."

"She's Jewish?"

"No. She had left before. She was an actress. She speaks good English." I thought of her letters. "Fair English."

"So he was single and lonely."

"No. He was still married."

"Really? In 1945? But Peter is—what did you tell me?—nine?"

"Yes. He was born in 1943."

"Out of wedlock, as you say."

"Yes. My parents divorced in 1946, after my father came back from London."

"And he married Karla . . ."

"Later that year."

"And you lived with them . . ."

"Until 1948."

"But Peter was already three when they married."

"Yes."

"So he was over three when you moved in."

"Yes."

"A little boy. Why did he suddenly need his own room?"

"It got crowded."

"And your father decided you should move out. How old is Karla?"

"Um, let's see. Thirty."

"Thirty! And your father?"

"Forty-eight."

"Then she's closer to you in age than to him."

"I guess."

"How did she feel about your moving out?"

"I don't know," I said too quickly.

"Have you ever had any kind of counseling?" Redclaw asked.

"What do you mean?"

"You know, a talking doctor. Psychotherapy."

"No. Why should I?"

"Just curious."

"Are you saying I need it?"

"Not necessarily."

"Then why did you ask that?"

"You'd be a good subject."

"Why?"

"Don't get insulted. Most people are candidates for therapy. It doesn't mean there's something wrong with you."

"Well, I'm not . . . getting counseling."

"You know about Freud?"

"A little. The Oedipus complex."

"Among many other things."

"What about him?"

"He was a great thinker."

"Yeah?"

"His ideas would help you understand yourself, Jerry."

"What about you? Have you been—y'know—psychoanalyzed?"

"Oh, yes."

"Really?"

"Absolutely."

"Why?"

"To understand myself." He paused. "But also to understand you."

"Me?"

"Not you as an individual. I mean your people. You as a white person, a European."

"I'm not a European."

"Of course you are."

"Did you understand them?"

"Yes. But it was also to understand Freud himself." He leaned forward. "Everything in your head, Jerry, is European. In my head too, much of it is European, because your people put it there. I had to understand it and then go beyond it to what's real."

"Europeans aren't real?"

"Not for me. Not for my people. For us there's a reality beyond."

I couldn't pull my eyes away from his.

"That's what the white man has never understood. Never tried to understand. The other."

"What 'other'?"

"Their great crime was not taking our land or destroying our hunting grounds. It was the refusal to acknowledge the other."

"I don't understand."

"No, you don't. But maybe you will."

"Why are you telling me this?"

"Because I'm going to show you."

I felt a coldness in my gut. "Show me what?"

"First the structure they've given you. Then the reality beyond."

"What do you mean, 'beyond'?"

"You'll see."

"How?"

He stood up. "You better go now."

I started for the back exit, feeling depressed and confused, but at the same time elated. Redclaw had put his finger on a lot of things I was barely conscious of: my father's part in my moving out, my mixed-up feelings about Peter, my avoidance of my mother. He made me feel as if something was missing in my picture of myself.

"One more thing," Redclaw said.

I turned around. He was patting the dog.

"The next vigil you'll take more seriously."

"What does that mean?"

"I'm referring to last night."

"How can you say that? You just got through saying it didn't matter."

"Not to them it doesn't. But we know you didn't take it seriously, don't we? Neither you nor Kaufman."

"You were with Woody on the island?"

"I know what happened."

I was caught. My outrage now seemed a little hypocritical. "I did my best with him."

"He didn't wear his mask. He was never touched by his sorrow."

"I don't think there'll be a next vigil."

"The next vigil you will show the deepest respect."

I decided not to argue.

"Do I make myself clear?"

"I heard what you said."

"Have I answered all your questions?" He came toward me.

"No. Not really." It was hard not to keep backing up.

"I don't want you going back to the camp dissatisfied in any way."

"Oh, really?"

"You have no more questions?"

"I have lots of questions."

"Ask one."

I thought of all the things about him that made me curious. *The smoke that night. The snakes. The stories he had told Peter. Where he had come from. Where he had learned the guitar. How he had lit and put out the council fire. Why he built the rifle range contraption.*

"Go ahead."

"Okay. Outside, those two graves. Why are they open?"

He moved his head slightly, as if he were letting something fly past him. "Good question. The answer is they're latrines."

I didn't believe him. He had made it up on the spur of the moment.

"Okay?" he said.

"Fine."

"Anything else?"

"May I have my lighter back?"

"In time, perhaps."

"It's important to me."

"I know."

I waited.

"We'll talk some more. This was just the beginning."

I turned away and pushed opened the flap with the tip of my crutch.

"And Jerry."

I waited without looking back.

"You won't tell anyone about this place."

"If that's what you want," I said.

I wandered back through the woods in a daze. Why did Redclaw cast such a spell over me? His sudden friendliness in the longhouse now made the underlying menace feel worse, and to think about the menace opened up shafts of fear that I didn't want to go near.

He got me thinking about my family. *Is there something I don't see about the plan with Karla?* I wondered.

I managed to find my way out of the woods, emerging just behind the Kybo.

I had more questions now than ever before: *Is Peter in some kind of danger from Redclaw? Am I? Or is he really trying to help me? To make me see more? It's as if he was trying to bend my mind the way he bent my knee that day.*

I have to get us out of here, I thought again, with greater resolve.

In the shower area I gathered up the towel and shampoo I had left. It seemed as if a week had passed since I had been there. I found Jeff stretched out on the floor of the boiler room. Assorted tools lay beside him.

"Hey, Jeff."

He continued to work without acknowledging me.

"Anything wrong?"

"Needs a new relay, I expect."

"The burners cut off okay before."

"Might not the next time. Where you been?"

"In the woods. I found his hut, his longhouse."

He widened his eyes in an exaggerated way. "Whose?"

"Buck's . . . Redclaw's."

"You better watch it. That's s'posed to be secret."

"How do you know about it?"

"I knows what I knows." He went back to studying the boiler's interior.

"I read that passage in the book you loaned me."

"When you finished with it, stick it in my room."

"I am finished. It was horrible."

"Them's not such nice folks, is they?"

"But they were Huron, the tribe that tortured Joseph."

"Iroquois do it right back."

"I wanted to ask you about something else."

"Ask away." He reached for a screwdriver beside him. He wore no armband.

"It's a word: Win . . . Winnidigo . . ."

"Windigo."

"That's it. What's it mean?"

"Lots of things. Giant that eats you. Monster you turn into when you're starving. Why you ask?"

"Our friend told my little brother about it."

"More Indian legend." He brought his hand out of the opening; it held a piece of metal attached to a wire. "Reminds me." He rolled halfway onto his side. "Got something for you." With his free hand he reached into his shirt pocket, pulled out a folded piece of paper, and handed it to me.

I unfolded it. The words "Professor Herbert R. Klees" were written in pencil in what struck me as surprisingly sophisticated handwriting. Below the name was a telephone number. "Who's he?"

"Just who it says he is. Guy who knows our friend Mr. Redclaw, as you calls him."

"What's he do? I mean what's he teach?"

"American civilization. At Allegheny College, not far from here."

"Redclaw taught there."

"That's right. Call him."

I studied the paper as a dozen more questions occurred to me—all of which I was certain Jeff would refuse to answer. "Thanks a lot. I really appreciate it."

"But leave me out of it," he said.

"I will. Don't worry."

"You didn't hear nothin' from me."

"Of course. I understand." I stood motionless.

"That's all I got for you."

The first thing I saw when I left the shower house was the scaffolding, gleaming like fresh bones in the sun. It looked exactly as I imagined the structure described in Jeff's book to be, and it reminded me that it was another thing I should have brought up with Redclaw.

I felt hot and exhausted, ready for a nap despite the heat, but the Settlers were in the cabins now, resting and preparing for the next phase of the battle, and I had to go up to the mess hall to see if the mail had come in. I felt determined to do something about Redclaw. The farther away from him I got, the more I realized how much he had scared me. Would Win still be willing to help? I had to talk to her.

I took Jeff's book and went up to the mess hall. No one was there. The doors to the crafts room, Woody's office, and the infirmary were all closed. The only sign of life was in the kitchen, where the staff was preparing the next meal. The clock there read three-thirty.

I didn't know if Win had distributed the mail yet, but on the chance that she hadn't, I decided to wait there for her a little while. A newspaper lay on the table next to the crafts room.

I scanned the local news but found nothing about the missing boy, Sam Holden.

After waiting another few minutes, I returned Jeff's book to his room and went to look for Win. She wasn't in their cabin, so I headed for the farmhouse, joined on my way by Chunky.

I opened the screen door but made the dog stay outside. The parlor was neat. There was no trace of the mess Oz and I had made that night. In the cluttered front room I found Win lying on a couch, reclining against a pile of pillows. She had an open book in her lap, but she was smoking a cigarette and staring into space.

"Hey, Win."

She snapped to attention. "Jerry. You startled me. I didn't hear you come in."

"Sorry. Did the mail come yet?"

"Yes, but there was nothing for you. Shouldn't you be with your campers?"

"I have free time coming, because of last night."

"Oh, yes."

"I need to talk to you."

"I can't now."

"It's about Red—about Buck."

"I'm expecting someone."

"I need your help. I need to make a phone call."

"About what?"

"Our friend."

"To whom?"

"A name I got."

"From where?"

"Some research I did."

"Well, it's a bad time now. Besides there's no phone here."

"I know."

"The only one's in the office and you can't use that."

"I don't want to. What about the Causeway Tavern, tonight?"

"I told you that would be difficult."

I took a step toward her. "I just spent some time with Buck. He really scares me."

"Why? What happened?"

"It's hard to explain, but I'm convinced something's wrong. Can't you get me to a phone tonight? I think it might be important."

She took a pull on her cigarette and just stared at me. I watched the smoke drift toward the open window in back of her.

"I'm ready to have our talk," I added.

"I don't know. Maybe I can get away, but we can't be seen. Can you meet me up the road?"

"Where?"

"Go about a hundred yards and wait for me."

"To the right?"

"Yes."

"What time?"

"Ten-thirty. I'll pick you up in the Town & Country."

AT TEN-TWENTY by the clock on the kitchen wall—shortly after taps had sounded—I announced that I was turning in. No one present was likely to guess that I was faking; just the kitchen staff was there—Eve and Sukie, Chris and Wimpy—and Nurse Laird; and what did they care whether I was going to bed or not? The rest of the camp was either skirmishing in the woods or asleep.

Bordy had just given us an update on how the Sham Battle was going. The Injuns were ahead by maybe twenty to thirty armbands. Redclaw had organized his troops efficiently and made a series of daring raids, using Oz's and Steady's skills to the utmost. In his boldness, he was stretching the rules to the limit, even flouting them. Just after dark this evening he had surprised Woody in a strategy session with Mac and Artie in Woody's cabin, which was completely off-limits. Bordy and two Settlers had saved the three of them as they were being hauled off, strapped to those pole-and-frame conveyors that the Plains Indians call travois. Woody was steaming mad about it. None of this news surprised me at all.

As I walked to the point where I was to meet Win, I decided that if I got the chance I was going to call Irma, my father's secretary, and get a number where I could reach him and Karla in Germany. Karla had written not to do this unless absolutely necessary. I knew perfectly well that things hadn't yet gotten to the point of justifying a call to my parents, but I wanted to get their numbers, just in case.

I hadn't seen anything of T.J. since our encounter in the woods. She was probably making peace with Mac.

Finally headlights loomed out of the dark.

"Did anyone see you leave camp?" Win asked when I climbed into the passenger seat. She was wearing dark slacks and a dark jacket over a white blouse.

"I'm pretty sure not."

She offered me a cigarette.

"Thanks. I've got my own." I tapped a Lucky Strike from my pack and lit it with the car's lighter.

"Tell me why you suddenly want to make this call?" Her voice was soft.

"It's a guy who knows Buck."

"Yes, but what's the sudden rush?"

"I just got the name and number. My concern isn't so sudden. I just couldn't meet you last night."

"When you came to the farmhouse this afternoon, you said that Buck had scared you. Tell me what happened."

"Well, for one thing, we . . . I went into those woods and found his cabin."

"I know all about that house. Woody helped him build it."

"It's really something."

"I'm sure."

"He caught me there. He threatened me."

"Threatened you how?"

"In a dozen subtle ways. It's hard to explain."

"Come on, Jerry. This is a big step you're taking." She swung into the driveway of the tavern, stopped, but made no move to get out.

"You seem to be having second thoughts," I said.

"I don't like the man. But there's a difference between not liking him and trying to stir up trouble for him. Especially for doing his job."

"Did Woody ever check his references?"

"I told you; there were none. Woody fell in love. Who is this person you're calling?"

"A professor who knows him."

"What if he calls Woody? Have you thought about that? If he knows Buck, he could well contact *him.*"

"I'm going to try and explain the situation."

"You better think it through carefully beforehand, what you say."

The neon signs in the window looked comforting, a very different world from Redclaw's longhouse. Win had lit another cigarette.

"Well, there's this," I said. "Do you know about a boy named Sam Holden from Linesville who went missing earlier this summer?"

"Yes, of course. Chief Izenaur told us long ago."

"They still haven't found him."

"What are you saying?"

"I'm wondering if Redclaw had something to do with his disappearance."

She thought a moment. "That's pretty strong. What evidence do you have for suggesting that?"

I rubbed my eyes. "Nothing that doesn't also have an innocent explanation. But there are a lot of suspicious signs."

"You better come up with something solid before you start making any accusations."

"I know."

"The boy will turn up. You're imagining things."

"I still have to make this call. I don't see what's wrong with talking to someone who knew Redclaw."

She sighed. "All right. Let's go."

Inside the tavern, only a few tables were occupied. "Because You're Mine" was playing on the jukebox.

"Let's sit at the bar," Win said.

"I better make that call. It's getting late."

"Yes, it's almost eleven." She perched on a bar stool and ordered a scotch on the rocks. "Tell me who you're calling."

I took the piece of paper from my pocket and read her the name. "He teaches at Allegheny, where Buck once was. It's a local number."

"Do you have change?"

"No."

She handed me some coins. "That should be enough."

I looked around, spotting the phone booth at the end of the bar. "What do you want to drink?"

"A coke, I guess." I went to the phone booth and dialed the number. The phone rang, a woman answered.

"Hello. Is Professor Klees there?"

"Yes, he is."

"May I speak with him?"

"Who shall I say is calling?"

"Someone inquiring about a former colleague."

"At this time of night? My goodness!"

"It's sort of urgent."

"All right, I'll see. Just a moment, please." I heard footsteps fading away. "Herbert! Telephone!" After a short silence, more footsteps. Then a dragged out "Yeeeees?"

"Professor Klees?"

"Yeeees. Who is this?"

"My name is Jerry Muller. I'm a—um—I'm a counselor at Camp Seneca here in Linesville. I'm calling to inquire about someone working at the camp who you might know."

"Yes? I can't imagine who."

"It's someone named Buck Silverstone. He says he taught American civilization at Allegheny. Right after the war."

"Oh, yes. Extraordinary man."

"Really?"

"Brilliant. An American Indian, as I recall."

"That's right. Seneca."

"Original ideas. Where's he teaching now?"

"I don't know that he is."

"Why are you calling me?" An edge of irritation had entered his voice.

"Well, uh, I'm just curious about this man and—"

"This seems irregular. Why isn't your employer making this call?"

"Well, it's complicated, sir. I'm sort of on my own here. I'm sorry if I'm intruding."

"Yes, well, you sound kind of young."

"I'm seventeen, sir. I'll be a freshman at Swarthmore in the fall."

"Swarthmore, eh?"

"Yes sir."

"Well, it was a while ago that I knew, ah, Silverstone."

"About six or seven years ago. Right after the war."

"I do remember him. Handsome man. What's your interest here?"

"Well, as I said, I'm a junior counselor. But I have some reason to be curious about him."

"You know, I shouldn't be handing out information to just anyone who calls."

"Yes, I understand that. But as long as you're sure about him."

"I'd have to check for any details. What's he do there at your camp?"

"He runs the Indian program. Woodsmanship, crafts, lore."

"He'd be ideally qualified for that, as I recall."

"He has some unusual ideas."

"What do you mean?"

"He feels the land belongs to his people, that the camp's on sacred ground, that—"

"Yes, yes. Right. There are people here I could compare my impressions with."

"That would be a big help, Professor."

"Is there any place I can reach you?"

"Not really." I thought a moment. "Could I call you back at a convenient time?"

"All right."

"How about tomorrow evening around this time?"

"It's a little late, but I suppose that would be possible."

"I'll talk to you then, sir."

"Good night."

I looked over at Win. She had lit a cigarette and was watching smoke drift in the air. I dialed the operator and gave her a New York City number to call collect. After two rings I heard a woman answer. The operator gave her my name and asked her if she would accept the charges.

"No, I'm sorry," she said immediately. "I'm not permitted to take this call."

"I'm sorry," the operator told me. "The party won't accept."

"Did you say my name clearly?"

"I'm sorry," she repeated in a mechanical tone. "The party won't accept the charges."

"Thank you." My voice sounded strangled. I put the phone back on the hook. *Won't accept the call? Not permitted to take the call? Not permitted? What was going on?*

I tried again. This time when the operator began to speak, the phone disconnected.

I stood there for a full minute, trying to figure out what was happening. *Did I have the wrong number?* I was sure I remembered it correctly. *So why did my father's secretary say, "I'm not permitted to take this call"?*

When I got back to the bar, Win looked at me and frowned. "What's the matter? You look as if someone died."

"I'm fine," I said, although even I could hear the uncertainty in my voice.

"Sit down. You might as well drink your soda." She pointed at her own drink for a refill.

I climbed onto the bar chair. *Did I possibly make a mistake by writing to Karla instead of appealing directly to my father?* I wondered. *Is he mad at me now?*

"What'd he say, your professor?"

Could Peter have written them something? I suddenly realized that was a possibility.

"Jerry? Are you okay?"

I listened to the echo of Win's words. "The guy said Buck was brilliant."

"Good. What's wrong, then?"

"I don't know if he took me seriously."

"Why not?"

"He said I seemed young."

"You are." She took a swallow of her drink. "Do you have another cigarette for me? I left my pack in the car."

"Sure." I lit one for her off mine and laid my pack on the bar. "He's going to check with other people. I said I'd call him again tomorrow evening. Can you get away again?"

She blew out smoke. "I guess we'll have to. Jerry, you look sick."

"I'm okay." The clock on the wall said ten past eleven.

"I have to say something."

"What?"

"I'm disappointed in you."

"Why?" I suddenly felt dizzy, as though things were spinning out of control.

"About your trying to leave."

"Leave?"

"Yes. Leave camp."

"How do you know about that?"

"Why didn't you tell me?"

"Why didn't I tell you?" I was having trouble catching my breath. "I've been slowly going to hell. I didn't think it mattered to you that much." I heard the scorn in my voice.

"How can you say that?" She reached for my hand. "You're very important to us."

"How did you know I wanted to leave?"

"Your father called Woody."

"My father? From Germany? When?"

"Late last night."

"I don't believe it."

"The phone woke us up."

"What did he say?" *So this must have been why Irma wouldn't take my call*, I realized.

"Apparently he told Woody about your letter asking to leave. He was angry."

"My father was angry? About what?" I could feel my face turning red. "The bastard!"

"Whoa, there!"

"I'm not a horse!"

She squeezed my hand. "Listen, listen. Your dad was very concerned about the two of you. But when Woody reassured him, he was annoyed about his trip being disturbed."

"Woody reassured him?"

"Yes. Of course he did."

"And you let him?"

Her eyes wavered.

"You went along with it? What's going on with you? First you were on my side! Now you've changed your mind? What the hell is going on with you?" My hand hit my glass and knocked it over.

"Take it easy, son," the bartender said, wielding a cloth.

"Give him another."

"I'm getting out of here." I grabbed my crutch.

"Wait. Give him another coke." She clasped my wrist. "Calm down. Please listen to me."

I stood there. Anger made my whole body tremble. I'd completely screwed things up at home, and now I'd made it next to impossible to stay on at camp.

"Sit down."

"I'll stand."

"Everything's all right now. Woody calmed him down."

"How did he do that?"

"They made a deal."

"A deal?"

"Try to understand something. Your family is very important to us. To me too."

"Why?"

"You can get us campers from your part of the country."

"My family?"

"It's hard for you to see." She had finished her second drink and was signaling the bartender again.

"I don't believe any of this."

"Your dad is going to bring us new campers next summer. Four or five."

How is he going to do that? I wondered.

"And he'll earn something for it. He's happy with that."

I nodded. *He would be,* I thought.

"But one condition is that you stay this summer."

I just stared at her.

"Promise me. You have to stay."

"I don't get any of this. How in hell could you have gone along with this bull? The last time we talked honestly you were as upset by all the crap that's going on as I was. What happened?"

She turned back to her drink. "I have my obligations too."

"To my father?"

"No. To my marriage."

"I don't see what that has to do with my father."

"I'd like you to stay for my sake."

I drained my coke.

"Promise me, Jerry. It's important."

"Do I have a choice? It won't be that easy to leave, even if I want to."

"Do you want another?"

"I guess so."

She signaled the bartender.

"Will you be able to drive?" I asked her.

"This'll be the last. Cigarette."

I pushed the pack of cigarettes toward her.

"Thanks. What went on with Buck?"

"I don't know."

"What upset you so?"

"I told you. It was a lot of things."

"But you're reassured now? By the professor?"

"I guess. I'll know more tomorrow."

"I'm sorry about the other night."

"What do you mean?"

"When we were dancing. I had too much to drink."

"Oh. Yes."

"These are kind of bad times for me."

"It's okay."

"How old are you, Jerry?"

"Seventeen."

"A child," she said to herself. "But old enough. Have you ever liked a man . . . Or a boy?"

"Liked?" *Does she know about Oz?* I wondered suddenly.

"Yes. Sexually."

"No. I'm not that way."

"Well, you never know," she said.

"I know. What are you driving at?"

"Take it easy. I'm trying to tell you. That photograph in Buck's file, the one of him naked?"

"Yes?"

"Woody took it."

"I figured."

"I think it scared him to death."

"What do you mean?"

"The feelings he had. I think a part of him has fallen in love with Buck."

"Woody?"

"Yes, and I think it's become a problem in their relationship, driving a wedge between them."

"But he seemed to worship Buck. Before you got here he was defending him to everybody. He said Buck was going to change the camp."

"He has," Win said. "But Woody still has conflicted feelings about him. Their friendship has cooled, I think."

"Is that why he played the bear trick on me?"

"Maybe." She laughed. "Woody's a kid at heart. He probably has conflicted feelings about you too."

"What the heck does that mean?"

"Nothing that he's conscious of." She laughed softly. "Nothing for you to worry about."

I didn't know what to say. "Shouldn't we be heading back?"

"Do you have bed wetters' patrol?"

"No."

"Then what's the hurry?"

"It's getting late." The skin on my face felt numb.

"Listen . . ." She caught herself. "Are you hungry?"

"I had something to eat in the kitchen."

She drained her drink and looked at the bartender.

"Please don't have another."

"You're right." She moved her hand back and forth over her glass.

"We really should go," I said.

"Yes." She grasped my upper arm and leaned against me. "You won't run away from camp, then?"

"I'll see." I had to catch my breath. "No promises. It depends on Peter."

"But Peter's fine." She placed some crumpled bills on the bartop.

"Maybe. We should go."

"Yes." She sighed, pulled away from me, and climbed slowly down from the bar chair. I took her arm to steady her.

She leaned against me. I stooped to conceal my erection.

She fumbled in her purse for the car keys.

"Are you okay?"

"Of course." The air was cool and it seemed to be sobering her. "Do you want to drive?"

"I don't have my license yet."

"Then you'll have to trust me."

I climbed in. Win started the engine and let it idle. "We forgot something," she said.

"What?"

"I was going to tell you what you missed on Buck's application."

"I completely forgot." I could feel my heart pounding.

"It may not mean that much. But it could. His résumé says that he left military service in February 1945. He served in the marines, in the Pacific theater."

"I remember that. I didn't notice the date."

"The A-bombs weren't dropped until August, so Japan wasn't about to surrender in February. Why would he leave the service then?"

"Was he honorably discharged?"

"It doesn't say anything about that. You would think that if he was, he would say so."

"How can we find out?"

"I don't know."

"We could call someone in Washington. Who?"

"I don't know." She put the car in gear and gunned the engine.

"Now you've got me worried again."

"But you'll stick it out, right?"

I said nothing.

"For me? And Woody?"

"I'll try."

"Good." She patted my leg.

I watched the road nervously. "How are you going to explain your absence this evening to Woody?"

"Woody has no idea where I am. He probably won't even notice. He's too involved in the battle."

WHEN I SAT DOWN on my bunk to undress, Teddy whispered to me from across the aisle. "Jerry?"

"What is it?"

"I gotta go."

"Didn't somebody walk you?"

"Yes, Bordy did. But I gotta go again."

When we got outside I led him around to the side of the cabin.

"I gotta make number two."

"Oh, Teddy!" I sighed in mild exasperation. "Let me get my flashlight."

"We don't need it. I can find my way. Carry me."

I picked him up. He was too light to bother my bad leg. "How's the arm doing?"

"Good. But it itches a lot. It's coming off soon." When we got near the Kybo, he stopped. "Check inside for me."

"I thought you said you could find your way."

"I can. But check it for me first."

I approached the dark door. Inside, as always, the smell made me gag. I felt for the nearest corner of the bench.

In the far corner, a low laugh sounded and a light went on, revealing the hideous rubber face of the Mad Cook of Pymatuning.

I let out a cry, backed toward the door, and tripped, falling painfully on my back. Teddy was running up Cabin Row, laughing gleefully.

"Fuck you, Woody," I said to the figure approaching me. *He knows where I've been!* I realized.

The figure pulled the mask off. It was Mac. "You got that one wrong. It's me."

"For Christ's sake, Mac."

"I owed you one for T.J.," he said. "Teddy owed you for breaking his arm. So fuck *you*."

7

THE RAID

AT BREAKFAST the next morning, Mr. Lister told me
Woody wanted to see me in his office. My stomach tightened; I wondered if he'd found out about my outing with
Win last night, or maybe about Mac's trick on me in the
Kybo. I had spent half the night having nightmares and the other half
going back and forth between plotting some form of revenge on Mac
and searching for some new way of escaping the camp. I felt hopelessly trapped. Obviously I wasn't going to get any sympathy from
Woody now that he knew he had my father on his side, although I
had to keep in mind that I couldn't let him know I knew about my
dad calling, because to reveal that would betray Win. I would have to
watch my step while talking to him.

"You look tired," he said when I walked in.

"I'm fine."

"I hear you had a little trouble last night."

"I'm not complaining." I sat down stiffly in the chair near the door,
my back still aching from the fall.

"That's good." He offered me his pack of cigarettes and I took one.
"I didn't like your reaction to the bearskin."

"I didn't like the bearskin."

"It was another sign that you're not on board."

"*Another* sign?" I snapped his lighter shut and put it down. *Here it comes,* I thought.

"I got a call from your dad last night."

I tried to hold his gaze without reacting.

"All the way from Berlin."

I let out my breath. "What was it about?"

"You know darn well. He got your letter."

"Actually, I wrote to my stepmother."

"Beside the point. You're not leaving camp. Is that understood? He wants you and your brother to stay."

"I guess I don't have a choice, then, do I?"

"I guess you don't." He tapped his cigarette over the ashtray. "I wish you felt better about it."

"Well, I don't feel good at all."

"You've been fighting me from the start of camp this summer."

"There's been a lot to fight."

"Maybe we can start fresh. You got any plans today?"

"Not really. I'm a bystander, remember?"

"I want you to go down to the Big Woods and do a little reconnoitering for me."

"Fair enough," I said. "Can I ask why?"

"No reason in particular. I just want you to find out what's going on down there."

"What sort of thing?"

"Where their main encampment is. Their headquarters."

"Isn't it the tree house?"

"Maybe it's the tree house. Maybe it's not. And I want the lay of the land."

"Of course I'll do it, if you want. But aren't I supposed to be, you know, neutral?"

He blew out smoke. "How would this change that?"

"Well, if I found out something, whom would I tell it to?"

"Me, of course."

"Wouldn't that be taking sides?"

"It might be viewed that way. But as you may have noticed, the rules are not being strictly observed."

"They're not?" *As if I didn't know.*

"Remember, they know our layout better than we know theirs. The camp lives and works here, not in the woods."

"I understand."

"And Buck's taken advantage of that. He tried to take me prisoner, you know."

"So I heard."

"We're just leveling the playing field a little. Besides, you work for me."

"Okay," I said, slowly nodding my head. Then I decided to take the plunge: "On that subject: may I ask you for an advance . . . on my pay? I need some money."

"What for?"

"Expenses that've come up. For college."

"Let me think about it. I'll talk to Win about it."

"I'd appreciate it."

"All right." He slapped the desktop. "Let's march, then!"

I stood up.

"By the way. Why *did* Mac spring the Mad Cook on you?"

"I don't know. Something about T.J., maybe."

"You interested in her?"

"He seems to think so."

"Well, that's healthy enough."

What does he mean by that? I wondered. I went to the door.

"Oh, and by the way," Woody said. "See if you can find out where they're storing their armbands."

I WAS GLAD to have something to distract me. When I'd finally fallen asleep I had dreamed of Peter again, a menacing, threatening Peter, with staring, vacant eyes. It was reassuring in the morning to find the familiar Peter, soft and youthfully energetic. I wanted to talk to him about leaving—even though the chances seemed hopeless at the moment—and I wanted to urge him to avoid Redclaw, but I couldn't get him to pay attention. He was too fired up about the Sham Battle and couldn't wait to get started on the day, so he could help his team get even in the count of prisoners. He had definitely grown from the timid little boy I had first brought to Camp Seneca.

I limped down Cabin Row, Chunky by my side, past the new, scaffoldlike structure, which appeared to be completed, and into the Big Woods. The scene there reminded me once again of the horrific book Jeff had made me read: all it lacked was black-robed missionaries praying for the souls of the damned. That and a torture victim. Everywhere I looked there were half-naked, war-painted boys, practicing forms of combat, including throwing makeshift tomahawks.

The campfire site had been cleared of all wood and ashes and was being used as a training area for hand-to-hand combat. A dozen pairs of combatants were practicing tosses and falls. They were being supervised by a hardly recognizable Oz, who had not only given up his jaunty cap but also shaved most of his scalp, leaving only a Mohawk crest in the middle. He was naked to the waist, wearing a loincloth and leather leggings. The skin of his head, face, and torso was splotched with colorful designs. He didn't acknowledge me as Chunky and I approached.

Off to one side of the campfire ring a small fire was burning, tended by two older campers. One of them had skewered what looked like a squirrel on a short metal rod, and was turning it slowly over the flames. About fifteen feet away, four boys were yanking down on a rope tied to the top of a tree, bending it to form an inverted J, struggling as they secured the end of the rope to a stake driven deep into the ground. An older camper, also with a Mohawk haircut, was directing them. It took me a moment to realize that it was Steady Bomber.

"What in hell are you doing?" I asked him.

He looked at me with surprise, apparently not happy to see me. "Building a man trap."

"Seriously?" *Even though there were a couple of people I wouldn't mind seeing caught in it, it looked extreme, and perhaps even dangerous.*

"It's gotta be so the lightest touch releases it," Steady said.

"We're just trying to secure it first," one of the boys said. "Then we'll fix it up so a fly will set it off."

"Okay, good," Steady said.

"How's it going to work?" I asked.

"When we get it right, we'll attach a loop to it and a trip wire, then hide them in underbrush."

Smaller campers had begun to gather around.

"You mean whoever trips it is going to get caught in the loop and strung up in the air?"

"That's the idea."

"Isn't that dangerous?"

He shrugged. "It's not my idea."

"Whose is it, then?"

"The commander's. Buck's."

"I see. Where is he now, uh, Buck?"

"At headquarters, I guess."

"Where's headquarters?"

"The tree house."

It wasn't possible to see it through the foliage. "You know anything about that thing in the meadow?"

"What thing?"

"That wooden scaffolding at the edge of the trees."

"It's supposed to be for training."

"Training for what?"

"I don't know. We just followed Buck's plans."

No one said anything for a couple of beats.

"Well, you did a good job," I said to ease the tension. "It looks impressive."

"Thanks," Steady said, turning his attention back to the job of the trap.

I stood and watched a few minutes more. Chunky stood beside me, panting. I didn't at all like the atmosphere in the woods. The kids seemed angry and threatening, as if infected by some ugly presence. My desire to grab Peter and escape was being replaced by a greater unease. I could sense a growing momentum of menace, a feeling of being headed toward disaster. I knew I should try to do something to divert it—but what?

Brooding, I headed off in the direction of the tree house. A few more young campers were coming down the path toward me. When Chunky bounced ahead to lick the face of one of them, I recognized Teddy Wentworth, like the rest of them wearing a loincloth and covered with body paint.

"How're you doing, Teddy?"

"Good," he said in a small voice. Hugging Chunky, he squinted up at me shyly.

I took a couple of steps closer and then stopped in astonishment. His cast had not only been painted to resemble flesh, it had been turned into a detailed illustration of the arm's underlying structure. The rendering had an authentic look, down to the finest nerves and arteries and tendons, reminding me of illustrations in anatomy textbooks I had seen.

"My God," I said, stepping closer to him. "Who painted your cast?"

"Buck did."

It was amazing. The surface was burnished, making it look like an old oil painting. "When?"

"Yesterday."

How in the world did he find the time? I wondered. "How long did it take him?" I asked.

"Just a little while. He did it fast."

"What did he copy it from? A book?"

"No. Nothing."

"Nothing? No picture or painting?"

"Nothing. He just painted it on."

"What kind of paints did he use?"

"Little tubes from a box."

I couldn't stop staring at it. "Do you like it?"

He wrinkled his nose. "It's sort of strange."

"Yes, it is." I tousled his hair, and began to move up the path toward the tree house again.

"Well, well, well, well, well! Look who's come to pay us a visit. It's Jerry Muller himself."

Redclaw was standing on the path ahead of me, wearing his leather outfit and, over his shoulders, a cape of feathers. His hair was falling loose around his head and his face was painted in bright colors. Several younger campers surrounded him. Over his head I could see the gray boards of the tree house nestled high in a big maple. Both ends of the dumbwaiter rope were hanging down.

What other place beside the tree house would they store the arm-bands? I wondered.

"Hi," I said tentatively. Chunky stopped in the path and began to growl.

"Tsk, tsk, tsk. Still leaning on that crutch?" Redclaw pursed his lips and shook his head.

"I've had to do a lot of walking."

"That's no excuse. You should push yourself more without it."

"I do. Sometimes."

"That's good. Now, what do you think?" He looked at the campers around him. "Jerry has come to inspect us, my braves."

"Think about what?" I asked.

"About all of this." He waved his arm around him. "My team. The training. The morale. What impressions have you formed."

"It's pretty . . . intense."

Chunky's barks got louder, as he backed away.

"Intense?" He laughed dryly. "Of course it's intense."

"The dog still doesn't seem too fond of you," I said.

"Something's troubling him," Redclaw said. "Excuse me." He extended the fingers of his right hand in front of him, as if he were inspecting his nails, and moved along the path toward Chunky. Chunky bared his teeth and stood his ground. Redclaw's hand suddenly shot out and seized the scruff of his neck. With his left hand he pulled the leather thong from around his waist, whipped it around Chunky's neck, tied it in a knot, dragged him to a small tree just off the path, and secured him to it. Chunky leapt at him and barked viciously. But it was too little too late.

Redclaw turned back to me. "Where were we?" he asked. "Oh, yes, intensity. But how else should it be? How else can we become stronger if we aren't intense?"

"Stronger? But your team is way ahead, I heard."

"The war's not over. We have a day to go yet. A lot can happen."

"Like what? You seem much better set up than the Settlers."

"I'm glad you're impressed. But we have to anticipate anything."

"Like what?"

Redclaw probed the inside of his cheek with his tongue. "A raid on our captured armbands, for example."

I looked in the direction of the tree house.

Redclaw followed my glance. "You wouldn't be spying on us?"

"I don't think I'm allowed to do that," I lied. "Even if I wanted to."

"Well, you can be sure our armbands are secure." He looked at the children again. "Do you think he's a spy, men?"

A small chorus of yesses.

"So the tables are turned, right?"

"What do you mean by that?"

"We're suspicious of you in the way that you suspect me. Come on." He gestured with his head toward the tree house. "Let's take a walk, alone."

The boys scattered. Redclaw started up the path toward the tree house. I followed him reluctantly, wondering why he was playing with me.

When I joined him, he took my arm and guided me off the path. I could see the top of the new scaffolding through the trees off to our right.

Redclaw saw that I was looking at it. "How do you like it?"

"I don't even know what it's supposed to be."

"Why, it's for torturing prisoners."

My head snapped around to look at him.

He was smiling. "See? This is what I mean. You think I'm serious, don't you?"

"I can't tell." I looked back at the scaffold. "It's quite a thing." The craving for a cigarette came over me. I put one in my mouth.

"The children built it." He took the cigarette from my lips, crushed it. "You shouldn't smoke down here."

"What about my lighter? When will you give it back?"

"In time, perhaps." He looked at the scaffold. "The children have done everything. My job is just to create the right setting. That's Woody's philosophy, isn't it? Create a situation where the kids will sink or swim. My campers are swimming."

"They told me those things were your ideas."

"What things?"

"The scaffolding. The trap Steady's building."

"I'm channeling their energy. That's my mission."

"That's not what you said at the campfire that first night."

"What did I say?"

Facing him, I found it hard to gather my thoughts. "You said it was your mission to redeem the land stolen by the white man."

"Well, you're right. That's part of the Indian program. That's what Woody hired me to say."

"But you sounded so serious, so angry."

"And I am. My people are angry and I'm taking their part. You have to understand that."

"Uh . . ." I tried to find words.

"But we can be friends. We have a lot to offer each other. I understand you."

"Maybe."

"What else is bothering you?"

"What do you mean?"

"Tell me what you're thinking. Right now, this instant."

"I don't know," I said quickly. "Teddy's cast?"

"Teddy's cast? What about it?"

"How did you do that?"

"I painted it. I'm a painter. I told you that about the tree."

"You painted it from memory."

"I did. But everybody has seen what our bodies look like."

"But they don't carry that kind of detailed information around in their heads."

"I like to look beneath the surface of things." He closed his eyes. "And I have a very strong visual memory."

"Of human anatomy?"

"Of everything I see."

I lowered my eyes.

"Is that it, then? Nothing more?"

"Oh, there's lots more."

"Why did you ask me about the graves?"

"They're pretty strange. I was curious."

"What were you thinking? Come on. Let's get everything out in the open."

I wondered about the missing boy."

"Aaah. Sam Holden."

"Right."

"You think I had something to do with that?"

"Yes."

"Why?"

"Your being in the woods some nights. There was a fire one time. I saw the smoke in the sky."

"And?"

"The bag you were carrying the night of the Snipe Hunt. The small grave. And the bones."

"Animal bones in the drawer of my hut. My God! What must you think of me!"

My face was burning.

"Well, I'm glad you told me. Anything else?"

"Isn't that enough?" I felt slightly faint.

He squeezed my shoulder. "Those are heavy thoughts to be carrying around. We'll get to know each other better now."

I braced myself with my crutch.

"I want to know about your family."

"Why?"

"It interests me very much."

"Why?"

"Because it produced you. And Peter. Tell me what Karla looks like."

I paused, wishing I were with her now. "She's pretty."

"Like Marlene Dietrich?"

"What makes you ask that?"

"The words on your lighter."

"Oh, yeah."

"Describe her face for me."

"She's got an angular jaw . . . not masculine, but firm. And a mole high on her cheekbone."

"A beauty mark. Is she very fair?"

"Fair?"

"Blond."

"Yes."

"So that's where Peter gets his coloring, his white, white skin and hair." He took a deep breath and looked up at the sky. "Time is passing. I have to go and set up defenses. I think Woody may be planning something. Do you want to join us?"

"No. I want to head back."

"Tired?"

"A little." I turned toward the path that led back to the entrance.

"You can go back this way." He pointed toward the softball meadow. "It's shorter."

"I know. I was going to get Chunky."

"I'll take care of . . . Chunky."

"I should take him back with me."

Redclaw stood without moving. "It was a good talk," he said. "We'll get to know each other."

THE FOLIAGE WAS thick for a few paces, but I suddenly broke through and found myself in the meadow, as if I had stepped from one world into another. In the distance I could see the softball backstop and, beyond it and a little to the right, Cabin Row. The scaffolding loomed over my right shoulder.

Why does he want to know more about my family? I wondered.

The smell of gasoline was in the air. I moved closer to the structure, so that it towered directly over me. Planks ran along three horizontal poles to form a platform about two feet wide and ten feet long. In the middle of the platform was a hole through which another vertical pole stuck up from the ground about ten feet into the air. To this pole, above the platform, was nailed a crosspiece that made the structure resemble a crucifix.

I put my hand on one of the poles. The wood was soaking wet. I brought my fingers to my nose. Gasoline.

What in hell does that mean? I wondered.

I moved to the end of the platform nearest the tree house to get a better look at the cross. Directly above me two lengths of wire ran upward into the foliage that surrounded the structure. They were about six inches apart and attached to two eyelets at the edge of one of the platform's planks. One wire was thicker and tauter than the other; in fact, the thinner one was sagging a little. Judging from the angle of their incline, I guessed that they led to the general vicinity of the tree house, which was about twenty-five yards away.

I looked around to see if anyone was watching me.

The wires didn't appear to be providing any kind of support, so I concluded they might be radio antennas. But where was the radio? Maybe in the tree house, I decided.

I started across the meadow, trying to make sense of what I'd just learned. The gasoline had to be there to make the structure burn, but why the wires? Suddenly, I saw a possible explanation. Rather than a radio antenna, the wires could be there to carry the flame to ignite the structure, just like the opening-night campfire. Someone in the tree house could light a rag or a toilet paper roll or whatever and let it slide down the wire and set the whole structure ablaze.

But then why were there two wires? I asked myself. *And what would be the point of it all?*

To set a dummy on fire?

Or a person?

I saw Jeff walking down Cabin Row, and I waited to see where he was going: the shower house.

I crossed the meadow and found him once again looking into the boiler. He had a dirty rag in his hand.

"Hey, how're you doing?"

He frowned. "'Bout the same as always."

"More problems?"

"Always problems."

"Can you fix it?"

"That's what I'm here for."

"I talked with your Professor Klees."

"Ain't my Professor Klees." He lowered his voice. "I best not hear about that."

"He had nothing but good things to say about Buck. But he's going to check further."

"Okay. Something else on your mind?"

"Have you noticed the thing they've built down there?"

"Hard to miss."

"I asked Buck what it's for."

Jeff's arm stopped moving in the boiler. "And?"

"He said it was for torturing people."

Jeff said nothing.

"He made out as if he was joking," I added.

"Like I said: it's all jes' fun and games. Why, you think he meant it?"

"I don't know. It was hard to tell. But the wood is soaked with gasoline."

Jeff whistled. "Gasoline, huh? What for?"

"I think they've rigged it so that it'll burst into flames, like at the campfire. But I can't figure out why."

"Could all be for show."

"But it's dangerous."

"Everything they do is dangerous. That's what I keep telling you."

"Yes. I wanted to ask you: we looked at that tree."

"I don't know about any tree."

"A tree in the woods by the longhouse. I talked with Buck about it. He said something about the creation of the world. Do you know what he's talking about?"

"Tree was called 'The-Tree-That-Is-Called-Tooth.'"

"That's what Buck called it," I said, excited.

"Right," Jeff went on. "Shows we're talkin' about the same thing." He lit a cigarette. "That tree led to the creation of the twins I was telling you about. The Good Twin, who created the first man and woman in the world; the Evil Twin, the giant Shagodyoweh, the keeper of the masks."

"So the tree was the beginning, like a tree of life."

"That's right, only it had to be pulled down for the world to get started."

"But Redclaw wants to keep his tree standing. Why would that be?"

"You got me there. Turn good and evil upside down?"

"What about the masks? He has a bunch of 'em hanging in his hut."

"Part of the story too."

"Why are their noses bent?"

"When the world was finished, the Good Twin went to look it over and run into his brother, who was now in the form of the giant Shagodyoweh. They argued about which of them made the world and decided to settle the dispute in a contest to see who could move the Rocky Mountains. The giant tried first and couldn't do it. The Good Twin said, 'Okay, now it's my shot. You turn around.' When the giant turned his back, the Good Twin moved the mountains right up behind him, so when the giant turned around he hit his nose on them and bent it."

"So the masks are the giant's face?"

"Listen. They made them a deal then. The giant said, 'Okay, I give up; you're the creator.' The Good Twin said, 'You give me that, I'll give you something in exchange. If people wear masks representing you and burn tobacco for you, then you got to give them certain powers.'"

"What powers?"

"Power to express all these forbidden emotions and not be punished for it. With the masks on, they could be anything, say anything. So wearing the masks became a ritual for expressing forbidden things, a way of clearing up conflicts in your mind."

"So that's what Buck's doing when he sends these boys on vigils and tells them to get in touch with their animal spirits?"

"Something like that."

Maybe Redclaw was right about making me do a vigil, I thought. From outside, in the direction of the Big Woods, we heard the sound of children yelling.

"I found out one other thing about Redclaw," I said. "He was in the marines during the war."

"Lots of folks were."

"That's where he got his gun, I guess. It says 'military property.'"

"That the thing he been shootin' at the range?"

"Yeah. A twenty-two."

"Not military issue," Jeff said.

"What do you mean?"

"That's a target pistol for training. They didn't issue twenty-twos for combat."

"How would he have gotten it?"

"Coulda stole it. Bought it at the PX. No big deal."

"And he left the marines in February 1945."

"Yeah?"

"He was in the Pacific. The war there didn't end till August."

"I know that."

We were interrupted by the sound of a child's voice calling out my name. I looked outside; a small boy was running toward me.

"Why would he leave the service so early?" I asked, anxious to keep Jeff talking.

"Beats me."

"Can't you find out?"

"How'm I gonna do that?"

"Jerry Muller!" the younger camper called, finally reaching me. "Woody wants you in his office."

"I'll be right there." I turned to Jeff. "Come on. Isn't there someone in Washington you can call?"

"You gotta be kidding, man. I done everything I can."

"I have to go."

Jeff went to work on the boiler again.

WOODY WAS SITTING behind his desk. He pointed to the phone. "We had a call," he said.

"We?"

"Some guy named Klees. A professor. Actually he wanted to talk to me. But he said you had his number."

"Yes. I do." I reached into my shirt pocket. The paper Jeff had given me wasn't there. My heart thumped. "So why didn't he talk to you?" I searched my pants pockets. No paper.

Woody look perplexed.

"He knew who you were, didn't he? The camp's owner?"

"I might have cut him off."

"Jesus."

"What's this about? Who is this guy Klees? He sounded very upset. What's he teach?"

"I don't know. If I ever did, I've forgotten."

"Where's he a professor?"

"He lives near here. He teaches at, um, Allegheny College."

Woody frowned and looked out the window. "Allegheny College, Allegheny College," he repeated.

Is he going to make the connection to Redclaw? I wondered. *Not yet, I hope; I don't want to put him on the defensive.*

Then he shrugged, as if giving up on some puzzle. "Oh well. You better get me the number. I better call him back."

"Okay." I left the office and headed for my cabin.

When I got back to Woody's office, the door was closed and locked. Although lunch was being served to the Settlers in the mess hall, neither Woody nor Win was seated at the head table. T.J. wasn't around either.

I had to eat something. I got myself a plate of food at the kitchen counter and found a seat at Peter's table. The boys talked obsessively of how the battle was going. In their sharp exchanges over possible maneuvers they seemed just as driven as the Injuns.

"Listen, men," Peter said in a raspy voice that made him sound as if he had been shouting too much. "We're at least thirty-two arm-bands behind. It's gonna take more than a raid or two to catch up."

"It's only a game," I said. "Don't forget that."

"Maybe it is," Peter croaked. "But I want to win."

I looked at my brother, at the flush in his cheeks, the anger in his eyes. *Why had I ever thought this would be a good thing?* I wondered.

I HEADED TO THE farmhouse to look for Woody and Win. As I passed the women-staff cabin, T.J. came out. I hadn't seen her since she had left Redclaw's longhouse the day before, and with everything that had happened in the meantime, she seemed like an attractive stranger now. I felt a flash of irritation at her that I quickly realized had to do with Mac's trick on me in the Kybo.

"Hey! Where're you going?" she said.

"Up to the farmhouse."

"Can I tag along?"

"Sure, but I gotta hurry."

She fell in step with me. "What happened?"

"I can't really talk about it."

"Hey, come on! I was there with you."

For an instant, I had no idea what she was talking about. "What do you mean?"

"With Buck . . . in that hut?"

"Oh, that." I thought back to the day before. "How come you ran off?"

"I thought you were coming with me. Was he mad?"

"Not really."

"Where were you last night?"

"Last night?" We were approaching the farmhouse. "Out."

"Where?"

"At the Causeway."

"What's the matter with you?"

"I've got to deal with something." I knocked on the screen door. There was no response. I opened the door and we went in. "Hello?" No one answered. Both the parlor and the living room were empty.

"Who you lookin' for?" T.J. asked.

"Woody or Win. You seen them?"

"No, I ain't. What you want them for?"

"I gotta talk to them." I started back for the mess hall.

"Why're you mad at me? I didn't have anything to do with last night." I stopped. "What do you mean?"

"The trick Mac played on you. In the Kybo."

"How did you know about it?"

"Mac told me about it. After."

"Don't worry about it," I said, pausing to look at her.

"You don't blame me, do you?"

"No. It's okay." I headed for Woody's cabin. "We'll talk later."

She didn't follow.

WOODY'S CABIN WAS empty, but I found Win sorting the mail in the crafts room. "There you are!"

She looked up. "What is it?"

"Professor Klees called back."

"Really! What did he have to say?"

"I don't know."

Win shook her head in bewilderment. "Make some sense, Jerry." She lit a cigarette.

"Woody took the call. Klees wanted to talk to him. But it sounds as if Woody hung up on him."

Win nodded slowly, as if she got the picture.

"Maybe I should call him back," I said, "but the office door is locked."

"I don't have the key."

"Can you drive me to the Causeway?"

"Now?"

"Yes."

Win pursed her lips. "Why don't you just wait for Woody? He should be back any minute."

"Where is he?"

"He went off with Bordy and Mac. To the woods. 'Scouting,' he said."

"Scouting in the Big Woods?"

"I think so."

"That's strange."

"Why?"

"He sent me down there this morning, and then never asked me for my report."

"Well, you can give it to him later. He shouldn't be more than a half hour."

I thought for a moment. Win went back to sorting the mail. I said,

"Will *you* call him, Win?"

"Klees?" She thought a moment. "No, Jerry, I won't."

"Why not?"

"I can't get directly involved."

"Woody really cares that much about Red—Buck?"

"No," she said. "In fact, he seems a little annoyed with Buck at the moment. But he wouldn't forgive my interfering."

"Will you drive me to the tavern? So *I* can make the call?"

She chewed her lower lip, then shook her head. "I can't. Not now."

"Why not?"

She took a deep breath. "Woody will wonder where I went." There was an edge of irritation in her voice. "You'll have to wait till tonight."

"Okay." I let out my breath. "Tonight, then. What time?"

"It'll have to be late. Eleven. Be in the same place on the road."

"I'll be there."

"Unless there's a problem, Jerry. If there is, I'll let you know."

"Someone has to call him, Win."

Her eyes met mine. "I'll do whatever I can."

I turned to leave.

"Do you want to take your cabin's mail?"

"Sure." I took it from her and looked through it. There was a letter from Karla. I wondered if she was responding to my call for help. "I asked Woody for an advance on my salary," I said abruptly.

"What for?"

"Expenses. College bills I have to pay. He said he would talk to you about it."

"He hasn't, but when he does I'll tell him no."

"Why?" I tried to affect mild outrage. "I really need it."

"Because I don't believe you." She closed her eyes. "And I don't want you to leave."

I couldn't think of anything to say.

"By the way, have you seen Chunky?" she asked.

I stopped and thought a moment. "He went down to the woods with me this morning. He's down there. With Buck."

"Okay, then he'll be along sooner or later."

———

AFTER I DISTRIBUTED the mail, I lay down to read Karla's letter.

My darling Jerry,

I'm afraid we made a big mistake with your writing to me about wanting to leave the Camp Seneca. Believe me, Jerry, I understand how you are feeling and I am so very much concerned with how things are going for you and our little Peter. But you see when I tried to express your feelings to your father he was very upset that you have written to me about it not to him or both of us. He said it was something we had "cooked up" together to disturb the peace of his summer. You know how sensitive he is about these things.

On top of this Peter has written to both of us to say what a good time he is having and how good things are going for both of you. How can this be? your father quite understandingly wants to know.

Of course he is always concerned about your well-being, you must understand that, Jerry. When he calmed down a little—and at my urgings—he called up Mr. Wentworth to find out for himself how things go for the two of you. As I am afraid you must know by now, Mr. Wentworth was full of praisings for you and Peter, and very enthusiastic about the summer that you are having. Your father was very reassured. And I must say I was also.

Where does that leave us now? Jerry, I can only comfort myself with the thought that in your letter you said that things *might* get impossible for you and you would have to leave. When I put this together with the reassurances from the Wentworths (she has also talked to your father), I feel a little better. As for our plan, with Peter so happy it is still working out very well. And so long as you can stay and work things out, your father will be happy too.

So let's hope that things have straightened themselves for you and that Peter continues having a wonderful summer. Remem-

ber that it's not too long before we all see each other again and
be together.

Please give my love to Peter and tell him to write again soon.
Much love, Karla

Disappointing as the letter was, it was not really surprising. I probably had made some sort of mistake by writing only to Karla, but that
was irrelevant now. Things were changing too quickly.

I lay on my bunk and listened to my campers arguing about how
they were going to get even with the Injuns. Peter continued to be at
the center of it, bold, aggressive, demanding. The kids were listening
to him with respect. I called him over.

He was wearing his holster with his wooden pistol. "We're s'posed
to go scouting with Bordy."

"He's out with Woody right now," I told him.

He shifted from one leg to another. "Can I go back to my bunk?"

"In a minute. First I want to hear some more about shooting with
Buck."

His face lit up. "It was great."

"How did it happen? I thought you were on a raid with the Settlers."

"I was." His eyes shone at the recollection. "We were sneaking
through the woods. Buck captured me."

"How?"

"He snatched me right out of line. Then he took me to the rifle
range."

"You shot his pistol."

"I was good. I hit the target."

"That's great. And he talked to you about this thing, the Winni . . .
Windigo?"

"Yeah, it makes you eat people. Can I go?"

I reached for his arm. "Tell me more."

He squirmed in my grip. "That's all."

"I don't think it would be such a good idea for you to go with him
again."

"Awww! Come on!"

"Promise me."

"What if he captures me again?"

"Don't go on any more raids."

"But I have to."

"When?"

"Tonight."

"Who with?"

"Woody. He asked me."

"When?"

"Before."

"I don't want you to."

"You can't stop me. You're not the boss of me here."

"Actually, I am."

"It's fun. I'm going." His jaw jutted with determination.

"I may not let you. I'm going to talk to Woody."

"Then I'll tell Mom and Dad."

We both froze into silence for a few moments. "Is that what you want?"

He seemed to be working out something. "What do you mean?"

"Do you want to get me in trouble with Mom and Dad?"

"Not really." He frowned. "I want you to move in with us."

"So do I. But I also want to do what's best for you."

He shifted from one foot to the other again. "I'll go on the raid, but I won't go with Buck if he tries to catch me again."

"How about you go scouting with Bordy, but not on the raid tonight?"

"Okay." There was a glint of mischief in his eye.

"I mean it."

"I'm going now."

I lay back.

Peter ran off. "Let's wait for Bordy outside," he said to his comrades, excitement in his voice.

I stared at the ceiling.

I WOKE UP with a start. The cabin was empty. I looked at the clock; it was nearly four. I had slept for almost two hours.

I went in search of Woody and saw him coming out of his cabin, heading for the waterfront.

"Woody!"

He stopped to wait for me. "What's up?"

"I've got that phone number for you."

"What phone number?"

"Professor Klees's. The guy who called you this afternoon. You're going to call him back."

"Oh yeah." He continued to walk toward the waterfront. "I'll do it later. When I'm in my office."

I hopped along beside him. "How come you didn't wait for my report?"

"What are you talking about?"

"My report on the Injun team. Win told me you went down there yourself."

"That was about something else." He adjusted his sunglasses. "You made it down there this morning?"

"Of course. You ordered me to."

"Where do you figure they're hiding the armbands?"

"I don't know," I said. "The tree house seems too obvious."

"That's true. But no other place would be as easy to guard."

"If they hid them someplace else down there, they wouldn't have to guard them at all."

"You're right," he said. "It would be like looking for a needle in a haystack. But I still think it's the tree house. That's the target."

"What do you mean?"

"Nothing. I'm just thinking strategy. Did you find out anything?"

"Not much. Buck was suspicious of me being down there."

"Doesn't matter. What'd he think?"

"That I was spying to find their armbands."

"Well, he's smart."

"Yeah. But I didn't like—"

"Is this more complaining about Buck?"

"I guess."

"I don't want to hear it, Jerry. Buck's now off-limits as a subject of discussion between you and me."

"But this is more than just Buck."

"What do you mean?" He kicked one of the piles supporting the wharf. "This is getting rotten. Remind me to have Jeff replace it." He stretched his arms and yawned. "What do you mean, more than just Buck?"

"Well, the whole atmosphere down there. It's—I don't know—savage, like they're preparing for a war."

A look of mock surprise came over his face. "Unlike the Settlers? Unlike your brother, for instance?"

He's right, of course. "But they're building things down there."

"Like what?"

"A trap. And that scaffolding."

"Yes, I've seen that." He moved toward the canoes. "Give me a hand here."

I followed him. "The scaffolding is soaked with gasoline."

"Really? Well, they've got something special in mind, I'll bet. Grab the other end, will you?"

I grasped the canoe. "There's a wire rigged up to set it on fire, I think. Like at the campfire."

"You see? They're going to put on a show."

We lifted the canoe and flipped it over. Woody swung his end around and led me the few steps to the pond. He slid the canoe halfway into the water before setting it down.

"Where're you going in that?" I asked, going back to get my crutch.

"Nowhere." He fetched two paddles from the rack and put them in the canoe. "Anything else on your mind?"

"What's the canoe for?"

Woody slid the canoe all the way into the water, picked up the painter, and began to walk toward the dam. "Tonight. Big raid."

"In a canoe? I don't get it."

He secured the painter to one of the rungs of the ladder next to the diving board. "On the other side of the lake there's a back way into the woods. Nobody knows about it."

"Why not just walk around the lake?"

"It's blocked by undergrowth on one side, and it's swampy on the other. Canoe's easier and quieter."

"This raid," I said. "What is it?"

"Just an exercise to give the Settlers a chance to even the score."

"Where?"

He walked back toward the wharf. "Has to be a secret."

"Well, who's going on it?"

"Just a few people. Uh, one of them's Peter."

"I don't think that's such a good idea," I said, trying to sound calm.

"May I ask why?"

"He's just a kid. He's small."

"He's rarin' to go."

"But see—"

"Look," he said impatiently. "This is just what I mean. He's completely in the spirit of the camp. He's a poster boy for the summer."

I took a ragged breath. "I know, but—"

"This is what your father would want. I can guarantee you that. Look, it's just reconnaissance he'll be doing. We need a little guy."

"There are other small kids."

"Peter's excited to do it."

"I know."

"So have him here at ten-thirty tonight."

"Here?"

"That's right. They'll be using the canoe."

"Who else is going?"

"Just Bordy and Mac."

"I don't know about Mac."

"Come on." He poked me in the shoulder. "He's even with you, so be a sport. Anyway, Bordy'll be in charge. Ten-thirty. You have an alarm?"

"I want you to find somebody else." I tried to hide the tremor of anger in my voice.

"It's going to be Peter." He started toward the mess hall.

"When will you be in your office?"

He stopped and turned back to me. "Oh, yeah, the phone call."

"Yes."

"His call was about Buck, wasn't it?"

My heart began to thump. "Yes, I'm sure it was."

"How does he know Buck?"

"He knew him at Allegheny College, one of the places Buck taught."

"Why would he call here? I don't get it."

"I think he's upset about something he found out about Buck."

"How do you know that?"

"Because I called him to ask about Buck."

"Why? How did you get his name?"

My mind went blank for a moment. "I thought you didn't want me to talk about Buck."

"We're talking about him," he said impatiently. "How did you find this guy?"

"I did some research."

"Why?"

"I don't think Buck is telling us the truth about himself. I think he's hiding something."

Woody's head recoiled. "What's this professor gonna say, that Buck's a fag or something?"

"Why would you think that?"

"That's the kind of nasty gossip people dream up."

"Well, I don't know what it's about. But I don't think Buck's being that way would make Klees so upset."

"What then?"

"I don't know. But he knows Seneca is a summer camp for children."

"So what?

"So you have to talk to him." I reached into my shirt pocket for the phone number Jeff had given me.

"Where is he?"

"Somewhere in the Linesville area."

He looked at the paper and put it in his shirt pocket. "Look," he said, "you can dig up stuff on anybody if you try hard enough."

"I know, but—"

"It doesn't have to mean anything."

I sensed suddenly that Woody knew more than he was letting on, *and* that he was afraid of what he knew. "Will you just call him?"

He swallowed. "Yes. I'll call him tomorrow, if I can." He turned to go.

I followed, feeling something important slipping away. "Can't you call him now or tonight?"

"No. Sham Battle. The raid."

"Really—"

"Don't worry; I'll call your professor back. I'll listen to what he has to say."

He turned back to face me and pressed his sunglasses against his nose. "Reminds me, there's something else I have to tell you. It's about your friend Osborne."

"Yes?"

"I'm afraid he won't be coming back next year."

"Why?" My scalp prickled. "You fired him?"

"Yes. That's why we went down there earlier."

"He's gone?"

"No. I'd like to get rid of him now, but I need him."

"Did he want to come back next year?"

"Irrelevant."

"I don't understand."

"No one will be told. He'll simply announce that he won't be returning. At the end of camp."

"But why?"

"He's queer. He's been carrying on with the Stemmer boy."

"Who told you that?"

"I see what's going on."

"They're just friends. Steady's that kind of kid. He's no closer to Oz than he was to me when he was my C.I.T. And I'm not—"

"Mac told me."

"Told you what?"

"He's seen things."

"Come on! Mac's doesn't like Oz."

"Never mind. It's done."

"Well, I feel a little responsible."

"Why? You didn't know, did you?"

"No. Of course not." *At least, not when I invited him to camp,* I thought.

"Well, then . . ." He was backing away. "Oz is still going to help us out."

"With what?"

"This raid."

"How?"

"Oh, just some things he's agreed to do." He waved his arm vaguely. "It's too bad about him. He represented something Seneca needs."

"In what way is he going to help?"

"And I know he was your friend, so I'm sorry about that." He pointed a finger at me. "Have Peter at the dock at ten-thirty."

I watched Woody as he walked away, wondering if I should be protecting Oz. I guess I still wanted to believe that he was just drunk that night when he kissed me. I did feel responsible, and I was worried about what Mac knew and had told Woody, although my concern was probably pointless. After all, Woody hadn't dismissed *me*, had he?

No, and that was a pity, I reminded myself. *That would be a way out of this mess.*

I SPENT THE rest of the afternoon lying on my bunk. I felt I had lost control of things. My campers came and went, busy with the Sham Battle. After supper I took Peter aside outside the mess hall. "What happened this afternoon?" I asked him.

"We just wandered around in the woods. Nothing happened. But we had fun."

"Did you see Buck?"

"No. Not once."

"This raid tonight—"

"I'm going on it!"

"No, Peter—"

"I'm supposed to be at the pond at ten-thirty tonight."

"I'm sorry, but I'm not going to let you go."

He moved away.

"I'm serious."

"So'm I."

"Do you know where the raid is supposed to go?"

"No. It's a surprise. Just me, Mac, Bordy, and Woody."

"Still—"

"Woody wants me to. He has a special assignment for me."

"Somebody else can do it."

Tears filled his eyes. "Why? You let me go this afternoon. What's the difference?"

"I don't want you down in those woods in the middle of the night."

"I'll be fine."

"I don't think so, and I'm responsible for you."

"But what can happen?"

"I don't know."

"Then I'm going. You can't stop me."

I squatted down beside him. "I'm just trying to protect you."

"From what?"

"I have to do what I think is right for you."

"I'm going anyway." He ran off.

AFTER LOOKING FOR Woody in his office and finding the door still locked, I went back to cabin one and decided to go to bed early, setting my alarm for ten-twenty so that I would be awake if Peter tried to leave. I slept restlessly, dreaming of Redclaw and Oz and Woody. The voice of Klees kept telling me to watch out for them.

I awoke in pitch dark. The clock read ten-thirty-five. Someone had turned the alarm off.

Peter!

His bed was empty.

I slipped on a pair of jeans and a sweatshirt, grabbed my flashlight, and headed for the pond. The night was overcast, with a slight breeze blowing.

At the waterfront, they had the canoe close to the ladder, helping Peter climb in. He had on his red cap and shoulder holster with the wooden pistol in it. He even had some sort of blacking on his face.

"Turn the light off!" someone hissed.

I moved toward the ladder.

"Is that the fancy boy?" The voice off to my left sounded like Mac's. "Well, well. Looka who's here." It *was* Mac, wearing a black sweatshirt under his bandolier, and army fatigue pants. His face was covered with something like soot.

"I'm getting Peter," I said.

He grabbed my light and turned it off. "No, you ain't, college boy."

"Hey, pipe down," Bordy said.

"You ain't spoiling this raid."

"This is none of your business, Mac."

"If you weren't on that crutch, I'd knock you on your ass."

"What the heck's eating you?"

"I don't like you messing with my girl."

"You don't own her." My head was beginning to throb with anger.

"No?" He stuck a finger in my chest. "When I'm finished in the woods, you're next." His finger jabbed painfully.

"Get me now, shithead!" I hissed. With a flash of rage, I chopped at his finger with the side of my hand, catching him on the knuckle.

"Hey, watch it!" Mac said.

The feeling of solid contact released something in my chest. I cocked my left fist and swung at his head, catching him high on the temple. It hurt my hand like hell, but my punch staggered him.

"Why, you son of a bitch!" He recovered his balance, raising both fists.

I lifted my crutch to swing it at him, but several hands grabbed my arms.

"Easy," Woody said.

"Let him go," Mac said. "I'll kill him."

"Easy, boys! That's not the way we do things here."

Mac dropped his fists. "I'll tell you something else, college boy. I know about you and your friend Osborne."

"You're full of shit!"

"I know what happened in the farmhouse with you two."

"Nothing happened." *Was he there?* I wondered.

"Oh? Really?"

"Get going, Mac!" Woody said.

Mac did an about-face and went to the canoe. I tried to follow him, but Woody stood in my way.

"I'm getting Peter." I said.

"Peter's going." He grasped my shoulders firmly.

I was so angry I couldn't catch my breath. Bordy followed Mac to the canoe and clambered aboard. There was a sound of paddles in water and the canoe began to move away. "Butts out," Woody called. An ash arced through the air and hissed on the water.

"I thought you were going," I said.

"We'll meet you here at midnight, men," Woody called out, still grasping me. "Good hunting."

As it began to dawn on me what this meant, a wave of nausea hit me. I bent over.

I felt his hand on my shoulder. "You shouldn't let Mac get to you."

I stood up straight. "I thought you were going on the raid." My voice was pitched half an octave too high.

"I gotta meet Win." He started to guide me along the path back to camp. "You'll have to be the one to meet them."

"What do you mean?" I couldn't hear the paddles anymore.

He kept his hand on my shoulder. "You'll be here at midnight to debrief them."

"Me?"

"Right. Win wants me to take her to Cleveland for the night. I can't get out of it."

"This just come up?" I asked. My heart was pounding. *Win was supposed to meet me in about fifteen minutes,* I thought.

"She's all stirred up."

"But the raid! You're supposed to . . ."

"Bordy's in charge now."

I started back toward the diving board. "I'm going to call them back."

He came after me and grasped my arm. "Take it easy."

"It has to stop." I was sweating in the cool air.

"They won't come back. If you call out, you'll just alert the enemy."

"Did you call Klees?"

"Didn't have a chance."

"Will you at least do it now?"

"In the morning when I get back."

"For Christ's sake, Woody! Buck's out there!"

"That's the whole point."

"The whole point of what?"

"The raid! Look, just be here at midnight when they get back. Find out how it went."

"You still haven't told me what it's all about."

A puzzled look dawned on his face. "Peter didn't tell you?"

The skin of my face began to tingle with dread. "Peter didn't know."

He took a step toward me. "The objective of the raid is the tree house. The mission is to capture their armbands. You helped convince me they're there."

"I did?"

"But the main thing is to take Buck."

"*Take* Buck?"

"Do to him what he tried to do to me."

"You're crazy!" I was feeling sick again. I thought of Bordy and Mac trying to overpower Redclaw, remembered Redclaw nearly killing Bordy in the boxing ring. "How?"

"It's all set up."

"How are they even going to get up there?"

"Easy. Nobody sleeps deeper than Buck. I should know."

"He'll still wake up if people go up there."

"Doesn't matter. We have a spy to warn the raid off if there's a problem."

"A spy?"

"Osborne. He'll be at the foot of the tree."

"What was the point of sending Peter?" The blood in my head was draining away.

"Peter's going up the dumbwaiter. Bordy'll pull him."

"How does Bordy get up there?"

"No. He pulls Peter up from the ground."

"Peter goes up there alone to face Buck?"

"Right."

"I don't believe this."

"We know from Osborne that Buck locks the trapdoor. Peter opens it. It's perfect."

"This is insane. You're insane!"

"What's the matter?"

"What if Buck's awake and Osborne doesn't know it?"

"Then Peter warns them."

"And then what happens to Peter?"

"Bordy and Mac go up and tie Buck up."

"Buck'll go crazy!"

"He'll be surprised, for sure."

"You're fucking nuts!"

"I have to go. If you must know, Jerry, I gotta save my marriage."

I started toward the canoe rack.

"Where are you going now?" Woody asked.

"We've gotta go after them and stop the raid." I lifted one end of a canoe off the rack and lowered it to the ground.

"You can't do that."

I lowered the other end to the ground, flipped the canoe over, and started to drag it.

He blocked my path. "You go, you're fired."

"Fine. I'm fired."

"That means you pack up right now, and we put you on a bus in Cleveland."

"Good." I tried to step past him. "But first I get Peter."

He grasped my arm. "No Peter."

"I have to take Peter."

"No Peter. That's what I promised your dad."

I stood there breathing heavily. He had checkmated me.

"Come on, Jerry. Calm down. There's nothing to worry about."

"Nothing to worry about?"

"Look how Peter's changed. Why, he's stronger than you are now."

"I don't care." The words barely came out. "I think this could be a disaster."

Woody flapped his arms in exasperation. "Just be at the dam at midnight. Explain why I couldn't be there."

———————

I WAITED WITHIN sight of the farmhouse until I saw the Wentworths' car pull away. Then I went down to the mess hall and snuck through the front door. A few people were gathered in the kitchen but the dining room was too dark for them to see me. Woody's office was still locked.

I went quietly out the front door again and walked the short distance to Woody and Win's cabin. A soft light was glowing on the desk. In the drawer I found a lanyard with a key that I was certain was the one to the office door. I was halfway through the cabin door when a numbing thought hit me.

I had given Klees's phone number to Woody.

I stepped back inside the office and looked around. On a chair next to the bed lay the T-shirt and shorts Woody had worn earlier. In the pocket of the T-shirt I found the slip of paper.

I went back to the mess hall and found that I was right about the key. Once inside the office, I gently locked the door again and sat down behind the desk. The bearskin's eyes reflected the light from Woody's cabin.

By the light of Woody's Zippo, I dialed Klees's number. After half a dozen rings, I was about to give up when a woman's voice said, "Hello?"

"Is Professor Klees there?"

"Oh, dear. It's awful late."

"I know. I'm sorry to bother you."

"Well, let me see," she said in a resigned voice.

Minutes seemed to pass. Finally, there was a shuffling sound and a man's voice said, "Errrrrrrrhhhmp, hello?"

"I sorry to be calling so late, Professor Klees."

"Is this Mr. Wentworth?"

"No. It's Jerry Muller."

"I need to talk to Mr. Wentworth."

"He's gone to Cleveland with his wife."

"I see. I really should be talking to him. When will he be back?"

"Can you please tell me what it is, Professor Klees?"

"Well, I've been making some calls about your man, uh, Silver-stone."

"Thank you for doing that."

"I've talked to three or four people who remember him. They pretty much confirm what I recall: that Buck, uh, Silverstone was a talented, brilliant man. Original."

"Yes. That's what you said."

"I remember him quite well, now that I've jogged my memory."

"That's good."

"But there's one thing that's disturbing."

"Really?"

"It's complicated and a little off the beaten path."

"Um, I'm alone here and I can listen."

"If you're the only one available now, I suppose I'll have to talk to you."

I swallowed hard. "I really am the only one who can talk right now."

"There was a case, you see. A rather bizarre case, involving a mother and her two young children."

"Yes?" My mouth went dry and my heart began to pound.

"It happened during Silverstone's time at the college. It was thought to have been a routine case of murder-suicide. A desperate mother."

"Yes?"

"The children were never found."

"Go on."

"As I say, it was declared a case of murder-suicide; the police were satisfied."

"Yes?"

"But recently, one of our young instructors started looking into it. His investigation began as a class project on how an event becomes mythicized."

"Really?"

"Yes. The poor woman is now the subject of folktales. The house the family lived in is said to be the site of strange goings-on, and so forth. You know?"

"Yes? And?"

"The instructor has written a paper, and while I haven't read it, and he hasn't gone public with it yet, I'm told by mutual friends that it's highly plausible. Makes good sense."

"Yes." I found myself standing up, trying to catch my breath.

"He's convinced the mother was murdered, and that it involved some sort of ritual. And here's why I called you: I'm told he has connected it all to Silverstone, and plans to take it to the police, to see if they'll reopen the case. I've put in a call to the instructor, but I haven't heard back. I probably should have waited to hear from him before I called you, but you had mentioned children, and—"

"Professor Klees, can you call him right away?'

"In the middle of the night?"

"It could be very important. Desperately important. Please . . ." My voice broke.

"Well, I suppose I could try."

"And if you're right, could you call the police in Cleveland? Have them find the Wentworths? They're at some hotel."

"Well, that's a little . . ."

"I know. But it could be that important."

"I don't know about calling the police. We'll see. Now I don't want my name connected to this, but I thought you ought to know, since you people asked."

"Please call."

"It could be nothing, you know."

"But if he thinks there could be danger for anyone here from Silverstone, please call."

"We'll see. Good night, now."

"Good night."

I hung up and looked around for a clock, my heart still pounding and cold sweat covering my face. *It must be getting on toward midnight,* I thought.

I locked the office door, returned the key to Woody's cabin, and headed for the waterfront. As I passed beyond the cabin, I heard soft footsteps.

"Hey."

I stared into the shadows. "Oh. T.J."

"That's not a friendly hello," she said, touching my arm. "You still mad at me?"

"I never was."

"Where you headed?"

"The pond. You?"

She fell into step beside me. "What's at the pond?"

"People coming back from the woods. I hope."

"Who?"

"Bordy, Peter . . . Mac. That's all I know of."

"At the pond?"

"Yeah, it's another way into the woods. Why're you out?"

"I'm worried about Mac. He said he'd meet me."

"Where?"

"In the kitchen."

"What time?"

"Late. He didn't say exactly."

"He's not due back till midnight."

"What time is it now?"

"A little before midnight, I think." I went to the water's edge and listened for the sound of paddling. All I could hear was frogs croaking and the wind as it rustled the leaves. A slight breeze chilled my damp face. I felt dizzy with panic.

"Whatcha doin'?" T.J. asked.

"Trying to hear if they're coming back."

"Let's go out on the dock. We'll hear better from there."

She was right, so I followed her. She took off her sneakers and sat down with her feet in the water.

"It's nice here," T.J. said.

"I just wish they'd come back."

"They will. Relax. Sit down."

"I can't."

"What's the matter?"

I took a deep breath, trying to calm myself. There was no point in panicking T.J. "I'm a little worried about this raid. And I had a fight with Mac."

"What do you mean?"

"He was jabbing his finger in my chest, saying I'm next for punishment because I messed with you. I punched him."

"Why do you let him get to you?"

"It's hard to ignore him."

"When did this happen?"

"Just before. When they were leaving."

"What was it about?"

"I was trying to keep Peter from going with them. Mac blocked me, started saying things."

"Mac's a blowhard."

"He said one thing . . . Do you know if he was in the farmhouse the night of the Snipe Hunt? Or were you there too?"

"Forget about Mac."

"No. Tell me."

"Sit down."

I lowered myself awkwardly and sat with my legs stretched out and my arms braced behind me.

"Come on. Sit next to me."

I moved closer.

"I really didn't know Mac was going to play that trick on you in the Kybo."

"Okay. But what's the deal with you and him? Really."

"Well, he loves me."

"Do you love him?"

"He wants to marry me."

"He asked?"

"Lots."

"You going to?"

"What?"

"Marry Mac."

"Maybe." She spoke dreamily. "He wants to join the navy."

"I know. What about you?"

"What do you mean?"

"What would you do?"

"I'd work. Live in Newport News, or some other naval base."

"Are you going to do that?"

"I don't know. Depends."

"On what?"

"Oh, this 'n' that."

"Have you thought about college?"

"Are you kiddin'? Who would pay for that?" She lit a cigarette. "Hah! For that matter, who would take my tests? I'm not a real great student."

"What'll you do if you don't marry Mac?"

"I can type good." She picked something off her lower lip. "What about you?"

"Me? You mean what am I going to do?"

"Yeah. What are your plans?"

"I'm going to college."

"But you could get a good job right away. You're smart."

"But why would I? I'm all set for school."

She slid next to me. Her body was warm. "But supposing you had to . . . y'know . . . like, support a family?"

"But I don't."

"But you could."

"No. Why would I do that?" *Where is this headed?* I wondered.

She lowered her head. "You know I like you a lot."

The warmth of her body felt uncomfortable now.

"You feel something for me, don't you?" Her breath was sweet.

"Sure. Sure I do."

"Well?"

"But we're just kids."

"I'm not. I'm seventeen years old, ready to get married. Have a baby." Her face came close to mine. I felt her soft lips engulfing my mouth and her tongue circling the inside of my lips.

I pushed her gently away. "I can't do this now." I looked into the distance. "Where are they?" *Why am I screwing around?* I asked myself.

"I thought you liked me."

"I do, but I'm not ready for what you seem to want."

She made what sounded like a half sob, half laugh. "Aw, shoot. Who are we kidding? I just wanted you for now. I wanted you real bad."

"I want you too. But . . ."

"You do?"

"Yes."

"For real?"

"Sure. But . . ." I stood up.

"Then let's . . . go somewhere." She got to her feet. "Right now. No strings." She came close to me and kissed me softly in the crook of my neck, sending a shiver of dizzy pleasure through me, despite all my tension.

I felt her ribs and the beginning swell of her breasts. My cock was at full attention.

"Hold me tight," she said.

Something splashed in the distance and I jerked away from her. "We can't now. I gotta meet the boat when it comes back." I pulled away from her. "And what about Mac?"

"What about him? To heck with Mac." She followed me. "Where *are* they?"

"I don't know. They're late."

"What're they doin', anyway?"

"A raid. Trying to capture Red—Buck."

"Where?"

"In the tree house, I think."

"Oh boy!"

"That's right. Not so easy."

"They'll get killed."

"I know."

"Let's go find 'em," she said.

I thought about her suggestion for a moment. "No."

"What're you gonna do, then?"

"I'm going alone."

"When?"

"Right now." I went to the canoe that I had started to pull out earlier. "Give me a hand."

T.J. bent to lift her end of a canoe. "I'm coming with you, Muller."

I lifted my end and we staggered to the water. "On three, turn it over. One, two, three. You can't come."

"Aw, why not? It's gonna be fun."

"I'm disobeying Woody by going. I'm not going to involve you."

"He won't know."

"Yes, he will." I stowed the paddle and my crutch in the canoe. "Buck'll tell him."

"I'll take my chances."

"And I don't want to stir up Mac anymore."

"That's my problem."

"It's mine too." We were standing face-to-face on the little beach. "When I saw the raiding party off, he was boiling mad at me."

"I'll take care of him."

"It'll be quieter if I go alone."

"We were quiet before, when we went to Buck's hut in the woods."

"I mean it. I've gotta go alone."

"How're you gonna get up that tree house with your leg?"

"I'll manage." I got into the canoe and pushed off with the paddle.

T.J. didn't fight me. "Be real careful. If you're not back soon, I'm coming after you."

"Don't worry," I called.

If she answered, I couldn't hear her.

The air felt cool on my skin. The stars lit up the sky. Before I knew it, I was gliding through reeds whispering against the hull. I saw the other canoe beached in a tiny inlet, and steered alongside it. There was no sign of anybody.

I pulled the canoe partway up into the undergrowth, and using the flash with my hand cupped over the beam, I found an area where the tall grass was beaten down to form what looked like a path. I set off, feeling good that I had found the way.

The path led away from the pond for about 150 yards, then turned left toward the woods and went along the remains of a stone wall that probably defined the limit of the camp's property. I was able to see my way by keeping the flashlight beam close to the ground, but I was worried about finding my way once I reached the woods.

Would somebody be waiting for me? Would they see my crutch and recognize me?

Where the path entered the Big Woods it jogged to the left again, heading me in what I figured was the direction of the tree house. Because the path was more distinct here, I was able to turn my flashlight off and feel my way slowly in the dark.

Each time I came around a bend I expected to find the tree house, but instead there were only more woods.

The sound of an owl hooting broke the silence. I wished I had a cigarette. The darkness around me was total; no flashlights or campfires anywhere.

I decided to turn on my flashlight. What did it matter if someone saw me? I almost wanted some company now.

After another fifty feet, my beam picked up a clearing in the distance. To the left of it was what I was sure was the tree with the tree house. I stopped to think. The woods felt oddly empty. There should have been a hundred eyes watching me. If the raid had failed, someone would have come back to camp.

Where is everybody? I wondered. *Why is it so quiet?*

I trained the light beam directly on the tree house. Its gray, weatherworn walls looked both familiar and threatening. There was no light coming from inside.

The only sound I could hear was my own breathing.

I took a few steps into the clearing and looked up. All I could see was the underside of the house. Why was there no sound?

"Bordy?" I called.

There was no response.

"Peter? Peter?"

Silence.

"Mac?"

Nothing.

I concentrated my gaze on the spot where the tree trunk passed through the platform. Next to it was the small opening you had to squeeze through when you climbed the ladder. The trapdoor seemed to be open.

So Peter had been successful! But where was Oz now?

I let my eyes descend the ladder rung by rung. On the ground, a few feet away from the trunk, lay a small sneaker.

Is it Peter's? I wondered. *Maybe there's been some kind of accident.*

I was going to have to climb up to the tree house, and I had to do it right away.

Leaning my crutch against the tree trunk and hitching the flashlight in my belt again, I placed my hands on the highest rung I could reach, took a deep breath, and began to climb. Shadows danced around me crazily as the light from the flash jerked back and forth. Because my right leg was stiff and weak, the going was hard, and the knuckles of my left hand were still throbbing from hitting Mac. I had to stop every couple of rungs to rest. The higher I climbed, the farther away the opening in the platform seemed. I felt as if the air was growing heavier in resistance to my progress. I kept straining to detect signs of life above, but all I could hear was the ladder protesting my passage. Each time I paused and looked down, I hoped to see someone standing below, but the woods all about remained unnaturally quiet.

About three feet from the opening, my left hand grasped a rung that was slippery with something thickly wet. *Oil?* I wondered. *Fuel dripping, maybe from some kind of container that was supposed to slide down the wire to the scaffolding and start a fire?* I spread my hand. Something dark had stained my palm and fingers. I took the flashlight off my belt and shone it on the underside of the tree house floor. Near the opening was a dark area between two planks where droplets of liquid were slowly forming.

Blood.

I nearly lost my hold on the ladder. I found myself gripping it too hard—with my face pressed against the rung in front of me—as if it had tried to fling me off. My first instinct was to go back down, but I thought that if anyone was up there, he had already seen me, and it would be stupid to try and run away now. I might as well confront whoever it was. At the same time I felt a horrified and shameful curiosity, mixed with a sick, sinking feeling about Peter. Karla would never forgive me if anything happened to him.

I gripped the last rung below the opening with my right hand and lifted myself up. With my left hand I raised my flashlight and shone it on the area that was now just below my eyes.

I couldn't understand what I was seeing. At first, I saw Bordy Udall's face, frozen in a look of great sadness. His T-shirt and jeans, torn so badly they barely covered him, were splattered with a great deal of blood. He was lying on the floor of the tree house, with his right forearm doubled back the wrong way at the elbow and his left leg so twisted that its foot was pointed backward.

I felt a distinct sense of unreality, as though I were dreaming.

As I tried to understand what I was looking at, I felt as if someone was hammering a huge nail into my temple.

Somebody was lying on top of Bordy—somebody whose head had been cut halfway off at the neck and whose face was so covered with blood that it was only from the bandolier across the torso's chest that I could guess that it belonged to Mac.

This isn't really happening, I thought. *This can only be a nightmare.*

I felt suddenly sick to my stomach, and realized I was peeing in my pants. I took my right hand away from the rung and reached for the one below it, but as I did I felt cool metal touch the side of my neck, and I heard a voice just behind me saying in a soft whisper, "If you want to go on living for another minute, Jerry, you'd better not even breathe."

Redclaw.

The flashlight fell from my hand and I watched it go bouncing down the ladder. I closed my eyes and held myself as still as I could, my open hand in midair. I hoped that my heart wasn't beating too loudly. I waited to be told what to do next.

What seemed like an entire minute went by. I opened my eyes. The thing touching my neck was the squared-off blade of a meat cleaver, dark with blood.

"I have to throw up," I said.

A hand grasped my left shoulder. "No, you don't."

"I can't help myself."

"What you're going to do," the voice whispered in my ear, so close I could feel breath, "is climb up to the next rung . . . now." The blade eased away a little and the hand pushed me upward. My right hand reached out and grasped the higher rung.

"One more," the whisperer said, and I obeyed, bile continuing to rise in my throat.

"Now step out onto the floor."

"I'll fall down. My legs . . ." But my shaking legs somehow held me up. The hand turned me to the right—I could feel the person standing right behind me now—and when a light clicked on in back of me, I saw what was beyond the tree trunk. A bench ran along the wall that enclosed the tree house. Lying on the bench was Peter . . . still alive! His mouth was covered with tape that wound all the way around his head and pinned him to the boards of the bench. His wrists were taped together. His eyes were wide open in terror, looking at me imploringly. His T-shirt and white armband were splattered with blood, but I saw no signs of injury to him. He still was wearing his shoulder holster, though the wooden pistol was gone. He had on only one sneaker. His face was so pale, and he was lying so still, that I was sure he was in shock.

I began to sob.

The hand let go of my shoulder and Redclaw moved away. I felt dangerously exposed, standing in the middle of the tree house without anything to hold on to. For a moment I stared at two wires attached to a branch above the tree house, barely realizing what I was looking at. Then I remembered the scaffolding and felt a sudden longing for the innocence with which I had wondered about their purpose.

"What should I do now?" I asked. "I need something to hold on to."

"You can sit down by your brother," said the voice, speaking in a normal tone. "But not too close."

"I'll have to turn around and see you."

"Be my guest. But don't think about calling for help, because I'll kill you both if you do."

"I won't." I tottered forward until I reached the bench, my bad leg barely holding me up. With my head lowered and my eyes shut I turned around and sat down in the corner opposite where the voice was coming from. A wave of shaking passed over me and I braced my forehead on the heels of my hands until my head cleared. Finally I opened my eyes and by the light of a lamp hanging from a large limb above us I looked at the person who had created this horror.

Redclaw was sitting opposite me with his left foot up on the bench, his leg bent double against his chest, and the arm holding the cleaver draped casually over his knee. He wore a beaded leather vest, a loincloth, and moccasins. He still had on his red armband, but now his long silver-and-black hair was held back by a purple-beaded head-band with a single black feather sticking up in back. His face was streaked with red and white paint.

He looked at me calmly, smiling faintly. For a moment I felt relief, but then I remembered the bodies on the floor.

"Hello, Jerry," he said.

"You're crazy," I sobbed. "You're really fucking crazy."

"I told you we'd get to know each other," he said.

THE LONGHOUSE

ARE . . . ARE YOU GOING TO KILL US?" I asked. I kept
switching back and forth between attacks of uncontrol-
lable shivering and waves of dizziness and nausea. Still, I
fought to keep control of myself, for Peter's sake.

"No." He had turned off the light.

"What are you going to do?"

He was quiet for a moment, as if listening. Then: "First we're going
to wait until I'm sure everyone's settled down again."

"What then?"

"We'll get out of here."

"What about sentries?"

"No sentries," Redclaw said. "Why do you think no one challenged
you?"

"How did you know I was coming?"

"I figured."

"Did someone tip you off about the raid?" *Like Oz?* I wondered.

"Enough talk now."

"What if I call for help?"

"You won't. And if you do, anyone who could help is too drugged to
hear you."

"Woody will come for us."

"Woody's in Cleveland. And by the time he gets back we'll be long gone from here."

I tried to concentrate on the blank darkness to keep my panic at bay, but I couldn't help imagining that Redclaw was about to cut my throat. My arms kept twitching. My neck and shoulders ached from the tension of having to keep still.

Useless thoughts kept racing around and colliding inside my head. I could hear the rustle of foliage in the night breeze. My voice would probably not carry very far if I did cry out. I snuck a look at Peter. His eyes were closed. The wild idea occurred to me of tearing his tape off, picking him up, and jumping over the side of the tree house, taking my chances on catching a branch on the way down. *But what if we just fell?* I wondered. *We'd break our necks.*

I wondered too if I could find the wires that led up from the scaffold. If I grabbed them, maybe the effect would be to set off whatever was supposed to ignite the gasoline? Some chemical, maybe? *But what good would a fire do us,* I thought, *even if I could start one?*

As my eyes got more used to the dark, I looked around the interior of the tree house, careful not to move my head. Just below me to my left I could see the large pulley of the dumbwaiter, suspended from a chain attached to a branch. The pulley held a rope connected to a box that Peter must have come up in.

Did he have time to open the trapdoor for Bordy and Mac? Or was Redclaw already awake and waiting for them?

There was nothing else in the tree house except the bodies and a couple of empty sleeping bags.

In the distance, a train whistle wailed. It sounded so familiar yet far away that I had to fight back tears.

Where is Oz? I wondered. I imagined him somewhere out there, waiting to help us.

Probably not. Who told Redclaw that Woody was in Cleveland? Mac or Bordy before they died? Or Peter?

I shifted my weight to move closer to Peter.

"No," Redclaw hissed.

"I was trying to get more comfortable."

"Stay away from Peter."

I tried to judge the distance to the trapdoor. *There has to be a way out of this!*

"IT'S TIME TO get going," Redclaw said.

"Where?"

His form loomed in front of me. With a few quick gestures he removed the tape from Peter and picked him up in his left arm.

Peter made no sound.

"You'll be quiet and follow me," Redclaw said. "Don't forget: I have your brother. One sound from you and he's dead." He went to the trapdoor, lowered himself through it, and was gone. Despite having Peter in his arm, he made no sound as he descended.

I stood up and followed, trying not to look at the bodies. My knee and left hand had stiffened and the descent was slow and painful. When I got to the bottom, I found Redclaw with my crutch in his hands, and Peter standing next to him, holding the lit flashlight I had dropped. The cleaver, sheathed now, hung by a thong from Redclaw's belt.

"This is to help your leg," he said. Holding my crutch like a baseball bat, he swung it hard against the lowest section of the tree house ladder, shattering both the crutch and the lowest rung. He tossed the remains of my crutch into the bushes and, wielding the cleaver, finished destroying enough of the ladder so that it would be impossible to climb into the tree house until a new one was built.

I listened intently for some response to the noise Redclaw was making, but none came. I guessed he was right about Oz and the other counselors being drugged.

I tried to catch Peter's eye, but he seemed to be watching Redclaw. By the beam of the flashlight, I could see Redclaw stoop to retrieve the lone sneaker on the ground, slip it onto Peter's foot, and tie the laces. He took the flash from Peter, turned it off, and picked him up in his arms. "Let's go."

From the direction he took I was pretty sure we were headed to the Forbidden Woods and the longhouse. I wondered if Klees would alert the Cleveland police to find Woody and Win, and if they would possibly find us. The chances seemed hopelessly remote.

The going was simpler and faster than I thought it would be, even though I was limping badly. As we moved along, I thought desperately about a way to blaze our trail, as T.J. and I had spoken about so long ago. I had nothing with which to slash the trees we were passing. There was nothing to scatter on our path except a few cigarettes, and even if I tore them into tiny shreds there wouldn't be enough of them to last. I had no way to cut myself deeply enough to mark our progress with my blood, and anyway who would notice such markings in the dark?

As we passed the council ring off to our right, I realized we would probably be walking straight through the rifle range. The box full of bullet shells would be right by our path. The wild idea occurred to me of marking our trail with them, as if I were Hansel and Gretel scattering shiny bread crumbs.

I was right about where we were going. As we passed over the little bridge that led to the range, I slowed my pace in the hope of putting some distance between Redclaw and me.

"What's wrong?" he whispered, without slowing his pace.

"My leg hurts," I murmured in response.

"Push yourself, Jerry. Don't give in to it."

As we passed the shooting gallery, I pretended to stumble and fall. I grunted as loudly as I dared in an effort to cover the sound of my hand plunging into the box of empty shells.

"Can you get up?" Redclaw asked, not unsympathetically.

"I'm okay. I'm fine," I said, thrusting a handful of the shells into my pocket.

When we got to the fence that divided the two woods, Redclaw gave a low whistle. I could hear the sound of scuffling in the undergrowth, and then Redclaw's big dog, Steel, was beside us. He let out his high-pitched bark. Redclaw hushed him.

Where's Chunky? I asked myself.

Redclaw unfastened the top strand of the barbed-wire fence, and we set off into a part of the Forbidden Woods where I had never been before. Every few steps, I managed to drop one of the shells. I couldn't see any path, but Redclaw found a way that led easily through the underbrush and the many small trees. The ground was soft and spongy, as if the water table was close to the surface. My crutch wouldn't have helped me here, even if I still had it.

We walked for about half an hour. I had lost all sense of where we were, except that I knew we were moving toward the longhouse. I kept dropping the shells, praying that Redclaw wouldn't hear the muffled clinking sound that came from my pocket whenever my hand reached for another one. Dropping them was probably useless, but at least it was something hopeful to do.

Then suddenly we stopped. It was too dark to see anything, but I sensed from the feel of the air that we were standing before some kind of structure, probably the part of the longhouse that T.J. and I had first come upon that day, a day that now seemed so long ago.

WHERE ARE WE?" Peter asked in a small voice.

"Shhhhh," Redclaw hushed him. He turned on the flashlight, and I could make out the two of them a few feet in front of me. Redclaw was standing by the back entrance to the longhouse. He was still holding Peter with one arm, and with the other was pushing open the flap of the entrance and urging Steel through it. "Go on! Get in there, boy!" he said in a low but firm voice. Steel obeyed him. Redclaw dropped the flap and moved around the far corner of the house. "Follow me."

I walked around to the side we hadn't seen that day. My knee really hurt now. Redclaw was standing near the wall with the beam of his light focused on the ground next to a small tree. Something lying on the ground glittered in reflection of the light.

"Come here, Jerry," he said.

I limped over. The glittering came from several lengths of chain attached to the base of the tree.

"Put your hands behind you back and sit down."

When I obeyed him, he grasped my hands firmly and shackled them to the end of the chain. "You can lean back and rest, if you want. This'll only be for a while."

"What are you going to do?"

"Don't ask questions. I'll explain everything in time."

I leaned back and tried to relax. The ground was soft and the air felt heavy. Redclaw put Peter down in back of me. The sound of another chain moving told me that Peter was also being shackled.

Redclaw went away for a minute or two, and then returned, holding what looked like a cup of liquid and a roll of duct tape. He set the cup down, tore off a long length of tape, and wrapped it around my head, covering my mouth several times.

"Can you breathe?" he asked.

I drew air through my nose and nodded. Redclaw disappeared from my view and I heard what sounded like Peter drinking.

"You might choke if I gag you, Peter," Redclaw said. "But if you make any sound, I promise I'll kill you."

He reappeared. "I have some things to do, Jerry. Then we'll talk."

He went off around the other end of the longhouse, and we were alone again.

I stared upward through the limbs of the death tree. Their shiny surfaces shimmered softly, reflecting the dim light of the moon and the pale wash of stars overhead.

"What's going to happen, Jerry?" Peter whispered from behind me.

I shrugged hard with my shoulders, hoping he would understand, and I reached back with my hands to pat his hip, trying to reassure him. But without being able to see his face, I couldn't judge his mood. That he had dared to speak to me was a good sign, I thought.

He said nothing more. From the sound of his steady breathing, I guessed he must be falling asleep. *The drink Redclaw gave him,* I thought. I smelled a faint whiff of wood smoke. I squeezed my legs together, trying to keep myself from shivering.

After a few more minutes, Redclaw reappeared from around the side of the longhouse. He was stripped down to a loincloth that appeared to be made of leather, and he was carrying a shallow metal bowl with a small fire burning in it. He set it down in front of me and hunkered down beside it. His body was glistening, as if he'd rubbed it with oil. His war paint was gone.

I looked at the fire and must have betrayed fear.

"Don't be scared, Jerry. As I've been promising you, you're finally going to sit a vigil."

I felt a small flash of relief. *At least I'm going to stay alive through the night,* I thought.

"Except it's going to be a short one, just in case you think you can stall me."

I opened my eyes wide, trying to express puzzlement at his meaning.

He pushed the fire pit closer to me and sat down on his haunches, resting his forearms on his knees. He tipped his head back and stared upward, taking a deep breath and letting it out slowly. "Look up, Jerry," he said.

I lifted my eyes to stare up through the glittering limbs of the death tree. The light of the small fire danced among the lower branches, smoke wafting up toward the stars.

"It's calming, isn't it?" Redclaw said.

I shrugged and kept staring upward. I could feel tears coming to my eyes. They ran down my temples, tickling me, and though I tried to wipe them away with my shoulder, Redclaw seemed to notice.

"What's wrong?"

I shrugged again, still looking upward. My mind flooded with despair.

"The tree is comforting," Redclaw went on. "It will never, never rot or fall. That's why we varnished it."

I dropped my eyes to look at him, and shook my head from side to side.

"I'll take the tape off if you'll promise not to cry out," Redclaw said. "All right? Agreed?"

I finally nodded.

He leaned close to me and tore the tape away. It stung, but I found it a relief to get air through my mouth.

"Do you understand what I'm saying?" Redclaw asked.

"No," I said, my voice choked with despair. "I don't know what you're talking about. Can I smoke a cigarette?"

"No, you can't. In my people's story of the creation, the world begins with a tree."

"The Tooth tree."

"That's right. The-Tree-That-Is-Called-Tooth. You remembered."

"You told me just a couple of days ago."

He smiled. "The uprooting of that tree led to the creation of man and to the birth of good and evil."

"The twins."

"Very good. You know something about us. Now you'll understand why I keep this tree standing."

"Why?"

"If the tree remains upright, no evil will come into the world."

Hope stabbed at my despair. "Then why are you making us do this?"

"Do what?"

"This vigil."

"It will help you."

"How?"

"By bringing us closer together."

"You're trying to brainwash me."

"It might seem that way, but it's far beyond that, beyond the understanding of your white culture. I'm going to take you where our selves will converge."

"You're going to be like . . . a spiritual guide?"

He was quiet for a moment. "Something like that."

"Jesus!" I was trembling again and beginning to sweat.

"What are you afraid of?"

"This is crazy!"

He touched my forearm gently and let his hand rest there. "I'm not going to hurt you." He applied the slightest pressure. "How could I? We'll be connected to each other."

"You've got me chained to a tree! You've done something to my brother! You've killed two people! How can we be connected?"

"I didn't kill them."

"Somebody did."

"They committed suicide."

"How did they do that?" My voice was too loud.

"By attacking me. That was their death."

"Where's Chunky?"

"Who?"

"The camp dog. Chunky. I left him with you this . . . yesterday."

"The dog is gone."

"Gone? What does that mean?"

"He challenged my animal. That was—no good."

"So you killed him!"

"Not I. Steel, my dog."

"And you buried him in one of your graves, right?"

"Yes. I didn't like him."

"Win loves him."

"Too bad."

"And you want me to relax."

"You have to, Jerry."

"Why? What are you going to get out of that?"

"You have to concentrate on what *you* get out of it."

"You'd better explain."

"We've talked all summer about the things going on in your mind. I'm hoping you'll see what they are."

I felt a wave of panic. *Is that something else to be afraid of?* "Why would I see them now, when I've never seen them before? Does it have something to do with Peter?"

"I think so. Partly."

"What else?" *Karla? My father?*

"We'll see."

"What do you care, anyway?"

He said nothing for a moment. Then: "Do you remember in my cabin that day, when we flexed your knee?"

"We? You did it."

"Maybe so."

"What about it? What's my knee got to do with all this?"

"You didn't want to bend it beyond a certain point."

"Of course not. It hurt too much."

"Yes. But I forced it beyond that point, didn't I?"

I nodded.

"And there was less pain than you expected."

I waited for him to continue.

"In fact there was no pain."

"Later there was."

"Because of the strain. But if you'd kept flexing it, you would have gotten past it for good."

"This is silly. What are you driving at?"

"There's something else in your life that's causing you pain—that you need to get past, to the point where the pain will be gone."

He leaned closer and touched his finger very softly to my cheek. "I hate it that you're in pain."

I felt something give way in my chest.

"I love you, Jerry. I want to help you."

My face felt flushed. I stared at Redclaw's gleaming chest, as smooth and hard as mahogany. "What's causing me this so-called pain?" My voice cracked slightly.

"Your so-called brother."

"That's just not true. I've thought about it a lot."

"Peter is the scar tissue that's impeding your freedom to move."

"That's bull!"

"You think you love him."

"I do."

"You think you need him."

"I don't want to hear this."

"Listen to me carefully, Jerry."

"No."

"It's very hard for you to see. But often the hardest path to see is the one to freedom and happiness."

I looked away, at the woods beyond the little clearing we were in. "I don't know what you're talking about."

"Tell me this, Jerry. Why is it so important that you get along with Peter?"

I could feel my brother's heavy breathing. *He isn't hearing any of this,* I thought.

Redclaw moved a little closer to me. "Why, Jerry?"

I didn't look at him. "It just is."

"You want to ingratiate yourself with his family, don't you?"

"It's my family too."

"That's exactly where you're wrong."

"I don't believe that."

"Of course you don't. You think you can't."

"What's that supposed to mean?"

"I've thought a lot about this," Redclaw said. "You've told me more than you realize. I see the picture very clearly. Your father's old and selfish, unbelievably selfish. He doesn't mean to be, but he is."

I tried to ignore Redclaw's words, but they kept slicing at me like scalpels.

"That's the way he's built," Redclaw went on. "This is painful, I know, but it's true. Your father doesn't even care about Peter that much, but he needs Peter's mother, Karla."

"Shut up!" I said angrily.

"Karla knows this very well, so she's turning to you."

"Turning to me for what?" I asked, looking at Redclaw despite not wanting to.

He was stirring the fire with a stick. "Oh, for a couple of things. Someone for Peter. That's obvious."

I can't argue with that, I thought.

"And maybe someone to . . . not exactly replace your father, but to help fill the void his self-centeredness leaves in her."

"That's bullshit," I said weakly.

"You're closer to her age than your father is."

"So what?"

"You're hardly a child."

"Everybody's child grows up."

"But you're not her child."

"This whole thing is ridiculous," I said, looking away.

"You know, Jerry, it was a compromise for Karla to marry your father."

"How do you know that?"

"It's obvious from what you've told me. When you come right down to it, Karla's a war bride. Your father was the best deal she could get."

I said nothing, but the possible truth of what he was saying gnawed at me.

"There's other pressures on you too," Redclaw said.

"What do you mean?"

"There's your mother."

"So?"

"Why do you want to get away from her?"

"She drinks."

"Why does that bother you?"

"It's depressing."

"Why?"

"I don't know. It just is."

"Poor Jerry."

I kept looking away without saying anything, but I could feel a lump of tears behind my eyes.

"Everybody wants Jerry."

I felt disgusted with myself.

"Your mother desires you."

I shook my head.

"Karla desires you."

I kept looking away.

"Win desires you."

"What makes you say that?"

"I have eyes in my head."

"You're crazy," I said weakly.

"I desire you, Jerry."

Fear stabbed me again. My face began to burn.

"And yet despite all the people who want you, you're so lonely."

"I'm okay."

Redclaw shifted his position. "Listen, Jerry."

"What?"

"I can help you."

"How?"

"You don't have to ingratiate yourself with these people. You can solve your problems without your brother. You can be free of him."

I kept shaking my head. "I don't want to be free of him."

"Do you see what I'm saying?"

"No, I don't."

"You can solve your loneliness by yourself. You don't need these people."

I could hear the rising passion in his voice.

"You can be free, Jerry. That's how your loneliness and pain will end."

Despite myself, I began to feel a glimmer of hope. "What do I have to do?"

"Get rid of Peter."

I lifted my head and looked at Redclaw.

"Free yourself, Jerry."

"Look," I said. "What if I do that?"

"Do what?"

"What you're saying. Uh, walk away from Peter."

"Go on. What else?"

"You know—stop trying to win over my father and Karla."

"Good, good. Go on."

"I'm saying I think I see what you're getting at."

He seemed to be searching my face for something.

"I mean, maybe you're right about Peter after all."

"I know I am."

"What if I say you're right. What if I admit it?"

"Go on. Keep talking."

"What if I act on what you're saying."

"How?"

"By freeing myself from Peter. By giving up this plan to impress my father with how good I am for him."

"Yes?"

"What then?"

"It would be good," Redclaw said. "You could be happy."

"What if I agree with all you've said?"

"Yes?"

"Will you let us go then?"

Redclaw looked puzzled. "Go where, Jerry?"

"Go free."

"Free?"

"Yes, go free. Walk away from here?"

Redclaw stared at me.

"I would promise to do all you've said," I told him.

He began to shake his head from side to side.

"I would cut myself off from Peter. Go back to living with my mother. I would promise you."

"No, Jerry. You don't understand."

"But I do, I do," I said as eagerly as I could. "I really hear what you're saying. I agree with you. You're really right."

"You can't go away from here."

"Why not? If I did everything you've asked?"

"Because I would lose you."

My face began to warm.

"You would be gone from me."

"No, I wouldn't," I said feebly. I could feel drops of sweat on my face. "I could . . . see you again."

"I couldn't trust you to do that," Redclaw said.

"I could promise. I . . . I could give you some kind of guarantee. Security." I searched my mind desperately for something I could give him. I felt Peter's weight against my back.

"No, Jerry. You have to stay."

My mouth was dry. I couldn't swallow. "Why?"

"So that you can experience the freedom of being rid of Peter."

"Why . . . why do I have to experience that here?"

"So that your self can be free to merge with mine. So that we can understand each other."

My body began to go numb. Tiny pinpricks covered my face. "Okay," I said. My voice sounded hollow and far away, and the growing panic I felt was making it hard to breathe. "Okay. Then I'll stay. Just let Peter go."

"No, Jerry."

"I'll stay and Peter can go."

"No." His eyes reflected the fire.

"Why not?"

"Because Peter has to die."

"Why?" The bottom of my stomach felt as if it were falling.

"Why?" Redclaw echoed me. "So that you and I can eat him together."

I closed my eyes. Acid surged into the back of my throat and I began to choke. I coughed and tried to vomit the acid, but nothing came up. "You can't kill Peter," I heard myself say. Tears were running down my face again.

"I'm not going to kill Peter," Redclaw said softly.

"You're not?"

"No. You are."

I shook my head and wept.

"With my help."

I opened my eyes again. Through my tears I could see Redclaw still sitting calmly in front of me. Anger began to boil up in me. "So that's what you do! That's what happened to that boy Sam Holden."

Redclaw tilted his head to the side and looked me. He seemed sad.

"That's what happened to children at Allegheny," I said.

Redclaw opened his eyes wider.

"You're sick." I raised my voice. "You're a monster."

"Be careful, Jerry."

"I don't care." I tried to calm my voice. "I know all about you."

"You know nothing."

"And your discharge from the marines."

Redclaw just looked at me.

"Why?" I said despairingly. "Why do you want to cause such pain to people? Why do you hurt innocent people?"

He shook his head. "I don't want to hurt them."

"Then why do you do it? Why?"

"You'll understand, Jerry. You'll understand when we're together more. When you come to know me."

"That isn't going to happen."

"It will. And you will understand the desire."

"What desire?" I asked.

"The desire is everything." He was staring at the fire. "When the desire comes, nothing else matters. The desire comes and it's beautiful, the whole point of being alive. The gods would not have created us that way if it wasn't supposed to happen." He let his breath out slowly and looked at me. "You'll understand that soon."

"You're disgusting," I said. "You're repulsive."

"Enough, Jerry." He rocked himself forward into a squatting position.

I flinched as if he had struck out at me.

"It's time," he said.

"Time for what?"

"It's time for Peter to die." He stood up.

"No! Wait!"

"No more stalling."

"Let's talk more. I have a lot more to say."

Redclaw stood over me. "Peter won't know a thing. He's out." He stooped, ripped more tape from the roll, and gagged me again. Then he stood up and disappeared around the corner of the longhouse.

I sat still for a few seconds and tried to think, but nothing formed in my mind. When I tried to yank my wrists away from the tree I only succeeded in hurting them. I looked around and saw that Redclaw had left behind the little fire pit. Glowing coals had formed beneath two charred sticks with flames still licking around them. I could easily work my left foot under the pan and kick its contents into the air. *But what would that do?* I asked myself. Any fire I started would be just as likely to burn us as anything else. And if I could kick the flaming embers at Redclaw when he came back, I would probably only harm him enough to make him mad and even more dangerous.

I was looking around at other possibilities when I heard his voice again.

"I'm glad you were sensible enough not to kick over the fire, Jerry." He knelt beside me and worked at our shackles for a minute or two. My hands came suddenly free, but before I could do more than enjoy a sense of relief, Redclaw had laid the sleeping form of Peter on the ground in front of me and shackled my right ankle to the little tree.

"Now you're going to do it, Jerry."

I looked up and saw the huge meat cleaver in his hands, its handle free and moving slowly toward me.

"Take it," he said.

I ducked my head and shook it weakly. My entire body trembled, and sobs convulsed my chest. I retched again, but only the burning acid came to my throat. With the gag back on, I felt afraid of choking to death.

Fingers circled my left wrist and lifted it. I felt the handle of the cleaver sliding against my palm. Redclaw's hand enclosed mine and forced me to grasp it. My other hand was lifted and its fingers forced to join my left ones. When my arms went limp and I could feel the cleaver slipping free, Redclaw's hands tightened their grip on mine and began to lift them higher in the air.

I lifted my head weakly, opened my teary eyes, and confirmed what my other senses were telling me. Peter was lying on his back with his neck exposed directly in front of me. Redclaw was using me as a tool to grip the cleaver and chop down on his throat.

I had to resist him. Sheer desperation somehow gave me the strength. The cleaver slowed its descent and began to tremble like a leaf in the wind.

"Damn it," Redclaw said. "You're going to do this."

Because of either the determination in his voice or the strength of his grip, I felt my arms and hands weakening. The cleaver began to descend again.

Redclaw too felt the weakening. Instead of forcing the cleaver to continue its descent, he took advantage of my sapping strength by lifting my arms higher, to lengthen the arc of the cleaver's chop.

The pressure upward stopped when my arms were raised as high as they would go. The force on them began to bear down again. I had little strength left to resist.

At that moment, what sounded like a dog began a high-pitched barking and howling in the distance off to our left, from somewhere beyond the graves at the front of the longhouse. It sounded like Redclaw's dog, Steel, whom I had last seen about an hour ago being ordered into the longhouse.

Redclaw must have thought so too. I felt the downward pressure ease.

The cleaver hung in the air.

"It isn't my dog, in case that's what you're hoping," he said. "I locked him up inside."

My arms were lifted once more.

The barking came again. It sounded exactly like Steel to me.

Redclaw released my wrists, snatched the cleaver out of my hands, and stood up. He appeared on my left. The slickness on his body now looked like sweat.

"Don't get any ideas, Jerry," he said, stooping to move the fire pit out of my reach. "I'll be right back." He disappeared around the corner of the longhouse.

I looked down at Peter. He still appeared to be sleeping peacefully. Realizing my hands were free, I reached for his shoulder and shook it gently. He took a deep breath, but otherwise didn't respond.

In the distance to my left, Steel barked again.

"Hands off Peter," Redclaw said, approaching us again. Still wearing only his loincloth and holding the big cleaver, he stooped beside me and switched the shackles back to my arms. He lifted Peter with his left arm, bracing him across his buttocks with his forearm, and began to move off. "Just relax, Jerry," he said. "I'll be back before you know it, and we'll finish what we started." He moved away and disappeared around the corner of the longhouse again.

I listened intently for any sound of him in the underbrush, but I could hear nothing. Steel barked again, and added a series of short yips. *If it really is Steel, why did he run away?* I wondered. *How did he run away? Did Redclaw not lock him up right?*

I tried to think of something I could do, but nothing about my situation had changed. My wrists were shackled and my mouth was gagged. The fire, barely flickering now, was out of reach. The air was cooling and I shivered, but mostly the chill I felt was from shock and fear.

———

"Jerry," someone whispered softly from just behind me. "Are you okay?"

I turned my head to the right and looked back. T.J. was kneeling behind me, doing something to my wrists.

She continued to fumble for what seemed like an eternity. I was dizzy with anxiety and had to remind myself to take breathe slowly through my nostrils. I felt a click near my wrists, and my hands came free. I tore the duct tape from my mouth, ignoring the pain, and opened my mouth wide to gulp cool air.

"Hush," T.J. said, kneeling next to me.

I put my arms around her waist, feeling light-headed and slightly sick. My face, pressed against her stomach, was burning and cold at the same time. "How?" I whispered, not knowing where to begin.

"Shhhhh," she breathed, brushing my hair with her hand. "Let's get out of here."

"How did you find us? Where did you get the keys?"

She stood and pulled my arm. "I'll tell you later. Let's go!"

"I can't. He's got Peter." I stood up, felt my bad leg begin to cramp, and I tried to shake it loose.

"You going after him?" T.J. asked.

"No. That won't work. But he'll be back. We gotta hide. Quick."

She pulled my arm harder. "Let's get in the longhouse. It's dark in there, except around the fire."

As if in a dream, I followed her to the other entrance, opposite the one Redclaw had used. We pushed our way through the flaps and moved to the right wall, where the drawers and glass snake case were. Then I stopped to catch my breath and clear my mind. I could hear T.J. breathing beside me.

As my eyes adjusted to the dark, the familiar interior came into dim focus. Halfway to the opposite entrance a wood fire crackled brightly beneath the large cauldron, whisps of smoke curling around it toward the smoke hole above. Beyond the fire's perimeter, I couldn't see anything clearly.

"What'll we do now?" T.J. said softly.

"I don't know. He'll be back in a minute for sure."

"No, he won't. I locked the dog to a tree."

"How did you get near him?"

"He likes me, remember? That day we were here? He was glad to see me."

"You sure were quiet. Wasn't he locked up?"

"The key was in that bunch in the drawer."

"He's got another set, I'm pretty sure."

"Then you better think up something fast."

"I know. I know." I tried to piece together what would happen. "When he comes back, he'll see I'm gone from the tree."

"He'll tell the dog to find you," T.J. said.

"Right. And the dog'll lead him in here. Through that end." I pointed beyond the fire.

"No point in running, I guess," T.J. said. "The dog will find us in the woods in no time."

"And my leg won't let me run." I shook my head in despair. "What made you come after us? How did you know we were here?"

"When you didn't come back, I went to the tree house. I saw the ladder was gone. Then I headed to the rifle range and my flashlight picked up your trail."

"Since we can't outrun him, we gotta set a trap for him somehow."

"I tried to find Mac and the others."

My heart skipped a beat. "They're in the tree house. You're crazy to have come here."

"Think of something, Jerry. His gun is still in the drawer, y'know?"

A coal in the fire popped, making me jump. My heart was still pounding. "We can't just start shooting at him. He'll be carrying Peter, I'm sure."

"We can shoot him from behind," she said.

"You stay right here," I said. "I'll hide outside around the corner and come in after him. That way I can get him from behind."

"Shoot him," T.J. said.

"Are you game to be the decoy?" I asked.

"Sure."

"It's gonna be scary as hell." I took a step toward the cupboard to get the pistol.

"Jerry, he doesn't know I'm here."

"So what?"

"If you stay here and be the bait, he won't be expecting me."

"Can you shoot the pistol?"

"I can if I have to."

I went to the drawer and found the pistol in its case.

"Hurry up, Jerry!" T.J. said.

I released the magazine to see if the weapon was loaded. It was. The sense of urgency kept floating away from me. I checked to be sure the safety was off, then cocked the pistol by pulling the barrel back the way I had seen Redclaw do at the firing range so long ago. I went back to T.J. and handed it to her. "Hold it with both hands and don't jerk the trigger when you shoot."

"Geez, you think I don't know that?"

"After he goes through the door, count to ten before you follow him in. You gotta give him time to put Peter down and come after me."

"Okay, okay. I got it."

I heard her rubbing her hand against the flap. Then I was alone in the room.

My knee was aching. I looked for something to lean against to take the weight off my legs, but there was no place where my view of the far entrance wouldn't be obscured.

I moved closer to the middle of the room, so that the fire would make it easier for Redclaw to see me.

I concentrated hard on the entrance, trying to visualize Redclaw bursting through it. The silence in the longhouse seemed to throb.

I was suddenly convinced that I had it all wrong, that it was overwhelmingly logical that Redclaw would come through the entrance in back of me. He would go to the side first, to be sure I was still chained to the tree. When he saw that I wasn't there, he would know I was inside and figure out the more unlikely way to come in.

How dumb can I be? I thought in a rising state of panic.

I fought the urge to look in back of me, knowing that my mind was beginning to play tricks. But I couldn't resist turning around. At first I was convinced that the entrance flap was moving, but when I concentrated hard I saw that I was imagining it.

When I calmed myself down and turned back to face the other

way, Redclaw was standing just inside the entrance, smiling at me.

In his right hand, he was holding the big cleaver. In his left arm, Peter was still sleeping, with his head resting on Redclaw's shoulder.

Steel was standing to his right, studying me intently. A length of chain was attached to his collar. I couldn't see the other end, or if Redclaw was holding it.

"So here we are again, Jerry," he said. "Now the question we have to answer is, who took the dog and chained him to a tree in the woods? And who set you free?"

I was sweating now. Redclaw was calm, smiling slightly.

"Would you care to help answer that question?" he asked.

I said nothing. He was still standing too close to the entrance. *Let T.J. have the good sense to wait!* I prayed.

"I think it was the girl, Jerry. The one who was with you here that day."

I concentrated on keeping my face expressionless. Steel, sensing the tension in the air, began to growl, the sound coming from deep in his chest.

"Steel thinks I'm right, Jerry. So where is she right now?"

Steel barked one of his strangely falsetto barks.

"Very nearby, I suspect." He still refused to step away from the entrance.

Steel began to move slowly toward me, still growling. I saw that the other end of his chain was dragging free.

"Steel is upset, Jerry. You better tell me where the girl is, so I can call him off you. We don't want him to do to you what he did to that other dog, do we?"

I looked at Steel and tried to blank out everything else in the room. His eyes blazed red, reflecting the fire. He looked as if he was gathering himself to charge. Redclaw was saying something to me. I thought of getting one of the knives from the cupboard, but I knew that Steel would charge me if I moved. There wouldn't be time.

I held myself very still, looking at Steel's red eyes and willing him not to charge. Involuntarily, my hands moved slowly down to cover my groin. Steel took two more steps toward me, let out a louder growl, and crouched to spring. I heard myself say, "No!"

A piercing whistle split the air and froze Steel in his crouch. He flattened his ears and looked around at the source of the sound. When I was sure he wasn't going to attack, I too looked up.

Redclaw, no longer holding Peter, had forced T.J. to a kneeling position next to the platform where she and I had begun to make out that day. He was grasping her hair with his left hand. In his raised right hand he was holding the cleaver. There was no sign of the pistol in either of her helplessly flailing hands. Her face was a mask of terror.

Redclaw was looking at me. I couldn't take my eyes off his to look for Peter.

"Don't make me do this, Jerry." By pulling her hair, he was forcing her body back toward her heels.

"What do you want me to do?" I heard myself say.

T.J. was nearly on her back now, with her buttocks touching the backs of her heels. Redclaw was squatting beside her, with the cleaver at her throat. "You can put a stop to this, Jerry," he said.

"How? How?" I yelled. "What do you want from me?"

His face was twisted in seeming agony. I could swear that tears were welling up in his eyes.

"Where's Peter?" I shouted too loudly. "What have you done with him?"

Redclaw glanced at the other side of the room, to a spot that the cauldron blocked from my view. "Peter's still asleep." He looked back at me. "He's fine. He's fine."

I saw out of the corner of my eye that Steel was now sitting on his haunches beside me, also watching Redclaw. T.J. had her eyes tightly shut and was trembling violently.

"What do you want from me, Redclaw?" I asked, trying to sound calmer than I was.

His body slumped a little, though the cleaver was still at T.J.'s throat. "I want you, Jerry."

"Okay. What should I do?"

"Come with me. Come away with me."

"Okay, I will," I said. "Put that thing down and let T.J. go."

Redclaw shook his head despairingly. "No, Jerry. You're just talking to me, trying to save the girl. You won't go with me."

"I swear I will."

"No."

"We'll go right now."

"No."

My voice rose. "We'll walk out of here right now. I'll go wherever you want me to."

He shook his head.

"Alone together," I said. I took a single step toward him.

"You can't. You can't. It's too late." He raised the cleaver as if to chop T.J.'s throat, and a shot rang out, followed quickly by another. Redclaw stood straight up, an amazed look on his face, then threw the cleaver weakly away and, with two limping steps, hurled himself through the entrance next to him, and was gone.

I blinked and tried to recapture his image. I could swear that blood had been pouring down his right thigh.

I looked down at Steel in time to see him get up, whimpering softly, and charge out of the longhouse after Redclaw, the chain trailing after him. I looked at T.J., who was still lying on her back with her eyes closed, trembling violently, and beginning to sob.

I took a few steps toward her and peered at the corner beyond the cauldron. Peter was kneeling there with the smoking pistol in his shaking hands.

"I think I hit him," he said.

"Yes, I think you did," I said, trying to hold back the sobs that were working their way up my throat.

In the distance outside the longhouse, I thought I could hear shouting.

9

AFTERWARD

AFTER THAT NIGHT, what I remember seems like the broken fragments of a dream.

For days after we were rescued by Woody and Chief Izenaur, I stayed in the infirmary, either sleeping fitfully or sitting in a chair by the screened window, chain-smoking, alternately shivering and sweating, and staring out at the Forbidden Woods. I was okay physically: my left hand turned out not to be broken and my right leg was none the worse for my having lost my second crutch. But I was convinced that Redclaw was out there waiting to get me, and that he would follow me forever wherever I went.

Peter seemed better off than I was. Whenever he stopped by to visit me, he would babble excitedly about his role in stopping Redclaw, punctuating his account by pulling his wooden pistol from its holster and spraying the landscape with imaginary bullets, accompanied by explosive sound effects. He seemed unperturbed by having to stay at camp for a week or so longer, until my father and Karla, having cut short their vacation, could get to camp to pick us up. It wasn't until later that I was told that Peter had started to wet his bed. And of course it would take years of bad dreams and counseling to rid him of the ghosts that now were beginning to haunt him, though I didn't know that then.

I had little contact with the few other people who stayed on—to close down the camp or be interviewed by the police and, of course, the press. I guess everyone was trying to protect me. Most of the news I got came from Nursey, who either told it to me directly or passed it on to others in my presence. This was how I learned that Win had gone home to Pittsburgh with little Teddy, furious at Woody for allowing Redclaw to get out of control, distraught also over the death of Chunky, whose remains had been found in one of Redclaw's graves, and determined to see a lawyer about getting a divorce. Despite this blow, Woody was keeping up a semblance of good cheer, pretending that the early closing of the boys' camp and the cancellation of girls' camp were parts of Seneca's normal routine. I also learned that T.J. had left for home and Mac's funeral, taking with her a stricken Artie Mac. But I didn't care much about anything, not even a long letter from my mother expressing shock about what had happened and promising to improve how we got along, for one thing by cutting out her drinking. All I could do was worry about where Redclaw might be.

The only thing that felt real to me was the visits of Detective Kenneth Krell, who came to see me each of the four or five days I stayed in the infirmary. He wore light-colored wash-'n-'wear suits, smoked a pipe, and looked as if the heat of the day didn't bother him. He admitted that Redclaw had disappeared, that a search of the woods around the longhouse hadn't produced any signs of where he and his dog had gone. They'd found no trace of him, other than a few drops of blood suggesting that they had been moving away from the camp in the direction of the farm on the other side of the Forbidden Woods. The trail had gone dead near the edge of the woods and they had found no other signs of his whereabouts.

But they had set up a three-state dragnet to find him. The whole area surrounding the camp was being searched, including all the islands in Lake Pymatuning and the lake's bottom, which was being dragged. Residents all around had been alerted, among them the owner of the nearby farm, who was even quartering a couple of local police as lookouts. There was no way Redclaw could get away, Krell assured me. He was either dead in the woods or in such deep physical trouble that he wasn't any threat to me.

I didn't believe him at first. I said that Redclaw had been only superficially wounded by Peter's shots. I argued that he had hidden his trail by moving around in the treetops. He knew so much about surviving in the woods that he could easily evade the police. He believed too much in the protective power of his tree ever to abandon the woods. He was just too smart for the police to find him.

But Krell worked hard to reassure me. By the third day I found myself looking forward to his visits. He would bring me news of how the Yankees were doing, and about politics and the Olympic Games. He played honeymoon bridge with me, talking all the while about how well the investigation was going, how they were tying up all the loose ends of Redclaw's crazy career, how before I knew it the whole experience would be a distant memory.

Still, I kept looking out the window in the direction of the woods. Krell would tap my knee with his knuckles. "Don't worry, kid. He won't get you. We got so many police in those woods he couldn't move ten feet without being seen."

THEN THERE ARE things that I remember as if they happened yesterday.

On about the fifth day, I began to feel a lot better. Part of it was my mother's letter, which I reread carefully. She seemed finally to have gotten a grip on things, including an A.A. group she had joined. Even her handwriting was noticeably firmer. She insisted I take the apartment's one bed whenever I was home. Suddenly I didn't feel quite so trapped. I felt as if some pressure had been removed from inside my head.

The next day I decided to venture out of the infirmary. The camp had a whole different feel to it, with men in uniform and two police cruisers parked next to the station wagon by the Wentworths' cabin. But I soon fell into the camp's familiar cleanup routine.

This involved piling up the beds and mattresses in the cabins and sweeping the floors—except for cabin one, where the remaining campers and counselors were bunking, and, of course, Redclaw's cabin, which was considered part of the crime scene. Most of the work had been completed by the time I joined in. Next, we set to work on a project Woody had thought up, having us tear down the barn. It was a big job, but sort of fun, especially at night, when we would build a bonfire out of the wood we had piled up during the day.

WOODY, THOUGH OBVIOUSLY depressed, tried to bring a spirit of community to the barn burning, as if by rousing all of us he could revive himself. He would line all of us up to form a kind of bucket brigade to pile more wood onto the fire; when it burned down to embers he would sing his old songs. He even got Oz to come out of his shell and sing and play his guitar, Now that the campers were gone, Oz's firing seemed irrelevant, and Woody treated him as if nothing had ever happened. But despite his love of bonfires, Woody couldn't shake off his depression. It all seemed grotesque to me, like trying to build a carnival in the midst of a plague.

Still, he kept trying. He even got the idea of having a special farewell fire the following Wednesday, the night before the rest of us would be leaving. Except instead of barn wood, we would burn down the scaffold that the Injun team had built to "torture" its prisoners. Woody had been trying to figure out what to do about the structure, and the idea of torching it seemed the perfect solution. We would make a sort of Camp Seneca ritual out of it. First he got permission from Izenaur. Then he told Jeff to make sure the wiring and the mechanism to ignite the wood were still intact so that we could light the fire on command, and he ordered him to soak it thoroughly once more with gasoline. I suggested bitterly that we make a dummy and burn it as a way of getting rid of any lingering spirit of Redclaw. Woody agreed. He said it would be a spectacle we would remember for the rest of our lives.

I FOUND MYSELF thinking a lot about T.J. I would remember her running the base paths during that softball game the first evening, her buttocks pumping and her T-shirt riding up and revealing her tanned midsection. I remembered the day she had thrown her legs around me while we were swimming. I could still feel the wetness of her mouth that night on the island in Lake Pymatuning.

Then suddenly, with only three more days to go, she was back. Sunday morning, when I walked into the mess hall to read the paper, she was sitting at a table wearing white slacks and a navy T-shirt, talking with Detective Krell. She seemed somber but not distraught. She didn't look in my direction, so I went over to her, but she waved me off, saying that she was busy and would see me later. A couple of more times that Sunday I saw her in the distance, but we never spoke and she didn't show up at the bonfire that night.

I was hesitant to chase after her. I figured she had to work through her grief over Mac, even though she didn't seem all that upset. I would see her whenever I stopped by the infirmary. She would flash me a smile, but she didn't have much to say. I asked her how things had been at home, and she said they had gone about as well as could be expected.

THEN, ON MONDAY NIGHT, with two days to go before the end of camp, she came to the bonfire and sat next to me. Oz and Bernie were singing "Midnight Special." Soon her thigh was touching mine.

"How you doing?" she asked.

"Okay. I missed you."

"Can you go out tonight?"

"What do you mean?"

"Later," she said. "After lights-out. Are you free?"

"Sure."

"We could go for a swim. What time is it now?"

I looked at my watch by the firelight. "About nine-thirty."

"I'll meet you at the pond at ten."

A few minutes later, Nursey came out of the dark and told her she was needed in the infirmary for a few hours. As she stood up she put her hand on my shoulder and whispered, "We'll do it tomorrow then, same time, same station. Don't forget."

THE NEXT DAY I counted the hours until ten. Finally, when the chores were done, the sun went down, and the fireflies came out, we lit the bonfire, the last one in back of the mess hall, because tomorrow night we would be burning the scaffold.

T.J. showed up at about quarter to ten. "I'm going right now," she said. "Meetcha at the pond in fifteen minutes."

I waited a few more minutes, then stood up. I fetched one of the remaining planks from the dwindling pile of barn rubble, tossed it on the fire, and moved away as if I were going for more. Instead, I circled back toward the mess hall and hurried down to cabin one. Inside I stripped, got into my bathing suit, and put on my jeans and T-shirt over it, moving quietly because Peter was sleeping. Then I set out across the meadow toward the pond. The night was cool and filled with the sound of peepers and the distant singing at the bonfire. By the light of the moon I could see the dim shape of the scaffold. It looked less ghostly and threatening now.

With no strings attached. That's what she said that night on the pier, I recalled.

As I WAS about to round the shrubbery next to the pond, someone grasped me from behind. I heard soft laughter and felt hands slide around my chest, pulling me backward against the cool softness of breasts and thighs, and lips against the base of my neck. I turned and tried to take T.J. in my arms, but she danced away, laughing. She was wearing jeans and a light cotton jacket. "I brought a blanket," she said.

"What about our swim?"

"Forget about it. The pond spooks me now."

"What do you want to do?"

"Let's go down to the woods. I know a good spot."

I reached for her left shoulder. *I want her now,* I thought. "Can't we find a place up here?"

She pulled herself away from me. "Trust me, Jerry. This place'll excite you."

"You're not thinking of the tree house, are you?" I asked.

"No. Why?"

"That place spooks *me!* I'm never going up there again," I said.

"I guess I can understand that."

We angled down toward the entrance to the Big Woods. The beams of the patrols were way off to the left and right, barely visible. As the forest loomed up, my legs began to feel heavy.

T.J. squeezed my hand. "Come on. You're okay."

I FOLLOWED HER across the campfire site.

"This is it," she said, letting my hand go. "There's thick moss over there, and it's hidden." I could hear her spreading the blanket. "Come on over. Watch out for the rock."

I groped my way in the dark. Her hand caught mine and she pulled me gently down toward her. I took off my pants and sneakers and lay next to her with my bathing suit still on.

We fit together, my legs folded against hers, my cock against the swell of her buttocks, my chest pressed against her back, and my face buried in her fragrant hair. I felt all the tension draining out of me.

"Kiss me."

I found her mouth in the dark. Her tongue darted between my lips and seemed to swell. I pulled at the cloth covering her legs, hooked my fingers into the band of her bathing suit, and began to pull down.

"Wait," she said, pressing her hands against my chest. "Just lie down next to me." She patted the blanket again.

Oh, shit! I thought. "Why?"

"We gotta talk a minute."

"Later." I pressed my pelvis forward.

She twisted to one side. "Don't! Not now! I mean it, Jerry."

I moved away from her, feeling alone and furious.

"Have you thought about what I said?"

Desire began to leak out of me. "Said when?"

"The night of the raid? On the pier?"

"You mean about 'no strings'?"

"Yeah. That talk."

"Sure."

"What did you decide?"

"Decide about what?"

"I did some looking around when I was home."

I waited for her to say more.

"There are some good colleges down there."

"You mean you're thinking of going?"

"I don't know. I meant for you."

"Colleges for me?" I slowly sat up.

"Yeah. Good ones."

The night air suddenly seemed cooler. "Is this why you came back?"

"I wanted to see you again."

"That's the only reason?"

She pushed herself up. "Sure."

"The police didn't call you down there?"

"Well, yeah. But I didn't have to come back."

I turned my head away. "I told you. My plans for the fall are all set." I could feel the pleasure draining out of me.

"This school you're going to. It's near Philadelphia, right?"

"That's right." I didn't look at her.

"My ma says I got a cousin there."

"That's good. You could visit her."

"Him. I could move there. Maybe get a job."

I felt a flash of anger. "We don't know what our lives are going to be."

"We could try it."

"You can't move there for me."

I could almost hear her mind working. "Never mind." She lay back. Her left hand groped for me. "Do it to me. I know you can."

I didn't look at her. "I've lost the mood."

"Don't you want me?"

"Tell me something." I turned my head to face her. "The night of the Snipe Hunt. Do you remember?"

She was very still. "What about it?"

"Were you and Mac in the farmhouse?"

She didn't say anything.

"Mac said he heard me."

"With Oz, right?"

"You were there, weren't you? You did hear us, just as Mac said."

"It doesn't matter."

"You were in the other room. With Mac." I tried to see her face. "You were making love with him there."

"I didn't want to. He practically raped me. I didn't even have time to . . ." She stopped.

"You didn't even have time for what?"

"Never mind."

"You didn't have time to protect yourself, right?"

She didn't answer.

"And now you think you're pregnant, don't you?" I said.

"I don't know. He didn't use anything."

"You wanted to do it with me tonight so you could claim it's my child."

"I'm late," she said. "That's all I know." She slid her bathing suit back on. "You can go to hell."

I COULD SEE one of the policemen's lights approaching the rifle range. As I quickly dressed, I tried to think of something more to say to T.J., but couldn't. I put on my sneakers and pants, grabbed the blanket, and hurried after her. I wasn't sure I wanted to catch her.

A moment after I began to move, the light started bobbing in the direction of the gate. Even if I hurried, it would get there before me.

At the gate, the light flashed in my eyes.

"Hello there, son."

"Who is it?"

"You know you're off-limits out here?"

"I know. I got lost." I pointed to my left. "Way up there beyond the tree house. Since I know the path in the woods, I figured it was the best way back."

The light moved as if beckoning me. "Well, come on out now."

"I will."

"Lucky for you it's safe here now."

I recognized him—Chief Izenaur.

"Oh, yeah," I said. "Nothin' around here now."

"But don't be coming back here, son."

"I won't."

Izenaur grunted.

The stars overhead were comforting. The backstop of the softball diamond reflected the dim light. The pain in my knee was almost gone. I took a cigarette from my pocket and found that, luckily, I had one remaining match to light it.

I walked slowly back to the row of cabins. That first night seemed so long ago. I thought about Win and Woody. Oz. Mac. T.J.

"To hell with T.J.," I said out loud. "To hell with everybody in my life. I'm free now."

I shredded the cigarette and ground out the burning remains with my sneaker.

AT CABIN ONE I roused Peter. When I had guided him to the downhill side of the cabin so he could pee in the tall grass there, he said, "I gotta make number two."

"You sure?" I didn't feel like trudging all the way back down to the Kybo.

"Yes. My stomach aches," he said.

I took Peter's hand and set off down Cabin Row.

"Carry me," Peter said.

"You're much too big for that now."

"You always carry me."

"You don't need me to do that anymore."

He stopped. "But I need you."

"No."

He sniffed back tears.

I knelt down and took him by the shoulders. "Listen to me. You're a big boy now. You got us out of that terrible trouble."

He began to cry.

I hugged him hard. "You saved our lives."

He pushed me away. "Are you still coming to live with us?"

"I don't know. Maybe not."

"But I want you to."

"I'll still see you."

"No."

"You can always talk to me. You're big and strong enough to do fine without me."

"But I'm strong because of you, Jerry."

I couldn't find any words to say. Taking his hand, I set off for the Kybo again.

The smell hit me when we got close to it, and I pushed Peter toward the entrance. I didn't feel like braving the fetid darkness, and I figured Peter was tough enough now to face it alone. I aimed the light at the door to guide his way.

Peter let out a shriek, and raced back out. His head hit my stomach, staggering me.

"Someone's in there!"

I aimed the light at the Kybo. Peter stayed huddled against my legs.

The beam picked up the blackness of the latrine holes first—one, two, three, four, five of them—and then a dark shape looming up where the sixth one was, in the farthest corner.

I stepped to the door. It looked as if someone large was sitting there, leaning over, as if with a stomach cramp. Whoever it was had a black coat on with the collar turned up, so that the figure appeared headless. When the light hit it and cast its big shadow on the wall, it began to straighten up. It seemed to be a man.

"For Christ's sake, Woody!" I shouted. "How can you do this after what we've been through?" I told Peter indignantly, "It's just a joke."

"I don't know," he quavered.

He was right. It wasn't Woody. The figure rose up and I saw that it was a stranger, stooped like an old man and limping as he moved toward me. I remembered the old farmer in Garvey's Woods. The man coming toward me had to be Redclaw.

I THOUGHT OF Woody's arrogance in keeping up the camp's routine. I thought of the police's carelessness in being so sure they could protect us. I thought of Krell's reassurances. I felt the inevitability of Redclaw's having outsmarted them. And I felt a sense of doom: even though he was obviously wounded, it was useless to try to escape him. I felt terror.

I should have turned and run, dragging Peter with me, but I was transfixed. How could he look so old and hurt and still have survived all this time, with the police searching everywhere for him? How could he be alive *and still here?*

"Well, well, Jerry," he said. "Here we are again."

"How did you get here?" I could feel Peter shivering against my legs.

"Take the light out of my eyes, please."

Obediently, I lowered the beam. Underneath the black coat he was wearing a worn pair of blue jeans.

Where did he get fresh clothes? I wondered.

I came to my senses. "Run, Peter," I yelled, shoving him to one side. "Run! Run! It's Redclaw! Go to the mess hall and get help!"

Peter took off up the cabin path, screaming, "Help! Help! He's back. Redclaw's back!"

"Peter can go," Redclaw said softly, waving his hand as if to brush the light aside. "It's you I need now." His voice was full of pain. He had stepped down from the Kybo, matching the distance I had moved back.

I tried to calculate how far it was to the mess hall. What with my leg and the uphill slope, I couldn't possibly outrun him.

"We've come so far together," he said. "We have to go the rest of the way." The blade of the meat cleaver reflected my flashlight.

"I never did anything to you!" I cried out, sounding like a child even to myself. I moved to my right. *How did he get the cleaver back?*

"You'll come with me now," he said, matching my steps, although his legs didn't seem to be working right. "I'm dying."

The terrible empty space in my mind opened up again. "You can get help," I said. "You don't have to die."

"And then what?"

"You won't get away. You're surrounded by the police," I yelled, hurling the flashlight at his head. My aim wasn't good, and it bounced harmlessly off the flap of his coat. I began to run, heading in the direction of the softball diamond, roughly along the same route I had hobbled that first night when Teddy's arm had been broken. But going there wasn't doing me any good. I was better off running slightly downhill, so I angled to my left toward the Big Woods. If I could outrun Redclaw there, maybe I could hide in its protective darkness. Or maybe Izenaur could help me. I could see his light way off to the right, but it was much too far away to get to before Redclaw would catch me.

At first I seemed to be running all alone, my footsteps and my heartbeat pounding together in my ears. But quickly I could hear his big coat flapping. I shouted for help, but only a strangled cry came out. I could hear his footsteps behind me.

I didn't dare look back. I didn't have to see to know that he was only about ten feet behind me, and gaining ground. The gate to the Big Woods was about as near as the distance from home plate to first base. Even if I got there ahead of him, he would be too close to give me time to hide. And though Izenaur's light seemed now to be moving toward me, he couldn't possibly arrive in time to do me any good.

The scaffold stood just off to my right—the raw wood of its skeleton looming up against the moon—and a desperate idea began to form. I made for the structure. My lungs were beginning to burn and my knee was screaming with pain. I could hear the sound of Redclaw's heavy breathing, which meant he had closed the distance between us. But the nearer end of the platform was only thirty feet away. If Jeff had done his job of resoaking the wood with gasoline, there might be a chance that I could finally get free of Redclaw.

I stretched my legs forward against the biting pain, pumped my arms harder as if to rip away the air in front of me, and strained my chest forward into the darkness. Redclaw's breathing now seemed synchronized with mine, and the back of my neck tingled as if in expectation of his blow. The platform loomed up right in front of me.

Thrusting myself forward like a sprinter at the finish line, I grabbed the edge of the wood and tried to pull myself up onto the platform in a single motion. The moment I touched the wood I could tell by its dampness that Jeff had done his job. But the soaking made the wood difficult to grip, and instead of clearing the edge with the upper part of my body, I slammed my chest against the butts of the planking. As I fell, I grabbed ahold of them and found myself hanging by my arms as if from a chinning bar. Surprised that Redclaw wasn't on top of me, I was able to swing back and forward and then thrust my right leg up high enough to catch the long side of the planking with my foot. With another thrust I got my lower leg and forearm up on top, and by sticking my fingers into the space between the damp boards, I got enough of a grip to pull myself up onto the platform. The movement hurt like hell and the fumes in my face were sickening, but I was now free to stand and run the length of the platform to the wires that would help set the fire.

But as I took my first step I felt a large hand close around my right ankle. It threw me off balance, and I would have fallen had I not been able to grab one of the upright beams that supported the platform. Clinging to the wet wood, I looked over the side and saw by the moonlight that Redclaw had raised the cleaver.

Sheer terror helped me yank my foot free, just as the cleaver flashed through the air and buried itself in the wood with a thud that made the whole platform vibrate. I tried to run again, but after two steps my right foot hit an object that made a dull clanging sound, and I went sprawling again, this time landing prone on the wet boards and banging my head hard enough to make my ears ring. I scrambled to a sitting position and reached for whatever had tripped me: the gas can that Jeff must have used to drench the scaffold. I grasped its handle and began to pour its contents over the side, aiming for the shadowy form who was now trying to work the cleaver free of the wood. The sound of splashing and a grunt told me that I had found my target and I poured with hysterical determination, shaking the can until I could feel by its weight that it was close to empty. Then I flung it at Redclaw as hard as I could, heard it hit, and limped toward the end of the platform. I could hear shouting off to my right, up near the mess hall. A police car's siren sounded and headlights began moving toward us. Maybe I had a chance.

But Redclaw seemed to understand what I was up to, because he was now moving toward where the wires were. I stopped and stood frozen, staring up into the darkness of the trees and listening as intently as I could for the sound of something sliding down. When it hit the planking and broke, would I have time to jump before the fire engulfed me?

ANOTHER SHUDDER of the platform told me that something else was happening. I saw that Redclaw had clambered up. He had cut off my route to the wires and was moving toward me.

I reached in my shirt pocket. *If only I hadn't used my last match!*

Running seemed hopeless now; Redclaw and his cleaver were too close. I thought of screaming, of kicking at his crotch. I dug my hands into my pockets for a comb or a pencil or even a coin, any object I might somehow fight with. My pockets were empty.

Redclaw loomed over me. His hand grabbed my left wrist. Twisting my arm behind me and into a hammerlock, he began to pull me toward the end of the platform where the wires were. When I tried to resist him he gave my arm a painful upward jerk.

"Don't fight me, Jerry," he said gruffly.

"Okay! Take it easy." There were tears in my eyes from the pain.

Two headlights with a floodlight just above them were moving toward us.

Redclaw dragged me a few more feet—nearly to the end of the platform—then, still holding my arm painfully behind me, forced me to sit on the wet boards with my legs dangling over the side. He sat down to my left, close enough that our thighs were touching.

"What are you going to do?" I asked.

"We'll talk a little first. Then we'll see."

The pressure eased on my arm a little. I didn't say anything.

"Here's your lighter. So much for Karla Muller. It doesn't work."

I looked down. To my surprise, he was offering it to me. I took it from him with my free right hand. "Why not?"

"Probably out of fluid." His voice was gentle, though his grip on my wrist remained like iron.

The floodlight, now ninety feet away, stopped moving. An amplified voice began to speak. "Hold your fire," it said.

I felt Redclaw snort in amusement.

"We're sending someone to talk with you. Hold your fire."

Redclaw tossed the cleaver away. I heard it hit somewhere in the dark with a dull clank. He yanked my arm painfully so that I had to move nearer him. "Don't fight me," he said.

"I won't." I was like a rag doll in his grip. Then I felt him lean to his left, to grasp the lower wire, the one connected to whatever would light the fire, I was sure.

"Hold your fire," an unamplified male voice said from the dark about thirty feet in front of us. When I squinted my eyes, I could see his dark outline. "We have you surrounded," he said.

I glanced over my left shoulder, straining my already twisted neck. Flashlights were ranged in the woods behind us.

"Where's your dog?" I asked softly.

"Dead," Redclaw said. "I had to kill him."

"Come down peacefully," the voice continued, "and nobody will get hurt. Come down now."

Redclaw shifted his position slightly and called out in a strong voice: "If you make one disturbing move—or even fire a shot—the fire will come in an instant and the two of us will burn to death."

"No one will shoot," the voice said calmly.

"Turn off your floodlight, or I'll pull the wire. That's all I have to say."

"What lights the fire?" I asked.

"White phosphorus," Redclaw said. "In a jar of water. When the jar breaks, the phosphorus ignites spontaneously."

We waited as the silhouette turned and moved away. I lowered the lighter to shield it from Redclaw with my right thigh and pressed the lever. There was a spark but no flame. Redclaw was probably right about it being out of fuel.

The floodlight went out. I listened to the two of us breathing in the darkness.

"Have you thought about what I told you on your vigil?" Redclaw asked in a soft voice.

"What vigil?"

"When we were talking that night under the tree. About your family?"

"Oh. Yes." *Maybe I can soak the wick with gas from the planks,* I thought.

"What did you decide?" he asked.

"I think you're right." I felt around for a damp part of the plank. "I think people use me."

"You see that now, do you?" The pressure on my left arm relaxed ever so slightly, but the grip still held firm.

"Yes, you showed me a lot." I found a depression in the wood next to my leg where the gasoline could have pooled when first poured. It might be a little damper than the flat surface of the wood.

"The girl, too," he said.

"What girl?" *Will he sense that I'm stalling?* I wondered.

"The one who saved you that night."

"T.J.?"

"Yes, that one. She wants to use you too."

"I know that now."

"Really? Then I helped you, didn't I?"

"You really did." I depressed the lever of the lighter, turned it over, and pressed what felt like the wick into the depression. I prayed my right leg shielded the lighter from Redclaw's view.

"You see?" He pulled me closer to him. "If we had gone off together, we could have beaten the world. You and I."

"It was too late." *If only I could see what I'm doing!* I thought. "You killed Bordy and Mac."

"That wouldn't have mattered. We could have beaten that."

"How?" *Was the wick touching the damp wood?*

"Plenty get away with murder."

"I don't believe that."

"You'd be surprised."

"I guess I would." I glanced over my shoulder again. The flashlights hadn't moved.

"The history of humans is murder. That's why we're doomed."

"Who's doomed?" I asked. I found a space between two of the planks, pressed the top of the lighter into it, and twisted it sideways, so that the wick would be sure to make contact with the damp wood.

"You and me. My people. All peoples wiped away by superior technology. That's the history of the planet. That's why the red man had to die."

"But why me?" I was being selfish, I knew, but I wanted to understand his reasoning.

"Your people are doomed too. The genius of Christianity was to proselytize and to populate. But now you've overdone it and are destroying the planet. So your doom is linked to mine."

If it's going to work, it'll work now, I thought. I released the lever and held the lighter against the outside of my leg.

"'A good day to die,'" Redclaw said softly. "Do you know who said that?"

"Something to do with General Custer and the Little Big Horn, isn't it?"

"The Greasy Grass, we called it."

"Okay."

"Near the beginning of the battle, a Lakota by the name of Low Dog said it."

"Low Dog?" *If the lighter works now, what do I do with it?* I wondered. *With only one hand free, there's no way I can depress the lever and feel if the wick is damp.*

Redclaw seemed to sense my wandering attention, and jerked me painfully closer. "Yes. Low Dog. I like that."

Do I light the scaffold, jump, and take my chances of not being burned to death?

"Low Dog called to his men, 'This is a good day to die. Follow me.'"

"But they didn't die, did they?" I said. "They won." I thought about giving the lighter one test, and then decided not to take the risk.

"Yes, Sitting Bull and his people won. But it was really their last stand, not Custer's."

Maybe I can burn Redclaw in a way to make him let go of me.

"The rest has been begging for crumbs from the white man's table. Pathetic."

"But I thought you were going to reclaim this land for your people. That's what you said at the campfire."

"I was dreaming, Jerry."

"You could have fooled me." I gripped the lighter more firmly and placed my thumb on the lever.

"See where my dreams have gotten me."

I began to move my right arm backward.

"It's a good day to die," he said softly.

"No. Wait!" The lighter was behind my back now. I took a deep breath.

"Follow me," Redclaw said.

I could feel him reach for the wire. In a moment the incendiary jar would be hurtling on its way. Raising my right arm behind my back I pressed down on the lighter's lever, not having the faintest idea if it would light. I groped for where I thought Redclaw's right elbow might be.

He let out a cry and his grip on my arm loosened. The lighter had lit, and I had burned him enough to distract him. I thrust myself to the right, rolled free of him, and began to crawl along the platform, the lighter still clutched in my right hand.

The sound of his grunting made me look back at him. Even in the dark I could see that he was having a hard time pushing himself up out of his sitting position on the platform. He seemed to be using both his arms, so he had apparently let go of the wire.

I opened my mouth to speak and had to cough to clear my throat. "If you come any closer," I croaked, "I'm going to set us on fire." I raised the lighter and placed my thumb on the lever.

Redclaw had gotten his feet under him and was slowly standing up. I could see his huge figure against the night sky, beginning to move toward me. "We're both going to die now, Jerry."

"Not me," I yelled. "Not me." I stooped and pressed the lever of the lighter.

A tiny flame flickered.

On my knees and left hand, I crawled a foot forward along the platform.

Redclaw, realizing that something threatening had happened, stopped to size up the situation. I reached out with my right hand and applied the tiny flame to the cuff of his jeans, praying that it would ignite before he could step back.

I had forgotten the gasoline I poured on him.

As if I had opened a furnace door, he exploded into flames, in an instant becoming a tower of fire. At the same moment, flames went licking beneath me along the gasoline-soaked planking.

My hands were burning.

I found myself falling.

"Help me," I called.

A THUNDEROUS "whump" was followed by a powerful roaring sound. My legs and sneakers and arms were on fire and there were flames all around me.

The ground hit my back, knocking the wind out of me. For a moment everything went black. But I knew to press myself into the ground and to roll along it. When I tried to push myself up and run, I saw that my feet were still burning. I tore my sneakers off, further singeing my hands, and flung them away. They bounced in the grass like tumbling fireballs.

The scaffolding was a wall of fire flowing upward, like a waterfall upside down. At the heart of it staggered a figure outlined by flames. It moved to the edge of the platform and fell, a giant ember breaking loose from a fireplace log. Flame trailed out behind it until it hit the ground in an explosion of sparks, then it seethed with white-hot intensity.

I swear I could hear flesh bubbling and boiling.

People were gathered around me, murmuring.

ABOUT THE AUTHOR

Christopher Lehmann-Haupt is the author of the novel *A Crooked Man* and *Me and DiMaggio,* a baseball memoir. Formerly senior daily book reviewer for the *New York Times,* he lives in the Riverdale section of the Bronx, New York, with his wife, the writer Natalie Robins.